"You're used to getting your way with women, but I'm out of your reach."

"Not at all," Paul murmured, the warmth of his breath touching her lips.

Kendra stepped around him. "I came to New Mexico to retrieve a suspect. That and staying alive are my only priorities."

"Life is short. Enjoying special moments is all we've got," he said. "Don't pass them up."

"I'm not your type, Paul. I want a lot more from a guy than a good time in bed."

"So you're looking for your forever guy?"

She nodded. "As I see it, the real danger is settling for something less." She needed to believe that, but Paul had awakened a new yearning inside her. It remained deep inside her heart—a temptation couched in two simple words. *What if?*

Acknowledgment

With special thanks to the following gentlemen who were there when I needed their help. You're all terrific.

Art Lester, Retired Deputy U.S. Marshal

Duffy Spies, Retired Deputy U.S. Marshal

Sergeant Ryan Tafoya, Bernalillo County Sheriffs Department

AIMÉE THURLO

SECRETS OF THE LYNX

HARLEQUIN®

entertain, enrich, inspire™

To Amy Bennett because her cupcakes and cake decorating
skills always make people smile.

Recycling programs
for this product may
not exist in your area.

ISBN-13: 978-0-373-74715-3

SECRETS OF THE LYNX

Copyright © 2012 by Aimée and David Thurlo

This edition published by arrangement with Harlequin Books S.A.

For questions and comments about the quality of this book,
please contact us at CustomerService@Harlequin.com.

www.Harlequin.com

Printed in U.S.A.

ABOUT THE AUTHOR

Aimée Thurlo is a nationally known bestselling author. She's a winner of a Career Achievement Award from *RT Book Reviews*, a New Mexico Book Award in contemporary fiction and a Willa Cather Award in the same category. Her novels have been published in twenty countries worldwide.

She also cowrites the bestselling Ella Clah mainstream mystery series praised in the *New York Times* Book Review.

Aimée was born in Havana, Cuba, and lives with her husband of thirty-nine years in Corrales, New Mexico. Her husband, David, was raised on the Navajo Indian Reservation.

Books by Aimée Thurlo

HARLEQUIN INTRIGUE
988—COUNCIL OF FIRE‡
1011—RESTLESS WIND‡
1064—STARGAZER'S WOMAN‡
1154—NAVAJO COURAGE‡
1181—THE SHADOW‡
1225—ALPHA WARRIOR‡
1253—TWILIGHT WARRIOR*
1316—WINTER HAWK'S LEGEND††
1333—POWER OF THE RAVEN††
1394—SECRETS OF THE LYNX††

‡Brotherhood of Warriors
*Long Mountain Heroes
††Copper Canyon

CAST OF CHARACTERS

Paul Grayhorse—A sniper's bullet had killed his partner and ended Paul's career as a U.S. marshal. Now the shooter was back, planning on finishing the job. Paul's only hope of putting his demons to rest was by teaming up with a sexy marshal who'd already made her own share of enemies.

Kendra Armstrong—Just as she was closing in on a fugitive, she'd been pulled off the operation and reassigned. Was this just a ploy to protect one of their own playing both sides in a gun running operation? Unfortunately, the only man she could trust right now was a dangerous distraction who might just get her killed.

Preston Bowman—A dedicated professional, he was a tenacious police detective who lived for the job, but Paul was his foster brother, and family always came first.

Evan Thomas—Thomas was Kendra's supervisory inspector, a career man well respected in law enforcement. He'd lost faith in her abilities and wanted her on desk duty. If she couldn't bring in the fugitive trying to kill a former U.S. marshal, he'd come down from Denver and do the job himself.

Chris Miller—The former military sniper turned hit man had changed his appearance more than once, so he had an edge. He'd been paid to kill only one marshal, but if somebody else got in the way, he'd take them out for nothing.

Yolanda Sharpe—A young woman with a criminal record and an ex-con boyfriend, she'd made the short list after setting an officer up to be killed. Yolanda claimed to be innocent. The only problem was, her alibi was on the run from the cops.

Garrett Hawthorne—He'd escaped the law enforcement net, though his brother was now in prison. With enough money to hire the best wet-work specialist in the country, Garrett stayed in the shadows, waiting for just the right moment to exact his revenge.

Annie Crenshaw—She'd fallen on hard times and now worked the streets. She'd do anything to feed her drug habit, even if it meant selling out one of the few men who still treated her with respect.

Chapter One

Paul Grayhorse stepped back into the shadows as a jagged flash of lightning sliced across the darkened New Mexico sky. He had a bad feeling about tonight, and it had nothing to do with the storm raging around him.

Ignoring the pain coming from deep inside his right shoulder, he remained focused. The bullet wound had healed, but the nagging ache that remained was a reminder that even the briefest lapse in attention could have devastating results. In less than three seconds, a sniper had taken the life of his partner, Deputy U.S. Marshal Judy Whitacre. Her death, and the high caliber bullet that had torn through his own shoulder that day, had changed his life forever.

He shook off the bitter memory as he continued to keep watch. It was a typically cold, rainless New Mexico storm, one of hundreds he'd seen while growing up in the Four Corners. There was the usual blend of wind and stinging dust, but no rain or sleet to ease the parched desert.

Given a choice, most people would have stayed inside on an October night like this one. That's where he should have been, too, sitting in his armchair, beer in hand, watching the football game next to a bowl of corn tortilla chips and hot salsa.

Yet here he was, standing on the lawn beside an old brick office building in downtown Hartley waiting for an arranged meeting with a mysterious, prospective client.

The skies rumbled again and the ground shook, rattling windows all the way down the block. Tense and ever alert, he kept his gaze on the darkened street. He'd considered staying in his parked truck, but this wasn't a stakeout, and his visibility and mobility would be restricted inside the cab of his pickup.

Tonight was a first. Since leaving the U.S. Marshals Service he'd worked several cases that had involved teaming up with his brothers, but this time he was going solo, and he liked it.

The woman who'd called his agency asking for help had captured his interest right from the get-go. Yolanda—at least that was the name she'd used—had dialed his office late last night. She'd spoken in a harsh whisper, her words coming out in a rush. Certain that her abusive, soon-to-be ex-boyfriend, an officer in the Hartley P.D., would be at his own home tonight watching the game, she'd insisted on meeting in this tiny downtown park after hours. It was near her workplace, she'd said, and on her way home.

All things considered, Yolanda, or whoever she was, had come to the right P.I. He'd never had much patience with bullies, particularly those who preyed on women.

As the minutes stretched by and the temperature continued to drop, he reached into his pocket for his cell phone and dialed his foster brother, Preston.

Like it was with all his foster brothers, Preston and he had come from completely different backgrounds. Yet, once they'd been taken in by *Hosteen* Silver, the traditionalist Navajo medicine man who'd become their foster father, they'd grown as close, or closer, than blood brothers.

Preston Bowman, now a Hartley Police detective, lived for his job. Even though it was getting close to seven, Paul knew his brother would still be clocked in.

Preston picked up on the first ring and barked his name.

"It's me," Paul said.

"What's up?" Preston asked.

"I'm supposed to meet a client—Yolanda—no last name. She contacted me last night claiming she'd been trying to break up with her boyfriend, a Hartley cop. He's apparently started using her as a punching bag, so she's asked for my protection."

"Hook her up with the chief's office or Internal Affairs. We have ways of dealing with this kind of thing," Preston answered immediately.

"I suggested that, but she doesn't trust the police. She thinks they'll cover for one of their own."

"No way. We try to keep things in-house, sure, but we make sure the situation gets handled. We take a dim view of domestic abuse," he said. "Give her my number and tell her to come see me."

"I'll pass that on when she shows up, but if she says no, I'm taking her case."

"You're waiting for her right now?"

"Yeah. She's late. She said six-thirty."

"You thinking maybe her boyfriend found out she was looking for help?"

"The thought occurred to me, yeah," Paul said.

"She wouldn't give you a last name?"

"Nope. She was whispering when she called, so wherever she was, she was worried about being overheard. All I got was a description so I could spot her," Paul said.

"Go on."

"Blonde, five foot seven, average build. She said she'd be driving a green Ford SUV, wearing a denim jacket and jeans, and carrying a red handbag. She sound familiar?"

"You mean do I know an officer with a girlfriend named Yolanda who fits that bill?"

"Yeah."

"Sorry, doesn't ring a bell. Give me her number and I'll run it through the system."

Paul gave him the number straight from his caller ID, then waited.

"That matches a residential landline for a woman named Yolanda Sharpe. The address is on Hartley's south side—485 Conejo Road. Hang on a sec. Here's more. Yolanda's got a record—shoplifting, check fraud and a few misdemeanors," Preston said. "She's served six months jail time."

"Interesting background, but she still doesn't deserve to get batted around."

"True, but I think you should back off, at least for now. Look at the facts. She didn't give you her full name or even the first name of her boyfriend. Now she's late. Who knows what might have gone down? What if the boyfriend shows up instead, mad as hell and looking for a fight? With that bum shoulder, if he comes at you, you're going down hard."

"Like hell."

"Look, bro, something's off. You felt that too or you wouldn't have called," Preston said. "Anyone who checks you out on the internet knows you like riding to the rescue. Remember that roughneck you threw out the window after he cornered the waitress at the Blue Corral? Made the cable news."

"That was self-defense." Paul chuckled softly. "And my shoulder didn't hold me back. He flew a good ten feet."

"Okay, so you're not backing off. Give me your location and I'll join you. You might be able to use a little backup."

"Just don't get in my way," Paul growled. "I'm standing behind the pines in the park beside the Murray Building on Main. My truck's across the street."

"I'm in my cruiser now. My ETA's only three minutes or less, so try to stay out of trouble till then."

Paul hung up, his gaze still on the empty street. His

brother was right. He had a sixth sense about some things, and right now his instincts were telling him trouble was close at hand.

Muscles tensing up, Paul reached for the lynx fetish he wore around his neck on a leather cord. The slivers of pyrite that comprised its eyes glittered ominously. He'd never been able to figure out why, or how, but whenever danger was near, the eyes of the lynx would take on a light of their own. Tonight, maybe it was the lightning or the cold playing tricks on his senses, but either way, he'd learned not to ignore the warning.

After checking his watch one last time, Paul decided to walk back over to his pickup. He'd just stepped out of cover when a blue truck pulled up to the curb and the driver leaned toward the passenger's side window. As a brilliant flash of lightning lit up the night sky, he saw the pistol in the driver's hand.

Paul dove to the ground just as two loud gunshots ripped through the air.

Paul rolled to his right, and using a tree trunk as cover, he rose to one knee, pistol in hand, but it was too late. The truck was already speeding away. Making a split-second decision, he ran after it, hoping to read the plates.

He hadn't gone fifty yards when he heard the wail of an approaching siren. A heartbeat later Preston rounded the corner and pulled to a screeching stop beside him.

"You hit?" Preston asked, leaning over and shouting out the passenger's side window.

"No." Paul opened the door of his brother's unit and jumped in. "Blue pickup, turned south down Applewood."

"Make and model?"

"Ford 150, I think," Paul said, reaching for the shoulder belt as Preston hit the gas. "Or maybe a Chevy. The tailgate was down and it happened in a flash."

"Let me guess. No Yolanda?"

"I never got a look at the driver. All I saw was the pistol sticking out the passenger's window. If that lightning flash hadn't lit up everything at just the right time, I would have been on the ground right now, a soon-to-be chalk outline."

"You were set up, bro." Preston turned the corner at high speed, yanking Paul to one side. "The shooter can't be far. Keep an eye out for taillights on the side streets."

Paul kept a close watch on the area as his foster brother raced down the street. Traffic here was light. Hartley was barely a city. Most downtown businesses were closed before six, and the area restaurants and bars were all farther east or west.

"In your gut you knew all along that this wasn't just another domestic abuse situation. I'm right, aren't I?" Preston said as he took another left, then slowed down and directed his spotlight into the darkened alley they passed.

"I didn't *know*, but I had a feeling something wasn't right," Paul said. "I'd just decided to call it a night when it went down."

Preston slowed as they passed a bank parking lot, giving them time to study every inch of the well-lit area. "I think we struck out. The pickup's gone."

After another ten minutes, Preston picked up his radio and called off the other patrol cars in the area.

"So, you gonna report this to the marshals service?" he finally asked Paul.

"Yeah. I have to because Miller is still at large." Paul understood his brother's lack of enthusiasm. Local departments hated dealing with the feds. But locating Chris Miller, the man who'd killed his partner and wounded him, was a priority. "It's been ten months since the shooting, so this is probably unrelated, but no matter. I still have to report an incident like this."

Silence stretched out between them.

"What's eating you?" Preston finally asked.

"What happened tonight matches the prediction *Hosteen* Silver left for me," Paul said. A traditionalist medicine man, *Hosteen* Silver had respected his culture by avoiding the use of proper names. Instead, he'd gone by a nickname that fit him perfectly. *Hosteen* meant mister and Silver alluded to the color of his long, shoulder-length hair.

"You're talking about the letters we all got after his death?"

"Yeah."

Preston nodded thoughtfully. "The old man...he knew things. At first I thought it was just tricks, him picking up on subtle clues, like some savvy street hustler. But it was more than that. He had a real gift."

"Yeah, he did, and whatever he foretold was usually right on target," Paul said.

"So what did he say would lay ahead for you?"

Paul recited it from memory. "'When Dark Thunder speaks in the silence, enemies will become friends, and friends, enemies. Lynx will bring more questions, but it's Grit who'll show you the way if you become his friend. Life and death will call, but in the end, you'll choose your own path.'"

"You saw the pistol because of the lightning, that's what you said, right?" Preston said, then seeing him nod, added, "And the business district was pretty quiet."

"Yeah, but this time, our old man's prediction is going to be somewhat off the mark. Face it, the day Grit greets me as a friend will be the day after never." *Hosteen* Silver's horse hated him.

"Yeah. Whenever he hears your name his ears go flat and his eyes bug out."

Silence stretched out again.

"I'll call the marshals service as soon as I get home," Paul said. "A landline will get me a better connection, particularly on a night like this."

"Better not wait or go home either, if it's really Chris Miller. You should stay at a secure location with backup nearby. Let me get hold of Daniel and Gene and have them meet us in Copper Canyon. For us, that's the most secure place on earth."

Paul nodded. All five of his brothers knew that formation like the back of their hands and, there, in a narrow, dead-end canyon, the tactical advantage was theirs.

Paul thought back to the phone call from Yolanda that had led up to this. He had no regrets. He'd been growing restless these past few months, eager to do something more than watch surveillance monitors, the bulk of his business these days.

Now, maybe, fate was finally giving him a chance to get back to the work he loved and pay his debt to the past. Throughout those long months of rehab, he'd kept going by telling himself that someday he'd find Miller, that it was inevitable their paths would cross again.

The possibility that Chris Miller had actually come after him now seemed almost too good to be true.

"Don't expect me to hide out," Paul said, then after a second added, "If it's Miller again, our face-off is long overdue. This is personal. Come morning I'm heading back to town."

U.S. DEPUTY MARSHAL Kendra Armstrong was nearly exhausted after another eighteen hour day. It was two o'clock in the morning, pitch-black outside, and she was alone in a remote corner of New Mexico's bad-lands. The headlights of her tiny rental car were the only illumination within miles.

She should have been back in Denver, in on the takedown of the fugitive she'd been after for the past six months. With effort, she pushed back her anger.

According to reports, it was possible that Chris Miller, a high-threat outlaw, had finally surfaced here. Her record for tracking down and capturing run-aways fugitives was second to none, so she'd been immediately ordered to New Mexico. Still, the sudden reassignment had taken her by surprise. She hated surprises.

As she eased the tiny rental sedan along a dried-up stream bed, the car's tires began to lose traction. Feeling the sedan bogging down, she decided to leave the soft, sandy track.

She'd traveled less than one hundred yards when the undercarriage scraped loudly, the screech so loud it hurt her teeth. The car suddenly stopped, her tires spinning from lack of grip. The wobbly tilt of her vehicle told her she'd high centered on bedrock.

Kendra switched off the ignition and climbed out. The light in the distance teased her—the ranch house where former Deputy U.S. Marshal Paul Grayhorse awaited her arrival, no doubt. She was reaching inside the car for the bottle of water on the seat when she heard something moving in the brush behind her. Kendra instinctively reached for her weapon and turned in a crouch, gun in hand.

Three armed figures were standing several feet away from her, but it was too dark to make out their faces. The tallest of the three quickly blinded her by aiming his flashlight at her face.

"U.S. Marshal. Lower your weapons," she snapped, shifting her aim to the person holding the flashlight. If she went down, she'd take him with her.

"We were expecting you to stick to the road," the

man with the flashlight said, instantly lowering the beam and putting away his gun. He stepped forward. "I'm former Marshal Paul Grayhorse. These are my brothers, Detective Preston Bowman and Daniel Hawk."

"Kendra Armstrong, Deputy U.S. Marshal," she said, remembering not to offer to shake hands. Navajos preferred no physical contact with strangers.

Kendra opened her car door, allowing the glow of the dome light to illuminate the area. Even in the muted light she could see the gleam of cold steel in Preston's eyes, the world-savvy gaze of a seasoned cop. Daniel Hawk had an easy smile, but he stood erect with his shoulders rigid, like someone who'd served in the military. Having grown up with a full bird colonel for a dad, she knew the stance well.

Yet it was Paul Grayhorse, the man with the flashlight, who'd captured and held her attention. Now, *there* was a man who seemed to be far more than the sum of his spectacular parts. He stood tall, with strong, broad shoulders, and had an amazingly steady gaze. Through sheer confidence, he commanded the situation.

"I was afraid I'd bog down in the sand, so I decided to veer off the path," she said, holstering her weapon.

Paul gave her a heart-stopping smile. "You're not the first visitor to get hung up on the sandstone out here."

"I'm glad we're all on the same side at least. I would have hated having to take on all three of you," she said, her gaze studying the men.

Paul smiled. "Preston's the smallest and he can't fight his way out of a paper bag. I bet you were planning on taking him on first."

Daniel laughed. Preston scowled but said nothing.

"What strategy would you have used? Attacking the good-looking brothers, or the one with the flashlight?" Daniel pressed, cocking his head toward Paul.

"None of the above," she said with a tiny smile. "I'm going to need all of you to help me get off that rock."

Paul laughed. "We'll get it back on solid ground for you. Just give us a minute."

His reassuring, confident tone was soothing. Without thinking, her gaze drifted over Paul's shoulders. She'd seen him favor his right shoulder slightly when he'd put away his weapon, so she knew it was still causing him some pain. According to what she'd read in his file, that gunshot wound had shredded muscle and forced him to take an early retirement.

"No need for heavy lifting. If we can get a shovel we can scoop up dirt, add some brush, and form a gripping surface beneath the drive tires," she said.

Paul, who'd already moved around to the back of the sedan with his brothers, looked up quickly. "So you've heard about my injury. Don't let it fool you. I can do whatever has to be done."

She heard the dark undertone in his voice and realized she'd struck a nerve. Paul was fighting the consequences of his gunshot wound by not allowing himself to accept limitations. Although she didn't know Paul very well, she liked him already.

She closed the car door, placing them all in the dark again. "I was more concerned about you standing out here in the open when there's a gunman on your tail, Paul," she said.

Paul shook his head. "No one's around."

"And you know that...how? There's no telling what could be out there in the dark," she said.

"Trust me, if anyone was here, we'd know," Paul said.

"An elephant herd could be out there, and we'd never see them," she said.

Paul chuckled. "This was—is—our home. Once you're in tune with the land, you can see beyond the deepest shadows." He handed Preston his flashlight.

She stared at him for a moment, wondering if he truly believed that metaphysical nonsense. No matter how you felt about the land, no one could see into the night, not without special gear anyway.

"You're not convinced," Paul said, not making it a question.

As his brothers crouched by the car, using the flashlight to check out the extent of the problem, Paul gestured back up the dirt track. "Nature itself lets you know if there's trouble. Look down the road. See that coyote crossing from north to south?"

She strained to peer into the long shadows of night and caught a glimpse of something low, moving fast. "Over there?" she asked, pointing.

"Yeah. If there were human beings skulking around, the animal would have known and never crossed the road, putting himself in full view like that. Coyote survives by staying attuned to his surroundings just like the other animals here in Copper Canyon. That's also how we knew someone had come into the canyon long before we heard your vehicle. Everything became still—too still."

"Hey, you two gonna chat all night?" Daniel called out.

Kendra realized that for a few moments she'd totally forgotten about the car and her situation. Paul's low, gravelly voice and his intense gaze had completely sidetracked her.

"Got a plan yet?" Paul called back.

"Yeah, if we lift the rear tires off the rock, it'll roll down onto level ground. Kendra, you'll need to get behind the wheel and put it into neutral," Daniel said.

"Preston, you take the middle, I'll take the left, and Daniel can take the right," Paul said.

"No offense, Paul, but maybe we should trade places so you won't have to stress your shoulder," Kendra said.

"No need," Paul said with a quick half smile. "I can lift more with one hand than my brothers can with two."

Preston laughed as Daniel answered, "Next time I need to unload a van full of tactical gear I'll give you a call, bro."

"Once the car's free, I'll drive all you guys back to the house," Kendra said, then got behind the wheel and placed the sedan in neutral.

A few seconds later, the car rose and began to roll forward. It rocked a little as they set it back down but continued to move forward.

"Okay, guys, jump in," she said. "We need to get to the house as soon as possible. I don't think anyone followed me here, but you can't be too safe."

Paul's brothers entered the two-door sedan from the passenger side, and climbed into the back.

"Expect some bone-jarring bumps along the way," Paul said, taking the seat on her right.

His words repeated themselves in her mind. Something told her this case would play out the same way.

Chapter Two

Kendra drove at a slow and steady pace to avoid losing traction in the sandy ground. Amazingly enough, there were no more mishaps. Although she repeatedly scraped the wheel wells against the brush, a sound like fingernails being raked across a chalkboard, the rest of the drive was uneventful.

Within a minute or two she saw the rectangular stucco frame house nestled against the wall of the canyon. Moonlight shimmered off its metal roof—a touch of civilization in an area that appeared to be largely untouched by man.

"It looks kind of lonely out here," she said quietly.

"You're a city girl, I take it?" Paul asked. Seeing her nod, he continued. "Life moves at a different pace in this canyon, but there's plenty of company. Big cats hunt here, and bears include the canyon in their territory, too, along with coyotes. Then there are all the smaller creatures. Copper Canyon is teeming with life."

"But no humans beside us, right?" she asked.

"There are several Navajo families within a dozen

miles of here, but they're all pretty scattered. What makes this place an ideal safe house is that there's only one way to approach it, and the canyon itself transmits sound like a tunnel."

Kendra pulled up beside the house and parked next to a big blue Dodge pickup.

"You two should probably go inside. We'll bring in some firewood," Daniel said, signaling Preston and gesturing to a cord of wood stacked beneath the roof overhang.

Paul led the way to the front door and invited her in. "Make yourself at home."

As she entered the living room/kitchen combination, she glanced around. The interior had a casual, rustic, Southwest elegance.

To her left along the far wall were kitchen appliances and a wide counter. A half dozen feet away from there stood a dining table and some straight-backed chairs that were handcrafted from knotty pine.

Farther in, near the center of the large open space, was a sofa covered in heavy, rich brown leather. The pine frame, with its decorative grooves and diamond-shaped patterns, matched the design on the table and chairs.

Beautiful red, black, and indigo Navajo rugs were hung on the walls facing the big stone and iron fireplace. A smaller one woven in red, black and white was draped over the back of the couch.

"I like this place," she said. "It feels...welcoming."

Paul smiled. "Over the years I've heard it described

in many ways. Each person sees something different, but the consensus is always the same. Our foster father's home agrees with people and sets them at ease."

"I love the pattern on that Navajo rug draped over the couch," she said.

"That's an antique blanket our foster father was given in payment for a ritual he performed for one of his patients. Almost everything woven prior to 1890 is a blanket. Navajos had little use for floor coverings since keeping warm was their priority. Then trading post owners started encouraging The People to weave rugs instead. Those were thicker and more appealing to the tourist trade." He went over to the couch. "Touch the blanket. It's soft and very warm."

She ran her fingertips over the woven fabric. "It feels wonderful, and so beautiful, too."

As Daniel and Preston came back in with armloads of firewood, talk naturally shifted back to business.

"I've read through your files, Paul," Kendra said. "From the reports I saw, you were on protection duty, fully prepared. Things went south for you and your partner after you reached the DC courthouse's steps."

He nodded. "I'd checked the whereabouts of the judge's known enemies, including the ex-soldier Chris Miller, the Hawthorn cartel's wet-work specialist. Our intel said he was hiding out in Mexico, well out of reach. That turned out to be wrong. Later, video surveillance cameras across the street from the shooting revealed he'd been on the scene."

She nodded slowly. "Our problem's been that

Miller's a master at changing his appearance," Kendra said, glancing at Daniel and Preston who were stacking wood. "Following an auto injury that took place just after he left the military, he had substantial facial reconstruction. The only subsequent photo we have of him is a very low-quality one taken from that video. It was actually thanks to a partial fingerprint lifted from a parking meter, combined with facial recognition software, that we were able to confirm his ID at all."

"That faulty intel cost my partner her life," Paul said. "What's worse, Miller's still in the wind."

She could feel the pain vibrating through his words. Though it hadn't been in his file, she'd interviewed other marshals before coming here and been told that Judy and Paul had been very close. Some had speculated that the two had become lovers.

As her gaze drifted over the man before her, she could understand the temptation he might have posed to his late partner. There was something about Paul, an intangible that went beyond those long legs, narrow waist and a chest any woman would be tempted to nestle into.

Yet all things considered, what drew her most was the mercurial quality reflected in his gaze. Those dark eyes could sparkle with intent, determination, or even gentleness, in a flash.

Paul Grayhorse intrigued her, but this wasn't the time for distractions. She looked away immediately, refocusing on her mission.

Having replenished the fire, Preston patted his brother on the back. "Police work is always filled with the unexpected, bro. What we do only comes with one guarantee—a lousy paycheck."

"We all go into this kind of work knowing the risks," Daniel, a security consultant, said, "but at least we don't die by inches, chained to a desk."

Paul crossed the room, stopped at the coffeepot on top of the stove, and poured himself a cup. "That's exactly why I had to expand my business to include actual cases. Sitting in front of surveillance monitors all day was driving me nuts."

"No one's arguing that, but you should have waited until you had full mobility in your arm again." Preston checked the handgun at his waist, then zipped up his jacket and brought out a set of keys from his pocket.

"You leaving?" Paul asked.

"Yeah. I want to find Yolanda Sharpe, then run tonight's events past my informants. I also want to know if any new talent, Chris Miller in particular, has shown up in the area recently."

"That's why I won't be staying here long either," Paul said. "If someone's gunning for me, I won't be hard to find. Next time, I'll be waiting."

"I can't stop you, but that's a bad idea, Paul. You're too close to this," Kendra said. "I'm here to bring Miller in, so we both want the same thing. Give me a chance to work this case first."

"Are you officially taking over the investigation?" Preston asked her.

"Not yet," Kendra said. "Until we figure out who we're dealing with I'll be working closely with your department, but it's still your case."

Daniel grabbed his jacket next, then nodded toward a rifle case barely visible beneath the sofa. "I'm leaving you my AR-15, with three full magazines. It's got a thermal imaging kit you won't believe. Just take care of it. I've got to hit the road, too. I'm conducting a training op at New Horizon Energy, the tribe's secure facility. Lots of VIPs coming in to observe."

Kendra waited for the two men to leave, then spoke. "Now that it's just the two of us, brief me on what went down earlier this evening."

"You must have seen my report," he said, taking a seat at the kitchen table. He removed his pistol and holster, leaving them within reach.

"Of course, but I want to hear it directly from you, Paul, particularly anything you may have remembered since then." She scooted her chair back, then took off her dark blue cardigan. As she did, sparks of static electricity lit the air. Her shoulder-length auburn hair stood out, twirling erratically, some strands tickling her nose. She brushed her hair back with a hand, trying to tame it into place.

As he recounted the events, Kendra jotted down the new details in a small spiral notebook, noting how sharp his instincts were.

Kendra tried hard to focus exclusively on Paul, but one strand of hair kept evading her and tickling her nose. She jutted out her bottom lip and blew hard, trying to force it away.

"Why did you stick around once you realized that something was off?" she asked, wanting to know more about the way he thought things through out in the field.

"I couldn't be sure that she was setting me up, and I didn't want to bail on someone who needed my help."

Kendra watched Paul as he spoke. She couldn't help but notice how calm he was. It was normal for people to shift and move around when they were being questioned, not necessarily a sign that anything was wrong, but Paul remained perfectly still.

The rigid control he held over himself reminded her of her father, the colonel. Never show anyone what you're thinking—that had practically been the colonel's mantra. She and her brother had learned that lesson well.

When he finished his account, Paul waited as she walked to one side of the window and studied the area outside. "You don't have to keep checking," he said as she returned to the table. "We're safe here. If you're unsure, all you have to do is listen."

Kendra did. After half a minute, she heard the cry of a coyote baying at the moon.

"Coyote wouldn't be indulging its instincts to call to the night if intruders were in the canyon," he said.

"I never heard him at all until right now."

"No problem. I did."

She got the message. They were on his turf, and

here, Paul held the advantage. "Strategically, Copper Canyon is a great place for you, but not for me. I came to do a job, and the sooner I find what I need, the better it'll be for everyone."

"Do you have a specific plan in mind?" Paul said.

"First, I need to find out if Miller's really here, and if he's the one who came after you today. I could really use your help with that part of it—but only if you can follow my lead and stay on target. I won't allow my work to be compromised by someone planning to cowboy up."

"I can handle it." He unplugged the coffeepot, then leaned back against the counter and faced her.

"Okay, then. After I grab a few hours' sleep we'll drive back to Hartley. I have to find a way to get the cooperation of the local businesses so I can gather up any of the local surveillance camera video within range of the shooting incident. If we have to resort to warrants, that'll cost us time. I'll also have to coordinate my efforts with your brother and the Hartley P.D. so we don't end up tripping over each other."

"You're hoping one of those cameras will reveal Miller was the shooter or, at the very least, in the area?" Seeing her nod, he continued. "I can help you get what you need. My company specializes in electronic surveillance, and some of those businesses are clients of mine. The others, well, chances are they've heard of me and my agency."

The logs in the fireplace were burning down, and feeling cold, she jammed her hands into her slacks.

"What concerns me is that your right shoulder is still giving you problems. You sure you're ready to be out in the field?"

His eyes darkened ominously, and she had to force herself to hold her ground.

"Muscle damage restricts my mobility somewhat, that's true, but investigations are mostly legwork." He paused. "If what's really worrying you is that I'll forget I'm not the one carrying the badge, you're wasting your energy. I want answers and a resolution to my partner's murder. I don't care who gets the credit."

"Tell me this. Are you looking for revenge, or justice?"

He paused for several moments before replying. "There was a time when there was nothing I wanted more than revenge, but I've moved past that. What I need now is to see the case closed and whoever killed Judy behind bars."

Though he remained calm, Kendra heard the undercurrent of emotions in his words. He was a man on a mission, and she didn't blame him. Yet the question foremost in her mind remained. Paul was on the hunt for a man who'd killed someone dear to him. Would he be an asset to the investigation or a liability?

"You can accept my help or not, Kendra, that's up to you. But I'm leaving here early tomorrow and I'm investigating the case."

"You can't go home, Paul, not yet. Think about it. If the gunman is still after you, that's the first place he'll look."

"I don't plan on sitting around. I'll be on the move, digging for answers."

She narrowed her gaze. "So, what you're telling me is that I either accept your help or you'll go solo and probably get in my way."

"I won't give you reason to charge me with obstruction, but unless it's hard evidence, I'll be keeping whatever I learn to myself." He straddled one of the chairs and regarded her patiently. "It's your call. I've got some great sources in town who'll help me if I ask, but they won't give you, an outsider and a stranger, the time of day without a warrant. If you want answers quickly, I'm your best bet."

There was something infinitely masculine about the way he was sitting, his steady gaze on her. Paul was all testosterone wrapped in a nice tight package of muscles, courage and pride.

"You're trying to push me into a corner," she said.

"Nah. If I were, we'd both enjoy it more," he said, giving her the most amazing lopsided grin.

She glared at him, a look she'd learned from her dad, the colonel, but Paul never even flinched. He calmly gazed back, challenging her with his easy smile and iron will.

This was getting her nowhere, and the fact was, he held all the cards right now. "All right, we'll work together, but I'm wearing the badge, so follow my lead."

"You've got yourself a deal," he said, standing.

He'd agreed a little too quickly for her tastes, but she'd take it as a win. "I'm good at what I do, Paul.

You'll find that out soon enough. If Miller's here, I'll take him down." Once again she blew the annoying strand away from her face.

He strode up to her, stopping so close she could feel the warmth of his body. A shiver touched her spine, but refusing to step away, she threw her shoulders back and met his gaze.

Paul smiled, brushing his hand over the side of her face and pushing away the strand of hair. "There you go. I saw you crinkling your nose and trying to blow it away. I thought I'd help."

He towered over her. Awareness, the raw and totally inappropriate kind, made her heart begin to race. "Static electricity. No humidity here in the desert." She stepped around him quickly. She'd glom it down with a half can of hair spray if necessary from now on.

"All right then," she said. "We leave in the morning. You lead the way out so I won't get stuck again."

"Why did you rent a sedan? That wasn't a very practical choice for the Four Corners."

"No kidding. I flew into the Hartley airport planning to rent something with four-wheel drive, but the agency had most of their vehicles on reserve for an event over at the power plant."

He nodded. "Daniel's training exercise. They put on a show for politicians and investors."

She walked around the big room, putting more distance between them and pretending to admire the decor. Paul was a living, breathing temptation. It had been a long time since she'd met a man who could make her pulse start racing just by stepping close to her.

"As long as the sniper is out there, one of us should stay awake and keep watch. We need a schedule," she said.

"We are safe," he repeated with his usual calm. "But, okay, what do you have in mind?"

"How about four-hour rotating shifts?" she said.

"Fine. I'll take the first watch," he said. "I'll need to be a lot more tired before I can doze off anyway."

As he reached down to adjust a log on the fire, she saw him rub his shoulder. "Do you need painkillers?" she asked, wishing she'd considered that possibility earlier. If his senses were occasionally lulled by medicine of any kind…

"My shoulder aches a bit from time to time, but I don't take anything for it. There's no need," he said. "The reason I wouldn't be able to sleep right now is because I'm not tired enough. I've never required the same amount of rest most people do—a plus in my former and current professions."

"If I don't get enough sleep, my brain doesn't work right, and at the moment, I'm exhausted," she said. "It's almost three a.m. now, so let me sleep till seven. Then you can wake me and get some sleep yourself while I get in touch with your brother and see what he or his people have found out. Once you're up we'll drive in to Hartley."

"Preston will have something for you by morning,

count on it. When he's working a case, he sleeps even less than I do."

"One more thing," she said. "If you need to go outside for *any* reason, be sure to tell me. I tend to go on the offensive if an unexpected noise wakes me up."

"You're always on alert?"

"Yeah. When I'm running down a fugitive or I'm on a protection detail, a part of my brain is always on duty."

"Good instincts. They'll keep you in one piece."

As he glanced away to turn off a lamp, she unhooked her holster. Leaving her weapon inside, she placed it on the coffee table within grasp.

"Use the blanket," he said, taking the closest chair. "It's comfortable *and* warm."

She pulled it over her. Wrapped in a comfortable cocoon of warmth, Kendra closed her eyes. Without visual cues, she became aware of Paul in a more primal way. She could hear the even sound of his breathing and enjoyed the outdoorsy scent that clung to him.

Though he was quiet, she heard him get up to stoke the fire. The crackling of the logs and the comfort of the blanket worked a magic all their own and soon she drifted off to sleep.

Paul smiled, his gaze resting on Kendra. Although he knew no one was out there, he remained seated on the easy chair closest to a window. Taking off the lynx fetish he wore around his neck, he held it in his palm and gazed at it for a moment. Like all of *Hosteen* Silver's gifts, the hand-carved wooden artifact was far more complicated than it appeared to be at a glance.

Lynx was said to be able to peer into the soul of man or beast and see the secrets hidden there. As the owner of the fetish, he knew that gift was his to use, but for many years he'd refused to accept such things were possible.

Slowly, as his mind had opened to new possibilities, he'd discovered that he could always sense when someone was lying to him, or even holding back. In time, he'd stopped searching for logical explanations and grew to accept his newfound ability.

The gift had served him well during his days as a U.S. Marshal and continued to do so now, even though he no longer wore the badge. He leaned back and relaxed, confident that the terrain around the house held no secrets from him or Lynx.

Hearing the rhythmic sound of Kendra's breathing, he focused on the woman. The blanket had slipped to her waist, and her simple wool sweater, though loose, accentuated her full breasts. Like many women in the marshals service, she did her best to underplay her curves, but thankfully, some things were impossible to hide.

Kendra was an irresistible blend of toughness and gentleness. She was clearly a fighter who'd refused to back down, even when staring down three gun barrels. Yet, in this unguarded moment, she was the most feminine of women.

He'd known all types of females and enjoyed their

company, but he'd always had one rule. He never stayed with any particular woman for long. Some had accused him of deliberately keeping his heart out of reach, and there was some truth to that. He didn't trust relationships. Promises made in the night didn't last when exposed to the light of day.

He'd only had one relationship that had stood the test of time, the one with his former partner, Judy Whitacre. The reason was plain. Though they'd cared deeply for each other, the job had always come first to both of them. They'd worked together for three years, and although gossip within the ranks had suggested otherwise, they'd never acted on their feelings. They'd both known that crossing that line would have jeopardized their working partnership.

Paul heard the faint rustling of something moving through the brush outside. Although that type of sound usually indicated the presence of an animal, he'd have to check it out. Seeing Kendra was still sound asleep, he slipped noiselessly out the back door.

Chapter Three

Paul moved silently around the outside perimeter of the house, pausing often to listen while searching the trees just beyond.

He'd made his way to the front corner of the house when he saw the source of the sound.

Paul smiled as the lynx took a step forward, almost as if in silent greeting. The last time he'd seen his spiritual brother had been during a particularly low point in his life—his rehabilitation process.

He'd been wandering aimlessly around the canyon during a long, sleepless night, his shoulder a throbbing reminder of the challenges ahead. Anger and pain, his constant companions in those days, had conspired to undermine him at every turn.

Struggling to find the courage to face what still lay ahead for him, he'd stood alone, waging his solitary battle, when he'd heard the low, throaty growl of the cat. Lingering in the shadows, unwilling to come out into the open, was a lynx.

In the animal's caution, one born of fear, he'd seen his own inability to move forward, and realized then that life was all about choices. His days as a U.S. Marshal were over, but he was still very much alive. He could choose to let his injury define him or build a new future for himself.

Facing the best and worst in himself that night had given him the ability to go on. A few months later, he'd opened his own private investigations firm.

Tonight, as he looked down at the cat and saw the kill the creature had just made, Paul realized that the animal's focus was his meal. The moment was all that mattered to him.

He, too, wanted to live in the present and stop looking to the past. Yet the sound of Judy's startled gasp as the bullet passed through his shoulder and into her body continued to haunt him. Until her killer was caught, he'd never be able to move on.

He clutched the lynx fetish in his hand until the wood bit into his skin.

"Don't move!" Kendra snapped from right behind him.

The animal disappeared in an instant. As it always had been, the cat showed himself to no one except him.

Having recognized Kendra's voice, he turned around. "Relax—"

She reacted automatically, raising her gun.

Instinct kicked in, and he countered without thinking, sweeping her gun hand, twisting her around, and pulling her back against his chest. With her gun hand pinned to her side, he held her steady, his arms locked around her.

"It's me," he repeated, dodging a kick to his instep.

She relaxed instantly. "Paul? I *told* you to tell me if you left the house. I thought you were in another room and that someone was tampering with the vehicles—or worse! What the heck are you doing out here?"

"I came to see an old friend," he said, noting that she wasn't trying to break free.

"Where?" she asked, trying to wriggle out and look around.

Reluctantly, he let her go, noting she had fit just right against him. "Not a person, an animal."

"You feeding the coyotes or something?"

He shook his head. "No, it's more complicated than that."

She searched the area trying to see what he was talking about, but it was too dark. "Come on, let's go back inside. I don't want to stay out here any longer than necessary. This is the best time for a sneak attack."

"Yeah. It'll be dawn soon," he said, letting her take the lead in the walk back around the house. "Why don't you get a little more rest?"

"Can't. I'm wide awake now."

"So, how about a real early breakfast then?" he asked.

"Thanks, but, no. It's too early for me to even think of food," she said, glancing at her watch. It was a little after five. "Unlike my brother, I'm not a big fan of breakfast. But our father, the colonel, used to insist on it. Personally I feel more primed for work if

I have a mug of strong coffee and something sweet, like a doughnut."

He laughed. "Not much for health food, are you?"

"Hey, I grab a sandwich at lunch. My anchor is a good dinner, when I'm not on the run."

When they stepped back into the house, Paul walked over to his chair and picked up his jacket. "Since we're both up, why don't we get an early start and head back?"

"If we start too early, we'll have to wake people up. We want them relaxed, not cranky, when we ask for their cooperation," she said. "Besides, you need to get some rest, too. I need you alert."

"I grabbed some shut-eye before you arrived here. I'm not tired, and right now there are some things I need to do, like contact Nick and tell him I won't be at home. I need him to steer clear of my apartment."

"Nick?"

"He's the son of the man who owns my rental unit, which is over his coffee shop. Nick also cleans for me and makes sure my fridge is stocked."

"With my crazy work hours, the food at my place is usually leftover takeout with a coating of green fuzz."

"So you're not exactly a domestic goddess, I take it?"

She laughed. "Not even close. You know what it's like, working double shifts, pulling all-nighters, traveling the red-eye with a prisoner at your side. When I first started out, I put in long hours, but there was time off the clock, too. Then somewhere along the way, the balance shifted."

He nodded, setting his jacket down again. "It happens like that."

"One day I discovered that whether I was on the clock or not, my mind was always on the job."

"Law enforcement is like that. It starts out as a job you love, but pretty soon it's your life," he said.

"It gets under your skin," she said, nodding. "What I love most about it is that every day brings its own challenge."

"I miss the constant change of pace," he said. "When I started my agency, my shoulder was still holding me back. All I could really do was set up security, conduct interviews, and manage surveillance monitors for my clients. I spent most of my time pushing paper or watching screens."

"And it drove you crazy?"

"Oh, yeah," he said. "I'm a lot happier in the field."

"I asked you about painkillers before. How much trouble does your shoulder give you these days?"

"It aches from time to time, but it's nothing I can't handle. It's healed up nice." Rather than have her wonder, he stepped over by the fire and shrugged out of his wool shirt. "Take a look."

She drew closer to him, started to touch his shoulder, but then changed her mind and dropped her hand to her side. "Through and through, though it must have taken out a lot of muscle. A rifle bullet can do a lot of damage. Rehab must have been tough," she said softly.

He nodded. "It was, but the daily grind of exercises helped me get everything working again."

He saw her gaze drop from his shoulder and run slowly down his chest. Women generally liked what they saw, and he was man enough to know when they did. As Kendra licked her lips, a flash of heat shot through him. His shoulder had taken a hit, but the rest of him worked just fine.

"It's cold. You better put your shirt back on," she said, her voice husky.

Following an instinct as old as time, he curled his fingers beneath the curtain of her auburn hair and pulled her closer to him. His kiss was gentle, coaxing, not forcing, and as her lips parted, he deepened the kiss, tasting the velvety smoothness inside.

Kendra moaned softly, then pulled away, sucking in her breath. "Whoa!"

"My fault," he said.

She shook her head. "If I wasn't working a case I wouldn't have pulled back. That felt…really nice," she said, then took a steadying breath. "Paul, you're a player. I've already picked up on that. But I'm here to take down a high-threat fugitive. Getting sidetracked could cost us our lives, so this stops now. What happened is just the result of tension and fatigue. You know that, right?"

He said nothing, but in his gut, he knew differently. The attraction between them was real, and it was strong. He watched her for a moment longer. It was exciting to see the play of light and shadow in her hazel eyes. Kendra wanted more, just as he did, but she was right, the timing was all wrong.

"I'm going to get myself something to eat. Fresh coffee for you?" he growled, walking toward the back counter.

"Please."

"No doughnuts in the house, so how about leftover fry bread and honey?"

"That sounds great," she said.

An hour later, though it was still early, she'd finished her report, stowed away her laptop, and was on the phone with Paul's brother, Detective Preston Bowman, who was en route to the station from his home. "If you turn up any connection between Ms. Sharpe and Chris Miller I want to be there for the interview. Let me know what you get as soon as possible."

When Paul came into the front room moments later, Kendra was putting her cell phone back into her jacket pocket. As her gaze took in his backpack, she stood. "Shall I follow you into town?"

"I have an idea. We've already agreed to work together, so it makes a lot more sense to ride together, too. My four-wheel drive pickup will get us anywhere in the Four Corners that a vehicle can go. Your sedan—not so much. Why not just leave it here?"

"All right," she said after a beat.

They collected her gear and headed to his truck. "While you stow away your stuff I want to make a quick call to the kid who takes care of my place," he said. "I already left a voice mail for Nick, but I want to talk to him and make sure he got the message."

"Sure. Go ahead," Kendra said, placing her luggage behind the front seat.

Paul placed the call from his truck while the engine was warming up, and a few seconds later Nick answered. "Hey, Mr. Grayhorse, you want me to bring breakfast up now?"

"No, Nick, I'm not at home. There's something else I need you to do. If you notice anyone hanging around my place, or if someone comes by asking about me, call my brother, Detective Bowman, ASAP. Then call me," Paul said, and added, "Avoid anyone who looks the least bit suspicious or dangerous. I've made some enemies, and I don't want you involved. Got it?"

"Yes, sir."

Paul ended his call, but before they were halfway down the dirt road to the gate, Kendra's phone rang.

"Armstrong," she clipped, then listened for a moment. "Good job, Preston! Keep an eye on her, but hang back till I get there if possible. If Miller's at the apartment, I want in on the takedown."

Kendra placed her phone back in her jacket pocket. "Your brother's got it together. He's tracked down Yolanda Sharpe. She's home right now and, according to her neighbor, has a new boyfriend visiting. Preston doesn't have the guy's name, but the description he has of the subject doesn't exclude Miller." She paused, then continued, "The way Miller managed to disappear until now makes me think he's changed his appearance again, but what's hard is faking height. Miller's six foot one."

"So you want to meet Preston at Sharpe's place?" Paul asked.

"Yeah. Let's head there," she said, giving him the address.

"When you question them, let me sit in. If either Yolanda or her boyfriend lies to you, I'll know," he said.

"You sound awfully sure of yourself."

"I am," he answered, feeling the weight of the lynx fetish around his neck.

Chapter Four

Although she'd placed her small carry-on in the rear of the cab, she'd kept her laptop with her. While Paul drove, Kendra worked on the updated report she'd have to file tonight.

They'd reached the outskirts of Hartley when Paul finally broke the silence between them. "I know you've been working and that's part of the reason you've been so quiet, but I have the feeling that something else is bothering you. If you tell me what it is, maybe I can help."

"One thing at a time," she said, closing the laptop. "Right now let's concentrate on the operation underway." She checked the GPS on the dash. "Turn right. Yolanda's apartment complex should be just ahead."

"There's Preston," he said seconds later, and gestured to an unmarked police car parked behind a cable company van.

"From that location, the complex's vehicle entrance and exit are both covered," Kendra said with an approving nod. "They can be blocked off in a few seconds."

"You can bet he's got backup already in place too," Paul said, and parked.

Preston glanced at them as they approached on foot, then got out of the cruiser. "Yolanda's apparently been traveling and got in early this morning. According to the DMV that's her SUV over there—the green Ford with mud on the fenders. Not a blue pickup, obviously."

"Which one's her apartment?" Kendra asked.

"Two-oh-four, second floor, toward the middle," Preston said.

"Have you found any connection between her and Miller?" Kendra asked.

"Not so far. I also haven't been able to confirm the presence of a second person inside the apartment. My men are watching her, and she's been unloading the vehicle by herself."

"All right. Let's go upstairs and pay her a visit," Kendra said.

She led the way, walking briskly. As the three of them approached apartment 204, Kendra pushed back her jacket so that both her service weapon and badge were clearly visible.

Paul remained beside Kendra. Preston, who'd crossed to the other side of the doorway, gave Kendra a nod. She knocked loudly, but before she could identify herself, a female voice from inside called out.

"Hold on, Alex. I'm putting the beer in the fridge."

There was a clanking sound, then steps across the

floor. The door opened a second later and a dark-eyed, long-haired blonde in her mid-twenties answered.

Seeing them, her expression changed from a grin to a scowl. "Whadda ya want? I haven't done anything wrong."

"I'm Marshal Armstrong, Ms. Sharpe. This is Detective Bowman of the Hartley Police Department, and I believe you've already spoken to Mr. Grayhorse." Not giving her a chance to reply, she added, "We need to ask you a few questions."

"Show me your ID. Anyone can buy a badge these days," Yolanda snapped at Kendra.

Kendra reached into her pocket and brought up her ID.

Yolanda shrugged. "Yeah, okay. So what's this all about?"

Kendra watched her closely. "You can start by telling us why you wanted to hire Mr. Grayhorse."

"What do you mean, 'hire'? I've never seen or spoken to that guy before in my life." She took Paul in at a glance and smiled. "Looks like I may have been missing out."

"Are you telling me that you'd never heard of Mr. Grayhorse?" Kendra pressed, watching the woman's expression.

"That's right, but if you want to set us up…" She winked at Paul.

"Where were you yesterday between four p.m. and, say, nine at night?" Kendra continued, undaunted.

"Camping up at Navajo Lake with a friend. We

spent the past three days there. The weather was cold and lousy, but it was plenty hot inside the tent, if you get what I mean," she said, giving Paul another smile.

Paul, who'd deliberately hung back, heard footsteps coming up the stairs. As he turned his head to look, a short, barrel-chested man wearing a plaid shirt came into view.

"Hey, Alex," Yolanda said, "tell them where we've been."

Alex looked at Paul first, then as his gaze traveled to Kendra and Preston's badges, he spun around and raced back down the stairs.

"Police officers. Stop!" Preston yelled.

Paul knew instantly that it wasn't Miller. The guy was too short. Though unsure who Alex really was, he raced after him.

Alex had a lead and was as fast as lightning. By the time Paul reached the stairs, the man was stepping onto the parking lot. Paul took the stairs in three steps, but Alex was already climbing into the Jeep.

"Preston, he's heading north!" Paul yelled as he ran to his pickup.

The guy's vehicle was already on the move. The Jeep's tires squealed as Alex swerved, scraped a carport support pole, then sideswiped a parked motorcycle.

Suddenly a police cruiser raced up, blocking his exit.

Alex hit the brakes, sliding to a stop inches from

the squad car, and ducked down, reaching for something on the floorboard.

"Gun!" Kendra yelled, approaching in a crouch from the passenger's side of the Jeep, her pistol out.

"Police!" Preston yelled, taking aim over the hood of the cruiser. "Put your hands up where we can see them."

Alex's arms shot up into the air. As he rose to a sitting position again, Kendra rushed up, pistol aimed at his chest.

"Who *is* this idiot?" Preston said as he came around the front of his unit.

"Not Miller, that's for sure, but from the way he took off, I'm guessing he's got a record." Paul glanced at Kendra. "Where's Yolanda?"

Kendra cocked her head back toward the staircase. "Unless she's got a lock pick, she's still handcuffed to the railing."

After Alex had been read his rights, Kendra examined the ID Preston had fished out of the man's pockets.

"Alex Jeffreys, make it easy on yourself and explain why you ran," Kendra asked.

"I want a lawyer," came the clipped, clearly practiced reply.

As Preston turned Alex over to a uniformed cop on the scene, Kendra holstered her weapon. "He's all yours, detective. That isn't the fugitive I'm after."

"Let's see who we're dealing with." Preston went back to his cruiser and ran Alex's name through his computer. "Jeffreys has an outstanding warrant for check fraud and ID theft. He's never been with the department," he added, obviously remembering Yolanda's story about her boyfriend being a cop.

"We still need to know how Yolanda's connected to what happened to Paul last night," Kendra said.

"I'll place her under arrest, then meet you at the station," Preston said.

Paul remained silent long after they were back on the road. "Alex is going to be a hard nut to crack," he said at last. "And I'm thinking that Yolanda may not be the same person who called. Her voice sounds different, for one."

"Maybe she was disguising her voice on the phone," Kendra said. "Either way, it's still possible Alex used his girlfriend to set you up."

"Maybe," he said. "If you let me sit in during questioning, I'll be able to tell you for sure."

Kendra remembered one report she'd read. Paul's first partner, the one before Judy Whitacre, had claimed that he had an almost uncanny ability to separate lies from the truth. "Your foster father was a medicine man, and I know there's a lot of psychology involved in healing rituals. Did he teach you how to read people?"

"No, it's not like that." He paused for a moment before continuing. "What *Hosteen* Silver did was open my mind so I could use the gift he'd given me."

She gave him a curious look. "I don't understand.

When you say 'gift,' are you talking something supernatural?"

He shrugged. "I can get you results. Do you want my help or not?"

She hesitated, then nodded. "Okay, but I'll take lead. Agreed?"

"Sure." He pulled into the parking lot beside the police substation. "You don't really trust me, do you?"

She weighed her answer carefully. "Intuition tells me that there's more to you than meets the eye, and intangibles make me uneasy."

"Just remember we're on the same side."

"I know. That's the only reason I've allowed you to get actively involved."

"No, there's another reason—one you're keeping to yourself."

His insight was right on target and took her by surprise. She suspected that Paul held the key to taking down Miller. If Miller was really in the area, and he'd come after Paul ten months after his initial attempt to kill the judge, there had to be a reason. Providing she could figure out what that was, she might be able to use it to draw Miller out of the shadows.

She looked at Paul with new respect. No one had ever been able to read her like that, yet Paul had somehow guessed that she'd been holding out on him.

"See? That's part of what I do," he said.

"How? Will you ever tell me how you developed your…skills? I'd be interested."

"Maybe someday," he said quietly. "For now, let's

go see what we can learn from Yolanda and her boy-friend. Hopefully, they'll actually know something of value."

THE ROOM USED to question suspects was purposely kept just a little too warm. The subject was meant to be uncomfortable. The straight-backed wooden chair and simple wooden table were other ways of cutting creature comforts.

Paul and Kendra were in an adjacent room with Preston. Standing next to the two-way glass, they watched Alex, who was sitting alone in the room.

"He's an old hand at this," Preston said. "He's only said one word—'lawyer.' You'll have more leverage with Yolanda. She wants to cooperate. It's clear to her that she could go to jail if convicted of harboring a fugitive."

"It's good that you have her thinking about that. I'll interview her now," Kendra said.

"You going in, too?" Preston asked his brother.

"Yeah."

"Down the hall, second door on the left," Preston said, indicating the direction with a nod.

They walked into the room several seconds later and found Yolanda pacing like a caged lion.

"Sit down!" Kendra snapped.

Yolanda obeyed instantly. "You've got to believe me. I had no idea there was a warrant out on Alex. If I'd known, I wouldn't have gone within a mile of him."

"The fact remains, you *were* harboring a fugitive. We could send you right back to jail."

"No, listen, I didn't know!"

Kendra sat across the table from Yolanda while Paul leaned against the wall, watching them.

"You called Paul Grayhorse yesterday afternoon and asked for his help. You claimed to be afraid of your boyfriend, a police officer, but Alex isn't a cop. So what's the deal, Yolanda? What were you trying to pull?" Kendra demanded.

"I didn't call *anyone* yesterday. My cell phone didn't even work up by Navajo Lake," Yolanda said.

"You weren't at Navajo Lake. You were home. You telephoned me from your house phone," Paul said. "I recorded the call, which came at 4:27 p.m."

"I never made that call! I wasn't here," she said, her voice rising. "And I don't have a boyfriend who's a cop. I hate cops. N-o offense," Yolanda told Kendra quickly, clearly regretting the comment. Looking back at Paul, she added, "Dude, I never even heard of you before today."

"Did anyone actually see you over at Navajo Lake?" Kendra asked her.

"No, we were in the tent most of the time. Remember I told you—" She stopped, then added, "Wait a sec. You said I called you yesterday *from my apartment?*"

"Yeah," Paul said.

"Then someone must have broken in," she said. "That's the only thing that makes sense. Maybe it was the landlord. He's kinda creepy."

Kendra said nothing. Sometimes, unnerved by the silence, a suspect would talk and in the process reveal something important.

Prepared to wait, Kendra glanced casually at Paul and saw that, although his face was void of expression, his eyes were alert. He was taking in everything around him.

For a moment she wondered what lay just beyond that steel-edged resolve. Paul kept his emotions well hidden, yet she knew just how close he'd come to being killed twice in the past year. He'd also lost his partner, and she suspected that beneath the surface he was concealing a lot of anger. Paul carried himself well and was the sexiest man she'd ever met, but was he also a dangerous man, now on the edge?

Kendra stared at the floor for a beat, forcing herself to concentrate, then focused back on their suspect.

The interview continued. "I'd like to believe that you had nothing to do with that phone call to Paul Grayhorse, but you're going to have to convince me, Yolanda," Kendra said. "A woman called, so it couldn't have been your landlord. He's male."

Paul came up and stood behind Kendra. "She's not lying," he said, his voice barely above a whisper.

Surprised, Kendra turned and saw the utter calm she'd come to associate with Paul etched clearly on his face. With effort, she tore her gaze from his and looked back at Yolanda.

"You said you had a recording of the call I supposedly made to you?" Yolanda asked Paul.

"Yeah, it's in my voice mail," Paul said.

"Let me hear it."

Paul pulled out his cell phone and played it for her.

"That's not my landlord, and not his wife either. Her voice sounds gravelly. But you can tell it wasn't me!" Yolanda protested.

"She *was* whispering," Kendra said. "For my money, it was you."

Yolanda shook her head. "Play it again, louder this time," she asked Paul. As he did, she smiled. "Now I know who it is. That's Annie, Annie Crenshaw. We used to be friends, but she's got so many problems now I can't stand to be around her. I forgot she still has a key to my place." She took a deep breath and let it out slowly. "Now I know what happened to some of my Navajo jewelry. I thought I'd misplaced it, but Annie probably ripped me off. She's hooked on meth and always needs cash to make a buy."

"Tell us more about this Annie Crenshaw," Kendra pressed.

"She got clean about six months ago, then her boyfriend dumped her and she started doing drugs again. She ended up losing her apartment. Now she's working the streets."

"Where does she hang out?" Paul asked.

"You might try the old brick building where Hensley's Gym used to be. It's supposed to be empty now. Last I heard she was sneaking in at night and crashing in one of the old locker rooms," Yolanda said. "But I doubt she's there right now. Once she's on meth, she finds it hard to stay still. Last time she was using she hung out in the alley between the bus station and the free clinic."

"Do you happen to have a photo of Annie?" Paul asked.

"No, but I'm sure you've got a mug shot somewhere," Yolanda said, looking over at Kendra.

"What about Alex? Does he know Annie? Could they be working together?" Kendra asked.

Yolanda stared at Kendra as if she'd suddenly lost her mind. "No way. They can't stand each other. Last time they were in the same room, they went at each other major league and she threatened to have him killed."

"All right, then. We'll look into this," Kendra said.

"So, can I go?" Yolanda stood, looking toward the door.

Kendra shook her head. "Not yet. Detective Bowman still wants to talk to you about Alex. What happens after that is up to him," Kendra said.

They walked to the door, Kendra knocked, and Preston let them out. He'd been standing in an adjacent room, listening and watching through the one-way glass.

Preston nodded to Kendra, then looked at his brother. "So what's your take on Yolanda? Do you think she's telling the truth?"

"I do, which means we need to track down Annie Crenshaw. My guess is that she was paid to make that call, and we need to know by whom," Paul said.

"That person is probably our shooter, maybe Miller, so finding Annie is our top priority now," Kendra said, glancing at Preston. The man was a hard-assed cop, yet he never questioned Paul's take on Yolanda's credibility. Something told her there was more to Paul's ability than he'd said.

Maybe he'd trained with covert ops somewhere, working closely with their professional con men and other highly skilled consultants. Federal law enforcement agents often had interesting, varied backgrounds.

Kendra looked at Preston, then at Paul. "How about going behind closed doors right now and tossing around a few ideas? Whatever we say stays there."

Preston nodded. "My office."

PAUL FOLLOWED KENDRA into Preston's spartan office, which held only a small desk, file cabinets and two folding chairs. There were no photos on the wall, only documents listing Preston's credentials.

Once they were seated, Kendra began. "What evidence did the crime scene team find at the site where Paul was ambushed?"

"Two slugs from a .45 were found embedded in the bricks of the Murray building."

"I was standing with the building at my back when the shooting started," Paul said.

"The shots were grouped tightly, the sign of an experienced marksman," Preston said.

Kendra leaned forward, resting her forearms on her legs. "My theory is that the gunman who came after

Paul is probably someone with a personal grudge, maybe someone linked to his P.I. business. With a rifle, Miller can hit a target at a thousand yards. With a .45, he can make a head shot at one hundred feet. The only reason he failed to kill the judge last November was because two U.S. Marshals got in his way. This can't be his work."

"I get what you're saying," Paul said. "When I got shot at last night I was the only target around and I was less than fifty feet away from the gunman. Miller's weapon of choice is the rifle, but he shouldn't have missed at that distance with a handgun either. I'd just been illuminated by a lightning flash—like I was standing beneath a flare. It was an easy shot for anyone with his level of training."

"Maybe he choked," Preston said.

Kendra shook her head. "Professional hit men don't choke and still group their shots that tight."

"Well, if it wasn't Miller, I have no idea who it could have been. Grayhorse Investigations primarily handles routine video and electronic surveillance," Paul said. "The reason I got involved in this last case was because a police officer was allegedly involved in domestic abuse." He paused, then added, "Anyone who wears a badge should be held to the highest standard."

She heard the barely concealed anger in his voice and realized the case had clearly struck a chord with him. Another idea suddenly popped into her head. What if the shooter had known Paul would react exactly as he had and used that knowledge to set him up as a target?

"Who would know that's how you feel about those who carry a badge?" she asked.

Preston answered her instantly. "Anyone who knows Paul or has worked with him."

"That's not going to narrow things down much for us," Kendra said.

"To track down whoever set me up, we've first got to find Annie," Paul said.

"I'll get you a booking photo of Annie Crenshaw. If you need backup, call," Preston said.

"Do you know the alley that Yolanda spoke about?" Kendra asked Preston.

Preston looked up from the computer screen and nodded. "Downtown, between Third and Fourth streets. Strictly small-time dealers hang out there, but they watch each other's backs and usually see our people coming. It's hard to set up a sting there."

"I hear you," Kendra said, then glanced at Paul. "Street people are usually unpredictable and half the dealers are high themselves. You want to sit this one out? Someone's likely to pull a weapon once I show a badge."

"A lot of people around here know I'm private, not a cop, and I'll get farther than you can flashing your badge. Let me help out."

"All right, then. Let's go," she said, leading the way out of the building.

"Unless we actually see Annie, let me pick who

we approach. We're more likely to avoid trouble that way," Paul said.

Kendra didn't answer. In situations like these, only one rule applied. Whatever could go wrong would— and at the worst possible moment.

THEY WERE BACK in Paul's truck moments later. "Before we head over to the alley, let's stop by Hensley's Gym. It's on the way," Paul said. "I'd like to check out the place where Annie supposedly crashes at night. It might give us some insight into her current situation that'll help when we question her."

"If we go onto private property without probable cause we'll be trespassing, and that'll place us on shaky legal ground. Do you know someone who could give us access?" Kendra asked.

He nodded. "I went to school with Bobby and Mike Hensley, the sons of the late owner. I'm sure I can get a key from one of them."

Several minutes later they arrived at a large sporting goods store on Hartley's west side. The place was bustling with customers.

"Looks like a sporting goods store is more profitable in Hartley than a gym," she said.

"No, that's not it. The gym was *Jim* Hensley's dream. He was really into bodybuilding and training. After their dad passed on, Mike and Bobby followed their own interests and started this business instead."

"Paul, is that you?" a voice called out.

A man in his early thirties came out from behind the

counter and shook Paul's hand. "I heard you'd moved back home. I've been wondering how long it would take for you to come by and say hello. Man, it's good to see you again."

"Sorry, Mike. I've been getting things sorted out and haven't had time to touch base," Paul said.

"Yeah, I heard. It sucks having to give up your career like that," he said. "You were the only one in our class who knew what he wanted before college. It took guts, reinventing yourself like this."

"At least I was able to walk away," Paul said.

"True enough." Mike took Kendra in at a glance and smiled.

"This is Marshal Armstrong," Paul said, introducing them. "We came hoping you might be able to help us out."

"Of course. Whatever you need, buddy. Let's go into my office and talk."

Once the door was shut and Paul explained what they wanted, Mike reached into the open safe behind him. He pulled out an envelope and slid it across the desk. "The key's inside. Guess Bobby and I should have boarded up that place."

Just then the door flew open and a boy who looked about three came bouncing in. He leaped into Mike's arms, and squealed with delight as his father lifted him into the air. "This is little Mike, guys."

Kendra smiled. She loved kids, but particularly ones close to that age, full of energy and innocence. The thought filled her with a familiar yearning, one that had become a permanent part of her these days.

For the past few months she'd been looking into the possibility of single parent adoption. She'd never met Mr. Right and wasn't sure he even existed, so she'd checked out other options. As she'd researched the adoption process, she'd discovered a series of hold-backs, some due to her profession, and all valid issues she'd need to resolve before she could take things any further. Unfortunately, she still hadn't come up with any solutions.

Paul shook Mike's hand and thanked him. "You've done really well for yourself, buddy. I'm glad to see it."

"My wife, Cynthia, and little Mike changed my life. I never thought I'd get married, but it was the best thing I ever did."

As they walked back out to the pickup, Kendra noticed how quiet Paul had become. "What's up?"

"I've seen two of my brothers settle down and I know they're happy, but the marriage scene...." He shook his head. "It sure isn't for me."

"How come?"

"I'm a confirmed bachelor," he said, then before she could press him for more of an answer, he added, "What about you? Is there a guy back in Denver?"

"Not in Colorado, not anywhere at the moment, but in case you're wondering, I have no intention of becoming one of those career marshals married to the job. I want...more...for myself."

"Like what?"

She shook her head, signaling him to drop it.

"A woman of mystery..." Paul smiled slowly.

The impact of that very masculine grin spread an enticing warmth all through her, and she avoided looking at him, afraid she'd give herself away.

Paul was big trouble, no doubt about it. He was a man who loved flying solo, yet he was built to perfection and could entice any woman with a pulse. Everything about him, from those wide shoulders to those huge hands, spoke of raw masculine strength. The steadiness of his gaze mirrored courage.

"I imagine you've got no shortage of girlfriends," she said.

"I can usually find a date," he said.

She suspected that was the understatement of the year. A man like Paul probably left a trail of broken hearts in his wake wherever he went.

TEN MINUTES LATER they reached their destination, an old brick building just one block south of Main Street in the business district. Paul drove his pickup down the alley, then parked beside what had been a loading dock. The big steel back door had a massive padlock attached to it. This entrance had clearly not been the one compromised.

"Let me go in first," Paul said, pointing toward the door and interrupting her thoughts. "If we come across squatters, I don't look like a cop, so we're more likely to avoid a confrontation."

"I don't look like a cop either. I'm in plainclothes, just like you."

He shook his head. "You're wearing business district clothes—dressy slacks and a matching jacket to look professional and cover up your handgun. You're also wearing sensible shoes, not heels, so you can fight or chase a perp. I'm wearing jeans, a denim jacket, worn boots and a working man's shirt."

"Okay," she said, glancing down at herself and shrugging. "Remind me to dress country. For now, take the lead."

She smiled as he moved ahead of her. He was long-legged, slim-hipped, and had the best butt she'd seen in a long time. Sometimes being second in line had definite advantages.

Chapter Five

Paul unlocked the door, then slipped inside noiselessly. He heard a faint scuffling and saw a mouse dart behind a discarded cardboard box. Against the wall stood an array of damaged exercise equipment, most missing key parts, like the treadmill without a walking surface.

They went through the two-story building quickly, verifying no one was about. Checking inside a large closet, they found that a weight bench had been placed beneath an access panel in the ceiling. The bench was dusty and revealed the imprints of small shoes—probably a woman's.

Paul climbed up and lifted the access panel. There was a built-in ladder there leading to the roof. "This is how she's been getting into the building. My guess is she's pried open the hatch on the roof, and climbs down." Paul stepped off the bench and brushed away the dust, not wanting to leave his boot prints behind.

"Hopefully we'll find Annie before she realizes that we're on her trail," Kendra said.

"If she comes in after dark, she probably won't notice the absence of dust on the bench," Paul said.

They resumed searching and after a few minutes they found signs of an occupant in the men's locker room.

Paul tried the faucet at one of the three small sinks opposite the shower area. "No water, but it looks like Annie has made herself at home." He gestured to a mirror that had been wiped clean.

"She probably chose the men's room because it's closest to her exit," Kendra said. "What we still don't know for sure is whether it's Annie who's living here or someone else."

Kendra walked around and saw the roll of blankets on top of an anchored wooden bench opposite a row of metal lockers. Farther into the room, two matching weight benches placed side by side served as a table. An empty can of soup, plastic spoon, and a bottle of soda had been placed on top of it.

Paul opened the locker closest to the blankets. "Take a look, Kendra."

Taped to the back of the locker was a small photo of two women in their late teens.

"That's Yolanda," Kendra said, pointing to the tall girl on the left.

Paul nodded. "I'm guessing that's Annie next to her. This must have been taken ten or fifteen years ago."

Kendra edged up next to him and studied the photo. "Memories may be all Annie has to hang on to these days."

"Do you want to wait around and see if she shows up?" he asked.

"I don't think she's coming back anytime soon," Kendra said, picking up a small plastic bag on the top shelf of the locker. It held minute traces of a white, crystalized substance. "She's either out looking for another hit or trying to raise the cash."

"Next stop, that alley over by the bus station?"

"Yeah," she said.

Paul's phone rang as they reached the door. He listened for a second, then spoke. "Whoa! Slow down, Nick. I'm going to put you on speaker, then start again from the beginning. Tell me exactly what happened."

"Okay, Mr. Grayhorse. It's like this. A stranger came into the coffee shop while I was bussing tables. He said you weren't home and asked me if I'd seen you around. He had a badge, but it wasn't from the Hartley P.D. and didn't look like the ones the federal marshals carry. When I asked him who he worked for, he said he was a cop with the Bureau of Indian Affairs," Nick said, and scoffed. "But he was paler than me."

"Nick's blond," Paul mouthed to Kendra.

"You didn't let him think you didn't believe him, did you?" Paul asked Nick.

"No way, I didn't want to piss him off. I just nodded."

"Smart move. Have you called Preston?"

"Not yet. I followed the guy outside to take a look at his license plate, but he drove off before I could get his number. He was driving a dark green pickup, not one of those generic white sedans or SUV's, and he didn't have government plates."

"Maybe my surveillance cameras picked him up. Here's what I want you to do for me, Nick," Paul said, then gave him precise instructions. "You got all that?"

"Yes, sir. I'll see you in ten minutes."

"Be careful, okay?" Paul ended the call and placed the cell phone in his jacket pocket. "Because my apartment is over the coffee shop, I want to avoid it for now. Nick will bring me what I need to access footage from my cameras. With luck, we'll be able to make a positive ID."

"Do your cameras cover the area outside the coffee shop, too?"

"They track most of the parking lot," he said. "There are a few blind spots, but the guy would have to have had some serious training to spot those."

"Let's go meet Nick then. The kind of clients Annie's looking for probably won't show up until the end of the work day, dinner time or later, so Annie probably won't be there yet."

"My thoughts exactly."

KENDRA KEPT HER eyes on the rearview mirror. "Nick sounds like a sharp young man."

He nodded. "He's a good kid. He's had some rough breaks, but he's managed to weather them all. I have a feeling he'll go far in life."

A long silence settled between them as Paul drove through town toward the northeast part of Hartley.

"The guy who's after you isn't coming across like

a pro," Kendra said at last. "A professional hit man gathers intel below the radar."

"And seldom misses—unless that's his intent," Paul said as he passed a slow-moving bus. "I've been giving this some thought, and the fact that the rounds came really close and were tightly grouped tells me that it wasn't meant to be a hit. It was a warning."

"A warning against doing what? You can't testify against Miller even if he did kill your partner. You never got a look at the shooter. Are you involved in another case you haven't told me about?"

"No, nor have I investigated anything that hasn't been solved—except the hit on the judge."

She said nothing for several long moments. "I'm getting a real bad feeling about this."

"Yeah, me, too," he answered. "There's more to this attack than we're seeing, and in our line of work, the unknown is what always gets you."

As Kendra glanced at Paul and their eyes met, she felt a spark of awareness. Almost instantly, she pushed that feeling aside. She was here to do a job, and nothing could be allowed to interfere with her work. The colonel had drilled that into her until it had become a part of everything she was.

"Nick wants to go into the marshals service someday," Paul said, breaking into her thoughts. "He's only sixteen and has a long way to go, but I think he'll make it."

"You really like that kid, don't you?" she said, noting the slight gentling in Paul's voice whenever he spoke of him.

"Yeah, he reminds me of my brothers and me in a lot of ways. Nick was in a truckload of trouble this time last year. His mom had died six months before and his father had buried himself in work," he said. "That's why Nick started running around with the wrong crowd. Before long, he was in over his head. He wanted out, but the street gang was putting a lot of pressure on him."

"So you helped out. How did you deal with it?" she asked.

"The gang leader's a punk with a bad attitude, but I'm badder." He gave her a quick half smile.

THEY PARKED IN front of Bookworm's Bookstore ten minutes later. The hand-painted sign out front advertised their coffee bar and Wi-Fi connection in big, bold letters.

"Bookstores have really been impacted by the economy. These days they have to diversify just to stay alive," she said.

"All the small businesses in this area have taken a hit, especially the mom-and-pop places, like Bookworm's."

"Yet you started your own agency," she said.

"Yeah, but it wasn't easy staying in the black, particularly at first. I've got my pension and disability, and I had to rely heavily on those to get by."

They'd just stepped inside the shop when they heard someone calling out.

"Hey, Mr. Grayhorse." A teenager she assumed was Nick stood and waved, then hurried over to greet Paul. "I brought your laptop. It's over there," he said, pointing to the corner table.

Paul took one of the three seats around the square table and opened his laptop. "Nick, did you look around your dad's coffee shop before you came over?"

"Yeah, but that guy hasn't come back," he said. "I also warned my dad to watch out for him. If he comes in, Dad'll give you a call."

"Great. Now think back carefully and tell me exactly what this guy looked like," Paul said.

"Like I said, he was just a regular guy. Tall, about your height, brown hair, brown eyes. I don't think he spent a lot of time outside, because he had light skin. He'd roast in the sun. Oh, yeah, I think he had freckles."

"Did he have any kind of accent?" Kendra asked. Miller had been known to speak with a slight Texas drawl. The light skin also fit. Miller was a natural redhead, though he repeatedly dyed his hair.

Nick, obviously unsure whether to answer her or not, looked back at Paul.

"Excuse my manners," Paul said. "This is U.S. Marshal Armstrong, Nick."

Nick shook her hand, then said, "He spoke just like everyone else—normal, you know, no accent."

"Was his voice higher or lower pitched than Paul's?"

Kendra asked. People often knew far more than they realized.

"Um, higher. And he talked faster, too, like he was in a hurry."

"Thanks," Kendra said. Reaching into her jacket pocket, she brought out her notebook, took out a photo of Miller, and showed it to Nick. "Could this have been him?"

Nick studied the photo. "Hard to tell. This guy's wearing a cap and sunglasses and the photo's bad. Looks like it's been Photoshopped, too."

"Yeah, but it's the best we've got," she said, disappointed.

"Were you able to direct the feed from my surveillance cameras?" Paul asked Nick.

"It took a while, but I got it to work," he said. "I tested it out, too, so it's all set. No matter where you log in you'll be able to monitor everything from your laptop."

Paul powered up his computer and entered his password. After a few keystrokes, he had the screen he needed. There was a small compass on the lower right hand side. "With this software I can redirect the cameras with the touchpad and conduct a real time 360-degree sweep of the area. If I catch anyone watching my apartment, I can zoom in on their location, lock on the cameras, and they'll track that person as long as he stays in range." Paul manipulated the touch pad to demonstrate.

"Sweet," Nick replied.

"One more thing, Nick," Paul said. "If you see the guy again, don't approach him yourself, you hear me? We have reason to believe he could be dangerous."

"Okay, no problem, Mr. Grayhorse."

After Nick left the shop, Paul remained at his laptop, sipping coffee while Kendra finished off a cheese Danish.

"I've looked at the prerecorded feed from all the angles. He's either incredibly lucky or he knew where to find the cameras and stayed away from them." Paul took his final swallow of coffee, logged off his laptop, and closed it up. "I've also checked real time surveillance, and things are clear over at my place. There are lots of people in and around the coffee shop underneath my apartment, so I think it's safe for us to make a quick stop by my place."

"Why take the risk? If we're going to have a face-off, I'd rather it go down away from a crowd of civilians."

"You need a place to change clothes, otherwise the people who hang out around that alley will take one look at you and scatter," he said. "They survive by avoiding anyone who might be a cop."

"I can stop at the MallMart and buy myself something less businesslike."

"Then they'll notice that what you're wearing is brand-new," he said, shaking his head. "You need to fit in."

"So what's your plan?"

"Borrow a pair of my jeans. You'll have to roll them

up a bit, but they should fit. You can also wear one of my pullover sweaters. It'll be big on you, but you can conceal your badge and gun beneath it easily."

"Okay," Kendra said after considering it for a moment. "But I'm calling your brother and asking for extra patrols in your neighborhood while we're there. If the guy shows up, I want backup close by."

"I can live with that."

As she called Preston, her gaze continually strayed back to Paul. Though she knew it would only complicate matters, the more she got to know Paul the more she liked him. After all he'd been through, she'd expected to find a jaded former marshal, sour on the world. Yet Paul wasn't like that at all. He still cared about people and had shown remarkable loyalty to the marshals service and his former partner.

"What's on your mind, pretty lady?" he said, his voice a gravelly whisper that ignited her senses.

For a moment she felt herself drowning in the dark, steady gaze that held hers. Certain he knew precisely how that look could make even the most sensible of women go a little crazy inside, she forced herself to look back down the street.

"It's not going to happen," she said firmly, pretending to be watching traffic.

"What?"

"You're not going to charm me, or tempt me to forget I'm here on business," she said.

"You're wound too tight," he said, chuckling. "I'm just being myself."

She didn't answer. She liked Paul way too much and he knew it. If she didn't keep her guard up, she'd end up in a world of trouble.

Chapter Six

They arrived at Paul's second-story apartment a short while later. "Living above a coffee shop has definite advantages," she said, noting the wonderful aromas that filled the air as they climbed the flight of stairs. "How did you find such an interesting place?"

"The apartment belongs to Nick's dad, Jerry. He gave it to me free of charge—minus utilities—as a trade-off for my surveillance services. It's worked out for both of us, too. Ever since I put up the cameras, his place hasn't been held up," Paul said. "Of course that's not the only reason he wanted me close by."

"I get it. You're a good influence on Nick," she said, and saw him nod.

"Jerry and Nick aren't close, but the gap between them widened even more when Jerry found out that Nick was in a gang. He had no idea how to help his kid."

"So what made you get involved?"

"Nick was headed in the wrong direction just like I was at one time. If it hadn't been for *Hosteen* Silver, my life would have been a real mess. I figured it was time for me to step up and do the same thing for someone else."

"Pay it forward," she said with a nod.

"Exactly." He entered a set of numbers on an electronic keypad lock, opened the door, and invited her in.

As she looked around Paul's combination living room, office and kitchen, Kendra realized that this wasn't so much a home as a place Paul lived in while he worked.

A large wooden desk held three computers, a multifunction printer and a monitor with a webcam. Two larger monitors with split screens and speakers hung on the wall behind and above the desk. Beside them, on a second rolltop desk stood a larger printer and a nineteen-inch flat screen TV. Across from that was a comfortable-looking leather recliner.

Beneath two small windows on the south side of the kitchen area was a counter that held a microwave oven and a coffeepot. On the adjacent wall stood a small fridge and narrow stove.

"It's small," he said as if he'd read her mind, "but it's easy to keep and serves my purpose. What's your apartment like in Denver?" he asked her.

"It's large, an old office loft, close to the federal building. It took me forever to find it. I needed lots of shelves for my…stuff."

"What kind of stuff?"

"Mostly knickknacks and collectibles I've bought over the years. Life with the colonel took us all around the world. Sometimes we'd move as often as twice a year. With his rank, we didn't have much trouble getting our stuff from post to post, but making each new place feel like home could be tough. Eventually I learned to surround myself with familiar things that had special meaning to me."

"You've referred to him as 'the colonel' before. You didn't call him Dad?"

"He preferred 'colonel.' He told Mom that it helped maintain a sense of discipline in the family."

"So he was strict?"

"Oh, yeah. For my brother and me, our house was like boot camp. You did things his way—no argument. Rules were everything to him. It was even more so after Mom passed away. By then I'd turned seventeen and I was marking off the days until I could leave for college. My brother received an appointment to West Point the year before. The first time he came home for Christmas, he told me being a plebe was easy, compared to home."

"Tough, huh? Do you ever visit the colonel these days?"

She shook her head. "He spends most of his time overseas, and a Christmas phone call is enough." Realizing she'd said too much, she suddenly grew silent. Paul was way too easy to talk to; she'd have to watch that from now on.

"It's been a while since breakfast," he said, stepping across to the fridge. "Hungry?"

"A bit, yeah."

"I have some frozen TV dinners. Take your pick—Mexican or Asian."

"Mexican."

"I'll nuke yours in the microwave while you go change clothes. Help yourself to whatever's in the closet. The shelves on the right hand side have my pullover sweaters."

"And the bedroom is…?"

"End of the hall—on the left."

As she walked to the back of the apartment, she found herself wishing she could have met Paul under different circumstances. Another time, another place, they may have become good friends…or more.

Kendra stepped inside Paul's bedroom and looked around. It was orderly but sparse—good thing, too, because it was tiny. The closet, with its two narrow sliding doors, was nearly empty—as opposed to hers, which was crammed full. She looked at the shelves fitted into the sides and saw the sweaters he'd mentioned.

She selected the top one, a blue wool crewneck, and slipped it over her blouse. It was warm and comfortable.

Kendra then chose a pair of jeans he'd draped over a hanger. Like most men, Paul had slim hips. The pants fit snugly on her, but they weren't uncomfortable. She rolled up the legs, creating cuffs, then looked at herself in the mirror attached to the closet door on the left.

She looked more like Paul's girlfriend than a cop now. For a moment, the very fact that she was wearing his clothes made her feel wonderfully wicked. It was like a warm, naked hug from the big man in the next room.

She smiled wistfully. Maybe someday she'd find a guy like Paul who could spark all her senses with just a glance. With luck, he'd also turn out to be a man who wanted the same things she did—a home and kids.

She shook free of the thought. She'd settle for a dinner date where nobody came packing a gun.

When she walked back to the front room Paul gave her a slow onceover. Although she was sure that it was a well-practiced gesture, it had the intended effect. The thoroughness of that look left her tingling all over.

Needing to focus on something safer, she pointed to the tea brewing in a cup on the counter. "Smells good. What kind of tea is that?"

"It's a special medicinal blend. *Hosteen* Silver taught us to fix it whenever…we needed it."

"That's the real reason you wanted to come here."

He shook his head. "It was part of the reason, but not the only one," he said.

"Are you in pain?" she asked bluntly.

"When the wind and cold pick up, my shoulder aches. *Tsinyaachéch'il* makes it stop."

"Didn't your doctor ever give you something you could take for that?"

"Sure, but painkillers put me in a haze, and I need to stay alert. Aspirin helps, but only in large doses. This tea works better all the way around."

"What is it exactly?"

"The main ingredient is an herb known as Oregon

grape. It grows in the high country." As he stretched his arm and reached into the back of the freezer for the TV dinners, she saw him flinch. He did it again as he placed the dinners in the microwave.

"Are you sure you're up to this search for Annie tonight? I could get your brother to assign me an undercover officer."

"In another twenty minutes, give or take, my shoulder will be back to normal. Don't worry, I'm fine."

She looked at the pouch that contained the tea. "Does Oregon grape taste as good as it smells?"

"Not by itself. The scent you're picking up includes some other herbs *Hosteen* Silver taught us to add to the mixture to make the tea more palatable."

"So what else is in there?"

He shook his head. "Knowledge like this isn't shared outside family. It wouldn't be appropriate for me to go into details."

The microwave dinged just then, and she didn't press him.

After a quick dinner, Kendra helped him pick up in the kitchen. "Are you good to go?" she asked, glancing at his shoulder.

He moved his arm in a circle. "See? No problems now."

Paul called Nick as they got ready to leave. "Keep an eye on my place, will you? I can't monitor the cameras where I'm going, so I'd like you to stay alert."

"You've got it, Mr. Grayhorse."

Hearing the howl of the wind outside even before

he opened the door, Paul turned to Kendra. "You're going to need a coat. Take my black leather jacket. It's on the back of the bedroom door."

He grabbed another, a well-worn, brown leather jacket from the hall closet.

"We're going to have to watch each other's backs in that alley," Kendra said after they were on their way.

"Just stay cool and don't tense up," Paul said. "Some of my informants hang out on that street, and I expect they'll come right up to us."

Ten minutes later they parked a block down from the alley, then strolled up the sidewalk. Drive time traffic had picked up since their bookstore trip.

They were on the side of the street that was sheltered from the wind by the tall buildings. Comfortable, Kendra fell into step beside Paul.

"Slouch a little more, and pick up some street attitude. You're walking like a cop," Paul said softly.

"Okay," she said, trying to correct her lapse.

They turned the corner beside the bus terminal and continued down the block. The alley between Third and Fourth streets was just ahead.

A tall redhead in a loose open coat, wearing a short skirt and a skintight top, greeted Paul with a huge smile. "Hey, Paul. How's it going?" she said, standing at an angle to emphasize her assets. "I didn't expect to see you downtown. You looking for some fun?"

"Hey, Brandy, how are you doing? Cold evening to be working."

"Pays the bills," Brandy answered with a shrug.

"So you looking for a threesome?" she added, giving Kendra the once-over.

Kendra forced a smile, glad she hadn't choked.

"Thanks, but, no," he said, placing his arm over Kendra's shoulder in a familiar, yet casual gesture. "Actually I'm looking for Annie Crenshaw—slim, blonde and a little shorter than you. I heard she hangs here sometimes."

Brandy made a face. "Oh, Antsy Annie? She's messed up. Don't waste your money. You can do a lot better."

"We just need to talk to her. Give me a call if you see her," Paul said, then reached for his wallet.

Kendra figured he'd give her his card but, instead, Paul handed Brandy a couple of twenties.

"You still got my cell number?" he asked her.

"Burned into my memory," Brandy said, giving him a big smile "555-1967."

A small, buxom brunette in jeans so tight they left nothing to the imagination came up and put her hand on Paul's arm. "Hey, handsome, it's good to see you."

"Hey, Kat," Paul greeted. "How've you been?"

Kendra watched Paul as he spoke to the women. He treated them with respect, looking past their present circumstances and seeing who they were at heart— women trying to survive. That kindness seemed to bring out the best in them.

Soon a tall, slender man wearing a stocking cap and a long leather coat climbed out of a parked Mercedes and came over. "These are my girls, so quit wasting their time with chitchat, Grayhorse. Make a deal or move along. Time is money—my money."

"Don't disrespect me or the ladies, Bobby. Get back in the car."

"Yeah, yeah. Talk big. Now look, man, you're hurting my business here, and my girls are trying to make a living. You got five minutes, then be gone before you scare away any customers, *comprendes?*" Bobby glanced at a passing car with a solitary driver. The man eagerly eyed the women, but when he saw Paul watching him, he accelerated down the street.

"There goes a regular. Am I gonna have to pay you to get lost, dude?"

"I'm looking for Annie Crenshaw. Seen her around this evening?"

"She ain't one of mine—too flat and skinny for my players. I saw her coming out of the Excelsior Drugstore about ten minutes ago, two blocks down on Fourth. If she didn't pick up someone along the way, she's probably at the far end of this alley by now."

Paul gave Bobby a curt nod and smiled at the women. "Take care, ladies."

"Come by anytime," Brandy said.

Paul and Kendra walked side by side down the sidewalk, circling the block instead of going up the alley. Despite their easy strides, Kendra stayed alert for trouble.

As the shadows deepened and darkness took over, the wind intensified. Cold gusts chilled their faces as they walked. Kendra pulled the zipper on the jacket all the way up to her neck. Remembering the scanty clothing Brandy, Kat and the other women had been wearing, she wondered how they could stand the cold. Maybe that was one of the reasons they remained around the corner, near the building.

As soon as they reached the far corner, they saw a slender blonde in a furry jacket, high heels and short skirt walking away from them down the sidewalk, her eyes on passing cars.

"I think that's Annie," Kendra said, "but we need to get close without spooking her. If she thinks we're cops, she'll probably ditch the heels and run for it."

"Why don't you cross the street and I'll hang back? Once you're past her, you'll be in position to cut her off if she decides to make a race out of it. Just don't make eye contact. Keep looking at your watch and pretend you're late for an appointment."

"Good plan. Let's do it."

Kendra crossed the street and then glanced back at him. Some men stood above the rest effortlessly. She hadn't known Paul Grayhorse for long, but something told her she'd never forget him.

Chapter Seven

While Kendra walked down the sidewalk on the opposite side of the street, Paul stood on the corner, pretending to text someone on his cell phone. Out of the corner of his eye, he saw Annie stop beside a lamp-post.

She turned in his direction, but he deliberately avoided her gaze, and she shifted her attention back to the street. Hopefully she wouldn't hook up with a customer or a dealer before they moved in.

Their luck held. Once Paul saw Kendra reach the end of the block and cross back to his side of the street, he made his move.

Paul walked toward Annie slowly, pretending to be focused on text messaging and looking up only sporadically to see where he was going.

By the time he got within twenty feet, she was waiting for him, assuming a sexy stance, with her hands on her hips, her chest out, her jacket open.

He put the cell phone back into his pocket and gave her an interested onceover as he approached.

She gave him a weary smile. "Hi, handsome. You

finally done texting, huh? How'd you like to party with a real live woman?"

"You read my mind," Paul said, smiling back at her.

Behind Annie, Kendra was closing in from the opposite direction. All they needed was five more seconds, and Annie would be trapped.

Suddenly someone in a passing car honked the horn. "Naughty, naughty," two or three teenage boys yelled in unison.

Annie turned, armed with an obscene gesture, and saw Kendra. As she looked back at Paul, her eyes grew wide.

"You're cops!" she yelled, spinning around.

Paul reached for her arm, but Annie slipped past him and shot down the alley. He sprinted after her, but the woman kicked off her heels, barely losing a step as she ran faster than a spooked jackrabbit.

He was closing in when she suddenly veered to one side, grabbed the chest-high end of a fire escape ladder and pulled herself up.

By the time Paul reached the ladder, Annie was already at the second story of the old brick apartment building.

Paul looked back. Where was Kendra? Ignoring the sudden pain radiating from his shoulder, he pulled himself up and began to climb.

"Annie, wait," he yelled. "We're not cops. All we want to do is talk."

"Screw you," she yelled from above, not slowing down. The ladder extended all the way to the roof, but instead of going to the top, Annie stepped onto a small balcony protected by a metal railing. Grabbing a big flower pot, she slammed it, plant and all, into the lock of a glass door.

By the time Paul reached the balcony, Annie was already inside the building. He slipped through the half open door and raced across someone's apartment just as a man in a bathrobe poked his head out from behind a hall door.

"What the hell?" Paul heard the man yell as he rushed past him and out the apartment's front door.

Hearing a bell, Paul turned his head down the dimly lit hall in time to see an elevator door closing. He raced for the stairs, taking each flight in three steps or less.

He reached the bottom floor in time to see Annie rush out the foyer, nearly knocking down an elderly woman at her mailbox.

The moment Annie left the building and stepped onto the sidewalk, Kendra cut her off. She grabbed Annie, spun her around and pushed her against the outside wall of the building.

"Stop struggling, Annie. I don't want to hurt you and you don't want to be hurt," Kendra snapped.

"All we want to do is talk to you," Paul said calmly, joining them outside. "We can walk over to the bus depot, get some coffee, and talk there, or we can do this at the station. Your choice."

"Not the station, please," she said, and stopped resisting.

Kendra eased the pressure on her wrist. "I'm going

to let you go, but if you run, I'll catch up and take you down hard. Your next stop will be a jail cell or the emergency room. I'm giving you a choice, so don't make me regret it."

"I won't run," Annie said.

"Good, now let's get out of the cold," Kendra said.

They walked down to the bus depot and went into the coffee bar. Annie sat down first, then looked at Kendra and Paul. "What do you two want from me?"

"We need some information," Paul said.

"I don't talk for free. Show me some money."

"Not going to happen. I'll give you a ride to the shelter, though," Paul said.

Annie shook her head. "I'll pass. So, what do you need?" she asked as Paul handed her some coffee.

"You made a call from Yolanda Sharpe's apartment the other night—to me. Why?" Paul asked.

"You're the mark. I thought I recognized your voice," she said with a sigh. "It was supposed to be payback for you sleeping with Chuck's girlfriend. He said you were a wannabe hero, and that you'd go nuts wondering what happened to the woman who called you. Chuck was sure it would keep you running around for days, hassling the cops."

Annie stared into the coffee cup, then back up at him. "Chuck was a loon, but I guess he was right about you, because here you are…."

"Back up a bit. Who is this Chuck character?" Paul pressed.

"Don't know…honest. He never told me his last name."

"What did 'Chuck' look like?" Kendra asked.

"Tall, brown hair, brown eyes, light skin, freckles, soft voice," she said. "Fit. Not bad-looking, I guess."

"Sounds like the guy Nick saw around his dad's coffee shop. Do you think you'd recognize Chuck if you saw him again?" Kendra asked.

"Maybe, but he kind of freaked me out, so I didn't look him straight in the face too long."

Kendra brought out the photo of Chris Miller and held it up so Annie could take a look. "Could this be Chuck?"

"Yeah…no…well, maybe. His hair looks wrong, and with the cap and glasses… Sorry, I can't be sure," Annie said.

"You sounded pretty scared when you spoke to me, Annie. Are you really that good an actress?" Paul said, watching her closely.

"I *was* scared. Chuck brought out this wicked knife. He told me that if I didn't make it sound real, he'd mess up my face real bad."

Paul didn't say anything, but his fist curled up. "So how did he find you?"

"I was working the corner by Central and Fourth. He pulled up, waved some bills, so I got inside his car. He said he didn't want sex, but he was looking for someone to help him mess with somebody. Pay-back, he said. He offered me two hundred if I'd make a phone call for him. After he handed me five twenties, I said yes. I should have known he was a sicko...."

"Why did he have you make the call from Yolanda's apartment?" Paul asked her.

"He didn't. That was my idea," Annie said sheepishly. "I wanted to get her into trouble. Chuck said that we'd need to use a throwaway phone because the guy I was calling was an ex-lawman with friends who'd trace the call for him. When I heard that, I figured using Yolanda's phone was a great way for me to get back at her."

"I thought you and Yolanda were friends," Kendra said.

"Not anymore. She won't have anything to do with me these days. She won't even let me crash on her couch, even though she's got plenty of room," Annie said. "Guess she forgot I still have a key to her apartment."

"So you've gone by there when she wasn't home?" Paul asked.

"A few times, yeah, and I took some of her jewelry to sell," Annie said. "Serves her right for cutting me out of her life just 'cause I'm down on my luck."

"A real friend won't let you go downhill without trying to stop you," Paul said, then gave her his card. "When you finally decide to get help to turn your life around, call me. I can connect you with the right people."

Annie took the card but didn't comment.

"A few more questions, Annie, then you're free to

go," Kendra said. "Did Chuck tell you what to say, or did you come up with that?"

"He gave me a script he'd written out and had me rehearse it until he was satisfied."

"What about his car? What make and model was he driving?" Kendra asked.

"It was a dark color, black or blue, that's all I remember. I don't know cars real well, but it was a two-door and it wasn't fancy."

"After he paid you the second hundred, he just let you walk away?" Kendra asked.

"No, it wasn't like that at all. Chuck was crazy, I'm telling you. By the time we were walking back to his car, all I wanted to do was get away from him and that knife. He offered me a ride back downtown, but I told him no, that I'd just take the bus. I even told him to forget about the other hundred he owed me, but he grabbed my arm and was pulling me back to his car when a cop drove by. He eased up a little then and I jerked free. I ran to the bus and rode all the way across town. I kept watch all the way, too, but he didn't follow. I haven't seen him since."

"We need a more detailed description of the guy you met, Annie," Kendra said. "Would you be willing to work with one of our techs and help us come up with a computer image of Chuck?"

"If I do, you'll let me go?"

"I don't think you realize just how much trouble you're in, Annie," Paul said. "We're the best chance you've got of staying alive. If I'm right, and I think I am, Chuck's also involved in the murder of a federal agent. Right now you're a liability to him. Without our help, you're as good as dead."

"I'll hide out and move to another part of town," she said quickly.

"That won't be enough. Think about this, Annie. You're a witness who can identify him, and you walk the streets, wanting to be seen. He's going to find you again, sooner or later. To stay alive you're going to need our help."

"I'll take care of myself. The cops can't help me," she said, a trace of uncertainty woven through her words.

"The weather's going to continue to get colder," Kendra said. "You'll be sleeping in places without heat, going hungry, and constantly looking over your shoulder for a killer. Is that really what you want for yourself?"

Annie shuddered and pulled her jacket around herself. "No," she whispered.

"Accept our help," Paul said. "You'll have a warm, clean place to sleep and food on a regular basis. Give yourself a chance."

Annie looked at Paul. "Why do you care what happens to me?"

"Everyone deserves a chance," he said reaching for his cell phone and dialing Preston. "That's all I'm offering you, Annie. What you do with it is up to you."

PRESTON PICKED UP Annie a short time later. "No jail, right?" Annie repeated.

Preston nodded. "As we agreed, Ms. Crenshaw. I'll take you to a rehab facility. Later today we'll send over our tech. He'll work with you to create a computer sketch of the suspect."

After Preston said goodbye and he and Annie had driven off, Paul walked back to his truck with Kendra.

"What's on your mind?" Paul said, noting Kendra's silence.

She didn't answer right away.

"Something's bugging you, so you might as well get it out in the open. Otherwise it'll stay in the back of your mind and remain a distraction."

"Okay," she said with a nod. "Here's the thing, Paul. I've noticed that you have a way with women."

"You think so?" He flashed her a quick half grin.

"I'm a Deputy U.S. Marshal, Paul. I'm immune. So focus," she added, working hard not to smile back.

"Okay, go on. What's your point?"

"You're a bachelor with no shortage of women friends, the kind who can lead a guy into all sorts of trouble. I'm thinking that it's time we took a real close look at your past...playmates," she said after a beat. "Maybe one of them hired the shooter, and this has nothing to do with Miller. Or it could be a boyfriend, like Annie said. This Chuck character came across as a jealous lover, at least to her."

"You want to rule out my personal life, that's procedure, but you're way off base there. Only one thing shares my bed right now—my Glock .40. I keep it under my pillow."

"I'm not passing judgment on you or your lifestyle, Paul. I'm just trying to find answers."

"I know. I would have asked you the same question if our positions had been reversed," he said, meaning it. "But I'm telling you, you're looking in the wrong direction." After a beat, he added, "I'm not convincing you, am I?"

She didn't answer. "Kendra, there's something you need to know about me. It's true that I enjoy the company of women. I'm a healthy, normal male, but you could count on one hand the number of serious relationships I've had."

He noticed her raised eyebrow and tried not to smile.

"You think I'm snowing you, but it's the truth."

"Okay, so tell me this. Who was the last woman you were seriously involved with?"

"She's not part of this, not anymore."

"How can you be so sure?" she pressed.

He looked her straight in the eyes. "Because she's dead. The last woman I really cared about was Judy."

She nodded, finally understanding. "Your former partner."

"Yeah." He remained silent until they climbed back into his truck. "What she and I had was special, maybe even one of a kind."

"I imagine you took some serious flak over that from your supervisory inspector," she said.

He shook his head. "There was nothing for him to

object to," he said. "Judy and I were close, yeah, but neither of us ever took it to the next level. We knew our place."

"Because you wanted to remain partners and that would have been a conflict?"

"Yes, exactly, but there was also more to it than that. Neither one of us was the kind who stepped into relationships easily. Judy had an ex-husband and a failed marriage in her history, and me, well, all I'd ever had was my foster family. She and I were a great team out in the field, but back then we were all about the job. Sure, our feelings for each other ran deep, but neither one of us was in a hurry to open the door to more."

"I know all about priorities and how important timing is in life," she said softly. "This job is never easy on relationships or families."

"True, but I loved the work. The first few months after I left the marshals service, I didn't know what to do with myself. It took me a while to find a new direction."

"And now?"

"I like working for myself and calling my own shots," he said. "My only regret is that I wasn't allowed to officially continue investigating the case that took my partner's life."

"If Chris Miller's here in this community, I'll have my collar, and you'll have your closure. I won't back off till my work's done."

"So let's get busy," he said.

"Before we do anything else I need to find out if

the local P.D. has software that'll reconstruct the angle and trajectory of the bullets the gunman fired at you. I've got this nagging feeling that we're missing something important."

"It's a small department, so even if they did, it's likely to be an old version, but not to worry. I know where we can get access to a computer with state-of-the art everything." He switched on the ignition and put the truck in gear.

THEY RODE IN silence until Kendra apparently ran out of patience. "Is this a covert op or are you going to tell me where we're going?"

"My brother Dan's place," he said, laughing. "It's like a fortress there, so the added benefit is that we'll be safe while we work. My gut tells me that Chuck and Miller are the same man, so we have to keep our guard up."

"Everything I've read about Miller tells me that we're chasing a ghost. He constantly changes his appearance, and he's good at playing chameleon."

"That's why he's been a high threat/high priority fugitive for such a long time."

"I've got one advantage no one before me has ever had. You're with me, so if Miller's really after you, I won't have to find him, he'll find us," she said.

"You're still not convinced that Miller was the gunman, are you?"

"There's no way for us to know, not yet, but here's

the thing. If it is Miller, the evidence says he's playing with you and we've got to figure out why."

Paul said nothing for several long moments. "You remind me of Judy in some ways. When things didn't line up just right, she'd keep digging until something turned up. I never saw her back off a case."

"I'll take that as a compliment," she said.

"It was meant as one."

She took a deep breath, then let it out in a long sigh. "It's hard, isn't it, when someone you care about is taken from you so abruptly. One minute they're there, the next they're gone."

"It sounds like you lost someone, too," he said.

Kendra nodded and swallowed hard. "My mother died of an aneurism when I was a senior in high school. I left one morning for school, and when I came home in the afternoon, I found her on the kitchen floor, dead," she said. "None of us were ever the same after that. She was the heart of our family."

He heard the sorrow in her voice and instinctively reached out for her hand. It was small and soft, and as he looked directly at her, he felt an unexpected warmth touch the cold emptiness inside him.

He brought Kendra's hand up to his lips and brushed a kiss over her knuckles. In their profession, survival meant being tough. Yet even the strong weren't above feeling pain.

When she drew her hand back at last, he gazed at her for a second longer. "When I wore the marshal's badge I rarely did anything that wasn't connected to work, one way or another, but I loved it. Is that the way it has been for you?" He had a feeling that there was a side of Kendra he'd yet to see. When he saw the shadow that crossed her eyes, he knew that he'd hit a nerve—one she didn't want exposed.

"I am what I am, a Deputy U.S. Marshal who's very good at her job."

He nodded, noting that she hadn't really answered his question. But he was patient. In the days ahead, he'd learn more about her. Something told him that Kendra was worth the wait.

Chapter Eight

"Are we going to your brother Daniel's office or his home?" Kendra asked as Paul drove down an industrial area at the western end of Hartley.

"Both, actually. His home is at the rear of the building, with a view of the mesas to the south," he said. "His wife has been insisting that they buy a house, but I just don't get it. They've got plenty of room. The place is just inside the city limits and used to be a farm equipment business." He wanted to get to know Kendra, and figured her response to his comment might tell him something more about her.

"Maybe Dan's wife wants a place that's exclusively her home—a place completely separate from her husband's work," she said, then added, "And who wants their kitchen to be a converted tractor showroom?"

Paul shrugged. "It sounds like you agree with my sister-in-law."

"I do. When I put away my gun at night, I want to relax in a setting that reminds me that I'm more than my work. My place is peaceful, filled with things that reflect the other side of me—the woman without the badge."

"When I was with the service, the work *was* my life," Paul said.

"And you still sleep in what's basically your office, so you haven't changed much," she said, flashing him a quick smile. "But I need the separation. Of course, there are times when work doesn't allow you any down time."

"Tell me about it," he said, laughing.

They arrived at Daniel's complex ten minutes later. Paul stopped, twenty feet from the metal gate that stood at the end of a driveway dividing two dark expanses he knew to be alfalfa fields.

"The lock looks like its impossible to tamper with, embedded in that big concrete post. What do you do, punch in a code?" she asked.

"Yeah, Dan's setup defeats bolt cutters or torches. Take a look."

As Paul looked past the gate toward Daniel's place, he felt the lynx fetish around his neck grow heavier. He pulled it out, thinking it had become caught in his sweater, but when he did, he saw the lynx's eyes glimmer.

He tensed and looked back toward the highway, where there was a lot of ground cover. Out of the corner of his eye he could see that Kendra's attention was focused elsewhere, and she'd wandered over close to the gate.

"It's so dark I can't even see my shoes." She reached

for the penlight in her pocket, but her cell phone came out too and fell to the ground. "Crap. Where'd it go?"

He glanced over at her. "Need my help?"

"No, think I found it." As she bent over to pick up her phone, Paul caught a flash of movement in the brush to his left, then a faint beam of red light illuminated by road dust. Turning, he discovered the bright ruby dot of a laser sight on the gate just above Kendra's back.

"Gun!" he yelled, racing toward her. Faint pops came from the field to their left, and they both dove to the ground.

Paul rolled onto his side, grabbed his Glock, then returned fire, aiming low to avoid reaching the highway beyond. Kendra also fired her weapon, twice.

The attack stopped as abruptly as it had begun. They held fire, then remained motionless, listening and searching the night for a target. About twenty seconds later, they heard a car motor revving up in the distance.

"Cover me!" Paul yelled, jumping to his feet. He ran in a zigzag pattern down the road, searching across the field for the vehicle. When he finally reached the cattle guard, it was too late to get off a shot. All he could see was the red taillights and rear end of a green car—no plate—screeching down the highway.

He cursed, then turned to look at Kendra, who'd run with him and stopped a dozen feet behind him. "You okay?" he asked, stepping closer.

She returned her pistol to the holster at her hip, then

reached up to touch her cheek. "Gravel and a scrape, but no gushing blood, so I guess I'm in one piece," she said thinly. As she turned up the collar of her jacket, shielding herself from the wind, she inhaled sharply.

"What's wrong?" he asked instantly.

"I'm not sure…maybe I'm wrong." She slipped off Paul's jacket and held it up in the moonlight for a closer inspection. There was a small hole at the back of the collar. "I wasn't wrong. That buzzing that grazed my face—it *was* a bullet."

Paul placed his hands on her shoulders, looking her over carefully. "Good thing you dropped your phone."

"By yelling at me when you did, you probably saved my life," she said, trying not to shake. "I'm a deputy marshal and I've had people shoot at me before, but no one's ever come this close."

The gate swung open with a loud squeak and they turned to find Daniel rushing forward in a crouch, assault rifle in one hand. "Get inside quickly."

"He's long gone, bro," Paul said, shifting his shoulder and biting back a groan at a spasm of pain.

"Come on," he said. "Hurry up anyway."

Less than two minutes later they were inside the big metal building, standing well away from the windows.

Daniel glanced over at his brother. "What is it with you, bro? You're a real bullet magnet these days."

"Thank you, I'm fine," Paul shot back.

"Hey, am I wrong?"

"This time, I wasn't the target," he said, then glanced at Kendra.

She brushed the gravel from her cell phone with an unsteady hand. "We need to call the Hartley P.D."

"Already done," Daniel said. "I'm also calling in some family help."

Kendra sat on the leather couch and opened her phone, verifying it still worked. "If Paul hadn't pushed me to one side when he did, the sniper would have locked in on me for sure."

"Fate always has the last word," Daniel said.

"This…incident," she said slowly and swallowed hard. "It's given me an idea, and a new angle we can pursue."

Paul knew she was using police speak to help her push back her fear and bring herself back under control. He'd had to do the same thing countless times when he'd worn the badge.

"So fill me in," he said.

"I will, but first I have to report what's happened to my supervisor in Denver."

KENDRA STOOD IN an adjacent office. Alone, she took several deep breaths before making the call. Once she was ready, she dialed and spoke to her supervisory inspector, Evan Thomas.

Kendra paid particular attention to the details, keeping any hint of emotion out of her voice. It was part of her training, and she knew what was expected of her.

"If you're really up against Miller, then I'm guessing he was aiming for Grayhorse, but you got in the way," Thomas said in a flat, no-nonsense tone. "Of course, if Miller found out that a marshal had been sent there to bring him in, it's also possible he targeted *you* first. You're the bigger threat."

"Well, Paul was closer, yet the rounds seemed directed at me, not him. This was the work of a professional, at least in my experience. I think he *was* after me."

"DON'T RELY on just your gut. You said there was a breeze, and the perp used a silencer. Wind and the low velocity of a suppressed round make for inaccuracy, and it was dark. Work with the Hartley crime scene people, check out the evidence, and see what you can come up with, then we'll talk again."

Kendra hung up, her thoughts racing. She'd been scared before, but now she was angry. She did trust her gut, and whoever had come after her was going down. After that initial burst of fear, only adrenaline remained.

She was pumped and ready for action. As a Deputy U.S. Marshal, she'd put some really dangerous men behind bars and made the world a little safer for everyone else. It was time for her to do what she did best.

Feeling more confident, she took a few moments for herself.

No matter how bad things got, she loved her work. What she did every day made a difference, and that's what kept her going.

Of course someday she'd have to make a choice— her work as a marshal or becoming a single mom. The crazy hours and the danger were all part of what had drawn her to the job, but her child would need security and deserved a parent who'd be home more often than not. That was one of the holdbacks she'd yet to figure out.

Sooner or later she'd have to find a new career, hopefully one that wouldn't make her feel she was just punching a time clock somewhere. She'd never be able to open an electronic security firm like Paul's. The work was too routine. Watching monitors or doing background checks all day would make her crazy. She was made for more active work, and if she didn't remain true to herself, what kind of mom could she hope to be?

She shook her head. All that could wait. Right now she had work to do.

As she stepped back into the hall, Paul was there to meet her. "My brother Preston is here now to help out. What's the news from Denver?"

"Evan Thomas, mysupervisory inspector, thinks you were probably the primary target, but I got in the way and needed to be taken out."

Paul said nothing for a moment, his gaze so steady it was unnerving. He seemed to be looking right into her soul.

"Yeah, and I know Thomas and where he's coming from. But you know he's wrong, and you've got solid reasons for believing that."

Paul was right on target. He could read her thoughts with amazing accuracy, and it was a bit unnerving.

"You were a Deputy U.S. Marshal once, Paul. You know there are details I can't discuss, not even with you."

"You still need help, Kendra, and you're going to have to start thinking outside the box. My record's spotless. You can trust me. Talk to me."

"Not here."

"Yes, here. My brothers are the most reliable backup you can possibly hope to have, but we can't work with you effectively if you're going to keep information from us." He paused and took a long breath. "I know you've read my brothers' files. They're men of honor. If we're going to stand in the line of fire, we deserve to know what's going on."

It took her several beats, but at length, she nodded. He had a point.

As they entered the room where two of Paul's brothers—Daniel and Preston—were waiting, she'd already decided that trusting them was the only way to go.

Kendra sat down at the big conference table and looked at the men already seated there, coffee mugs in hand. As Paul suspected, she'd read all their files. She knew about each of Paul's foster brothers.

Besides Preston, the city cop, and Daniel, the business security expert, there was Kyle, who was with the NCIS at Diego Garcia. Rick was with the FBI, but his current overseas work—location not listed—had been redacted in the one paragraph summary she'd been able to access. Reading between the lines, she assumed Rick was working undercover. All of the men, raised in a foster home by a tribal medicine man, were connected to law enforcement in some way. All except for Gene, who was a truck driver turned rancher in southwestern Colorado. From the documents she'd seen, they were a tight-knit group, and she could certainly use trained, trustworthy manpower.

"I'm going to need some help, guys, but what I say here today can't leave this room." She took the offered mug of hot coffee.

Paul looked at her and nodded.

Daniel did the same.

Only Preston hesitated. "I can't withhold information from my P.D., not if it's something that affects them directly."

"I understand, but this has more to do with the marshals service than it does with your department."

"Come on, Preston. I need you in on this," Paul said.

She saw the look that passed between both men and knew that nothing would ever trump their loyalty to each other.

"All right," Preston said at last. "I'm in."

Kendra nodded, and with a steady voice began. "The shooter who came after me tonight may be linked to a case I was working before coming here. He and Miller may even be working together."

It took her a moment to gather her thoughts, but no one interrupted the silence. Grateful, she considered her words carefully. The colonel and the marshals service had taught her to present facts as clearly and as succinctly as possible, leaving emotion—in this case her fears and sense of betrayal—out of the narrative.

"Before I was sent here to search for Chris Miller, I was working a different fugitive retrieval case. The felon I was after, John Lester, is a convicted gunrunner and a suspected member of the Hawthorn cartel. He served six months, then broke out of a Texas lockup. Since then he's always remained a step ahead of us. Last time we got a lead, I prepared for the takedown by restricting information to our office only. I also held off filing any reports that would give away the salient details. There was no way Lester could have guessed our next move, yet somehow he was tipped off. By the time we got to where he'd been staying, the only things left were his fingerprints."

Paul, Daniel and Preston exchanged glances again, but remained silent.

Kendra continued. "That's when I began to suspect we had an informant in our offices, someone inside the service," she said. "In view of what's happened, I think it's possible I was taken off that case because someone wanted me out of the way. Miller is the Hawthorn cartel's wet-work specialist, and Lester is a gunrunner for them. That connection may explain why I'm now a target."

"But what you've said also leads back to me," Paul said. "The judge my partner and I were protecting was presiding over Mark Hawthorn's trial. He's Garrett Hawthorn's brother, the leader of the Hawthorn cartel. I'm in the crosshairs because I prevented the death of the judge, and Mark was eventually convicted of murder."

"Do you have any evidence that proves the Hawthorn cartel has an informant inside the marshals service?" Preston asked.

Kendra shook her head. "All I've got is this. Right before I was sent here, while I was still hot on Lester's trail, I spotted someone tailing me after hours. I tried to double back more than once to catch the guy, but he was good, and I never did get a look at him—or her. I finally fell back on procedure and reported it."

Preston nodded approvingly. "Sometimes following protocol is the only way to go."

She shrugged. "Evan Thomas, my supervisory inspector, put two deputy marshals on me, but they couldn't find any evidence that I was being followed. Neither did I. Eventually I was called to Evan's office. The consensus that came down the chain of command was that I'd been working the Lester case too long and hard. I was given a choice. I could take leave and see the shrink, or accept another case, like the hunt for Miller."

"You were making certain people nervous," Paul said.

"Yeah, that's the way I saw it, too, but all I had was a gut feeling and a few random glances at a careful stalker—a man."

"Could it have been Miller?" Paul asked.

"Maybe, I only got a glimpse or two. Without solid evidence, there was no way for me to prove any of it.

But the guy had some serious training. Three of us couldn't work him into a corner."

"And now your supervisory inspector is assuming you're paranoid," Preston said. "But based solely on the facts, his theory about tonight's shooting at least has some merit. In the shooter's eyes, Paul's an easier target once his backup is taken out."

She shook her head. "Experienced snipers learn to focus and filter out distractions. If Paul had been his target, the bullets would have been directed toward him first. He wouldn't have wasted the opportunity to take him out. More details—Paul was closer, and I was moving away from the shooter's location. If Paul was the target, I certainly wasn't in the way, blocking his line of fire. If anything, it was the other way around."

"I agree with your conclusions," Daniel said.

"So here's what I think we should do, though admittedly, it carries some risk," she said. "I want to gather up photos of local criminals with the right weapons training and background, then take those to Annie. Let's see if she can ID any of them as 'Chuck.' If she can't, then we go back to searching for Miller."

"That's a good idea," Paul said.

"Why don't you access the photos from my computer here?" Daniel asked Preston.

"Yeah, might as well. It'll save time," he said.

"I'm going to call the rehab center and get an update on Annie," Paul said, reaching for his cell phone and moving away.

Kendra remained with Preston and Daniel, and a

few minutes later, Paul rejoined them, a somber look on his face. "Bad news."

Something in his tone made Kendra's blood turn to ice. "What's wrong?"

"Annie's gone."

Chapter Nine

Kendra swallowed hard. "What do you mean 'gone'?"

"It looks like she just split," Paul said. "She was at a group counseling session when she excused herself. They never saw her after that, so they think she may have slipped out the side door."

"That wouldn't have been hard to do," Preston said. "She was in protective custody—she wasn't a prisoner. A street-wise person like Annie Crenshaw would have found it easy to give them the slip."

"The center reported her absence to the P.D. about an hour ago. The D.A. was notified since Annie is a material witness to a crime," Paul said. "Officers checked out the gym where she'd been crashing, but they didn't find her."

"What about her cell phone?" Kendra asked. "Let me call her, or better yet, Paul, you do it. You had more of a connection with her."

He dialed, but no one answered. "All I'm getting is her voice mail. Let's stop by the alley where we first found her. Maybe she's working the streets again. Or maybe we can find somebody who's seen her and pick up a fresh lead."

"Good idea," Kendra said. "Let's go."

"I'll put a BOLO out on her," Preston said.

Daniel was the last to speak. "Wait a minute, guys. I've got an idea. Give me her cell number, Paul. If her phone's still on, I may be able to track the signal."

"You've got equipment that can do that?" Kendra looked over, eyebrows raised.

Daniel shrugged.

"Don't ask," Paul said, leading Kendra to the door. "Let's go. If he gets something, he'll let us know."

They were on their way a short time later. "We'll be getting there while people are still out on the streets so that'll help. If she's not there, we can ask around," she said.

They arrived a short time later and walked the alley from Third to Fourth Street, but couldn't locate Annie. Although they searched the area themselves and talked to the working girls, no one had seen her.

Soon they began cruising the neighboring streets in Paul's truck. There was heavy traffic around a city park sheltered on all four sides by multiple-story buildings.

"This is a good place for the street people to hang out away from the cold," he said.

"This park is more sheltered than the area around Fourth Street. With those scanty outfits, the women must be freezing this evening," she said. "I just don't understand what makes them choose the life."

"They tell themselves it's temporary, and that things are going to change for them real soon. That hope is sometimes all they've got to hold on to. Remember the movie *Pretty Woman?* The little girl who dares to dream of bigger and better things is still inside these women. That's what gets them through the day."

It was the gentling of his voice that captured her attention most. The way he'd treated Brandy and the others may have been rooted in something more than compassion. She had a strong feeling that there was a lot more to Paul's story. She wanted to ask him about it, but this wasn't the time for distractions.

"There's Kat, the brunette we saw before," Kendra said. "She just came out of that apartment building."

Paul pulled over to the curb. Kat and two other women were standing near the street corner as he and Kendra approached.

Kat looked over at them and managed a shaky smile. "Slow, cold night," she said, crossing her arms in front of her chest. "You still looking for Annie?"

Paul nodded. "Have you seen her?"

"She came by about ten minutes ago. She said she needed quick cash to get out of town. Got lucky, I guess, 'cause she scored a 'date' almost immediately."

"You get a good look at the vehicle—and the john?" Kendra pressed.

"It was an old van, Chevy or a Dodge. The guy had a beard, neatly trimmed, matching dark hair and wire-rimmed glasses."

"What about the van? Can you describe it?" Paul asked her.

"Like from the eighties. It was faded blue with one of those chrome ladders in the back and a luggage rack on the roof."

"Did you happen to catch the license plate?" Paul asked.

"No, sorry," she said, shivering.

Paul fished a few bills from his wallet. "Here you go, Kat. Call it a night, go home, and get warm."

"Thanks, Paul. If you ever need anything, information…or whatever…just drop by."

"Take care of yourself, Kat."

As she walked off, Kendra gave Paul a gentle smile. "You're not an undercover minister or something like that, right?"

He shook his head, chuckling. "No. I just know what it's like to be alone, miserable and afraid. It's something you never forget."

She wanted to know more, above and beyond the cold compilation of facts that were in his file, but before she could ask, he got down to business again.

"We need to work this block and talk to anyone who might have seen that van," he said.

"Let's split up. It'll go faster."

Kendra asked everyone she saw on her side of the street, but no one wanted to talk to her or get involved. By the time she joined Paul again, she knew at a glance he had nothing new to share either.

"I have a real bad feeling about this," Kendra said.

He nodded slowly. "There are hundreds of old vans in the Four Corners. Finding one based solely on the description we got is going to be tough."

"Even if we did, it doesn't mean the owner was driving it. It could have been stolen."

"Let's follow up on it from that angle, but meanwhile let's get out of this wind. I'll call Preston as we walk back to the truck and have him check the hot sheet. He'll put out a BOLO on the van, too," he said.

Paul brought out his phone but was forced to leave a voice mail.

Kendra's teeth were chattering by the time they got inside the truck. She wrapped Paul's leather jacket even more tightly around her and aimed the heating vent toward her. "Gusts like those get inside your clothing and chill you to the bone."

"The Navajo People say Wind's the messenger of the gods. Very little deters him."

"Is Wind supposed to bring good news or bad?" she asked.

"It brings…change."

"A nasty wind like this one, cold and bitter, can't bring anything good," she said, and shuddered, still cold.

"To those who'll remain outside, probably not. Be glad we'll have food to eat and a warm place to sleep tonight."

Again she heard that haunted tone in his voice. "You sound like someone who knows firsthand what it's like to be hungry and cold."

"I do. It happened to me more times than I care to remember."

She started to ask him more, but just then Paul's phone rang. It was Preston.

Kendra watched Paul, lost in thought. Before flying down to New Mexico she'd studied former Deputy U.S. Marshal Paul Grayhorse's file extensively. Yet the longer she was around him the more she realized that those cold facts didn't really tell Paul's story.

Paul glanced over at her as he was placed on hold. "Preston's checking the local and regional hot sheet. Let's see if he gets a hit on that van."

They didn't have long to wait, and with Preston's permission, Paul put him on speaker.

"Okay, here's what I got," Preston said. "We've had no reports of a stolen blue van in Hartley, but I broadened the search and found one in Durango, which is less than an hour away. The report is about two hours old, and, according to a witness, the van was last seen heading south."

"Toward New Mexico—and here," Paul said.

"So what are you thinking, bro?" Preston asked.

"Annie would have avoided 'Chuck' at all costs—unless he wore a disguise, which is one of Miller's areas of expertise," Paul said. "The fact that the john who picked her up had a beard and glasses…" He paused for a moment. "If we don't find Annie, she's as good as dead."

"I'll send additional units to the area, but we had a shooting outside a restaurant on the east side less than an hour ago. That gunman's still at large, so most of our available officers are there."

"Annie's an important witness," Paul said. "She's our only link to whoever's after me."

"I know, bro, but she's missing because she skipped out on our protection. We offered her a deal—we'd drop the B&E against her in exchange for her testimony and her ID'ing this 'Chuck' guy. Now that she's on the run, she'll lay low," Preston said. "I'll get a cruiser to work a grid pattern originating from the park, but for now that's all I can do."

After the call ended, Paul weighed their options. "I want to keep searching the area south of the bus depot for that van."

"Then let's do it."

Paul drove slowly around the old, run-down neighborhoods south of downtown. It was late. The few businesses around were closed, and most of the residences had only their porch lights on.

"The wind's really picked up," Kendra said as a hard gust slammed against the pickup. "I think we're in for snow."

He looked at the fast-moving, dark gray cloud bank low to the ground, coming in from the west. "The cold front is passing through, but all it'll bring will be blowing dust and virga—rain that never makes it to the ground. We're going into the third year of drought in New Mexico."

Paul hit three red lights in a row as he drove toward the old river bridge. As they approached the Turquoise

Lights Motel, he slowed down and surveyed the parking lot.

"Over there, on the café side, by the trash bins," Kendra said, pointing.

Paul turned the truck around, then approached the big green Dumpsters. As he drew closer, a faded blue van became clearly visible in the floodlight mounted above a small loading dock. "It matches the description perfectly, down to the luggage rack and ladder in the back."

"We need to move in," Kendra said, reaching for her weapon. "Call for the closest backup."

"No," Paul said. "Let's not divert a unit unless we're sure. No one's visible in the van, and it's just sitting there with the driver's side window rolled down. Maybe it belongs to someone who works in the café. Let's go take a closer look."

"Okay, but be ready for surprises," she warned.

After parking so his own vehicle provided cover for them, Paul brought out his pistol.

"Let's go," he said.

Slipping around, he advanced from the rear of the van toward the passenger's side, his head low. If anyone raised up to look out, he'd see them in the side mirror.

Seconds later, he reached the window and looked inside. The keys were still in the ignition, but the bench-style backseat was empty.

"Clear in front," he called out.

Kendra was at the back of the vehicle, her weapon ready as Paul came around to join her.

Giving her a nod, Paul reached for the back handle and yanked it open. Kendra stepped up, her gun aimed at the interior.

"Crap." She lowered her weapon slowly. "We're too late."

Chapter Ten

Paul expelled his breath in a long hiss as he looked at Annie's lifeless body crumpled on the floor of the van. She was fully clothed, her hair in disarray. The loop of wire used to strangle her had cut deeply into Annie's neck, leaving a caked over pool of blood on the thinly carpeted floorboard.

"She hasn't been dead for long, and she fought him. See the defensive wounds on her arms?" Kendra said softly.

"I'll call it in." Paul spoke to his brother, then after about a minute, ended the call. "Preston told us to stay and protect the scene until officers arrive. After that, he needs us back at the station so he can take our statements."

"Better step back. We need to preserve the evidence," Kendra said.

He did as she'd asked. "We can still take a look from here," he said, then went back to his pickup and returned with a powerful flashlight. Standing about ten feet away, they both studied the interior.

"There's no blood splatter or scuff marks on the

floorboard. He must have killed her outside the van, then tossed her into the back," Kendra said.

He turned off the light and stepped farther away. He was no Navajo Traditionalist, and he wasn't worried about the *chindi*, the evil in a man that was said to linger earthbound after death. Yet being around the dead still gave him the creeps.

Paul returned to his pickup with Kendra, then leaned back against the cab watching the van. From here, neither of them could see the body, which was a good thing.

Kendra sighed. "Maybe she'll find peace now. The life she led must have been pure hell."

"When you have nothing, you have to fight to get out of that hole. If you don't, all you'll find is misery, or worse."

Kendra watched him closely for a while. He was all male, rugged and hard-muscled, yet his masculinity came with an amazing gentleness that could touch even the most jaded of hearts.

She tore her gaze away. "We need a new lead. Maybe in death, Annie will point the way. She's got the killer's DNA under her fingernails."

"We don't have Miller's DNA, or at least we didn't when I was in the marshals service," he said, looking at her.

"We still don't," she answered, "but this crime fits his profile. In a close-up kill, he likes getting his hands dirty."

Before he could comment, a patrol vehicle raced up.

Behind it, halfway down the block, they could see the emergency lights of the crime scene van.

Kendra and Paul helped the officers secure the scene, then drove to the station.

Preston, who was talking to another detective in the area known as 'the bullpen,' saw them and waved. "My office, guys."

Kendra walked through the building, aware that she was under the scrutiny of every officer she passed. It was nothing unusual. No local law enforcement agency ever wanted a fed on their turf, especially a Deputy U.S. Marshal with jurisdiction virtually everywhere in the country.

"Don't let them psych you out," Paul said.

Surprised, she turned her head. She hadn't voiced the thought out loud, so she wasn't exactly sure what he was talking about. "What do you mean?"

"You're thinking the locals are giving you the usual mad-dogging stares reserved for feds, but that's not why they're looking at you," he said.

Just then Kendra reached the end of the hall. Preston waved her inside the open doorway.

"Take a seat," he said. "I'll be back in a minute. I need to talk to the captain."

Once they were alone and seated, Kendra answered Paul. "I'm used to getting some hostility from local departments. It goes with the job."

"They weren't sizing you up. They were checking you out, Kendra," he said with a smile. "Even wearing my clothes, you're a beautiful woman."

She was surprised by the impromptu compliment and his uncanny ability to read her. "You've got to tell me how you do that. I've never met anyone who can read people like you do. It's not just body language either. I know that already."

"It's Lynx."

"I don't know who or what Lynx is, but can I have some?"

He chuckled softly, but before he could say more, Preston walked back into the room.

"I need you both to make an official statement about what you saw at the murder scene. Paul, the desk sergeant in the bullpen will take yours. I'll handle Kendra's."

It was protocol to separate witnesses so they wouldn't influence each other's accounts, so this came as no surprise to her. "It'll go faster if you'll let me type out my statement," she said. "After you read it, I could also forward a copy to my supervisory inspector."

"Go for it," Preston said, waving her to his computer.

Kendra finished her report within five minutes. Preston then printed it out for her to sign.

"I'm sorry I don't have more to give you," she said.

"Our crime scene people are very good at their jobs, and they don't miss much. Even if this was the work of a pro, there may still be trace evidence we can use. Miller has a military record, so we can at least check for a blood type match."

Paul came in a moment later and took a seat. "Okay, that's done."

"Good. I've got some other news. The crime scene report on the incident over at Daniel's came in," Preston said. "The rounds came from a silenced thirty-two pistol. We found the casings. The defining thing is that while the shooter was positioned twenty yards away, he still came within a few inches of putting three rounds into your neck or skull. That indicates an incredible skill level, particularly with the subsonic rounds he was using."

"So this supports the theory that we're dealing with a pro," Kendra said.

"It's got to be Miller," Paul said. "High quality shooting like that requires extensive practice and training."

"There's also one big connection between the incident at Daniel's and what happened to Paul the night he went to meet Yolanda. Though different calibers were used, the rounds were all reloads, not factory made."

"So he has the foresight and ability to adapt his M.O.," Paul said.

Preston looked toward the door, where another detective was motioning to him. "Excuse me a moment," he said, getting up.

Now that they were alone again, Kendra stood, pushed her hands deep into her jacket pockets, and began to pace. Somewhere along the way, Chris Miller had managed to get inside her head. The truth was that he scared her in a way no other fugitive ever had.

Kendra straightened her back and forced herself to stand tall, her almost knee-jerk reaction to fear. She'd often been described as an exceptionally strong woman. Yet what the world defined as strength was simply her ability to bury raw emotions like fear deep inside herself in a place no one could see. For her, the cost of that had been loneliness. Not many understood that even the strongest woman could yearn to be held and comforted.

She walked to Preston's window, turning her back on Paul. She couldn't look him in the eyes right now. He saw way too much as it was. "I've been shot at before, Paul. It comes with the badge. But this man…"

"Drawing fire while trying to make an arrest is one thing, but being hunted—to be in a killer's crosshair—that's entirely different."

She turned around, but he'd come up from behind and she ended up bumping her nose against his chest.

He held his ground.

"How'd you get so close all of a sudden?" she muttered.

His nearness confused and excited her. Or maybe it was all a reaction to this case—knowing how close she'd come to death. All her senses were attuned to life and survival now.

"Could you step back just a little?" she said, forcing herself to meet his gaze.

He remained where he was. "I know what you're going through, Kendra. The knowledge that Miller, or whoever, wants you dead, is out there, waiting for his chance, is something that'll eat at you. What you need to do is make fear your ally. Use it to stay alert." He brushed his knuckles against the side of her face.

Maybe it was that gentle touch, or his tone of voice, or the way his eyes held hers, so steady, so sure. For whatever the reason, she didn't even bother hiding behind a string of denials. "I'm trained to hunt down fugitives—the worst of the worst—and I'm good at it. I do whatever has to be done. I shouldn't be feeling this way."

"Being tough doesn't mean we stop being human."

Hearing footsteps, Paul moved away, giving her space.

Kendra dropped back down into her chair just as Preston came into the room.

"Annie's body showed no signs of livor mortis, that darkening of the skin where the blood pools, so she'd been dead less than a half hour when you found her. That fresh a crime scene may give us some answers."

"Did the motel or restaurant have a surveillance system?" Kendra asked.

"Only inside at the front desk and cash registers," Preston said.

A short time later they walked back to Paul's truck. "You're a mass of compressed energy and tension right now, Kendra. You need to work some of that off so you can think clearly again. So tell me, when you're off duty, how do you deal with this? The gym?"

"No, I jog," she said.

"Okay, so how about going for a run with me right now? The wind's died down."

"It's close to midnight," she answered. "Where can we find a track that's not going to turn us into instant targets?"

"What I have in mind isn't a track, not exactly anyway. It's a beautiful trail, particularly by moonlight."

"Sounds like you've done this before."

He nodded. "There are times when running is the only thing that can help take my mind off things. When I'm running, the only thing I think about is my next step."

"Me, too," she said. "So stop someplace where I can pick up some gear. I can't run in these clothes."

"Hartley has an all-night MallMart. You can get some sweats there. As for me, I'm covered. I've got stuff in the back of the cab. If I ever want to go somewhere on the spur of the moment, I can."

"And that includes running shoes and stuff?" she asked, surprised.

He laughed. "I keep a little of everything with me. I don't like doing without."

It was the way he'd said it that made a million questions pop into her head. Maybe, while they were jogging, she'd get him to talk about himself. Then again, maybe it would take everything she had just to stay even with him.

Chapter Eleven

Some time later they pulled into an empty parking area next to the *bosque,* the wooded area flanking the river. "We're way past their posted hours," Kendra said, a trace of disappointment in her voice.

"No one will bother us. I know the park staff and they know me." He climbed out of the pickup, placing his weapon and other essentials inside the front pockets of his hooded sweatshirt.

As he stepped toward the trailhead she became delightfully aware of the way his sweats accentuated his height and hard muscles. She didn't know if he had gym shorts on beneath or not, but either way he had the best butt she'd ever seen. She bit back a sigh.

He looked over at her and grinned. "Window shopping?"

"I wasn't...."

He grinned even wider.

"I'm here for the run. I need to wind down," she said.

"Exercise? There are other ways...."

"Not for me," she snapped, wishing again things

could have been different. "When I'm working, I don't like distractions." She'd said it more for her own benefit than for his.

"Sometimes I think you're wrapped way too tight."

"You think too much," she countered, then took off at a fast clip, hurdling the low metal gate designed to keep vehicle traffic off the foot trail.

He caught up easily in a few seconds, laughing. "I *think* too much?"

She increased her speed, though it was tough going on that winding cobblestone trail, and evened her breathing. She intended to jog at least an hour. Unless she was close to exhaustion by the time they finished, she wouldn't be able to sleep tonight.

After ten minutes she realized that she was setting the pace. "Am I going too fast?"

"Not at all. I'm just enjoying the view from back here."

She slowed down immediately. "Why don't we run side by side...unless you want to drop out now," she added, immediately contrite. "I have no idea what kind of rehab program you're following."

"Why are you worried?" He came up beside her, his voice not at all winded. "Do I look out of shape?"

She didn't have to glance over to answer. "Far from it."

"Then don't worry about me. Choose whatever pace you're used to following. I'll keep up."

"I run three or four hours a week," she said.

"So it's not that far then."

Now she'd done it. Her competitive nature would never let her quit first—and clearly neither would his.

After another half hour, halfway around the big loop that wound up and down both banks of the cold river, she glanced over at Paul. To her annoyance, he wasn't even breathing hard.

"You look as if we've been out on a stroll, not running up and down these inclines. That's some stamina," she said.

"When I was living on the Rez my brothers and I would race each other up and down the canyon trails. It was a great way to work off excess energy and stay fit. The closest gym was at the high school, and that was thirty miles away. Most of the time we didn't have the gas money for trips like that, so we worked out at home."

"You mentioned that sometimes you were completely broke and had to go hungry," she said, hoping he'd talk about himself a bit more.

"That was before the foster homes, and before I went to live with *Hosteen* Silver."

"Life must have been tough when you were a kid." She slowed down without even realizing it, more interested in their conversation than in jogging.

"I guess. My mom did her best, but she was barely sixteen when she got pregnant. She quit high school to have me, so she never graduated. She took whatever jobs she could find, kitchen help, cleaning, stuff like that. By the time I turned eight she just gave up. I think she was ill, cancer or something like that. One day she dropped me off at a fire station, and I never saw her again. New Mexico Children, Youth and Families Department took custody after that."

He'd been matter-of-fact, and the only indication that the past still caused him pain was that he'd increased his pace, as if he were trying to outrun the memory.

"Eight years old is so young," she said, trying to keep up with him. She wouldn't offer him sympathy she knew he didn't want, but she could show him support by just staying beside him. "Did you know at the time that she wouldn't be coming back?"

"No. We'd taken the bus, and when she dropped me off, she handed me a sealed envelope. I was supposed to give it to the first fireman I saw. Later I found out it was a letter relinquishing custody of me. For a long time, I kept thinking she'd come back for me after she got better. It never happened."

"Did you ever find out what happened to her?" she asked, increasing her pace to match his.

"Not for years. I figured since she'd thrown me away, there was nothing for me to find." He slowed down, and their pace returned to a fast jog. "Eventually I found out that she passed away about six months after she left me at the fire station."

Although Paul's words held no trace of emotion, the revelation stunned her. She'd known about the wound on his shoulder, but the scars he bore inside went far deeper than any bullet ever could.

Somehow the moon, the darkness and the physical

exertion had worked a magic all their own and helped her see a side of him she doubted many ever saw.

"It's a beautiful night. Let's just enjoy the moonlight for a while," she said, slowing down to a walk.

"Tired?"

"Me? No, not at all," she said, unwilling to admit it. Realizing he was going to speed up again, she bit back a groan. "Slow down anyway. I'm tired of being in a hurry. The pressure to get there first is part of everything I seem to be doing lately."

"I get that," he said, and slowed to a walk. "The urge to see the payoff at the end of the line is always there. It can make the journey nothing short of a test of endurance."

"Yeah, it feels like that sometimes. Even in my private life I'm always racing to reach a new goal."

"Like what?" His voice was softer now, gentle.

"I've been looking into adoption," she said, liking the way he'd stepped closer to her. She could feel the warmth of his body wrapping itself around her, and the way he was looking at her made her tingle all the way down to her toes.

She looked away and struggled to clear her thinking. "There are some holdbacks I've yet to work out, but I'm not giving up on the idea."

"Why not just have a baby of your own?"

To her credit, she didn't sigh, but it took a concerted effort not to look at him. "I've considered that, but, to me, adoption is the way to go."

"How come?"

"It's complicated," she said.

"We've got time." Seeing her hesitate, he added, "We need to get to know each other, Kendra. Working as partners, even for who knows how long, means we have to learn to trust each other all the way. I don't like talking about my past, but I've told you a little about myself. Now it's your turn. Help us maintain the balance between us. By doing that, you'll also be honoring Navajo ways."

"All right," she said after a moment. "It all goes back to the days where 'home' was wherever the colonel's change of station took us. We traveled all over the world. One of the things I learned back then was that in an amazing number of countries poor kids have no chance, no future. Toddlers and their mothers would be living on the streets, and older kids sometimes completely on their own."

She paused, then in a soft voice, continued. "I know I can't change the world, but maybe I can make a difference in one life. International adoptions are complicated, but someday that's what I'd like to do."

"There are kids in our own country who could use a loving home. Look at my brothers and me. *Hosteen* Silver changed our lives. He gave us a future."

"I know," she said quietly, "but in the U.S. babies and toddlers are harder to find, and preference is usually given to two-parent homes."

"You're not planning to marry?"

"It's not that I've ruled it out, but there's no man in my life and I don't know if there ever will be," she

said. "A single-parent adoption, particularly for someone in my profession, is difficult. I've got practically
no chance in the U.S."

"Yeah, running down fugitives, transporting prisoners, and having to travel halfway across the country
at a moment's notice could be real tough for a single
parent."

"I've taken all that into account myself. That's one
of the reasons I haven't gone any further than fact-
finding. I have a lot of things to work out first."

Aware of how much she'd revealed about herself,
she suddenly grew quiet. It had been way too easy to
open up to Paul. His nearness, the sound of his low,
sexy voice, and the quiet beauty of the *bosque* trail
had conspired against her.

Soon after they'd rounded a curve in the trail, the
bosque became increasingly dense. She picked up
the pace. "We're hemmed in here, and I can't see into
the trees. Tactically, this isn't a good place for us."

She'd barely finished speaking when they both
heard a deep catlike growl coming from the brush to
the right of the cobblestone path. All she could see
was a dark shape and two amber eyes gleaming in
the moonlight.

Kendra reached for her gun slowly, glad she always
carried her weapon, even when off duty. If the animal attacked she'd be able to defend Paul and herself.

"Don't. We're in no danger," he said in a barely audible voice.

"It's a wildcat and it's coming toward us."

"It won't harm us."

Paul stepped in front of Kendra and pulled out the leather cord he wore around his neck. Something hung from it, but she couldn't make out what it was. A good luck charm? She preferred bullets. Her gaze shifted back to what appeared to be a bobcat that was advancing silently toward them with graceful but deliberate strides.

Paul took another step toward it, effectively blocking the creature's path. "Go your way and walk in beauty, my brother."

Kendra kept her hand on the grip of her pistol, but, to her surprise, the animal stopped its advance. It seemed to nod, though it was probably just a twitch, then turned away and walked off into the undergrowth.

It wasn't until the cat had disappeared completely that she finally drew in a full breath. "Guess we're too big to take on."

"That wasn't it. He never intended to attack. The cat came out to honor the connection between him and me. The animal kingdom is more attuned to things like that than the Anglo world is." Paul fell into step beside her. "What amazes me is that he approached even though there were two of us."

"I don't understand what you mean when you say you two are connected. Do you think the cat saw you as a friend?"

"No, not exactly. It's more, and less, than that." He took off the leather cord from around his neck and showed her the small fetish that hung from it. "It's a lynx, carved from oak. *Hosteen* Silver gave it to me right before I left to join the marshals service. Although all my brothers had their fetishes given to them on or around their sixteenth birthday, mine remained uncarved until that day."

"Was he punishing you for something?" They were walking side by side now, close enough to touch, but not doing so despite the temptation.

"No, not punishing—teaching. You see, I'd always played things close to my chest, and I guess that made me hard to read. On my sixteenth birthday he told me that I was still a work in progress. Until I became the man I was meant to be, he couldn't be sure which fetish would be the right spiritual match for me. Then, a few days before I was scheduled to report to the USMS training academy in Georgia, *Hosteen* Silver had a very vivid dream. He told me about it. He said he saw a beautiful lynx walking ahead of me as we went out on a hunt, so *Hosteen* Silver honored the sign and had the carving made for me from this piece of oak. I've worn it ever since, and as *Hosteen* Silver promised, it's proven to be invaluable."

"How so?" she asked. Paul's voice drew her. She wanted to stop, hold the fetish...and him.

"It's said that each fetish possesses the qualities of the animal it represents and shares them with its owner," Paul said, slipping the fetish around his neck again. "Lynx knows what others try to keep secret, and sees what's not readily apparent. That's why Lynx is the perfect match for someone in our profession. We have to find the truth, no matter how deeply it's hidden. We're also hunters."

"Maybe *I* should carry a lynx fetish," she said. "Do you think it would work for me?"

He shook his head. "Lynx isn't the right match for you. One of the things Lynx does is bring you knowledge that you may have forgotten about yourself. But you have no hidden past, as far as I can tell."

"No, I don't."

"I'll tell you what, then. Give me a chance to think this over, and as I get to know you better, I'll find the right fetish animal match for you," he said as they reached the end of the trail.

"Remind me never to say no to a run with you," she said walking with him to his truck. "It's been an amazing night."

"What still surprises me is that the cat allowed you to see him. That's not the way it normally works. I wonder what he was trying to tell me." Looking into her eyes, Paul stepped closer to her. "What does he know about you that I don't, Kendra?"

Everything about him enticed her and teased her senses. The fire in his eyes called to her, whispering temptation. More than anything, she wanted to feel his arms around her, to rest against his chest and enjoy the heat there.

He tilted her chin upwards, ready to cover her mouth with his.

Suddenly his cell phone rang, startling both of them.

Paul cursed, moved back a few steps, and glanced at the caller ID. "It's Preston," he growled.

While Paul spoke to his brother, she took a deep breath. Her body was still tingling and not from the cold. She sighed softly as she looked at Paul, wondering what his kiss would have been like. Would he have been tender at first, then rough? Would he have deepened his kiss slowly or would it have started that way?

She swallowed hard and looked at her surroundings for a moment. She had to keep her mind off Paul and on business.

"I have no idea where we'll sleep tonight," Paul was saying to Preston, "but it won't be Copper Canyon. Things are happening here, so this is where we have to be, close to the action."

The realization that, in order to stay alive, they'd have to spend the night standing guard over each other put her thoughts back on track. What had she been thinking? If there was ever a time *not* to let her guard down, this was it.

Paul hung up and glanced at her. "My brother suggested a motel that's not too far from here. The owner is an ex-cop, and the local D.A. occasionally uses the place to sequester a jury or hide away a key witness."

"Sounds good to me," she said.

He brought out his truck keys and opened the doors with the remote. "You and I are up against a pro who's getting paid for the hit. He won't give up till it's done."

As she looked into Paul's eyes, she saw a renewed

sense of caution mirrored there. As much as she wanted to prolong this tender moment with him, living to take their next breath had to take priority now.

Chapter Twelve

The Blue Mountain Lodge, a long, cinder block rectangular building with thirty guest rooms, stood at the edge of town. It backed up against a six foot concrete wall and could only be approached from the front and sides. It also faced a fairly busy street.

"The local cops like this place because of the layout," he said. "The halls are covered by security cameras. One of the exterior doors is next to the front desk, and the other is an emergency exit with an alarm. That one's always locked on the outside after nine pm. The halls are ceramic tile, too, so the sound of footsteps carries a long way."

"Good," she said, stifling a yawn. "I'm beat, Paul, so how would you feel about taking the first watch tonight? Unless I get a few hours of sleep, I may not be able to stay alert."

"No problem. I'm not ready for sleep yet, so I'll keep a lookout."

Paul parked on the side of the building next to the main entrance. To his right was a small, attached restaurant.

As they passed through a small glass-walled foyer and entered the lobby where the main desk was located, the husky man behind the counter grinned. "Hey, Grayhorse, how you doing?"

"Jimmy Masters? I thought you were still on the force." Paul stepped forward, bumped fists with the man, then turned around and introduced Kendra. "Jimbo and I went to high school together."

Kendra shook hands with him. Jimmy had blue eyes and dark hair. He was about twenty pounds or so overweight, but he still seemed way too young for retirement.

"I took a fall chasing a suspect and trashed my knee. After that I couldn't pass the physical. The department couldn't find me a desk job because of the economy, so here I am," he said, answering their unspoken question.

"That's a tough break, man. I'm sorry," Paul said.

"It's not so bad. I work nights and my wife days, so there's always someone home with the kids, and we have our weekends together. We're doing good."

"I'm glad you made things work," Paul said.

"Word is you're in a bit of trouble," Jimmy said. "I spoke to Preston a while ago, and he filled me in, so I got you a room halfway down the hall on the right. With the emergency door secured from the inside, the only way anyone can approach is to walk past this desk or break in the window. The curtains are also thick enough to keep anyone from tracking you from the outside. So no worries there."

"Thanks. That'll make things easier," Kendra said.

"I also put an extra carafe of coffee in your room, and some snacks in case you get hungry."

"We appreciate it, Jimbo," Paul said. "Mind if I take a quick look at your surveillance coverage?"

"No prob." Jimmy gestured to a small room just beyond the open doorway behind him. "We have very few late night drop-in guests this time of the year, so I'll be able to spot any activity right away."

Paul went in, looked around, then gave Kendra a nod.

"Okay then, we're good," Kendra said.

As they walked down the hall to their room, Paul gave her a quick half grin. "Good thing we're both beat. It'll keep us out of trouble."

She took a deep breath. "Paul, about what happened earlier…"

"I already know what you're going to say and you're right. We're working a case where one slipup could get us both killed. We can't afford to get sidetracked. Maybe after it's all said and done…"

She didn't answer. There was no need. It was clear to both of them that she was here to do a job. Afterwards, she'd go back to her life, and he, to his. If she could somehow manage to keep that firmly in mind, she'd be fine.

Paul opened the door and Kendra stepped into the room. Only one bed. It was as if fate itself was determined to tempt them. "We'll take turns keeping watch. Are you sure you're okay taking the first shift?"

"Absolutely," Paul answered.

"If you leave the room to catch up on old times with your friend, don't feel like you have to wake me. I really need some sleep and this is a secure location."

"No prob," he said.

Kendra went to the bed, pulled down the covers and, after kicking off her shoes, crawled in. The warmth and the weight of the blankets did the job, and she drifted off to sleep.

As her mind opened to the dreamscape before her, Kendra found herself on a hunt with a man couched in shadows, while the cries of a wildcat echoed through the darkness.

IT WAS 3:00 a.m., according to the digital clock on the nightstand.

Paul watched Kendra sleep, glad to see her looking at peace. As she smiled and shifted her hips, he wondered what she was dreaming about and if he'd come to visit her there. The possibility played on in his imagination, making him hard.

Expelling his breath in a hiss, Paul looked away and stood to stretch his legs. As he did, he spotted the flashing light on their room phone. He picked it up instantly, before it had a chance to ring.

"Paul, it's me," Jim said quickly. "I'm not sure if what I've got is important, but I thought I'd pass the information along. About a half hour ago, a dark-colored pickup parked outside for several minutes, then drove away. It's back again, and it's now parked on the south side between the Dumpsters. I think he's talk-ing on his cell phone. Do you want me to call Preston and have him send over an officer?"

"No, let me check it out first," Paul said, speaking in a whisper. "I don't see how anyone could have tracked us here."

Paul watched Kendra for a moment, listening to the even sound of her breathing. Last time he'd stepped away without waking her, she'd pulled a gun on him, mistaking him for an intruder. She'd told him that she slept light, but not tonight. The jog had done its job, allowing her to sleep soundly. She hadn't woken up despite his brief conversation.

He slipped out of the room quietly. He didn't need backup at this point, and Jimbo was keeping watch and would alert her, if needed.

The moment he was out in the hall, he used his cell phone to call Jim. "Keep a close eye on the hall and make sure no one approaches our door. While my part-ner's sleeping I'm going to take a quick look around. If I get any bad vibes, I'll call in the cavalry."

"Copy that," Jimmy said, his tone reverting to that of the officer he'd been once.

Paul was only a few steps from the lobby when he heard footsteps ahead. It was Jimmy, coming around the front desk.

"I'll cover the hall," he said softly, giving Paul a nod.

As Paul slipped outside, the cold air cut into him

like an icy blade. He hadn't worn his jacket, wanting ease of movement and free access to his holstered weapon.

Walking quietly down the sidewalk, he passed the restaurant, now dark and silent. Once he reached the corner, Paul stopped and looked out toward the Dumpsters, which were positioned about fifty feet down the six foot high concrete wall.

Between the two big trash bins he could see the tail end of a solitary pickup. The driver had parked at an angle so he could have a clear view of the main entrance and front corner of the building. It was a method someone with training in surveillance techniques would have used. The position concealed the driver's face and intentions while allowing him to utilize his side and rearview mirrors to give him an unobstructed view.

The cloud of water vapor escaping from the truck's tailpipe told Paul the engine was on, so the driver was undoubtedly inside. He decided to move in for a closer look.

As he inched toward the wall, screening himself with the large trash containers that also hid the pickup, he heard light footsteps coming up from behind.

Paul turned in a crouch, pistol in hand.

"It's me," Kendra whispered. "Jim said you'd be here checking out some pickup."

"You were sound asleep when I left. What woke you?"

"Jimmy's footsteps. Then he dropped his keys. I looked though the peephole, ID'd him, and got the story. Is that the pickup behind the trash bins?" she whispered.

He nodded. "The way he's screening himself and the fact that he's come and gone once already..."

Kendra nodded. "Let's go check it out. Split up. I'll go right, you go left."

"No, let's advance along this wall using the Dumpsters for cover. If it's our guy, he'll be packing," Paul said.

"Bad plan," she said. "If he has a gun, he won't show it till you're at point-blank range. I won't see it either, not in time to back you up. Or he'll just shoot through the door and you'll never see it coming. Let me angle back, circle the motel, and come in from his passenger's side blind spot. There's no way he can cover both flanks."

"Go." Paul reached the shoulder-high trash bin, weapon pointed down, and waited until he could see Kendra at the far corner of the motel. Moving quickly, he walked toward the driver's window, and as he closed in, he studied the driver's profile. He was sitting back in his seat, still unaware of their presence.

Kendra continued her approach from the right and was less than fifty feet away when the driver inside the truck turned his head toward the side mirror and spotted Kendra.

"U.S. Marshal!" Kendra yelled, crouching on one knee and bringing up her pistol. "Show me your hands!"

The driver instantly threw the pickup into reverse, spinning the steering wheel and racing backwards straight toward her.

"Bail," Paul yelled, pointing toward the Dumpster.

Kendra raced him to their only refuge, diving just ahead of him into the trash bin.

They landed on top of a section of flattened cardboard just as the pickup bounced off the metal corner. They were tossed around between trash filled bags but avoided the sheet metal sides. Before either of them could regain their balance, they heard the pickup race away, tires squealing.

"He's gone," Kendra said, pushing aside a trash bag. She tried to take a step but slipped and fell onto her hands and knees. "What is that smell?"

Paul made it to the edge and hoisted himself up and out. "I think it's a skunk," he said, grabbing Kendra's hands and helping her climb out.

"You okay?" Paul asked, taking short breaths and fighting to keep from gagging.

"That stench just rips the air out of your lungs," she said, coughing.

"We need to shower and change. Once we can breathe again, we'll sort things out," Paul said.

Jim ran to meet them. "I saw what—" He suddenly turned his face away and covered his mouth and nose with one hand. "You found the skunk."

"Yeah, seems so," Paul said.

Jim took another step back. "It wandered onto the parking lot just after dark and got run over. The restaurant manager had one of his people put it into a plastic bag and toss it in there. You must have ripped open the bag when you went Dumpster diving."

"Lucky us," Paul said.

Jim curled his nose. "You're going to need my special mixture. It's dry mustard and a few other choice ingredients." He glanced at Paul. "Works fast. You might want to shower together so the scent won't spread to the curtains and bedding."

Paul glanced at Kendra and grinned. "Hey, it's our duty to step up in an emergency."

"In your dreams," she shot back. Not that she would have minded. The thought of seeing him naked under a hot spray in the shower left her tingling all over. "No showering together, and it's too cold to hose off outside. What's plan B?" she said as they approached the main entrance.

"Paul, shower in the first room on the right. Kendra, take the one on the left. I'll let you in, then bring you both some odor remover and plastic bags for your clothing. And work fast, will you? Otherwise I'll never get that scent out of the hall—or the rooms. It'll get on everything."

"If we're in the shower, someone will have to stand guard out in the hall," Paul said.

"I'll do it. I've got a concealed carry permit and my .38," he said, lifting his jacket. "Just wait in the foyer for a sec, okay?"

"Go get the stuff," Kendra said.

IT TOOK KENDRA a full twenty minutes before she felt clean enough to finally step out of the shower. She'd used the descenter and the perfumed soap and had washed her hair several times.

Since she hadn't wanted to handle anything until she'd rid herself of that awful skunk smell, she hadn't brought a change of clothes into the bathroom. Taking one of the large, plush towels, she wrapped it around herself and stepped into the room.

To her surprise, Paul was there. She stopped in midstride and stared at him, unable to tear her gaze away from his loose, open shirt. She'd never seen that much of his bare chest before, and it was a sight to behold. He had the perfect build. From what she could see, he had just the right amount of muscle for her tastes and a flat stomach that rippled with raw masculine strength. Low-slung jeans sparked her imagination even more, making her wish she could see the rest. Soon her fingertips tingled with the need to touch him.

Using all her willpower, she looked away. That's when she saw the first aid kit on the table beside him. "Are you hurt?" she asked quickly.

"I got a few cuts and scratches from those big staples on the cardboard box. Do you have any scrapes that need tending? I'd be happy to put on the antiseptic." His gaze traveled over her like a slow, intimate caress.

"I need my clothes," she managed in a hoarse voice, suddenly remembering that her carry-on was still in Paul's truck.

"Jimbo brought in your things while you were in the shower. You'll find everything in the closet."

She hurried to her small suitcase, started to bend over, then abruptly changed her mind. "You can either get out of the room, or put the bag on the bed for me."

"How about if I put you on the bed first and check you over for cuts?" he said, his eyes never leaving hers. "I promise to be thorough."

Her breath caught in her throat, and her heart began to pound so loudly she was sure he'd hear it. "We're in trouble, Paul. Try to act like it."

He gave her a heart-stopping grin. "We're not in trouble…not yet."

To her own credit, she managed an icy glare. "I'm going back into the bathroom to get dressed," she said, bending at the knees and grabbing a handful of clothes. "Afterwards, we'll discuss what happened and figure out what's next."

Kendra dressed quickly. Slacks, a plain navy blue pullover sweater and a dark blazer were practically a uniform for her these days. She chose them now, hoping to remind herself that she was never off the clock when working a case like this one.

When she went back out into the room, Paul still had his shirt open. Those low-slung jeans seemed to fit even lower on his hips now, or maybe that was just her imagination.

"You planning to finish getting dressed soon?"

"I'm decent—or am I distracting you?" He gave her a slow, devastating grin.

"No, you're annoying me." Paul was relentless when he wanted something, and at the moment he appeared to want her. The knowledge thrilled her and made her ache for things she had no business wanting.

"You're not being truthful with me or yourself," he said, taking a step closer.

She held her ground, refusing to back away. "You're used to getting your way with women, Paul, but I'm out of your reach."

"Not at all," he murmured, the warmth of his breath almost touching her lips.

She stepped around him and gathered her things. "Paul, I came to New Mexico to do a job. That, and staying alive, are my only priorities."

"Life is short. Enjoying special moments is sometimes all we've got," he said. "Don't pass them up."

She heard the dark undertone woven through his words. His past was marked by the loss of people who'd mattered to him. Although she understood what drove Paul, she lived her life by a different set of rules. "I'm not your type, Paul. I want a lot more from a guy than a good time in bed. It may sound old-fashioned, but there it is."

"So you're looking for your forever guy?"

"I'm not really sure there's such a thing, at least for me, but without something solid to back it up, physical attraction fades away. I want the whole package, not just pieces of it."

"You might end up taking on more than you can handle."

"As I see it, the real danger is settling for something less." She said it firmly, needing to believe it, but Paul had awakened a new yearning inside her. It remained deep inside her heart—a temptation couched in two simple words— "what if."

Chapter Thirteen

They'd returned to their original room, and now it was Kendra's turn to watch Paul sleep. She'd had to insist that he try to get some rest. Finally, after tossing and turning for a long time, he seemed to have drifted off.

Kendra sat next to the small table at one end of the room, staring at the latest issue of *New Mexico Magazine*. On the cover was a photo of children playing in front of a picturesque *casita*.

She sighed softly. As much as she loved the marshals service, she knew the job would make it almost impossible for her to become a single mom. Yet investigative work was what she did best. She'd considered working in the private sector, but no job in her field would ever come with a guarantee of regular hours. She'd also need a decent paycheck that included good benefits. Without all that, she still wouldn't be able to qualify as an adoptive parent.

The obstacles that stood in her way seemed insurmountable. Maybe some dreams weren't meant to be.

As she leaned back and stretched, she heard soft,

padding footsteps in the hallway. She went to the door, her hand on the grip of her pistol.

Kendra listened carefully and heard what sounded like a scratching sound near the electronic lock. Maybe it was nothing, housekeeping or an inebriated motel guest, but too much had happened already for her to ignore it.

"Paul!" she whispered harshly.

He was up instantly, and from her position near the door, he seemed to figure out the rest.

"Throw it open," he said, his words barely audible. "I'll handle it." He flattened against the other side of the door.

Kendra slipped off the security chain, then held up one finger, then two. There was no three. In a lightning fast move, she pulled the door open.

Paul yanked the man into the room and threw him down onto the floor. Kendra moved in, her weapon aimed at his chest.

It was Preston. Kendra immediately lowered her weapon.

"What the hell do you think you're doing, creeping around out there, bro?" Paul demanded, offering his brother a hand up. "You have a death wish?"

"You never sleep, so I figured you'd be the one keeping watch. I used our signal."

"Signal? I didn't hear anything except footsteps and an odd scratching sound," she said.

"*That's* the signal," Preston said. "It was something we came up with back home whenever we wanted to sneak out of the house. Whoever stayed behind was supposed to cover for the other one. We had different rooms and if we'd gotten together to make plans, *Hosteen* Silver would have heard us."

"I think he knew and just chose to ignore it," Paul said.

Preston chuckled. "I came up with that particular signal because it sounds like a cat scratching, and Paul's like a stray with nine lives. The son of a gun lands on his feet no matter how many times you toss him across the room."

Paul laughed. "When was the last time you could do that?"

"Have you had these selective memory problems long?" Preston countered without missing a beat.

"Guys," she said, interrupting them. "Preston, I assume you're here for a reason. Has something new turned up?"

"Yeah," he said. "I paid John Lucas a visit this morning and my hunch paid off."

"I don't know the name," Kendra said.

"Lucas owns a gun shop and a very popular shooting range just outside the city limits," Preston said. "The rounds that were used against both of you were hand cast from linotype, so I figured the gunman might want to purchase additional supplies soon. Lucas is the only local source of metal for cast bullets."

"John's pretty closed-mouthed, particularly around cops. How did you persuade him to loosen up?" Paul asked.

"Enlightened self-interest," he said, not elaborating. "He told me to speak to Gil Davies. He said that if there was out-of-town talent working here, Gil would know."

"I've heard the name, but I can't place the guy," Paul said.

"He runs a survivalist training camp. He's also suspected of dealing black market guns, but no one's ever been able to get any evidence to back that up. What we've got is more rumor and gossip than anything, but I trust my informant. If he says Davies is the man to talk to, you can count on it. The problem is that Davies is out of my jurisdiction. You'll need to talk to him, Kendra."

"Where exactly do I find this Gil Davies?" Kendra asked.

"He has a small place just off Highway 145 north of Cortez, Colorado, about fifteen miles from my brother Gene's ranch. I've been told he's not friendly to uninvited guests, so watch your backs. You're more likely to be greeted with firearms than open arms."

Kendra glanced at Paul, and for the first time found she could read what was going on in his head. She recognized the signs—that initial rush of adrenaline, mingled with iron-willed control. It was the latter that he'd draw on to exercise restraint.

"You know where we're headed, right?" she asked Paul.

"Yeah, no problem. It's a little over an hour from here. Nine-thirty now, we'll get there by ten-thirty."

"Okay. Let's go," she said.

"Stay alert for surprises," Preston said as they walked out. "There's nothing but empty highway once you pass through Shiprock and turn north."

"We'll handle it," Kendra said, acutely aware of the weight of the badge on her belt.

A HALF HOUR later, beyond the reservation town of Shiprock, the road stretching north before them seemed endless. She shifted in her seat, absently noting the series of tower-like mesas to the east.

"Restless?" he asked.

"Yeah, the scenery is beautiful, but I need something to focus on. How about going over some contingency plans?"

Paul shook his head. "Planning every detail is just a way of fooling yourself into thinking you have control over the situation. That false sense of security can be dangerous."

"If you plan for the most likely eventualities, you have a better chance of achieving your objectives," she said.

He smiled at her. "That sounds like something the colonel taught you."

She laughed. "It is. The colonel always got things done, and he expected the same from my brother and me. He taught us independence and responsibility, and never tolerated excuses of any kind."

"You've barely mentioned your brother. I gather you two aren't that close?" he asked.

"No, we're not. In the colonel's household we looked out for ourselves and learned not to ask for help. He expected us to be leaders, not followers, so depending on someone else was considered a sign of weakness."

"So, you and your brother each went your own way?"

"Exactly." She smiled. "I know you're close to your brothers, but Gene went his own way, chose ranching instead of law enforcement. Does he still belong to the pack?"

He nodded. "Yeah, we're all there for each other anytime, no matter what. But you're right. Gene's always marched to his own drummer." He paused, collecting his thoughts. "The guy was practically born to be a rancher. He has an amazing way with animals, particularly horses."

"And you don't?" she asked, sensing what he'd left unsaid.

"That's the understatement of the year," Paul said with a wry grin. "That's why it made no sense when *Hosteen* Silver left his horse to me instead of Gene. His last request was that I learn to be friends with Grit."

"You own a horse!" she said, enthusiasm evident in her tone.

He smiled. "You like horses?"

"I love them, but excuse me for interrupting your story. Tell me more about Grit. Why is it difficult for you two to become friends?"

"There's really no story. We're not friends because, basically, the horse hates me. To date, he's never let me ride him. Every time I've tried I've ended up face-down in the dirt. I was the one who named him Grit because that's what ended up in my mouth each time I was tossed," he said, laughing. "I've done everything I can think of to get on better terms with that animal, but Grit's not interested."

"Maybe you're trying too hard," she said.

He looked at her in surprise. "That's exactly what Gene says, but I'd like to get this over with as soon as possible. It's important."

"I don't follow," she said.

"It's part of the puzzle *Hosteen* Silver left for me." A minute or two stretched out as he tried to decide how much to tell her. Kendra had a sharp mind and investigative training. The fact that she wasn't directly involved might mean she'd be able to offer him new insights on *Hosteen* Silver's letter. "I could really use your take on something, but it involves family business, so it would have to stay between us."

"I can keep a secret when it's not case related, and I enjoy working with puzzles. I'd love to help, if I can."

"I've already told you a little about *Hosteen* Silver and the kind of man he was. After he passed away, we discovered that he'd left each of us a letter. The ones that have been opened so far have contained both a prediction and a final request. What he asked of me was that I become friends with his horse. That also plays a part in what he foretold for me." Seeing the questions in her eyes, he gave her a shortened version. "He said that enemies would become friends, and

friends enemies, but Grit would show me the way, *if*
I became his friend."

"Maybe that was his way of making sure Grit would
always be looked after," she said.

Paul shook his head. "The horse was already in
good hands living at my brother Gene's ranch. Had he
asked Gene, it would have made perfect sense, but he
asked *me*. Gene thinks maybe *Hosteen* Silver wanted
me to learn patience, but I don't buy it. As an investigator, I've already got more than my share of that."

"And the horse has always given you problems?"

"From the very beginning," Paul said, nodding. "I
tried to befriend him lots of times, but he's never been
interested."

"I'm not an expert, but I know a little about horses.
They can kick, buck and bite if you make them angry
enough. Maybe the lesson wasn't about patience
as much as it was about not trying to force certain
things." She paused and took a breath. "What do you
think? Does that sound like him?"

He considered it for a moment, then nodded slowly.
"Yeah, it does. When I look at Grit, I see an animal
I'm going to have to outlast, intimidate or fight, and
that affects how I deal with him," he said with a wry
smile. "Thanks for your insight, Kendra. Figuring out
what *Hosteen* Silver was really trying to say has never
been easy for any of us."

"Thanks for letting me help."

A half hour later they drove up a long, narrow dirt
road in southwestern Colorado's ranching country.

At the end of their bumpy ride they found a closed metal gate with a sign that read Last Stand Ranch. No Trespassing.

"It's closed but not locked," she said. "Maybe he's expecting a delivery."

"Once he sees us, he'll be mighty disappointed."

"Let's drive in and find out, but let me lead. I'm not so threatening."

A ghost of a smile tugged at the corners of his mouth. "And you think I am?"

"It's the package. You seem to know how to work it." Biting back a smile, she didn't give him time to answer. "Let's roll."

Chapter Fourteen

The road just beyond the gate was so rutted it took them nearly five minutes to reach the freshly painted, white wood framed house. About fifty yards to its left stood a classic bright red barn. Paul parked next to a utility pole off to the side of the main house.

"Quiet and peaceful, not my vision of a survivalist's home," Kendra said after exiting the pickup. She checked the position of her weapon. "Let me take point. I'd like him to assume we're a couple who got lost. Once we're face-to-face and he can see my weapon, I'll identify myself."

As he got out of the pickup, Paul looked around. His fetish felt heavy, a sure sign that something wasn't quite right.

"Something feels...wrong." He held up his hand, asking for quiet. In the distance was the rumbling sound of metal clinking and clacking. "Reloading equipment—one of those vibrating case cleaners," he said, then gestured to the barn.

"If he's over there processing some ammo, that

might explain why he didn't hear us drive up," she said. "Let's check out the barn first."

Paul hung back like she'd asked, his gaze taking in the area, searching for the danger he felt but couldn't see.

"If he's around guns, I don't want to take him by surprise. I'm going to identify myself as soon as I walk in," Kendra said, then entered the barn. "U.S. Marshal—" she called, but suddenly a hand snaked out from behind a stack of hay bales and yanked her back.

"Don't like trespassers," the burly man growled, pinning her against him in a chokehold.

Kendra stomped hard on his instep, then slammed her elbow deep into his gut. He bent over, his hold easing slightly, and she twisted free.

In the blink of an eye, Paul hurled himself at the man, tackling him to the ground.

"U.S. Marshal," Kendra snapped, moving in, weapon in hand. "Stop." The two men were still struggling, so she couldn't get a clear line of sight.

The man punched Paul in the chest, trying to break free, but Paul grabbed his arm, twisting it painfully, and rolled him onto his stomach.

The man groaned, then finally stopped resisting. "Okay, you win," he mumbled.

Paul released him, then rose to his feet and stepped back, clearing the way for Kendra.

"Don't move," Kendra said, coming up, her pistol aimed at the man's spine.

"Relax, little lady," he said, raising his head off the ground a few inches, trying to see her.

"Deputy Marshal," she corrected. "You can stow the 'little lady' routine. Now roll over and sit up. Keep your hands away from your body."

"Yes, ma'am. I had no idea you were law enforcement. We've had home invasions and break-ins around here lately, so I was just defending my place, like any man would. You didn't identify yourself until now."

"I did, right before you began to choke me," Kendra said. "Bad move. Instead of asking you a few questions and moving on, I'm placing you under arrest. Looks like you're going to be doing your talking at the closest police station."

Paul stepped away and called the local sheriff's department while Kendra kept her gun trained on the man. "You're Gil Davies, I take it?"

"That's me, so now that we've been properly introduced, you gonna tell me what you want?"

"Some information," Kendra said.

He smiled slowly. "Forget what happened here, and you might convince me to cooperate. If you take me in, forget about it."

Kendra looked him in the eye, trying to read him, but before she could answer, Paul came up and touched her on the shoulder.

"He's got a stash of black market gun parts in a box over there that can turn assault rifles into fully automatic weapons," he said.

"Looks like we'll be finishing this off at the station," Kendra said. "If you want to trim off a little prison time, Gil, start talking."

"The parts your partner saw were purchased outside a gun show in Durango. If you look in the box, you'll see the ID badge that proves I was there."

"To be in possession of those gun parts requires a boatload of specialized ATF permits. Care to show me the paperwork?"

He shrugged. "I bought them from a guy selling stuff out of his trunk in the parking lot. Just one good ole boy to another."

"Enjoy prison," Kendra said.

"So you came here just to check out gun parts?" He shook his head. "That's not what you really want to know, is it?" He smiled slowly. "Your choice. Take me in, and that's the last thing you're going to hear from me."

"Then that's the way it is. You're under arrest," Kendra said. "Turn around, and place your hands behind your back. I'm going to cuff you."

"Hey, come on. You know this'll never hold up in court. Where's your search warrant?"

Kendra smiled. "Didn't need one. You gave us permission to look in the box, remember? He just took you up on that offer."

Davis responded with a one-word curse.

It didn't take long for a deputy to show up, and Kendra remanded Davies over to the uniformed officer. "He's under federal jurisdiction, so you need to notify the marshals service. Our department will be responsible for the expense of housing the prisoner. And expect a visit from ATF on those gun parts."

Kendra made a call to that agency and reported the situation. By that time, close to noon, two more deputies had arrived on the scene, along with a search warrant based on information Kendra had forwarded.

As one deputy took Gil Davies away, others began to tape off the area in preparation for the Bureau of Alcohol, Tobacco and Firearms agent now en route from Durango, Colorado.

While the deputies worked to preserve the scene, Paul and Kendra searched the barn for any more surprises. After several minutes they met outside the barn.

"There's nothing else here for us," Paul said. "You might want to leave word for the ATF agent to contact you if there's anything in the main house that connects to Miller."

"Good idea," Kendra said. "After that, there's another lead I want to follow up."

"What's on your mind?"

She took a deep breath. "Gun shows usually have security monitors for the safety of their vendors. We need to figure out who handled that, then take a look at what they recorded from that Durango event."

"Security is Daniel's business, and if he didn't handle it, he probably knows who did. Let me give him a call."

Paul moved away as Kendra spoke to the remaining deputies about the arrival of the ATF agent. A few minutes later, she joined Paul again.

"I've got the information we need," he said. "Daniel subcontracted the job to a guy named Mickey Carson. He lives in Cortez. We passed through there on the way here, so it won't take us long to drive back. Do you want to leave now?"

"Yeah. Let's go pay him a visit. If his video of the event includes any outside surveillance, I'm going to ask to look at the footage. I'd like to try and ID the guy selling black market gun parts. It's possible he may have done business with Miller, or he might be able to point us to someone who has. Miller gets his gear under the radar, so you can bet he's got contacts all over the country."

"We're getting close to finding answers," he said as they set out. "I can feel it in my gut."

"Yeah, but in my experience, that's when things can start going wrong," she said.

"Is that what happened when you were trying to track down John Lester, the gunrunner?"

She nodded. "Lester's a slippery son-of-a-gun who's always one step ahead of whoever's after him. The other dealers want him dead because he controls a very big share of the illegal weapons market. The problem is he's got too many allies and informants," she said. "Once I capture Miller, I'll try to get reassigned to that case. I want to bring Lester down next."

He smiled. "You've got a lot of courage, Kendra, and you hate backing off. That's what I like about you."

"Yeah, I'm a fighter." Yet even as she spoke, she

knew that was only partly true. In her heart she longed
to surrender, to be swept away by the fires she'd found
in Paul's arms.

As she glanced at Paul and saw his steady hands on
the wheel, she bit back a sigh. Paul was a man trapped
in the past, and he'd only break her heart. She had to
keep her emotions locked safely away.

A LONG SILENCE had stretched out between them, and
Paul didn't interrupt the quiet. He needed time to
think. For the first time since he'd left the marshals
service he thought he had a chance to find closure—
to put away the man who'd killed Judy. Kendra was
relentless, just the kind of partner he needed to close
the case that continued to haunt his dreams.

"You said you know Mickey Carson. Any chance
he's involved?" Kendra asked at last.

"I don't think so, but it'll be better if we don't assume anything."

"Yeah, better safe than sorry," she said. "The stakes
are too high."

More than she even realized. Trying not to look at
her, Paul kept his eyes on the road ahead. He liked
being with Kendra way too much for his own good.
Beneath her toughness lay a core of gentleness that
drew him to her.

Many women had passed through his life over the
years. Some had tried to mother him, others had offered him love, and sex, too. But his instinctive distrust
of women had always kept things from going too far.

Kendra had offered him nothing more than a temporary working arrangement. She wasn't interested in a relationship, not even a physical one, though it was clear the sparks were there. Yet his feelings for her had continued to grow.

Although he could have tried to work on her emotions and persuade her to give in to the attraction between them, the final outcome would still be the same. Kendra would eventually leave and go her own way. The only thing he could do was walk on. He'd forget her…eventually.

"The video…" she said, cutting into his thoughts. "Are you sure you're ready to deal with whatever we see?"

"I don't follow. Why wouldn't I be?"

"It's possible that someone in this community, someone you know and maybe trust, is one of Miller's suppliers."

As he glanced over at her, he suddenly realized what she meant. "Wait—do you think Preston's been feeding us false information? That he's dirty? No way. He lives and breathes the job. He sees police work in Navajo terms—as restoring the balance between good and evil."

"All right, then."

"Are you really ready to let go of that idea?" he asked, watching her reaction.

She nodded. "I never thought Preston was involved, I just wanted to know where *you* stood, and that I could count on you no matter what turned up."

"You have your answer."

They arrived at Mickey Carson's upscale home outside of Cortez a while later and drove up the long, paved driveway to the front door.

Kendra, out of habit, stood to one side of the massive double doors as she rang the bell, and Paul did the same.

Moments later the door on their right opened. A tall, light-haired man around forty, wearing expensive wool slacks and a V-neck cashmere sweater, greeted them with a pleasant smile.

"Paul, it's good to see you again. Daniel called a while ago, and I've got a flash drive ready with what you need. Sorry I can't stick around. I'm meeting a new client at two o'clock."

"No prob. I've got my laptop in the truck. I'll make sure it loads, then we're gone," Paul said.

"Okay. Here's the flash drive. Let's do this."

Mickey followed them to the pickup, and on the way Paul noticed three vehicles parked under a big carport. There was a white sedan, a gray SUV, and an older model black pickup. As he glanced at Kendra, he noted that she'd also been checking out Mickey's transportation.

"Hang on while I boot it up," Paul said, bringing out his laptop. Moments later, the data files were being transferred to the laptop hard drive.

"You can manipulate the images to accentuate whatever you want," Mickey said. "You have a little over eight hours of feed there, but the files are still manageable because we used time lapse photography. Images are taken one per second, not continuously."

"Thanks, Mickey," Paul said. "Appreciate it."

"You bet."

As Mickey walked back to his house, Kendra went around to the driver's side. "Let me take the wheel, Paul. I'll drive while you deal with the laptop. It's set up for you anyway."

"Sure." He went to the passenger side, carrying his laptop. "Treat Cassie gently, okay?" he said, climbing into the cab.

"Who?" she asked, then smiled. "You gave your truck a name?"

"Yeah. Cassie's as tough as they come, but she still deserves a gentle hand," he said and winked.

As Kendra reached down to turn on the ignition, he saw the tiny smile that tugged at the corners of her mouth.

THE GRAVEL ROAD leading back to the main highway was well maintained, but a giant rooster tail of dust still trailed in a thick cloud behind them. "The drought has really taken its toll this year, even up here in southern Colorado." Paul said, rolling up his window.

Kendra slowed down to thirty miles per hour as she saw an approaching SUV traveling down the center of the road.

Paul, engrossed in the screen, said nothing.

"Move over, dummy," she muttered, honking the horn.

Paul looked up and saw the vehicle. "He's probably used to being the only driver on this road." The large, older model, green Ford SUV was closing the gap at a rapid clip.

Kendra leaned on the horn again, then inched closer to the shoulder of the road. The empty irrigation canal on her right was less than ten feet away now.

Blaring her horn, Kendra touched the brakes and eased over to the side even more. "Maybe the guy had a seizure or something."

"Or he's drunk," Paul said.

Kendra swerved across to the left, but the SUV did the same. Seconds from impact, she cut back to the right. "Hang on!"

Her heart thumping in her chest, Kendra slammed on the brakes. As the truck skidded alongside the canal, she felt the right front tire drop off. "We're going in!" she yelled, swerving into the ditch and praying they wouldn't roll over.

The pickup dropped into the ditch upright, metal screeching as the sides of the truck ricocheted back and forth off opposing banks. With one final bounce off the bank, they hit sand, slamming their heads on the roof as the truck came to an abrupt stop. A vast dirt cloud enveloped them.

Paul looked over at her immediately. "You okay?"

Kendra still had a death grip on the steering wheel. "I'm in one piece. Now I need to find a way to stop shaking."

Paul lifted the door handle and pushed, but the door only opened an inch before hitting the steep inside wall of the canal. The top of the earthen wall was at least a foot above the cab. "No clearance over here, not even through the window. How about your side?"

Kendra released the wheel and tried her door, but it wouldn't budge. "Nothing. We're jammed, and the window is right up against the bank."

Paul turned slowly, sniffing the air. "Do you smell that?"

"Gasoline. We must have ripped open the fuel line or the gas tank." She took a whiff. "I think it's coming from behind the seat, not the engine compartment. Is that better or worse?"

"I have no idea, but we better find a way out of here." Paul turned in his seat and checked the rear cab window. Through the glass he saw a man wearing a hoodie and sunglasses standing at the top of the embankment. "We've got an audience."

"Maybe it's the jerk who ran us off the road. What's he up to?" Kendra said.

Paul saw the man pull something from his pocket. Acting on instinct, he yanked Kendra down. A heartbeat later the windshield shattered, and they heard two loud pops in rapid succession, followed by a third.

"Stay down!" Paul yelled, covering her with his body.

As two more bullets struck inches from them, they heard a whooshing sound, followed by a boom that shook the truck. A blast of heat and flame erupted from the engine compartment.

Raising his head slightly, Paul saw the hood had

blown open. Acrid smoke was billowing up around the front end of the truck, and vile fumes began seeping into the cab through the vents.

"We've got to get out of here right now." Gun in hand, Paul risked a look through the rear cab window, searching for the shooter, but thick black smoke obscured his view. As it was, he could barely make out the pickup bed, which was just on the other side of the glass.

"Our only chance is to break this window and squeeze through onto the bed of the truck—right into his field of view," he said, coughing hard as the air became increasingly thick.

"Go for it," she said.

"Hold my weapon," he said, handing her his pistol. He twisted around in his seat, placed his back against the passenger's side dash, and kicked the rear cab window with his boot heel. The glass cracked but held. He kicked it again, even harder than before. This time the entire window gave way, rubber seals and all, and fell into the bed of the pickup with a thump.

He took a quick look, but the guy had disappeared. "I'm going first," Paul said. "If he's still out there, I'll keep him pinned down. Hand me my weapon."

"No. I'll go first. I'm the one with the badge."

"I can get through the opening faster. You've got too many curves."

Before she could answer, he took the pistol from her hand, then angled his body up and through the narrow opening, leading with his weapon. A few seconds later, he landed on the bed of the truck with a thud.

"Still can't see him. I think he's gone," Paul yelled back, reaching for her hand. "I'll pull you through, but watch the edges. The metal is sharp."

"I'm gonna leave body parts behind for sure," she muttered, trying to protect her breasts with a forearm as she wriggled through the opening. The second half of her posed another problem. "You're built straight up and down, but I've got hips. It's just not fair."

"You're doing great," he said, standing on the flat-bed of the truck and lifting her up and out.

Something in her pants pocket suddenly caught, but with a painful twist to her left, she managed to slip through.

"Thanks," she said, then took her first good look at Paul. "Your arm's covered in blood," she said, her voice rising.

He glanced down at the long tear on his sleeve, and the scrape beneath. "Aw, hell, this is just a scratch."

Paul pulled her into his arms and held her for one precious moment. Then something up front popped, and the truck shook again.

"Time to bail." Paul took her hand, they ran to the tailgate, and together they jumped down into the sandy bottom of the dry irrigation canal.

"Keep running!" he said, tugging at her hand.

They were barely fifty feet away when a thunderous explosion rocked the air. The nearly simultaneous blast of hot air threw them facedown to the ground.

Paul covered her with his body as burning truck parts rained down all around them. Seconds stretched out, and each heartbeat became an eternity. Finally, all they could hear was the roar and crackle of the fire behind them.

Paul raised his head and looked back at what was left of his truck. "Goodbye, Cassie."

"We're lucky to be alive, and your first words are 'goodbye, Cassie'?" She shook her head and pushed him off of her. "Men!"

Paul laughed and gave her a hand up. "Our luck held and we're okay," he said, reaching to wipe away a trickle of blood that was running down his forehead. "That makes this a good day."

Kendra checked her weapon, making sure the barrel and action weren't clogged with dirt, then removed her holster from her belt and emptied out the sand. Finished, she looked him over and smiled. "I look like something a cat dug up, but even dirt and blood looks good on you. How do you do that?"

He laughed. This was the side of Kendra he was sure most people never saw. The girly-girl who wanted to look good and cared about things like that even now, after crashing, dodging bullets, and almost getting fried. "You look pretty good to me, woman," he growled playfully, pulling her closer and taking her lips in a deep, satisfying kiss.

This time she didn't pull away, and heat blasted through him. As she drew back to take a breath, he saw her moist lips part. He took her mouth again, devouring her slowly.

She whimpered softly, then nuzzled the hollow of his neck. "No more. We can't."

"Death came calling for us today, but we're still here. Celebrate life with me. No more wasted moments."

He took her mouth again, not giving her a chance to protest. The way she melted against him nearly drove him over the edge.

"No," she managed with a broken sigh and moved away. "We can't wait around here in the open. We have to find some place safe."

"The guy who did this probably thinks we're dead, but you're right. We need to leave in case he decides to come back and make sure," he said.

"Any suggestions? Your friend Mickey's not at home, so hiking back there is out."

"How about Two Springs Ranch? It's in the area and belongs to my brother Gene," Paul said. "He'll come get us and provide a safe place for as long as we need. I trust him—with my life and yours."

Chapter Fifteen

An hour later Kendra was riding in the back seat of Gene's four-wheel drive SUV. The Colorado state patrol officer had assured her that they'd sealed off the crime scene and that an ATL, attempt to locate, was out on the shooter and his green Ford SUV. The problem was that in this ranching community that was a common make of vehicle, and tracking down the right one would take time.

Gene soon braked to a stop and went to open the gate leading to Two Springs Ranch. He was still saying goodbye to someone on his cell phone when he returned. "Just checking. My wife keeps the bunkhouse ready for guests."

"So Kendra and I are going to rough it?" Paul said, grinning.

"Not at all. You haven't seen the changes we've made since you were here last," Gene said, then looked at Kendra and explained. "The bunkhouse was initially supposed to be the rancher equivalent of a man cave, but Lori had different plans." He glanced back at his brother. "So, should I get Doc Riley to drive over and take a look at you two?"

"Let me guess. He's your vet?" Paul asked.

Gene laughed. "No, he's an M.D. He had a big city practice, retired, then decided he didn't want to sit around doing nothing all day long. He bought the ranch north of here next to Deer Trail Creek and donates time to a clinic in Dolores. He even makes house calls a couple of days a week."

"I don't need a doc," Paul said, then glanced at Kendra. "I think you should have one look you over, though."

"No thanks. I'm scraped up and bruised, but nothing worse than a bad day at the gym," she said.

Paul didn't argue. She was back to being Deputy Marshal Armstrong now, and Kendra would call anything short of gushing blood a scrape. He smiled. She was some kind of woman—his kind of woman.

The realization slammed into him. He was falling in love with Kendra—hard. He stared at her for a moment longer than he should have.

"You okay?" she asked. "You look…confused."

"Nah, I'm just sorting things out." The truth of it was he had no business falling in love with anyone. Until Judy's killer was behind bars, his life wasn't his own. He owed a debt to the past—one that needed to be repaid.

"I've got a bottle of twelve-year-old single malt scotch in the cabinet for you," Gene said, glancing at Paul.

"Still the best painkiller I know," he replied.

As Gene parked in front of the bunkhouse, Paul looked over at Kendra and saw the smile on her face.

"You into country living?" Paul asked her.

"I wouldn't go that far, but this place is just so welcoming," she said. "I love the white painted wood, bright yellow chairs, and just look at that porch swing for two."

"That's mostly Lori's doing," Gene said proudly. "Before, there was only a log bench and hitching post. Come on, let me show you the inside."

Gene opened the door and invited them in with a wave of his hand. "There's not much in the mini fridge here, so come over to the main house when you're ready to eat."

"Where's Lori?" Paul asked glancing around. "Cooking up a storm?"

"Nah. She's shopping in Cortez, but she'll be back by eight. She left dinner for me, but, as usual, she made enough to feed an army, so you're invited to dig in. There's a batch of fresh homemade chocolate chip cookies, too."

"Bro, she's got you eating right out of her hand," Paul teased.

"Don't knock it till you've tried it," he said, then nodded to Kendra. "There's a shower in the small bathroom at the end of this hall, but you'll only get cold water there. The big bathroom with the claw-footed bathtub has cold and hot running water—and the tub fits two."

Kendra nearly choked. "I bathe alone."

Gene looked at Paul with raised eyebrows and shrugged.

"One more thing before you go," Paul said, playfully shoving Gene back toward the door. "Where do you keep the first aid kit?"

"Bathroom cabinet. You'll find plenty of supplies there. Lori insisted on it after Preston and Daniel put on the gloves and turned the corral into a boxing ring one evening. They'd decided to work out their frustrations after the fifty dollar pay-per-view match they'd been watching lasted less than two minutes."

"Who won, Preston or Daniel?" Kendra asked.

"Neither. Lori turned the hose on them as soon as Preston got a bloody lip," Gene said, laughing.

"Speaking of bloody," Paul said, glancing down at his clothing. "Can I borrow a change of clothing?"

"Daniel keeps a few shirts and pants in the first bedroom. You and Dan wear the same size, right?" He glanced at Kendra. "You're about the same size as Daniel's wife, Holly. She keeps some jeans and sweaters in there, too. Feel free to borrow whatever you need. They won't mind. I think there's some makeup stuff in there, too, but I don't know jack about that."

Paul walked outside with Gene. "Thanks for coming to pick us up," he said.

"No prob. Clean up and relax with the lady. I'll stay away."

"No need, nothing's going to happen."

Gene shook his head. "Maybe something *should*. I

saw the way you look at her." Not giving him a chance to answer, Gene walked away.

Paul expelled his breath in a hiss. Were his feelings for Kendra that obvious? He strode back inside and found Kendra running her hand along the tongue and groove, knotty pine walls.

"This is so beautiful," she said, standing at the doorway to one of the rooms. "It's real wood, and the grain's perfect."

"It used to be one big room with bunk beds and a potbelly stove in the middle. Lori has been pressuring Gene to make the place better-suited to adults. I can see she won that battle."

"She's done a great job. Look at this vanity table. I bet she made the organza skirt around it. It's so pretty."

"In a bunkhouse…"

"It's extra special precisely because it's *in* a bunkhouse. It welcomes women, not just men."

"I guess," he replied.

She glanced back at him. "What's wrong?"

"Just sore and crabby," he said, but as he tried to shrug, he winced.

"Is it your shoulder again?"

"Nah, I scraped my back when I crawled out of the pickup window," he said. "I recall I was in a hurry at the time."

"Take off your shirt and let me take a look. You might need that doctor after all."

"It's not that bad," he said, but he shrugged out of his shirt anyway and set his fetish aside.

"Turn around," she said softly.

As her fingertips brushed his skin, he suppressed a shudder—and not from the pain.

"You're more scraped up than me, so you get to clean up first. Once you're out of the bathtub, I'll put some antiseptic on those cuts."

"Then I'll do the same for you."

"My scrapes have sealed up. I'm fine," she said.

He pointed to her shoulder. "Not really. You're still bleeding a bit. See where your sweater's sticking to the cut? You don't want to get any of that soot and grime in there. Better take it off so we can have a look."

He saw the flash of excitement that lit her eyes, and that look pleased him far more than it should have.

"Never mind. I'll grab some clothes and go take a bath," she said, then looked at her hands and winced. "Ugh. On second thought, I need to wash my hands first. Pretty disgusting, huh?"

"I have to disagree." He pulled her into his arms and kissed her gently. "You're beautiful," he murmured, drawing back and enjoying the hazy look in her eyes as she gazed back at him.

"Why can't I stop wanting you?" she whispered, but this time she didn't pull away. "I know what I have to do...."

"You can't be strong all the time. No one can," he said, kissing her again.

"Not even you?"

"Particularly me," he said. "I need...you."

He kissed her shoulder, then her neck, loving the

way she melted into him. "Even the strong need love, sweetheart, more than we'll ever admit."

She drew in a breath as he gently lifted off her sweater, unclasped her bra and kissed her breasts. "My knees are about to buckle. I'm not that strong."

"You need me as much as I need you. Stop thinking. Just-feel."

He grasped her buttocks and pressed her into him. He was hard and ready, but he'd hold back. He'd burn these moments into her memory forever.

"Before you came into my life, I was cold and empty inside. You've given my heart a reason for beating again." He took her soft breast into his mouth.

Gasping, she wrapped her arms around him. "I want...." Her words trailed off as he nipped at the taut peak gently.

"Tell me," he demanded in a rough whisper.

"I want to surrender...then feel you go wild inside me."

The words lit a fire in his blood. He lifted her into his arms and carried her to the bed.

"Set me down," she said quickly. "You'll hurt your shoulder...."

"What shoulder?" All he could feel now was the fire—pure, sweet, and furnace-hot.

He eased her onto the soft mattress, brushing away what remained of her clothing and kissing her everywhere. He kept his touch gentle, wanting to bring her to the edge many times before they were through. He knew what would give her pleasure.

"This was meant to happen," he murmured, opening her to his touch.

She gasped with pleasure and arched upwards toward him. "No, not yet," she managed, struggling to hold back. "You've still got your jeans on. Let me see you."

He stood beside the bed, unbuckled his belt, and stripped. "Like what you see?" he growled, standing there, letting her gaze sear over him.

"You're so beautiful," she managed in a choked whisper.

"Nobody's ever called me that."

She opened her arms and reached out to him. "Look at me when you slip inside my body. I love the way your eyes darken when you want me."

Seeing her wanting and needing him made him crazy. Holding her gaze, he settled over her. "How could I not look at you now?"

SHE WASN'T SURE how long she slept, but when she awoke she found herself encircled in his powerful arms. His chest moved with each breath as she lay with her head on his left shoulder.

"You're awake," he said.

"How did you know? Your eyes were closed."

"Yes, but I wasn't asleep. I was enjoying the warmth of your body against mine."

She nestled deeper into his arms and sighed contentedly. "We can't lie here forever. It's seven o'clock in the evening."

"My brother won't bother us."

She laughed softly. "Have him trained, do you?" she said, sitting up.

"He knows I've got feelings for you," he said.

"Do you?" she asked softly.

He started to reach for his jeans, then stopped and turned his head to look at her. "I thought I was pretty clear about that." He gestured back to the bed. "Complaints?"

She shook her head and smiled. "You were gentle when you needed to be and rough and wonderful at other times," she said, getting up.

Only one thing had kept it from being perfect. He'd never really told her how he felt about her.

Almost as if Paul had read her unspoken thought, he pulled her against him. "I care about you, Kendra, and that's not something I say lightly. In fact, I've never said that to anyone before."

The revelation didn't surprise her. She looked up at him, sensing he had more to say.

"These days, people use the word 'love' too easily. To me, love means the willingness to make the other person a part of your life, but that's not a place you can be right now. My life will never be my own until my past is settled."

She nodded. That kind of loyalty was rare and beautiful. "No promises were made and none need to be kept," she said.

He stood tall, confident in his nakedness. "Regrets?"

"None," she said.

He took a step closer to her, his body growing hard again. But hearing a car pulling up in the gravel, he stopped.

Paul went to the window and, standing to one side, looked out.

"Two of my brothers are here," he said.

"I'll bathe fast, then you can go clean up."

"No hurry. I'll use the shower. The cold water will do me good."

Chapter Sixteen

Kendra bathed, then dressed quickly. Stopping to look at herself in the mirror, she studied her reflection. The pale peach turtleneck sweater and snug jeans accentuated her feminine curves.

"You look nice," he said, standing in the doorway.

"These clothes will have to do, but they don't really suit me," she said.

"They may not suit Deputy U.S. Marshal Armstrong, but they do suit the you I've come to know."

Kendra avoided looking at him. It was time to get down to business. To emphasize it to herself, she clipped her badge onto her belt. "Sexy and feminine clash big-time with my weapon and holster," she said with a quick half smile. "There's a jacket in there, and I think I'm going to put it over this sweater."

He nodded, then walked down the hall.

A few moments later, she met him in the living room.

"You look the part, Deputy Marshal, and you'll fit right in with law enforcement here in the Four Corners," he said.

"Good." She rolled up the cuffs another notch. "This jacket will hide my holster and badge—unless I choose to have them show."

Minutes later they walked over to the main house. As they went through the unlocked kitchen door, Paul heard the crackle of the fireplace and loud, familiar voices arguing in the next room.

"They're both targets," Preston was saying. "The evidence speaks for itself."

"Don't kid yourself. Without a clear motive, we're still just guessing," Daniel answered.

"They've been ducking bullets for days now. What else do you need?" Gene said.

"Guys," Paul said, walking into the room.

"Hey, good to see you're both okay. I figured I'd give you about another ten minutes, then call the paramedics," Gene said with a quick grin.

"Yeah, yeah," Paul growled then looked at Preston. "What brought you here? Did you turn up something?"

He shook his head. "I read the bulletin and knew you'd be here. The state patrol is still looking over the crime scene, so why don't you tell me how it all went down?"

"The gunman was above us on the bank, firing blind into the cab," Paul said. "There was a lot of smoke, and the side windows were below ground level."

"Which side of the cab took the bulk of the hits— driver's or passenger's?" Preston asked, zeroing in on the question foremost in their minds. "Do you know?"

"The driver's side took the first few hits. The rounds came through the lower roof and rear of the cab," Kendra said. "The steering wheel hub took a hit, and there were at least two more through the driver's side backrest. The way I see it, they were grouped to cover that half of the interior."

"Did the shooter know who was driving?" Daniel asked.

"Yeah, he knew. We passed by so close there was no way for him to miss that," Kendra said. "Paul pulled me down across the cab, and the bullets passed just over my legs. If I'd stayed behind the wheel I'd be dead."

"I still don't get it. What were you doing on that road in the first place?" Preston asked.

"We'd just picked up a flash drive from Mickey," Paul said, telling him about the gun show surveillance feed.

"So, once again, though it looks like we're dealing with a marksman, he still missed his target?" Daniel said.

"This time it wasn't for lack of trying," Paul said. "Combine that with the fact that he ran us off the road, and that alone could have easily killed us, and you're looking at what was clearly a hit."

"But why are you being targeted? What's the motive here?" Preston said.

"You tell me. I suspect an informant in the marshals service, but as I said, I have no proof," Kendra said.

"From where I sit, it looks like the informant is

someone close to both of you," Daniel said, looking at Kendra, then Paul.

"It's no one I associate with," Paul said. "I haven't had any special contact with the marshals service in eight or nine months."

"I'm sure you have your own source there, a friend who has kept you current on the status of the investigation?" Kendra said, taking a guess. "Who is it?"

He shook his head. "Couldn't be him. He's completely loyal to the marshals service."

"I'm with Kendra on this. We should still look into it," Preston said. "I could check him out—discreetly, of course."

"No, you don't get it," Paul said. "He retired two months ago. My guy's out of the loop, and what's been happening to us is recent."

"Okay, but keep thinking about it," Preston said. "Who could it be?"

Paul said nothing for several long moments, standing in front of the fireplace, staring at the flames.

Minutes stretched out. Kendra started to speak, but Preston shook his head.

She waited.

Paul finally turned to face them. "The hit on the judge happened ten months ago. No one's come after me since then. So why now? What's changed?"

"I asked myself that just the other day. I figured once I found the answer, I could use it to draw Miller out," Kendra said. "Nothing's come to light, so now I don't know. Do you think that maybe it's taken them this long to get to you because they figured you weren't going anywhere?"

"Not likely. That kind of business doesn't get put on hold," Paul said. "I've got another idea we need to consider. What if you were right, Kendra, and *you* were the primary target all along? The hit on me could have been arranged so that your supervisor would be pressured to send you here—away from where you might have done serious damage. Having you killed while hunting down Miller could have also permanently obscured the real motive for the hit."

Kendra stared at him for a moment, his words sinking in. "If you're right, that's a brilliant plan."

"So, now what?" Daniel asked.

"We go back to one of the primary questions," Preston said. "Someone has been feeding the gunman information on your whereabouts. Let's narrow it down. Who knows where you are?" he asked Kendra.

"My supervisor, Evan Thomas, his office assistant, his boss and anyone else in the chain of command who has access to the reports," Kendra said.

Her cell phone, inside the pocket of her shirt, began to ring. She glanced at the caller ID. "It's Evan, do you believe it? I have to take this. By now, he's seen the Colorado patrol's report."

"Don't give out your current location if you can help it," Preston warned.

Kendra nodded and stepped into the kitchen. "Armstrong," she said, answering the call.

"I just heard about the incident that went down earlier today, but there was no medical report. You okay?" Thomas asked.

"I'm fine, Evan," she said. "I was tracking down a lead to Miller when I got run off the road and into an empty irrigation canal. The suspect then shot the vehicle full of holes. He missed, and we got out just after the truck caught on fire."

"Were you able to ID your assailant?"

"No. It could have been Miller, but conditions prevented us from getting a good look at the suspect."

"I need results, Armstrong, and you're getting nowhere," he snapped. "I've got people breathing down my neck here, and I'm tired of making excuses. Unless you can bring Miller in, or at least track his location, I'm going to have to come down there myself."

Having her supervisor question her abilities for the second time in days hit her hard. "I'll find Miller."

"Don't let me down, Kendra. You've got a week," he said.

Hearing nothing but dead air, she realized Thomas had ended the call. She stared at the phone in her hand, her emotions flipping back and forth between exasperation and anger.

"What's wrong?" Paul said, coming up to her.

"Nothing."

"Yeah, right. Your eyes are flashing hot and cold, and you've got a death grip on that phone."

"My boss is a tool. Now my job—my reputation—is on the line." She recounted her conversation with Evan. "I've never failed to get results, not once. Sure, sometimes it took everything I had, but I always came through. Now, twice in a row, I've come up short." She gripped the countertop, lost in thought. "What irks me most is that by telling me he'll take over, he's saying he can do something I can't."

"Like I've mentioned before, I know Thomas. He was trying to motivate you, not rattle you. He'll play with your head if he thinks it'll make you better at your job." Paul said. "Evan was my supervisor, too, for a while. When my partner went down, he was right on the scene. He helped me get a handle on things. He's good at what he does."

Kendra exhaled slowly and glanced around. "He's still a tool. Any chocolate around here?"

Gene came in just then and laughed. "Sounds like you and my wife have something in common, Kendra, but I'm afraid I finished the last of the chocolate peanut butter cups. Lori was going grocery shopping today. I'm guessing she'll be getting a fresh supply."

"Then I'm going for a walk," she said. "Don't worry, I won't go far, and I'll keep my weapon handy."

"Even so, let me take a look around first," Gene said.

"I'll go with you," Daniel said, coming up behind him.

TWENTY MINUTES LATER, Kendra stood with Paul by the corral, illuminated by an overhead lamp on a post, and watched the trio of horses browsing through scattered alfalfa leaves on the ground.

"It's so incredibly peaceful here," she said, taking a breath of fresh air.

"Yeah, it is. There was a time in my life when I couldn't understand why Gene or anyone else would want to live all the way out here, running a ranch so far from the city," Paul said. "Standing here right now, I've got to say it doesn't seem like such a bad idea."

She turned around and leaned against the welded pipe fence railing. "When I first joined the marshals service I was in love with the idea of an exciting career, something far from the ordinary."

"And now?" he asked.

"I still love my work, but I've also discovered I need more than the job to be happy. Someday I'd like a family of my own." She looked at Paul and gave him a wry smile. "Don't panic. I'm not angling for a proposal just because we made love."

"Would that be so bad?"

"Bad? No," she managed, apparently surprised at his response.

"You know what our problem is?" she said, smiling. "Some people need fresh air, but our brains need car exhaust fumes to function right."

"Maybe so," Paul said, laughing. He placed a boot on the lower rail and leaned over, resting. As he did, one of the horses came up to him and nickered softly.

He glanced up, expecting to see Bud, or maybe Clyde, Lori's favorite horse. To his surprise, it was Grit.

"What a beautiful pinto! That jet-black head and

perfect white blaze down his nose is really eye-catching," Kendra said.

Paul stared at the animal, then patted his neck cautiously, half expecting Grit to spin and try to kick him, or make a bite threat. Maybe in the dim light the horse had mistaken him for someone else. Yet even as the thought formed, he realized how unlikely that was. Horses had a good sense of sight and smell.

Gene, who'd been coming toward them, stopped and stared.

"Can you believe this?" Paul said to his brother.

"You stopped forcing it, and things worked out on their own," Gene said. He glanced at Kendra, then back at Paul. "Remember *Hosteen* Silver's prediction."

Paul nodded, then looked at Kendra. "I only told you part of it. Would you like to hear all of it?" Seeing her nod, he continued. "When Dark Thunder speaks in the silence, enemies will become friends, and friends, enemies. Lynx will bring more questions, but it's Grit who'll show you the way if you become his friend. Life and death will call, but in the end, you'll choose your own path."

"We just escaped death, and Grit's here to show you the way...to life?" she asked, petting the horse.

Paul spoke softly, noticing how the horse nuzzled her. "I think *Hosteen* Silver was telling me to look to the future and not dwell on the past. If I continue fighting to find justice for my partner's murder, more blood may be spilled, but I've got no other choice. A killer is out there, one who won't stop until he's brought down."

"Then you've made your decision," Gene said.

"I've also got a plan," Paul said. "Let's go back inside. Kendra and I will need Preston's help."

Chapter Seventeen

Paul laid out the details of his plan, then looked at the others gathered around the room. "There are no guarantees, but if we follow through with this we'll find out once and for all if Kendra's the gunman's primary target. Once we know that, our other questions will be answered, too."

"I don't like this at all, but I don't see a way around it either," Preston said, then continued. "If we're going to do this, you should use one of our department's safe houses in Hartley. There are three, but the one I have in mind is unoccupied right now, and the houses on both sides of it are empty, too. That entire neighborhood has been hit with one foreclosure after another."

"You're asking me to lie to my supervisor, Paul," Kendra said slowly. "That kind of thing has serious consequences, and Evan's bound to find out eventually."

"That's true," Paul said, "but can you think of anything else we can do at this point?"

She said nothing for several long moments, and no

one interrupted the silence even as the minutes ticked by. "No, unfortunately, I can't," she said at last.

"Then it's a go?" Preston asked.

"Yes," Paul said, "but we need to make sure that the only people in the loop are ones we trust one hundred percent. That means the list will be short—Preston, Daniel, Gene, Kendra and me. Kendra and I will be at the safe house while the rest of you will be close by, providing backup."

"One second," Preston said. "My career is on the line and this is my turf, so *I'm* calling the shots. Agreed?"

As the others nodded, Preston continued. "Kendra, time to put things in motion. Call your supervisor and tell him that you'll be staying at one of our P.D.'s safe houses and you're waiting for directions. You can say that you've picked a place that's off the radar—not connected to any part of your fugitive retrieval assignment—since Miller's shown he can find you easily. If he asks about Paul, tell him that he's working out other arrangements, but you haven't been briefed yet."

"I'll do it right now," she said.

Kendra picked up her cell phone and dialed Evan Thomas. It was nine at night now, so she had to call his cell. He answered on the fourth ring, and she stuck to the script.

"File a report through channels," he snapped. "The next thing I want to hear from you is that you've found Miller."

She gritted her teeth and politely finished the call.

"Let's get going," she said, reaching for her jacket. "Evan isn't the only one running out of patience. If Miller's out there, his days as a free man are coming to a close."

ON THE WAY back to Hartley, Paul was quiet. They'd borrowed Gene's new truck for the time being, and as he drove, he constantly checked in the rearview mirror.

"Your brothers are always there for you. That must be a very nice feeling, to know someone always has your back."

"You have your brother and father. They're both military men who live by a strict code of conduct and honor. They'd do the same for you."

"If it came down to it, sure, but the closeness isn't there. Their lives are halfway around the world."

"Not all my brothers are living close by. As a matter of fact, two are overseas right now. Once they left home, Rick and Kyle wanted to go as far away from the Rez as possible," he said. "Now that it's out of their systems, they'll be coming home as soon as their rotation is up. Their roots are here."

"I think it's your cultural ties that really help strengthen the bond between all of you," she said.

"They do, that's true. The traditions of our people—concepts like 'walking in beauty'—shape our lives," he said. "Explaining our ways to outsiders is hard because when we try, it often comes across as stilted English—a bunch of odd-sounding phrases all strung together."

"Those who care enough to want to understand, will."

He smiled. "And if not, it's their loss. We're proud of who and what we are. That's part of *Hosteen* Silver's legacy."

"He sounds like a remarkable man," she said.

"He was. His death left a huge gap in our lives," he said. "It also took us by complete surprise."

"What happened, if you don't mind my asking?"

"He walked off into the desert one winter night without any explanation and his body was never found. That's the way of our Traditionalists when they believe death is near, but the thing is, he wasn't sick, not that we knew about anyway."

"Did he leave anything behind that might have explained why he did that?"

"There was one clue—of sorts. He left us a retelling of a Navajo creation story, one meant to show that good can be corrupted by evil, but that evil can always be defeated by those who remain strong," Paul said. "Now it's up to us to find the answer hidden there."

"He wasn't one for speaking plainly, I take it?"

"He would when necessary, but *Hosteen* Silver believed that when you grappled with a question, you often found answers to things you never even thought to ask."

"Maybe you need someone who can view it from an outsider's perspective. If you tell me the story, I'll try to help," she said.

"All right." After a moment he began to tell her the

tale, his voice soft, yet oddly compelling. "Changing-Bear-Woman was a beautiful maiden who had many suitors. Coyote wanted to marry her, but she wanted no part of him. Trying to discourage him, she gave him a list of impossible challenges. Coyote agreed to all her demands but, in return, made her promise that she'd marry him if he succeeded. Eventually, Coyote found ways to fulfill all of the tasks, so she became his wife."

"That was good, right? I mean, she kept her word."

"Yes, but soon Coyote began to teach her about the power of evil. In time, she learned how to change into a bear. That's when she stopped being who she'd been, an honorable mortal woman, and became an evil monster that needed to be stopped."

"Did Coyote do that himself?"

He shook his head. "Once she became evil, Coyote didn't like her anymore, so he walked out on her. Angry and feeling betrayed, she went looking for him. During her search she ended up killing everyone who got in her way, including most of her brothers."

"But not all?"

"The youngest one escaped, but seeing the lives she'd claimed, he realized that his sister was gone forever. To restore the balance between good and evil, he knew he'd have to destroy the creature that now stood in his sister's place. He prepared himself to do what was necessary, but wanting to somehow honor who she'd once been, he allowed her to live on in other forms that continue to serve the Diné, the Navajo People. A part of her body became the first piñon nut, another yucca fruit and so on."

"So in the end, evil was conquered and served the ultimate good," she said, understanding. "That could be said to be a cautionary tale, particularly for those of us in law enforcement. We tend to see things in black and white—legal or illegal. That's our job. Maybe this was your foster father's way of saying that good needs evil and evil needs good. The battle between the two defines each side."

He considered her words. "You may have something there. That's very much in line with Navajo thinking. We believe that everything has two sides. That's how balance is achieved."

"Maybe Mister Silver knew he had an illness that couldn't be controlled. His way of restoring harmony was to greet death," she said softly.

"No. Though what you're saying sounds logical, it doesn't feel right to me," Paul said.

"Sometimes it takes a long time to find the truth. We see that in investigations all the time."

"And like it was with Grit, I can't force it."

"Exactly."

"You've given me something to think about," he said. "Thanks."

"Glad I could help."

"Before I met you, I'd never spoken about *Hosteen* Silver's letters to anyone outside my family." He took her hand and gave it a squeeze. "There've been a lot of firsts for me since you came into my life."

She sighed. "And that's bound to make facing down Miller, or whoever comes after us, harder. You realize that, don't you?"

"Maybe, but we're trained for this and we're not alone," he said.

"If Miller doesn't show up and all we end up collaring is a minor player, I'll have to come up with a plan to force Miller out into the open. I'm not going back empty-handed," she said.

"I now know what your fetish should be," he said, a slow smile tugging at the corners of his mouth. "It's practically tailor-made for you."

"What?"

"Let me surprise you."

"If I promise to act surprised later, will you tell me now?"

He laughed. "You'll know when the time is right."

THEY ARRIVED AT the safe house in Hartley an hour later. It was in a middle class neighborhood filled with single family homes whose owners had fallen on hard times since the real estate market's free fall. Several of the houses were listed for sale and appeared to be mostly foreclosures, judging from their state of disrepair.

The safe house was in the middle of a cul-de-sac. There was a high cinder block wall in the rear, bordering a warehouse protected by dogs, judging from the signs, so the only real access was from street side.

A minute later Kendra and Paul were inside the

sturdy brick house. It was plain and utilitarian but well laid out and solidly constructed.

After finishing the delicious take-out Navajo tacos Preston had brought, Kendra and Paul were alert once again, weapons easily accessible, as they kept an eye on the street. Having already taken up their positions, Preston and Daniel were hidden outside. It was close to ten-thirty, so there were few cars passing by and no neighbors out walking.

As per the plan, Kendra made it a point to cross in front of the window periodically, allowing herself to be seen, but never walking slowly enough to turn herself into an easy target. Keeping the table lamp and a TV on with the sound down so they could hear anyone approaching, they still hoped to create the illusion that they were easy prey.

After two long, boring hours, Paul was at the fridge grabbing another cola for himself when the tactical radio positioned on the coffee table crackled to life. The next thing they heard was Daniel's voice.

"There's a four-door sedan coming up the street, going real slow."

"Paul, Kendra, stay out of sight," Preston said next. "I'm on the north side of the house behind cover, watching the street. It could be just a resident coming home from an evening shift, so stay cool."

Paul was already by the front window, off to the side, and behind the curtain as he watched the street with night vision binoculars. "He's slowing, like he's checking addresses," he told the others.

Paul reached down for the tenth time in the past two hours and rested his hand on the butt of his weapon. "I can't make out the driver, but I think he's male, judging from the short hair."

"He's going to stop...here," Kendra said, standing across from Paul behind the other curtained window.

"Hold your positions. Maybe it's an officer," Preston said.

The driver pulled up into the driveway and parked. As the car door opened and the dome light came on, the face of the driver became clear.

"I've got an ID. It's my boss, Evan Thomas," Kendra said quickly.

Paul came over, his binoculars lowered. "I thought you didn't give him your location."

"I didn't, at least not which one. He didn't ask, and I didn't volunteer," Kendra said. "I don't know how he tracked me."

"He must have hopped on the next available flight after you two spoke, or maybe he was already making the drive down from Denver," Paul said.

"Stand down," Preston called over the radio to the others. "He's not packing a weapon."

Thomas opened the passenger door on the driver's side and reached inside. "Give me a hand with this gear, Armstrong, will you?" he yelled. "I know you saw me pull up."

"I better help him out. Evan's the best special ops sniper in the Rockies, and he never goes anywhere without his weapon," Kendra said, moving to the door.

Kendra stepped out onto the front porch, her weapon holstered now, then walked across the remnants of the lawn toward Thomas's car. "How did you know where I was?"

"Gun!" Paul suddenly yelled from inside. "Driveway—across the street!"

Kendra dove to the grass, rolling as three shots rang out. Out of the corner of her eye, she saw Thomas flinch, then fall to the driveway, groaning.

Pistol out, she squeezed off two of the six or seven rounds that suddenly erupted from all around her, all aimed at the gun flashes coming from a hundred feet away. The shooter, barely visible before, tumbled to the ground.

"Cover me," Paul yelled to his brothers, then ran to Kendra's side. "You okay?"

Kendra was already on one knee, her weapon trained on the fallen target. "I'm fine, but Evan took a hit."

"Hold your positions! Look for a second shooter," Preston yelled, then ran out from behind the corner of the house.

Preston continued across the yard to where Supervisory Inspector Evan Thomas sat, his back against the side of the car.

"I'm fine," Thomas said. "The round went through my arm. Check out the shooter."

A porch light came on in a house farther down the street, and an elderly woman poked her head outside. "What's all that racket?"

"Go back inside, ma'am," Preston yelled out to her as he crossed the street. "I'm a police officer and there's been a shooting."

Preston reached the downed perp and, using his foot, pushed aside the Ruger carbine that lay next to him. "The shooter's alive. Call 911, Dan," he yelled to his brother, who was standing in front of the house to Kendra's left.

"Already on it," Dan said.

Kendra crouched by Evan, who was now holding a blood-soaked handkerchief against his upper arm.

"Wanna get a first aid kit? I'm losing a lot of blood here," he said, his tone a professional blend of anger and pain.

"I'll see what I can find," Kendra said.

Paul joined Preston by the gunman, who lay on the grass beside the concrete drive, his breathing shallow and labored. He'd taken multiple hits but was wearing a vest, and the rounds that had struck his torso hadn't penetrated. He was bleeding heavily, however, from two hits to his upper thigh. The man would live if he had immediate care, which was on the way.

Preston placed a handkerchief over the leg wounds, applying pressure to reduce the flow of blood. "Hold this in place if you want to live," he ordered. The wounded man complied without comment.

Paul looked at the gunman's sunburned face, concentrating on the eyes. "Miller," Paul said in a quiet voice. "About time we met up close."

The man made eye contract, but there was no discernible expression on his face.

"I'll need a positive ID," Preston said. Crouching down, he pressed the suspect's finger to his cell phone's screen, sending the image to a database thousands of miles away. "Chris Miller," Preston said a moment later. "A perfect match to his military prints."

"You're going down hard," Paul told the wounded man, who continued to stare back at him blankly. "You killed a federal marshal, which means life as you know it has come to an end."

Kendra came over and crouched next to Miller. "You're never going to see freedom again, but *if* you give us the name of the person who hired you, we might be able to cut a deal. Think about it. Maximum security prison time safely away from the cartel's hit men, versus lethal injection."

Miller said nothing.

"I know you came looking for me at the coffee shop, impersonating an officer," Paul said, but Miller still didn't react. "The evidence we've already got will bury you. Get smart and cooperate. You're a liability to your former employer now, with makes you a soon-to-be dead man. Without some form of protective custody, it's just a matter of days or weeks."

This time Miller looked away and closed his eyes.

"You're an excellent marksman, yet you failed three times trying to kill Paul, my supervisor and me," Kendra said. "The big question is, why? You gave me a chance, and now I'm giving you one in return. You need protection, and we need your testimony."

Miller opened his eyes and looked at her for the first time.

"That's all I can offer you," she said.

The sound of approaching sirens filled the air, and as the paramedics arrived, Kendra rose to her feet and waved them closer.

FORTY MINUTES LATER Kendra sat by Preston's desk at the station. Both Chris Miller and Evan Thomas were in the regional medical center, protected by local police officers and hospital security.

Preston placed Chris Miller's file in front of Kendra, but after a quick look, she realized she'd had nearly identical copies on her laptop for days. "There's nothing here I don't already know. Miller's strictly a gun for hire, a freelancer with no real ties or allegiances. With him, it's all about the money. We need the person who hired him, and that's information only he can give. Without that, we're only buying time. His employer will just send a new shooter after us."

"What I want to know is how Inspector Thomas found you. We never gave him your location," Paul said.

"Yeah, we did," Preston said. "Supervisory Inspector Thomas called my captain earlier today on another matter. Kendra's name came up, and Captain Johnson told him where she'd be. He knew I'd requested the safe house on her behalf."

Seeing Paul's expression harden, he glared back at him. "I'm part of a police department, bro, and we have protocols to follow. Without going through those channels, I wouldn't have been able to use the place."

"Okay, one mystery solved," Kendra said. "Now here's another. I'm guessing that the leak in the marshals service took Miller to Thomas, but I still don't understand why my boss suddenly became a target, too," Kendra said. "Anyone?" she asked, looking at Paul, then Preston.

Preston shrugged. "We need to gather more evidence and identify at least another player or two before motives become clear. For now, let's concentrate on the physical evidence we have," Preston said. "Miller's Chevy, which was stolen earlier today, is still at the crime scene. Officers discovered it parked one street over from the safe house. The tags were stolen, along with the car."

"So the crime scene unit is processing the car right now?" Kendra asked.

He nodded. "Here's what we've got so far." He looked down at the small notebook he pulled from his pocket. "With Miller, there was the carbine and two spare magazines loaded with nine millimeter ammunition. In the stolen vehicle we found a smart phone under the driver's seat, and a disguise kit—two wigs, a mustache with stickum on the back, and a beard with the same type of adhesive. There was also a tube of rubber cement."

"Anything yet on the carbine?" she asked.

"The serial number was run, and the weapon was traced to an estate sale in Arizona. We've got people trying to contact the seller to see if they kept a record on the buyer," Preston said, then shrugged. "Private sales…you know how that goes."

"Yeah. Usually impossible to trace. Was there a navigation unit in the vehicle?" Kendra asked.

"Yes, but Miller knew how to disable the system, which means we can't trace his travel route after the vehicle was stolen."

"I'd like to revisit the crime scene and take a look around," Kendra said. "Since I can't speak to Evan yet and Miller's still in surgery, maybe I find something that'll give us a few more answers. I came here to collar Miller, and I've done that, but now I've got to make sure he stays alive. He's a potential federal witness and the next likely target of whoever's running this operation."

"Yeah. It's clear Miller wasn't working alone. The fact that he was able to take his shot right after Thomas arrived proves it," Paul said.

"Exactly. Miller had to have known Evan's movements, down to the exact address of his destination," Kendra said. "He was already set up to take the shot by the time Thomas got there."

"Good point," Preston said. "One thing—since all this is taking place on my turf now, I want to be kept current on whatever you find."

"Consider it done," Kendra said.

"We know where he ended up, but where was Miller

staying?" Paul asked Preston. "Does the department know yet?"

"He didn't have any key cards or house keys with him, but we're on that now. I'll let you know."

Paul and Kendra left the station shortly thereafter and walked directly to Gene's truck.

"My gut's telling me that the answers we're looking for are staring us right in the face," Paul said.

"Once we're able to question Miller again we'll get what we need," Kendra said.

"I'm not so sure. He's a hard case. I've seen his type before. He'd rather rot in jail for the rest of his miserable life than give us anything," Paul replied.

"He heard my offer. When he wakes up and realizes how vulnerable he is now, unarmed and immobile, I think he'll come to his senses and cooperate," Kendra said.

After ten minutes of light traffic, they arrived back at the safe house. Yellow crime scene tape cordoned off the area where Miller had gone down, and the crime scene team was spread out, working under floodlights.

"Where do you want to start?" Paul asked her.

"The vehicles. Let's take a look at Evan's rental while the police are concentrating on Miller's car."

They walked over to the sedan, and Kendra studied the exterior. "The police will want to extract the two rounds that struck the door, but let's check out the interior."

Kendra put on a pair of latex gloves, then slipped

behind the driver's seat and looked around. While she flipped down visors and looked in the center console, Paul checked the glove compartment.

"We need something brighter than the dome light that's in here," he said. "Let me borrow something from the crime scene van."

As Paul strode away, Kendra saw Evan's hard-sided rifle case still lying on the back seat cushion. Beside it was a leather portfolio. Under the circumstances, looking inside for his notes seemed like a good idea. Maybe Evan had left a copy of a memo or correspondence that would reveal who else knew of his travel plans.

It was unlocked, and Kendra brought out several folders. The first was a file on a case she wasn't involved in, so she set it down. The next folder turned out to be a copy of her marshal service personnel file.

Kendra skimmed the top page, and as she did she felt a coldness envelope her. Evan's latest recommendation was that she be removed from the field entirely and reassigned to desk or training duty permanently. Anger filled her. He'd never believed she was being tailed, but with an informant still in place, things would continue to get worse.

As she glanced at Paul and saw the resolve etched on his face she knew that, like her, he was in this to the end. No matter how tough things got, Paul would remain beside her until they completed what had to be done.

Chapter Eighteen

Once she'd finished checking the interior of Evan's sedan, Kendra went to the crime scene van to look at the items removed from Miller's car. The first thing she did, still wearing latex gloves, was remove the cell phone from the evidence bag.

It seemed odd to her that Miller had chosen a smart phone instead of a cheap throwaway. Something like this could be traced, even if it had been stolen, as she suspected it had been.

She turned on the phone, but there were no saved names or numbers, only a huge collection of apps that came with the device. Seeing an unfamiliar icon among the rest, she activated it with a touch.

Kendra realized almost instantly what it was. Hurrying out of the van, she signaled Paul. "Miller has a GPS app on his phone, and it's indicating this location. See if there's a GPS sender in Evan's car somewhere."

"They're making them smaller and smaller these days, so it may take a while. Let me check the typical hiding places first." Paul walked around the car, checking the easily accessed wheel wells, and stopped as he reached the rear.

"I've got something." He pulled out a device the size of a pocket calculator and showed it to her. "Here's the tracker. It was glommed in place with what feels like rubber cement. Didn't Miller have a tube of that stuff in his car?"

"Yeah, but how on earth did Miller know which rental car Evan would be using? That sedan isn't from the motor pool." She paused. "I'm going to have Preston get a warrant so we can access Miller's complete call record—and another one to search his room, when we find where he's been staying." She placed Miller's phone back in the evidence bag and added her initials and the time to the tag.

"I'll call my brother for you," Paul said, but before he could dial, Preston pulled up. "That son of a gun has his own built-in radar. Even when we were kids, he was like that. Whenever I needed him, there he was."

"Maybe that's part of the gift that comes from his fetish. Yours is lynx. What's Preston's?" she asked.

Paul shook his head. "That's his secret to share—not mine."

As Preston joined them, Paul showed him what they'd found.

"Thomas picked up the rental car at a lot right across from the Hartley airport," Preston said, "so Miller must have arrived first and attached it, or he had an accomplice waiting and watching. Maybe the tracker was put there in case Thomas decided to change his destination. That way Miller could set up another shot."

"It helped that Evan wasn't on his guard and didn't spot the placement of the GPS. He also ignored my reports and refused to believe there was a problem," she said, then told him about the personnel file she'd found.

"If you hadn't stood your ground and fired back at the shooter, Thomas might be dead right now. I'll be happy to remind him of that for you," Paul said.

She barely managed to conceal a smile. Paul was a fiercely loyal, unwavering ally, and that was one of the things she loved most about him.

She'd never met a man quite like Paul. In his arms, she'd found both gentleness and strength waiting for her. His touch could make her burn with passion, or soothe her, if that's what she needed. That calm steadiness that came from his unflagging courage continued to draw her to him.

Kendra took a breath and forced herself to focus on the case. "Do you have anything new for us, Preston?" she asked.

"Yeah, as a matter of fact, I do. I found out where Miller was staying, a motel not far from here. That's now named in the search warrant. It's my next stop, and I thought you'd want to come with me and take a look around."

"You bet," she said without hesitation.

With Preston in the lead car, they made their way southeast across Hartley.

"We're close to finding the answers," she said softly. "Can you feel it?"

He nodded. "Yeah. It's something that starts in your gut, then all your senses become fine-turned. Smell, taste, everything becomes super sharp. There's no other feeling like it. Well, maybe one."

She laughed. "Stay on track. Even with Miller sidelined, we've never been in more danger. Whoever hired Miller will throw everything he's got at us now."

"I know."

"There's something I need to do." She took a long, deep breath. "If we run into trouble, you'll need the authority to act in an official capacity, using deadly force if necessary. I have special deputation authority, so I'd like to swear you in."

"All right," he said with a nod.

"As soon as we get to the motel, we'll make it official," she said.

Ten minutes later they arrived at an upscale motel at the junction of two main city streets that merged onto the highway leading out of Hartley. The five-story building was roughly stuccoed with a Mediterranean look that included balconies and a red slate roof. The landscaping was immaculate, even for this time of year, and a sign proclaimed the presence of an indoor pool, sauna and gym.

"Guess Miller doesn't like to rough it," she said.

"In his shoes I wouldn't have stayed in a cheap dump either. Those attract low-end criminals, generate trouble and, ultimately, the police. Here, the room rates alone guarantee him more privacy."

Once out of the car, Kendra saw Preston parked just ahead, talking on his radio. While he finished his business, she stood before Paul. "Are you ready to be sworn in?"

"Absolutely."

"Raise your right hand. Do you solemnly swear to faithfully execute the duties of a U.S. Marshal, so help you God?"

"I do," he said, his voice strong and clear. Something in the tone made Kendra realize just how much he still missed his old job.

"It's like a step back in time for you, isn't it? I'm—" She started to say she was sorry, but the last thing Paul wanted was her sympathy. She fell into an uneasy silence.

"I do miss the job," he said, "but I meant it when I said I wouldn't go back even if I could. When I first started my business, I saw it as a temporary thing, something to keep me distracted while I sorted myself out, but I've made a place for myself in Hartley. Now that Grayhorse Investigations is turning a steady profit, I'm going to accept the offer Daniel made me when I first opened my agency's doors. He wanted to merge our companies and make it a family-owned business. I didn't jump in back then because I didn't feel I was bringing enough to the table, at least in comparison to him, but he said he'd be ready whenever I was. Now I am."

"It sounds perfect, you two working together," she said. "It would also broaden your options, wouldn't it?"

"Yeah," he said with a smile. "I'd get to do more field work, which is something I've wanted."

Preston stood by the side door and waved. "You two coming, or taking a vacation?"

Paul laughed. "Let's go."

A few minutes later they entered a large, ground-floor room close to the rear exit of the main structure. "Fancy model laptop," Preston said, glancing at the corner desk across from them.

Kendra walked across the thick carpet, then stopped and studied the computer without touching it. "This could have information that'll lead us to whoever hired Miller. I'd like to take a quick look." Seeing Preston nod, she turned it on with a gloved hand.

As they waited for the computer to boot up, she helped Paul and Preston search the room. In the closet were two gun cases, one with two nine millimeter autoloader pistols and spare, loaded magazines, and the other containing a .308 caliber bolt action Remington rifle with fifty rounds of hunting ammunition. There were also several small pistol and rifle targets, a hunting knife, New Mexico large game hunting flyers and two forest service maps of area woodlands.

Kendra noticed the hunting jacket and red vest on a hanger in the closet. "With deer season coming up, no one around here would have questioned all this stuff."

Kendra returned to the computer screen and tried to access the files, but kept getting an enter password screen. "It's encrypted. I can't get in without risking triggering a program that'll wipe everything clean," she said at last. "Do either of you know anyone who can hack into this thing?"

"Daniel," Preston and Paul said at once.

"Your brother's a computer geek?" she said.

"That's not how he'd express it, but, yeah, you bet," Paul said. "He's also got some top-notch techs on his payroll."

"The fewer people involved, the better," she said. "Did you happen to include an electronic device search on that warrant of yours, Preston?"

"Sure did. With today's criminal element, it's almost automatic when we conduct a search. And there's no problem using Daniel. The Hartley P.D. hires him all the time to do specialized work, so it's mostly a matter of getting the right signatures on the paperwork."

"This should have gone to the marshals service directly, but without knowing the good guys from the bad, I don't want to risk it," Kendra said. "I've got to think outside the box now."

Preston reached for the computer, but just then his cell phone rang. He took a step back, spoke hurriedly, then hung up. "Miller's awake," he said. "The doc says we can question him, but not for long. Supervisory Inspector Thomas is already out of recovery and has been moved into a private room."

"Miller's a target now, and with an informant on the inside, his employer may already know where he's at,"

Kendra said. "We have to move him to a secure location before all hell breaks loose."

"Here's what I can do," Preston said. "If his doctor consents, we can move Miller to a small but well-equipped clinic on the Rez. I've got a place already in mind. I'll tell only a few key people, including my boss, and keep the relocation under wraps that way."

"He's my prisoner. I have to be in on the transfer," Kendra said.

"All right. I'll set it up. Where will you two be sleeping?" Preston asked.

"I hadn't thought that far ahead," Kendra said.

"I have an idea. You're both still in the crosshairs, and I'm betting neither of you has had a good night's sleep in days," Preston said. "I know a place where you'll be safe. The Wilson brothers have a large, secure house. One's a former cop, and the other two are currently with the department. They let us use the place whenever we have a high threat situation. It's strictly for emergencies, but you'll have two cops keeping watch, plus George."

"George Wilson went blind after an accident and was forced to retire, right?" Paul said.

"Yeah, but he can hear someone breathing at twenty-five yards. In the dark he's more aware than either you or me."

"Refocused senses. It works that way sometimes." Paul glanced at Kendra. "George's brothers, Jake and Hank, could bench press a horse, too. Those guys are *big*."

"No one messes with them," Preston said, "but you two won't be able to use the same room. The Wilsons are very straitlaced about things like that."

"I remember. Their dad's a preacher," Paul said, then added, "I see no problem with that. They've always shown respect for Navajo ways, and I can do the same for theirs."

"Me, too," Kendra said. "Give us the address."

THERE WAS A big iron gate at the walled entrance to the Wilson home, but as Paul and Kendra drove up, it swung open to the inside and Paul was able to drive in without stopping. Their headlights soon swept past an enormous, blue-uniformed cop standing on the far side of the covered porch.

"Talk about security, it's barely four in the morning and they've already got someone outside. Which of the brothers is he?" Kendra asked.

"That's Hank. He must have been pulled off duty." Paul parked his pickup next to a Hartley patrol car. "Come on. I'll introduce you," he said, stepping down from the truck as the gate clanked shut behind them.

When Hank came up to meet them, flashlight in hand, Kendra suddenly realized just how big he really was. Paul was over six feet tall, but Hank Wilson was half a head taller, and must have weighed two fifty. He was the kind of backup someone like her would have wanted when walking into a Denver biker bar. If Hank had played sports, she could easily imagine him as a defensive end.

Paul bumped fists with Hank, then introduced Kendra.

"Pleased to meet you, ma'am," Hank said, his voice almost soft despite the deep tone. "It's all copacetic out here at the moment. I'll be watching the grounds but I'll try not to make any noise. You two don't have to worry. Just catch up on your sleep, okay?"

"Thanks. Jake and George inside?" Paul asked.

"Copy that. Just ring the bell when you go to the door, okay? Anyone who knocks gets a pistol waved in their face."

"Good to know," Kendra said. "Nice to meet you, Hank."

"You too, ma'am. Good night."

As they stepped up onto the porch, Kendra waited while Paul reached for the doorbell. "If the other brothers are like Hank, they're really on the ball. And polite," she added with a smile.

The door opened just a crack, and they both turned at the sound. "Preston?" a deep voice asked.

"No, Paul and Marshal Armstrong," Paul said, noting Kendra's puzzled reaction.

"Just testing to make sure everything's okay. Come on in, you two," Jake said, opening the door. As they stepped in, the man, maybe an inch shorter than Hank, placed his handgun back into his holster.

"I'm Jake, Shorty to my brothers," he said with a smile, nodding to Paul, then offering his massive hand to Kendra.

"I'm Kendra, Kendra Armstrong. Thanks so much

for your hospitality on such short notice, Jake," she said, surprised by the gentleness of his handshake.

"Pleased to be of help, ma'am," Jake said. "Make yourself at home. You two will be as safe as babies tonight."

"Appreciate your help," Paul said, looking around at the big room. The overstuffed chairs and two sofas in the living room were arranged in a half circle around a cozy, blazing pellet stove a few feet from a brick wall. Mounted on the wall itself was a big screen TV, and against another wall were a digital music center and wooden shelves with CDs.

"Thought I heard a racket," a soft, pleasant voice called from the kitchen side of the room. Kendra turned and saw the oldest giant of the Wilson brothers. George wore shaded glasses and picked his way past a massive oak table and chairs with certainty.

"Would you two like something to eat? I'm a good cook, if I say so myself. When you can't see, taste becomes more important."

"Actually, I'm beat. If you don't mind, I'd rather call it a night, or morning, I guess, and get some sleep," she said.

"Sure." George led the way down a short hall, then opened the door.

There'd been no hesitation. "You knew precisely where the door and the knob would be," Kendra said, surprised.

"I know this house like my own heartbeat. I can tell when something doesn't sound right, or if anything's been taken away or added to any of the rooms," George said. "If anyone's outside beside my brothers, I'll know that, too, maybe even before Hank and Jake. When blindness took away my sight, the good Lord gave me other gifts."

"This room is great. Thank you," Kendra said, glancing around.

"Clean sheets, fresh towels. If you need anything else, just call. I won't be far."

"Thanks," Kendra said. "There is one thing. I'll need to be up at eight. Is there an alarm clock?"

"Jake will knock on your door at that time," George said.

"Great. Then we're all set."

As the men left, Kendra sat down on the edge of the king-sized bed. This could be the last night she'd be working with Paul. The thought felt like a heavy weight over her heart. She hadn't come to Hartley wanting, or even hoping, to fall in love, but her heart had made other plans.

After undressing down to her underwear, she crawled beneath the covers and switched off the light.

Despite her exhaustion, for a long while all she could do was stare into the dark. Everything inside her hurt. She didn't want to go back to her empty apartment in Denver, then try to tell herself that Mr. Right didn't exist. He did—he'd just come with pre-existing conditions.

Paul couldn't give her his whole heart, and even if she could have accepted it for herself, it wasn't fair to the family she'd eventually have. When it came to love and family, it was all or nothing.

With silent tears running down her face, she gradually faded into a deep, dreamless sleep.

SHORTLY AFTER BREAKFAST they left the Wilsons' home and headed to the hospital. Things were already well underway there, and soon, they were ready to transport Miller.

Two vehicles pulled out of the ambulance port, a sheltered bay that provided quick access to the emergency room. Preston and another officer led the way in a large black SUV with tinted windows. Paul followed, driving the ambulance, with Kendra at his side.

Kendra wore a protective vest, and the short barrel of a shotgun rested between her feet, visible to anyone who passed by on the passenger side of the ambulance in a high-profile truck or van.

"This time of the morning we won't be facing much traffic. Most of the coal mine and power plant employees have already changed shifts," Paul said.

"We've got a good plan, and even if we do draw fire, we have the advantage. They'll assume Miller's with us and that'll buy your brother time to get him away safely. I only wish we could have had an escort behind us, as well, but Preston's right. It would have looked like a VIP motorcade and attracted too much attention."

Soon they were rolling down the four-lane highway ten minutes west of Hartley. Traffic flow and bad tim-

ing forced them to stop at a light in the small community of Kirtland, just north of the Navajo Nation
boundary. It was the last stop before Shiprock, a dozen
or so miles farther west. Traffic was heavier here than
before, but their small convoy stayed together.

Paul checked the rearview mirror. "There's a white
van behind us. It's probably a service or utility vehicle, but I can't see a company or agency name from
this angle."

"There are two men inside wearing baseball caps
and big shades. We've got the sun at our backs, and
that makes the use of shades a bit odd. They look more
like spooks than anything else," Kendra said.

Kendra checked out the new-looking pickup that
pulled up beside them at the light. There were two men
in the cab there, also wearing ball caps and sunglasses.
"To my right," she said, "another pair of spooks in
heavy jackets."

Paul looked over. "Something's not right. They're
not the least bit curious about us."

"Yeah, and here we are in this ambulance."

As the light changed, Preston's SUV surged ahead.
Paul accelerated to keep up, but suddenly the pickup
beside them veered into their lane.

"Hang on!" Paul swerved the heavy ambulance to
the left, lessening a blow to the right front bumper, but
the ambulance still shook hard on impact. As he pulled
the wheel back to the right, he caught the pickup's rear
bumper as it tried to cut them off. The truck fishtailed,

almost catching an oncoming car, then straightened out, rocketing ahead.

"Behind us!" Kendra grabbed the dashboard.

The white van slammed into them with a bone-jarring thud. Kendra bounced forward, but the seat belt kept her from hitting the windshield.

Paul looked ahead. The passenger of the pickup was leaning out his window, pointing a gun. "Duck!"

A bullet shattered the windshield, striking the rear-view mirror, which broke loose and bounced off the back of the cab. Paul tried to hold the wheel steady, but the van hit them again on the right rear bumper and sent them skittering down the highway, tires screaming. Paul yanked the wheel to the right, avoiding an end-over-end rollover.

Kendra drew her gun as the van pulled up on her side, but it instantly dropped back into their blind spot.

Paul yanked out his pistol, back in control of the ambulance, but by then the pickup was speeding away. The van behind them cut its speed, whipped across the median, and also raced off.

"What the hell?" Paul looked at Kendra. "They had us pinned. Why did they bail?"

Kendra looked out the side mirror. "There's something stuck on our side panel back there. Get off the road, fast! There, that empty lot," she said, pointing.

Ten seconds later, she leaped out of the cab and took a quick look at the object.

"Bomb!" she yelled to Paul. "Run!"

They were barely twenty feet away when the blast

shook the ground. Enveloped in a wave of heat and pressure, they were thrown forward onto the gravel.

"You okay?" Paul said.

"Yeah," she said, coughing.

They rose to their feet slowly and turned to watch the mass of flames that covered the ambulance. Billowing black smoke rose upwards in dark waves.

Paul looked over at Kendra. "You can bet they're watching us with binoculars right now and think they killed Miller."

"Good thing Miller's safe and sound in Preston's SUV."

"We bought some time, that's all," Paul warned.

"It may be a small win, but it's one that counts."

Daniel, his head out the window, pulled up in a second SUV, this one blue. "Come on. Get in!"

Paul and Kendra didn't hesitate. "What are *you* doing here?" Paul asked, waving Kendra in first. "I never told—"

Daniel gunned the engine the second they were both inside. "Preston asked me to cover the move but stay well behind so I wouldn't be made. When I saw you running from the ambulance, I figured out what was going down. Now let's get out of here."

FORTY-FIVE minutes later they arrived at a reservation clinic south of Beclabito in the piñon/juniper hills. Preston was outside waiting for them.

Kendra looked around. "Good choice. No way to sneak up on this place. There's not much cover around here."

"That, and we're thirty miles deep on the Rez so a white man sticks out like a sore thumb," Preston said, leading the way inside. "One good thing—the bomb attack rattled our prisoner. He wants to cut a deal—immunity in exchange for his testimony."

"He killed a U.S. Marshal and Annie Crenshaw. Those defensive scratches found on his arms are going to seal a conviction when the DNA under Annie's fingernails comes back from the state lab. His only hope is a life sentence," Paul growled.

"Yes, but to survive even behind bars he'll need our help. That's going to be our leverage," Kendra said. "Of course *any* deal will be up to the federal prosecutor."

As they went down the short hallway, the doctor who'd ridden with Miller and Preston came out of a room to meet them. "Miller can be questioned whenever you're ready," he said, "but I'm going to stay in the room, monitoring his vitals, just in case there's a problem."

"Hold that thought, doc." Kendra took Preston aside. "How carefully did you vet out this doctor?"

"I'd trust him with my life. He's with the New Mexico National Guard and was wounded during a mortar attack on his medivac unit in Iraq. I chose him because I knew he could handle himself under fire."

"Okay." Kendra nodded to the doctor, then went inside the treatment room where Chris Miller lay on a hospital bed.

"You ready to cut me a deal?" Miller asked as Kendra came in. "I've got plenty to trade."

"Give me something big to take to the prosecutor, then we'll see what we can offer you." Kendra brought out her digital recorder and set it on the table next to the bed. After recording the date and time, she gave Miller a nod. "Okay, make it good."

Chapter Nineteen

Kendra waited as Miller sipped some water. He was taking his time. She wasn't sure if he wanted to back out or if he was just playing them.

"First, let me make one thing clear," Miller said at last. "I was hired to wound—not kill—your supervisor, Thomas."

"What?" Kendra sat up abruptly.

"You heard me," Miller said. "I was shown a photo, given the address, then ordered to make the hit once he got out of the car. I was paid to target an arm or leg—no head or torso shots."

Kendra shook her head in disbelief. "What a minute. Are you telling me that your client told you specifically *not* to kill Thomas?"

"Yeah. I was instructed to use a pistol caliber round with a full metal jacket. Less damage if it went through and through," he said. "It didn't matter to me, I got paid the same. But I was set up, too. I was told to expect one fed inside the house and the target, not a full security team."

"Your bad luck," Preston said. "How long have you been in town?"

Kendra knew he was trying to tie Miller to the earlier events.

Miller shook his head. "That's all I'm saying for now. What I've given you is just a taste of what's to come. Give me immunity—in writing—and we'll talk again."

"Were you responsible for the hit on Deputy Marshal Armstrong and Paul Grayhorse a few days ago?" Preston said, pressuring him anyway. "And the murder of Annie Crenshaw?"

"I'm only copping to a single charge of assault with a deadly weapon. The more you give me, the more I'll give you."

"Not good enough. Tell us who hired you," Preston said.

When Miller looked away and stared at the wall, Kendra stood and gestured toward the door.

Outside in the hall Preston glared at her. "That guy's playing us."

"Yeah, but he's got information to trade, and we need him," she said.

"All right then. I'll get in touch with the prosecutor," Preston said.

It took another hour and a half, but once they convinced Miller he'd be given protection behind bars and a new identity to protect him from hostile inmate retaliation, he relaxed.

"Okay, let's have it," Kendra said, staring her prisoner down.

"We're still talking *one* crime—the one where I winged Thomas. But here's something you didn't know. I was also hired to take you and the former marshal out permanently the moment the opportunity presented itself. Last night, today, tomorrow—ASAP. That was my next gig."

"So we were both targets," Kendra said quietly.

"My primary target was Thomas. You two were B-list."

Kendra didn't answer. "Now on to the big question. Who hired you for the job, Miller?"

He shrugged, then his lip curled into what might have been a smile. "I never ask for a name. That makes clients uneasy. But there's a way you can track him down. The carbine, clips loaded with ammo, and smart phone were all left for me at a prearranged location inside a discarded dog food bag and a paper sack. In the bottom of the sack, which contained everything except for the carbine, I found a sales slip for a cash transaction dated the day prior to my arrival, exactly one week ago. It wasn't for the stuff I picked up, but the name of the place was Roy's Happy Trigger."

"That's a gun shop on Hartley's west side just off the old highway," Paul said, looking at Kendra. "The owner's a good man, and even better, he's got a great security system. I provide it for him."

"Do you still have the receipt?" Kendra asked Miller, thinking of fingerprints.

"No, I threw it out."

Kendra stood. "We'll be back," she said.

"Wait a minute. Where's the protection I was promised?" Miller said. "One cop at the door isn't going to do it, you know."

"You're safe here," Preston said. "You'll have at least two armed guards outside 24/7, and others you'll never see. Considering your location, no one's going to sneak up either."

A few minutes later, after warning the doctor not to trust Miller, Kendra led the way back outside. "I want to talk to that Hartley gun shop owner as soon as possible."

"You two will have better luck if I'm not there," Preston said. "The proprietor and I have had our differences."

"That's because you keep telling him how to run his business," Paul said.

"All I've been suggesting is that he move his store out of that high crime neighborhood."

"So why's he staying there? You think he's involved in some shady side business, dealing illegal arms or something?" Kendra asked.

"No, it's not like that," Paul said. "Willie's dad started the gun shop and Willie doesn't want to move away and leave all his memories behind. When he looks around the neighborhood, he still sees it as it used to be, not run down like it is now."

Kendra was touched by the empathy in Paul's voice,

a man with more than his fair share of memories that continued to haunt him.

She didn't comment until they were back in Gene's truck, heading to Hartley. "I feel for Willie, but wanting things to stay the same…" She shook her head. "That's a losing battle."

"Sameness…. There was a time in my life when I would have considered that a curse of major proportions."

"Is that also part of the reason you've decided to accept Daniel's offer now? You want to stir things up a bit so the business will remain a challenge to you?"

"Yeah," he said with a smile. "Something like that. What about you? Are you ready for new challenges? If someone offered you a job with a decent salary and more regular hours, would you leave the marshals service and become a mom?"

She took a slow, deep breath. "It's not that simple. Salary's important and so are the hours, but there are other holdbacks I've yet to work out. For one, I don't have an extended family like yours who lives close by and could help me if I got sick or injured. I would also need to provide my child with some male role models, ones who would be around for more than an occasional birthday or holiday."

"Here's a thought. Come work for Daniel and me. You've got the training and skills we need, and I'll be close by and able to help you out if you're in a pinch."

She suspected that even a partial commitment like that one had been hard for Paul. He was a man who didn't open his heart easily to anyone outside his band of brothers. Yet halfway propositions weren't for her, and what he was offering just wasn't enough.

Paul was the kind of man she'd always dreamed of but never thought she'd find. When the going got rough, he'd remained right by her side. Yet although he was a relentless fighter, he could also show compassion.

Maybe those qualities also explained why Paul had been such an extraordinary lover. He was wildly passionate, yet he also knew how to take his time and prolong a woman's pleasure.

Paul had claimed a piece of her heart. When the time came for her to leave, she'd go, but the memories they'd carved out would be part of her forever.

THEY RODE IN silence until they reached their destination. "There's Willie's shop, straight ahead on the right side of the street," Paul said.

Kendra saw a small building ahead with bars on all the windows. The stores on both sides were closed and boarded up, but Roy's Happy Trigger seemed to attract a large volume of customers. The parking lot in front had just one empty space. "Looks like Willie's got a booming business."

"Yeah, he sure does. After his dad died, he inherited a shop that barely made ends meet. Willie turned it around and made it a huge success," Paul said. "He sees things differently, though. If you compliment him on the good job he's done, he'll just say that his dad did most of the hard work. He just improved a few things because that was what his dad expected him to do."

"Will he be leaving the place to his son?"

"Doesn't look like it. Willie says that he's married to the store. According to him, he's never even had time for dating."

"He sounds lonely, trapped."

He shook his head. "No, I don't think so. Willie just likes the status quo. By building up his business, he's honored his father's memory and found financial security. He has no desire to change anything."

"So rather than move locations and take a risk, he settles for the known."

He didn't answer right away. "Maybe. You know, sometimes it's hard to deal with memories that won't let go."

S<small>INCE</small> P<small>AUL AND</small> Willie already knew each other, Kendra asked Paul to take the lead. As they walked through the front door, ringing a small, overhead bell, Paul waved at the middle-aged man with the thinning hair and neatly trimmed beard. He was busy showing a hunting rifle to a customer.

"Just take a look around, folks," Willie called out without really looking up. "I'll be with you just as soon as we're done here."

Paul walked around, glancing at the shop displays as he waited. He'd taken his shot by asking Kendra to stay. He'd also been careful not to attach any strings to the arrangement or burden either of them with a slew of expectations.

Maybe if he'd had a different kind of life, he would have just gone for it, hoping for the best. That's what most people did, wasn't it?

What had held him back was knowing that she wanted to adopt. As someone who'd gone through the system, he knew firsthand how vulnerable kids who'd known rejection really were. If things didn't work out between Kendra and him, the same kind of scars he'd borne all his life could be imprinted on another child.

Happily-ever-after wasn't a concept he could believe in, so walking away had been his only logical option. He wouldn't make Kendra and the kids who'd come into their lives a promise he suspected belonged only in a fairy tale.

Paul tried to show some interest in a display of collectible infantry rifles from World War II, but his mind remained elsewhere.

Willie, apparently finished with his previous customer, came up to him. "Hey, buddy. What brings you in here before lunch? Are you going to pitch me a new upgrade to your surveillance system?"

Paul shook his head. "My lady friend and I need to talk to you privately," he said, catching Kendra's eye and motioning her over.

Willie waved to a clerk, then led them behind the counter to an office in the back of the shop. The small, windowless room held a wooden desk, two small LED monitors and several filing cabinets. There were three chairs, one on casters with a padded seat, and the other two, old-style metal folding chairs.

"My dad never liked white-collar offices. He said they made a man soft," Willie said, smiling at Kendra as she came in just behind Paul. "Now tell me what brings you two here. From your expressions, I gather it's serious."

Paul gave him a quick update on what Miller had told them, then showed Willie a photo of Miller's carbine.

Willie sat as still as a rock. "Dammit, you know I'm not responsible for what people do with the guns they buy here. I run the mandatory background check, and if the buyer comes back clean, I finalize the purchase."

"Relax, Willie, we know that," Paul assured him quickly. "The reason we came is that we need your help to track down this guy. The cameras will have a record of all your customers and we're hoping to find a familiar face."

He nodded. "Okay, have at it, while I go check my records and get the names of our cash customers for that day."

Seeing two more customers come in, Willie looked at Paul. "Give me another few minutes. Matt needs my help out there. You know where everything is, so go ahead and access the feed. Let me know if you find the guy you want. If it's someone I deal with regularly, I may be able to tell you where to find him."

As he left, Paul sat down at the desk and pulled back the keyboard stand. There was a mouse beside it and the proper monitor came out of sleep mode in a few seconds.

It took Paul a few minutes, but the feed soon began. "The images are pretty clear, and since the camera's not readily visible, no one bothers to turn away."

"Nice touch."

"Thanks," he said. "The surveillance business can seem really tame after working the field, but it provides tangible results. Willie used to get held up three or four times a year. Since the cameras went in and the stickers went up on the windows six months ago, he's had one robbery and the suspect was identified and arrested within a day."

"You don't always need a gun to fight crime. The right information is often all that's needed for the bad guys to get caught and the public to win."

"Navajos call it restoring the balance. That's how we walk in beauty."

"It's a good way to look at it," she said. "To me, what's always been important isn't the star or badge that comes with the job, it's the work itself."

"Does that mean you're considering joining our family business?"

"You're making it sound like the Mafia!" she said, chuckling but not answering his question.

"You've been in the city too long," he said, smiling.

Kendra, who'd focused on the screen, suddenly sat up. "Stop! Freeze that frame." Even though he was wearing a hat and sunglasses, she knew exactly who the man in the video was. Her body grew cold as she realized the magnitude of that one man's betrayal. "I can't believe this. He fooled everyone—including me."

Chapter Twenty

"Evan Thomas, my boss," Kendra said softly. "He knew we were getting close to catching Miller, so he arranged to get himself shot, knowing it would keep him in the clear a while longer."

"He was probably also hoping that we'd end up killing Miller. That would have practically guaranteed that his connection to the cartel would have never come to light," Paul said.

"I have a feeling we're right on all counts, but we still have a problem. The hat and sunglasses obscure too much of his face. I know that's Evan, but a defense attorney could successfully throw out my ID. The word of a professional hit man that led us to the buy isn't going to get us a conviction either. If Miller never saw him, Evan could weasel out of this in any of a thousand ways. We need more evidence," Kendra said.

"Agreed, but we're going to have to watch our step. If I'm right, Evan's been undermining operations for a while. Evan was my supervisor, and I'm beginning to suspect that one of his first jobs was setting up Judy and me. After Judy's...end of watch..." he said, using their service's term for the deceased, "I heard about other ops that went wrong. They blamed it on a lot of things, including mistakes by the marshals in charge, but I believe the pattern began back then."

Willie returned, took a look at both of them and smiled. "You got what you wanted, I see." He held up a piece of paper. "Matt, my clerk, made the sale. Here's the name of the buyer and an address. I've also got the serial number of the weapon he purchased, a nine millimeter Ruger carbine I picked up third-hand via an estate sale. I've also written down the name of the supplier, a friend of mine who shops for guns at estate sales and gets some great deals."

Kendra took the paper and held it so she and Paul could both read the note. "Right serial number, but not the right name for the purchaser. His ID was fake. Evan prepared something gathered from a federal database, my guess, or it wouldn't have passed background."

"Doesn't matter now. We got our lead." Paul looked at Willie. "I need to borrow one of your flash drives so I can make a copy of the footage. I'd also like to use your computer to email the image on that frame to Daniel."

"Do whatever you need," Willie said.

Less than five minutes later, Kendra and Paul were on their way across town. "Paul, I have to ask you something. Is your past connection to this case going to be a problem?"

"You think I want to catch up to Evan so I can blow him away?"

"No, that's not it at all. You live by certain rules, just like me. That's what makes us the good guys."

He reached for her hand, then brought it up to his lips. "I'm glad you believe in me."

"I do, but I also need to know that you'll play this by the book—no short cuts just to achieve the goal."

"We can do that, but we'll still have to push Evan hard," Paul said. "I say we confront him with the video and the sales record. Let him know that you're taking the information up the chain of command. Then we'll watch and see what he does. My guess is that he'll damn himself one way or another."

"Evan's not stupid, quite the opposite. How else to explain how he's managed to stay under the radar for so long?" she said. "He'll know we've got nothing that'll stick."

"Matt, the gun shop clerk, may be able to positively ID Evan as the customer who bought the carbine," he said.

"Or not."

"We have the serial number on that weapon," Paul said.

"That identifies the weapon, but we still can't conclusively tie that to Evan. We need to *prove* he was the purchaser and that he turned that gun over to Miller. Our biggest problem is that Miller never saw his client—Evan."

"Let's tell Evan that Preston is questioning Miller

right now and that Miller's claiming he's got a source inside the marshals service. We won't be accusing Evan of anything, but we'll be pointing out a problem that Evan may see as a direct threat. Then we'll hang back and see what Evan's next move is," Paul said.

"All right. We'll do it that way, and see what he does."

It didn't take Kendra long to find Thomas. He'd checked out of the hospital and was back in his Hartley motel room. "Before we go over there, we need to get a reliable tracking device. We don't want to lose Evan if he makes a run for it."

"He'll be on the lookout for that. He'll probably search his luggage and whatever vehicle he's got to make sure they're clean and stay that way," Paul said.

"That's why I want to use *two* devices—one that he'll find after a careful search and another he won't expect."

"Daniel can help us with that," Paul said, and reached for his cell.

By the time they arrived at Daniel's place he was waiting and ushered them inside quickly. "I've got what you asked for, and actually got you a third device so you can game the gamer," he said.

"Thanks," Kendra said. "I like it. We'll put one where he'll be sure to find it, then place the second somewhere he'll have to search hard to find. When he finally spots it, he'll assume he's outsmarted us and he's good to go. He'll never look for a third."

"Nice use of game theory," Paul said.

"Are you sure you don't want backup on this?" Daniel asked Paul, then glanced at Kendra.

"No. We have to give Evan plenty of room," she said. "If he senses a trap, he has all the training necessary to disappear for good. I'm sure he's got stashes of cash and identities he can assume at a moment's notice."

Paul checked out the three small devices. "You can plant the smallest one on him, Kendra. He won't be expecting that. I'll take the other two and put one inside the wheel well of his car, a place he's bound to check, and another in his gear."

"Okay, let's get rolling then." Kendra dialed the hotel and got Thomas after three rings.

Though it was difficult, she kept her voice steady and businesslike. "Miller's in custody," she said. "The local P.D. is questioning him now. Miller has told them that he's working with a partner inside the marshals service, but we don't have a name yet."

"Where's he being held? He's not in the hospital. I checked," Thomas said.

"For his own protection, I had him moved to an Arizona clinic," she said, deliberately misleading him. "He's still under heavy guard."

"You shouldn't have acted without my knowledge," Thomas snapped.

"It's my case—my fugitive."

"It *was* your case. Now it's mine." He stopped short, then, after a moment, continued. "Get over here. We'll talk about the evidence you've gathered and see where the case stands."

KENDRA AND PAUL arrived at the motel ten minutes later and went directly to Thomas's room.

Kendra sat on one of the chairs placed by a round table near the window.

"The evidence is sketchy, Evan," she said. "We have the name of the gun shop where the carbine and ammunition were purchased. The purchaser didn't notice a receipt lodged under a flap in the paper bag, apparently. We pressed the business owner for more details but apparently one of his younger clerks made the sale and can't recall the buyer. The clerk is reviewing hours of video, so once he identifies the guy, we'll have more."

"Miller probably wasn't the one who bought the weapon and ammo, so you could be on a wild-goose chase."

"If his employer or partner provided Miller with what he needed for the hit, it's possible we'll recognize him once we view the feed."

Thomas stood, idly adjusted the sling on his wounded arm, and stared at an indeterminate spot across the room. Paul also remained standing, positioned beside Evan's carry-on bag, which was on the carpet, unzipped. "I've kept you out of the loop as long as possible, but now I don't have a choice. There are things you need to know, Kendra."

Thomas looked at Paul.

"He's been deputized," Kendra said, "if that helps."

Evan nodded. "What I'm about to say can't leave

this room. Am I clear?" he said, looking at her, then at Paul.

"All right," Kendra said, then saw Paul also nod. He raised an eyebrow, as well, signaling that he'd deployed the first listening device. She guessed it had been tossed into Evan's open luggage.

Thomas had other things on his mind. "If Miller's talking, some of the things he'll say will eventually point back to me as his inside man. He's never seen my face, but if he made a recording of any of our conversations, voice identification software might also identify me."

"Are you admitting guilt?" Paul growled, taking a step closer to the supervisor.

Thomas held his ground. "You're off base, Grayhorse. I'm not the bad guy here."

"Yes you are." Paul moved like the wind, and in two seconds Thomas was pressed against the wall.

"You're interfering with a federal investigation, and you're going to blow my whole case. Back off—now," Thomas ordered, undaunted.

"What investigation?" Kendra forced herself between the two men, one hand on the back of Evan's collar and the other on Paul's forearm. "Back up, Paul."

Evan turned around. "I've been working undercover for nearly a year, worming my way into a criminal network that covers half the country."

"And selling out my partner and me was part of your job?" Paul snarled. "Nice try."

"What happened to you and your partner wasn't part of the plan," Thomas said. "That's the truth."

"I should be able to verify all this," Kendra said, picking up her phone. "Who's your department handler, Evan?"

"There's no way I can tell you that. I've got reason to suspect there's another informant in our office, one we've yet to unmask. Lives are at stake here, not just careers."

"So we're just supposed to believe this undercover story you're selling?" Paul said, moving in with clenched fists.

Kendra got in his way again, forcing Paul back.

"If you go off half-cocked, Paul, you'll destroy months of undercover work. Judy died at the hands of these jerks. Are you going to let it be for nothing?" Evan said, his eyes on Paul.

Paul lunged forward, his forearm at Thomas's neck, pinning him to the wall, but he avoided touching Evan's injured arm this time.

"Stop!" Kendra snapped. "Enough with the testosterone." She took hold of Paul's shoulder and eased him back again. "Let's sit down and reason this out."

Evan sat on the edge of the bed, then ran a hand through his close-cropped hair. "After the attempt on the judge that resulted in the death of Deputy Marshal Judy Whitacre, I began to suspect that the Hawthorn cartel had a well-placed informant in our office. We'd taken every precaution, yet they still managed to have a sniper in position to make the attempted hit."

"Did you report your suspicion?" Paul demanded.

"I had no evidence, and you don't bring up something like that unless you can make the case. To get the proof I needed I knew I'd have to go undercover," he said. "I eventually earned the cartel's confidence by passing along information, but it was always the kind I knew we could afford to lose."

"Like the fact that I was here in Hartley, and setting me up as Miller's next target?" Paul growled, his eyes cold and without expression.

"No. I never gave them your exact location. I also made sure you had one of our best marshals on the scene in case things got rough. That's the real reason I sent Kendra to retrieve Miller."

"You tried to discredit me when I reported that the cartel had an informant. Yet you knew I was right," she said.

"There was no way you could have accomplished what I could as an insider, so I protected my cover. All you would have done was get yourself killed, and you would have never even seen it coming. By sending you down here I gave you both a chance."

Paul stood, rock still, staring at Thomas. "You spin a nice story, I'll give you that, but it's nothing more than a skilled evasion unless we can verify it."

"Take a look at the facts. I never gave Miller your exact location, but he still found you. That proves the cartel has another well-placed source on the inside. Unless we ID that person, we're all in danger," Evan said. "My life is already on the line. The cartel suspects I've been playing them because my information is always missing key details. This is my last chance to finish what I've started."

"But if you've been compromised…" Kendra started, pointing to his arm.

"This wound is precisely why I'm still alive. I offered to take a bullet from the cartel's sniper. I convinced them that would help my credibility at the marshals service and allow me to continue to feed them information. That also proved my loyalty to the cartel since I was trusting them with my life," Evan said. "It was a calculated risk, of course, but I'll have more room to maneuver now and be able to penetrate deeper into their organization."

"You're asking me to trust you, but you've given me absolutely no proof of anything," Kendra said. "All I've got is your word."

"Do you really want to risk everything by sticking to protocol now?" Evan said. "I'm ready to make my move. Let me finish this."

"All right. I'm listening. What do you have in mind?" Kendra said.

"A large weapons stash is going to be shipped across the border into Mexico any day now. Garrett Hawthorne is going to be there himself to supervise the operation. If we raid the place today, we can prevent those guns from ever leaving the warehouse. We'll also be able to collar Garrett with enough evidence to put him away for life."

"Or we could be walking into a trap," Paul said.

Thomas looked at Paul, then back at her. "If I'd been working for the cartel, I could have taken either of you out long before now. I knew where you were and could have brought you into the open easily enough."

"Where's this warehouse?" Kendra asked after a beat.

"I don't know for sure yet, but it's local. I'm supposed to link up with one of Hawthorn's soldiers, get the location from him, and then go meet Garrett." Thomas checked his watch. "Crap, I'm already fifteen minutes late. I'm supposed to drive to Spencer's Superstore and meet him in the parking lot."

"Take one of us along," Paul said.

"No, that won't work. They don't like strangers, and they hate surprises of any kind." He paused for a few seconds, then continued. "What you *can* do is track me all the way via my cell phone's GPS. As soon as I get the warehouse's location, I'll text you with a quick single character, lower case k, as in okay. Stay out of the area until you get my signal, then make your move. Avoid using SWAT because their arrival is sure to tip off any spotters keeping watch on the neighborhood. Also, after it all goes down, make sure you take me prisoner along with the rest. That'll protect my cover."

PAUL WALKED OUT with Thomas while Kendra reported to Preston and brought him up to date.

"I'll deliver on this, don't worry," Thomas said.

As they reached the rented sedan, Paul suddenly grabbed Thomas and threw him against the driver's side front fender. "If you set us up, there'll be no place on earth where you can hide from me. I'll find you."

"If I'd wanted you dead, Grayhorse, you would have been a corpse already. Let me go."

Paul stepped back and allowed Thomas to get into the car.

As Paul turned to walk back to the motel, he wiped away the dust and road grime from the fingertips on his left hand. While roughing up Thomas and effectively distracting him, he'd used his free left hand to slip the second tracking device under the front tire well. The first one had been slipped into Thomas's luggage.

Thomas was bound to eventually find the two devices he'd planted, then probably ditch the electronics, including his phone. Depending on how prepared he was, Thomas might also end up abandoning the car he was currently driving.

The smallest, third device, the one they were counting on to track him, was planted in the back of his collar. Kendra had placed it there when they'd all been back in the room, and she'd stepped between Thomas and him, ostensibly to split them up.

After Thomas left, Kendra joined Paul and they were on their way moments later.

"Preston's ready?" he asked.

"Yeah. He'll wait for our call." She remained silent for several moments. "I don't trust Evan. Something about this feels…off."

"To me, too. It was almost too easy. His explanation was plausible, but it sounded too well rehearsed."

Paul stayed a half mile back, well out of visual range as they followed the three dots on the GPS screen targeting Thomas's location. "Do you have someone inside the marshals service you'd trust with your life?" he asked her.

She thought about it a moment, then nodded slowly. "Several, but one in particular, Tim Johnson. I was his partner for two years before he was relocated to Washington."

"A mover and shaker?" he said, pushing back the stab of jealousy. Had they been as close as Judy and him? A storm raged inside him as he thought of her with someone else.

"Tim demanded a lot from himself. Five minutes with him and you knew he was destined to climb the ladder."

"Is he the kind who goes strictly by the book?" he said, biting off each word.

"No, not really. He's more results oriented. What is it you want him to do?"

"The day Judy and I were shot, backup arrived within five minutes. Thomas showed up with the deputies who first came on the scene, too, though he wasn't part of their team. I never questioned it because, to me, he was one of the good guys. Now I'd like to know why he was in the area. You said he was your team's sniper?"

Kendra's mouth fell open, but she recovered quickly.

"You think he was the one who tried to make the hit on the judge?"

"He showed up out of thin air, and if memory serves me, he was on foot. Of course there was a lot of confusion, and I was flat on my back on the pavement at the time in a lot of pain."

"Was he part of your protection detail?" Kendra asked.

"No, but if he had official business in the area it should be on record somewhere," Paul said.

Kendra nodded. "Okay, I'll ask Tim to check that out for me. He won't hesitate."

Kendra made the call, and Paul heard her tone of voice change as she spoke to her former partner. She'd greeted Johnson like a friend, but the awkwardness that would sometimes result between former lovers—or partners who'd crossed that line—was absent. Still, it was clear that they liked each other and that irked him. He wanted her to get to the point quickly and end the conversation, but somehow held his peace.

An eternity later, she hung up. "He'll check."

"We've got another problem," Paul said, pointing to the screen. "Thomas ditched two of the bugs and his cell phone as I thought he would. The signals are coming from a strip mall ahead. The other bug, probably the one you stuck under his collar, has him heading north."

"I wonder if he's running to, or from, his cartel friends?"

"We'll find out soon enough," Paul answered. "Call

Preston and fill him in, and ask officers to check the strip mall. I suspect Evan had a second vehicle stashed there. Under the circumstances, it makes sense that he'd want to ditch the sedan. We know what it looks like."

"If the tracker indicates he's heading out of the city or to the airport, we'll have to pick him up," Kendra said.

"I don't think he'll make a run for it," Paul said. "He'll probably go to ground somewhere after linking up with the cartel."

Kendra updated Preston, then, keeping him on the speaker phone, added, "Looks like Thomas circled Main Street twice, then stopped. He's moving so slowly now, he must be on foot."

"There's a dry cleaners there—Smith's Finest—that seems to attract a lot of suspicious characters," Preston said. "We've been watching the place for weeks but we still don't have a clue what's really going on there."

"Tell us more about the cleaners," she said, glancing at Paul, who nodded.

"Hang on." They heard Preston sending an unmarked patrol unit to watch the cleaners, then seconds later, he returned to the phone. "It's a one-story cinder block building with a front entrance and one back exit into the alley."

"How about the roof? Any escape through there?" Kendra asked.

"A skylight, maybe, since it's a flat-roofed structure. We can have an officer cover that from the building next door," Preston said, then added, "But no way that's the warehouse Thomas told you about."

"I'm guessing that this is the first meet," Paul said. "Thomas will talk to one of Hawthorn's lieutenants and try to get the cartel's help leaving the country."

"Waiting around to see if he can lead us to bigger fish is too risky," Kendra said. "Evan's smart and knows how we work. Let's move now."

"You ready to make the arrest?" Preston asked.

"Ten-four," Kendra said.

Chapter Twenty-One

Ten minutes later Preston and several detectives entered the dry cleaners from the street. Kendra and Paul were positioned out back, weapons ready.

Within a few seconds a man wearing a suit jacket and slacks burst out the door and onto the loading platform, brandishing a sawed-off shotgun.

He spotted Kendra first and swung his weapon around. Paul leaped out from cover and yanked the barrel of the gun upwards, slamming the butt down into the perp's groin. The man doubled up, and Paul tore the shotgun from his grip.

Kendra moved in, sweeping his legs. The man crashed to the ground just as a second perp carrying a pistol rushed outside. His path blocked by his fallen companion, the suspect took aim at Paul.

Kendra shot first. The man grunted in pain, his own bullet going wild. Clutching his chest, he turned to run back inside, but found himself face-to-face with Preston.

"Don't give me a reason," Preston growled.

"No more," he managed through clenched teeth and

sagged to his knees beside his prone partner. He placed the pistol on the concrete platform, then assumed the position, locking his hands behind his neck.

"No blood. Suspects must have vests," Paul said. Kendra's gaze remained on the ex-owner of the shotgun.

"Where's Evan Thomas?"

"That bastard sold us out. He and Genaro crawled through the dryer tunnel," he said. "There's a fake panel in the back. If you hurry, you can probably grab them."

As another officer appeared outside to cover them, Preston handcuffed the men. "Go," he said. "We're good here."

Paul followed Kendra inside. One Hartley detective was guarding two employees lying facedown on the floor. He looked up just for a second. "Clear outside?" he asked.

"Yeah," Paul replied, "but we're one perp short, maybe two."

"Let's check the big dryer at the end," Kendra said, "the one with the 'out of order' sign."

Paul opened the door and, glancing inside the stainless steel bin, spotted a nickel-sized piece of green plastic sitting on the drum.

He recognized the device instantly. "It's the GPS tracker you placed on Evan's collar. So where the hell *is* this tunnel?" Paul reached in, put his hand on the circular end of the dryer drum, and pushed. It swung open, revealing an opening beyond.

"I'm going in first." Kendra stepped around him, jumped in, feet first, then eased down into a plywood-lined vertical tunnel. She could see a dim light at the bottom of a ten-foot drop.

She called to Paul. "I think this leads to an adjacent building. Go outside and look around. I'll check things out here."

"Not alone," Paul clipped and, seeing his brother approaching, added, "Preston, I'm backing up Kendra."

"Go. My people will check the surrounding buildings. Maybe we can locate Thomas out there above ground, or find his vehicle," Preston said.

"Copy," Paul said and followed Kendra down.

They were only about ten feet into the three-foot-high, horizontal metal culvert when Kendra entered a side tunnel. Glancing inside, she saw several big metal, ex-military ammo boxes but no suspects. She then heard shuffling ahead and a moan. Though it was hard to see, she could make out a figure leaning against a metal pipe perhaps twenty feet ahead.

She inched forward on her hands and knees, gun ready, and found an injured man pointing a pistol toward the opposite end of the tunnel.

"U.S. Marshal, put down your weapon," Kendra said.

The man eased his grip. The pistol slid out of his hand and clanked onto the metal floor. "Needed to stay alive till you got here…knew you weren't far," he managed in a raspy voice.

"Who are you?" The second Kendra saw the knife

still imbedded in his chest, she knew help wouldn't arrive soon enough to save him.

"Use…your cell phone…record…my last words."

Kendra had her phone out and recording within five seconds. "Go ahead," she said, holding the phone close to him.

"My name…Louie Genaro. Thomas, Marshal Thomas, stabbed me. Had the knife hidden in his sling. Traitor…to both sides. Wanted me dead, so he could get away with it, but…not his lucky day."

Genaro's eyes fluttered, but he forced himself to focus again. "Thomas…tried to kill Judge Yolen. I provided…the gun barrel…to replace one on his service weapon just for the kill. Supposed to destroy it later…but kept it…for leverage. Has his prints. My address…in wallet. Look in closet."

She started to ask him more, but Genaro gasped, then his eyes glazed over, and his head sagged onto his chest.

Kendra felt the pulse point at his neck. There was nothing. Aware that Paul had come up from behind, she looked back at him and shook her head. "Did you hear what he said?"

"Yeah. We need to move fast. Thomas isn't getting away this time." His voice, echoing in the tunnel, had grown stone cold.

Kendra placed the cell phone with the recording back in her pocket. "Thomas made a critical mistake when he failed to finish off Genaro. That's going to cost him his freedom and maybe his life."

Paul, taking point, continued down the tunnel and soon pushed up a manhole beside a trash bin. "We're between two buildings," he called back to her, then gave Kendra a hand up.

They ran to the sidewalk and looked around. They were now across the street from the dry cleaners.

"Hey, bro," Preston said, coming up to them.

"Any sign of Thomas?" Paul asked.

Preston shook his head. "Maybe he ducked inside one of the other buildings."

Kendra pointed back to where they'd reached the surface. "We found a small stash of what looks like ammo down there in the tunnel. I didn't see any weapons, though."

"I'll send in an ordnance officer to check it out ASAP," Preston said.

Kendra looked around and located a surveillance camera at the smoke shop just beyond the tiny alley. "Thomas isn't around, so I'm going to assume he drove off. Let's go check their surveillance footage."

The smoke shop owner, who'd gone to high school with one of Paul's brothers, was happy to cooperate.

"There's Thomas," Kendra said, pointing to the image. "Can't miss the sling on his arm. He went straight to that SUV, then headed east."

"I'll put a BOLO out," Preston said. "We'll catch him."

Paul walked outside with Kendra. Just then, Daniel drove up and came to a stop at the curb beside them.

"I've been monitoring police calls and following

the events. Don't worry about finding Thomas. He'll find you."

"What do you know that we don't?" Kendra asked.

"If Thomas turns himself in, he's facing the death penalty, so that's not his best option right now. The cartel isn't going to forgive him for bringing the cops here either, and Thomas knows that better than anyone else. The only chance he's got is to convince the cartel that he's still got something to offer. Then he can negotiate a quid pro quo and get their help leaving the country."

"Contacting the cartel at all will be extremely risky for him now, particularly if they find out what he did to Genaro," Kendra said.

"That's my point. He's going to need something really big to convince them of his loyalty and usefulness—like delivering both of you on a platter. The cartel could use two captive marshals as bargaining chips and buy time for the leaders to go to ground."

Kendra drew in a breath. "You're right, Daniel. It's the only deal he's got left."

"That means he'll try to contact us and arrange a meet," Paul said. "I'm guessing he'll approach us with an offer to testify if we can offer him life instead of the death penalty."

"Evan tried to kill a federal judge, and in the process murdered a U.S. Marshal—one of his own. He doesn't have much room to bargain," she said.

"We know that and so does he, but I still think he's going to try. He'll either set us up to be captured or killed by the cartel or maybe convince them he'll do it himself."

"Which means we need a plan," Daniel said. "Come back to my place. Preston will join us there as soon as possible. When Thomas calls, I'll try to zero in on the signal. My equipment is better than what they have at the police department. If you can keep him talking long enough, I can get a location."

"We're assuming he's going to call," Kendra said. "He may decide to go underground on his own."

"If he ends up running from the cops *and* the cartel, his life expectancy goes down to zero," Daniel said.

Paul agreed. "Makes sense to me."

"If he does come after us, we can count on one thing—he won't be alone," Kendra said.

"Neither will we," Paul said. "We'll have all the backup we need."

"Count on that. No way the rest of us guys are going to miss all the fun," Daniel said with a lethal grin.

WHILE PAUL, Gene, Daniel and Preston studied the large, aerial view of Copper Canyon on the computer display, Kendra went into the kitchen for some coffee. She needed to stay completely alert to face what lay ahead.

Paul joined her a moment later. "Preston heard from the DC police. They went to the address Genaro provided. It didn't look like anyone's lived there for a while, but he was telling the truth. They recovered a rifle barrel wrapped in paper and Thomas's prints are on it. If ballistics matches it up with the bullet that killed Judy, Evan's going down."

"I've got some other news," she said. "Tim checked out Evan's whereabouts when your partner was shot and killed. Evan was in DC, ostensibly on personal leave. He wasn't called to respond to the incident, either. He just showed up. Big coincidence, huh?" She placed a hand on his arm. "Looks like you're finally going to have the closure you wanted."

"I know, and there are things I need to say to you once this is over, but until then, there's something I want to give you." Paul reached into his pocket and pulled out a small leather medicine pouch. "I had Daniel pick this up for me. It's from the same Zuni carver *Hosteen* Silver used to craft our fetishes."

She pulled the tiny figure out carefully. "It's a... deer?" she asked, running her fingers over the delicate carving. It was made from turquoise and beautifully detailed.

"It's Antelope. Antelope people see with their hearts and have the ability and inner strength to accomplish whatever they set out to do," he said. "Antelope will guide you through the fight ahead and beyond."

"I will always keep this with me," she whispered.

"No matter where life takes you, whenever you look at it, think of me," he said, then brushed her face with the palm of his hand.

She leaned into him, allowing herself to bask in that moment of gentleness. "I—" She never got to finish her thought.

Her phone rang, and as Kendra reached for it, Paul's eyes held hers. "If it's Thomas, remember we'll only meet him at Copper Canyon."

Kendra answered, and noting that Paul's brothers had come in and were now watching her, she put the caller on speaker.

"It's Evan," a familiar voice said. "You've always played it smart, Kendra, so think about what I'm going to offer. I can hand over the leaders of the cartel, plus enough evidence to bring them down. In exchange, I want a deal that includes a new identity."

"Go to the Hartley Police Station on Airport Drive right now. We'll meet you there," Kendra said, following the strategy they'd mapped out.

"No way. The cartel's got informants everywhere, including the local P.D. I can't risk showing my face. I'd be as good as dead."

"That's your problem. You betrayed the marshals service. If you want to talk, those are my terms."

"What I'm trading is worth the price I'm asking. You can make your career on a collar like this. Don't throw it away," Evan said. "If you're worried, bring Grayhorse as backup. I've already got a site picked out. Meet me west of Hartley, about a mile down the power plant road."

"No. *I'll* choose the place," she said, then waited several seconds, as if trying to decide. "Meet us at the end of the road that goes up Copper Canyon—that's Grayhorse's old place. There's a big metal gate there. I'll make sure it's unlocked."

He hesitated. "That's a long drive and I'll be a sitting duck every foot of the way."

"Not unless you tell someone where you're going. That area gets only locals and a little oil worker traffic. That's my offer. Take it or leave it."

"All right." There was a brief pause, then Thomas spoke again. "Meet you there tonight at nine."

As the phone call ended, Kendra looked over at Daniel, who was standing beside his computer. He shook his head. "All we could get was the nearest cell phone tower. At least we know he's still in the area."

"But we knew that already," she said. "At least we got the meeting place we needed."

"I'm bringing two top-notch officers from our tactical unit," Preston said, "and Daniel will provide a few security people and some of their special gear. We'll be ready for whatever surprises Thomas throws in our direction."

"Trust me, and trust us," Paul said. "Tonight you'll have all the trained backup you need, Kendra."

"I know."

As she looked into Paul's eyes, she saw an emotion she didn't dare name reflected in the intensity of his gaze. Everything feminine in her yearned to call it love, to know that her name was forever written in his heart. Yet as a woman and a marshal, she knew that wishes didn't always come true.

She swallowed hard and focused back on business. "Let's go over those plans again."

Chapter Twenty-Two

Traveling at breakneck speed on the gravel roads, Thomas arrived fifteen minutes early. Paul and Kendra heard him long before he showed up on their night vision goggles. The old pickup he'd probably stolen bounced hard on the gravel track and barely made it across the cattle guard of their open gate, clipping a post on the passenger's side.

Despite only having one good arm, Thomas was driving as if the devil himself were chasing him. He nearly wrecked into the trees before he slid to a stop outside the main house.

Paul and Kendra were hidden outside, on the north flank behind some bales of old hay. They stuck to the plan and stayed behind cover, watching as Thomas jumped out of the pickup while it was still running, grabbed something from behind the seat, then sprinted toward the main door. Through his lens, Paul could see Thomas had a handgun at his waist and was carrying his department issue sniper rifle.

Atop the two hundred foot high mesa to their left, above the entrance to the narrow, horseshoe-shaped blind canyon, stood his brother Gene, watching with a powerful spotting scope. "Two SUVs are closing in on Copper Canyon now," Gene said into the mike of his headset. "They just left the highway."

The ranch house door opened just before Thomas reached it. One of Preston's officers greeted Thomas and motioned him into the darkened interior.

"They know what to do with him, right?" Paul spoke quietly into his mike.

"Copy that," Preston said. "Disarm Thomas before he catches on, check him for bugs, then handcuff him and put him in a corner so he can't move or call out until the op's over."

"That's the bad cop part," Kendra whispered, not taking her eyes off the narrow entrance into the blind canyon. "The good part is telling him that if he lives to testify, he might avoid lethal injection."

Paul didn't answer. He was looking to the left, across the floor of the narrow canyon to where Daniel and his two companions were making final preparations.

"The two vehicles have stopped about fifty yards outside the gate," Gene reported. "They're apparently going to advance on foot." There was a pause, then he spoke again. "Four men, wearing ball caps, body armor and night vision gear. I don't see radios, but they could be connected via headsets. All four have assault rifles and spare clips on their belts."

"Copy," Kendra said.

Kendra listened as Daniel and Preston confirmed

they were up to speed and ready. Gene, from his over-head observation post, was going to be their eyes and ears. Inside the canyon it was often darker than dark, especially on a night when a moonless sky and the high canyon walls created the deepest of shadows.

"At the gate. They're splitting up, with two men advancing down each shoulder of the road. They're spaced about twenty feet apart," Gene said.

Paul looked over at Kendra, smiled, then pushed his goggles away from his face and clicked on the night scope of his M-4 clone—an assault rifle descended from the old AR-15. Daniel had provided them with the equipment, standard issue for his security training operation. Those, and a few more surprises, would be available if needed.

Paul watched as the first two men walked briskly up on opposite sides of the road, apparently eager to get this over with. He kept his sites on the man farthest from them, knowing that, according to plan, Kendra would be targeting the closer of the two.

Paul spoke into the headset and signaled the house. Behind him a light came on in the cabin. An image silhouetted by a lamp crossed in front of the kitchen window.

The two men closest to them stopped, as did those across the road. Soft words were exchanged, too low to understand, then all four men picked up speed. Soon they were across the road, crouching low and angling toward the house.

A noisy generator started up just then, and three

large strobe lights came on, flashing in the faces of the advancing men, blinding their night vision devices. Two of them cursed, raised their weapons and opened fire on the lights. The other two ducked down behind some brush.

Daniel turned on the floodlights next to his position, illuminating the two trying to hide and drawing more misdirected gunfire from the confused attackers.

"We need prisoners," Kendra said. "Don't shoot to kill unless there's no other option."

The spotlighted men fell prone and returned fire, but they were caught in the crossfire, trapped out in the open.

Daniel added hand-directed lasers to his regimen of confusion, forcing the assault team to tear off their night vision devices.

Preston, speaking from beside the house, called out from a bullhorn. "You're surrounded and outgunned. Lay down your weapons."

One of the gunmen whipped his weapon around and fired toward Preston, but someone near Daniel's position took him out with one shot.

Two of the remaining assailants put their weapons down and sat on the ground, hands locked behind their heads. The fourth set down his rifle but, instead of sitting like the others, suddenly spun around and raced toward the gate.

Kendra jumped up to cut him off, Paul right behind her. The man was fast, but Kendra was between him and the gate. She stopped and fired into the ground right in front of him.

The man tried to dodge, tripped on a prickly pear cactus and fell facedown on the ground.

"Careful now," Paul said, rushing forward, his weapon aimed.

Kendra, barely ten feet from the fallen man, turned her head for a second as Paul came up.

At that instant the man yanked a pistol from his jacket. Kendra caught the motion out of the corner of her eye and swung her weapon around.

Paul fired first. The wounded man clutched his side, dropping his pistol.

"You knew before he even reached for the gun," Kendra said, this time not looking away from the target. "I'm glad you had my back."

"Always." Paul stepped in front of her, standing between her and the gunman, his eyes and weapon still on their assailant.

Kendra and Paul helped the rest of their team collect the captives as a medic tended the man who'd pulled the pistol on Kendra.

After all the prisoners were secured, Kendra went inside the cabin. Thomas was sitting, handcuffed, on the floor, his back against the kitchen counter. "It's over," she said.

"I still want to cut a deal," he said.

"Forget it. You set us up again, but now we have the evidence we need. You're going down this time, Evan, and there won't be a way out."

THREE PHONE CALLS later, however, Evan Thomas *had* struck a deal with the federal prosecutor and had been flown out by state police helicopter to Albuquerque.

"The ones responsible for your partner's death are going away for a long time," Kendra said.

"The fact that Thomas cut a deal doesn't make this feel like a win."

"I know, but he'll still spend life in prison for killing your partner, and look what we got in return. Thomas gave up the names of all his contacts in the weapons cartel and revealed the location of the Colorado mountain hideout used by Garrett Hawthorn, the leader of their operation. He also pinpointed two weapons stashes on a Google map and the entrance of a smuggling tunnel that leads into a Mexican warehouse just across the border. Combined agency strike teams are already en route."

Paul nodded thoughtfully. Deals were everyday compromises in the criminal justice system. "This is the end of a long road."

"Yes it is."

"Time to look to the future," he said, but before he could say more, Kendra was called away to work the scene.

HOURS AFTER the remaining prisoners and the crime scene had been processed, Kendra stood outside the cabin beside her dusty rental car. The sun would be coming up soon and the return trip to Denver would be a long one, so it was time for her to go. Yet she just couldn't make herself leave.

This was the moment she'd dreaded. Prolonging their inevitable goodbye wouldn't help either of them. She'd made her decision. Good friends with benefits would never be enough for her. Working with Paul every day, being part of his world yet knowing that she'd never be at the center of it, would break her heart.

She looked down at her hand, staring at the antelope fetish he'd given her just yesterday. The message was clear. To survive, she had to go.

"What are you doing out here? You getting ready to leave?" he said, coming over to join her.

"Yeah, it's time," she said, and swallowed hard. She'd always stunk at goodbyes.

"It's almost dawn. Can you hold off a bit and come with me? There's a place I want to show you, and we can talk there. Afterwards, if you really want to leave, I won't stand in your way."

"All right," she said. He wasn't going to make leaving easy, but she couldn't find it in her heart to say no. "Where are we going?"

"There's a place that has special meaning to me. I'd like to take you there. It's not far."

He took her hand, and together they walked into Copper Canyon. As the first rays of sunlight fell over the land, small animals stirred in the brush, scampering about in search of food. A hawk flew overhead, idly circling from rim to rim.

As they climbed up a narrow trail that cut into the

cliffs, Kendra told herself not to expect anything except one final, beautiful goodbye. Paul had already told her what he was willing to give her—everything, really, except his whole heart. She couldn't expect him to change who he was. She had to accept it and move on.

Soon they reached a ledge that overlooked the canyon floor. He gestured to the vista below them with a sweep of his arm.

"Look to your right," he said. "See that spot that gleams in the sun? That's the metal roof of *Hosteen* Silver's house. About six months after he brought me here, he and I got into an argument. He'd had us carrying water to the livestock and filling two stock tanks hundreds of yards away—by hand. I'd never worked so hard in my life. I accused him of taking us in just for the cheap labor, that he didn't really care about me and Preston."

"Harsh words," she said, eyebrows raised. "What did he do?"

"Nothing. He told me to go check the water in the trough behind the house." He smiled. "He wasn't the kind to explain himself. *Hosteen* Silver felt that by sharing his home and taking care of us, he'd said all that was needed," Paul said. "He was right, but I didn't understand that at the time."

"So what happened?"

"I walked off and came here. I sat down with my feet dangling over the edge and tried to figure out what I should do," Paul said, staring at the shiny metal roof, gleaming like a beacon calling them home. "*Hosteen* Silver tracked me here in less than half an hour."

"Was he angry?"

"No, he just sat down next to me and told me that he'd take me back to the foster home if I wanted to go. If not, I had a family waiting below. The next step was up to me, but if I stayed, I'd have to follow his rules."

Paul paused for several long moments. "That was the first time anyone had ever given me a choice, particularly on something that would determine my future." He turned to face her. "To me, this is a place of beginnings. That's why I wanted to bring you here."

"I'm not sure I understand...."

"It wasn't Lynx who warned me when the gunman you thought was down drew his weapon. I felt the threat to you inside my gut. I acted out of instinct, protecting the woman I love," he said, pulling her into his arms. "Everything that makes me a man tells me you don't want to go, but you think you can't find what you need here." He held her gaze. "Antelope People see with their hearts. Look into mine now. I'm no longer a man chained to the past. When I see you, I see our future. A home, a family, it can all be ours. Say you'll stay with me."

Her whispered yes became nothing more than a sigh as his mouth closed over hers.

Epilogue

Eleven months later

Kendra laughed as Paul dove into the hedge trying to catch the Nerf football flying end over end. Jason, the four-year-old Navajo boy they'd fostered since the death of his single mother, hadn't quite mastered the art of a spiral pass.

"Sorry, pop," Jason yelled, running around the end of the hedge for the ball, which was still out of Paul's reach.

"Paul, you're going to get grass stains all over your knees, and, look at you, Jason. Can't you keep your shoes tied for more than thirty seconds?" Kendra called out, smiling.

Paul laughed, catching Jason's surprise hike as it came over the hedge. "Get back here, boy. Your mom wants us to look our best when we sign those adoption papers today."

Kendra laughed as Paul picked up their feisty soon-to-be son and carried him on his shoulders across the lawn. "Now go put that ball back into the toy box, J.," Paul said, setting him down.

As Jason, the little boy who'd become the love of their lives, raced away, Paul stepped up and gave her a sweet kiss, one hand caressing her swollen belly gently.

"I'm glad we get to make the adoption official before our next little guy arrives," Paul whispered.

"Look on the bright side," Kendra said, resting her head against his chest. "It gave me time to get used to my new job as a working mom." She smiled. "And to think I actually got full maternity leave from your brother Dan so soon after he hired me. That was great."

"It comes from knowing the company's MVP," Paul said, smiling. "Life is as perfect as it can be for us right now, isn't it? I never saw myself as a family man, but now I can't imagine being happy any other way."

She reached up and touched his cheek in a soft caress. "Things didn't always go so smoothly for us. Remember the first time we met? I was stranded and you rescued me at gunpoint. Your confidence was so annoying."

Paul chuckled. "Hey, but in the end, Antelope tamed the Lynx."

"No, not tamed, gentled."

"Maybe so," he murmured, taking her mouth in a kiss as tender as the love that burned in his heart.

* * * * *

FAMOUS FAMILIES

YES! Please send me the *Famous Families* collection featuring the Fortunes, the Bravos, the McCabes and the Cavanaughs. This collection will begin with 3 FREE BOOKS and 2 FREE GIFTS in my very first shipment— and more valuable free gifts will follow! My books will arrive in 8 monthly shipments until I have the entire 51-book *Famous Families* collection. I will receive 2-3 free books in each shipment and I will pay just $4.49 U.S./$5.39 CDN for each of the other 4 books in each shipment, plus $2.99 for shipping and handling.* If I decide to keep the entire collection, I'll only have paid for 32 books because 19 books are free. I understand that accepting the 3 free books and gifts places me under no obligation to buy anything. I can always return a shipment and cancel at any time. My free books and gifts are mine to keep no matter what I decide.

268 HCN 0387   468 HCN 0387

Name _____ (PLEASE PRINT) _____

Address _____ Apt. # _____

City _____ State/Prov. _____ Zip/Postal Code _____

Signature (if under 18, a parent or guardian must sign)

Mail to the **Reader Service:**
IN U.S.A.: P.O. Box 1867, Buffalo, NY 14240-1867
IN CANADA: P.O. Box 609, Fort Erie, Ontario L2A 5X3

* Terms and prices subject to change without notice. Prices do not include applicable taxes. Sales tax applicable in N.Y. Canadian residents will be charged applicable taxes. This offer is limited to one order per household. All orders subject to approval. Credit or debit balances in a customer's account(s) may be offset by any other outstanding balance owed by or to the customer. Please allow 4 to 6 weeks for delivery. Offer available while quantities last. Offer not available to Quebec residents.

Your Privacy— The Reader Service is committed to protecting your privacy. Our Privacy Policy is available online at www.ReaderService.com or upon request from the Reader Service.
We make a portion of our mailing list available to reputable third parties that offer products we believe may interest you. If you prefer that we not exchange your name with third parties, or if you wish to clarify or modify your communication preferences, please visit us at www.ReaderService.com/consumerschoice or write to us at Reader Service Preference Service, P.O. Box 9062, Buffalo, NY 14269. Include your complete name and address.

FFBPA12

Reader Service.com

Manage your account online!

- Review your order history
- Manage your payments
- Update your address

**We've designed
the Reader Service website
just for you.**

Enjoy all the features!

- Reader excerpts from any series
- Respond to mailings and
  special monthly offers
- Discover new series available to you
- Browse the Bonus Bucks catalogue
- Share your feedback

Visit us at:
ReaderService.com

"So what's your agenda for bringing me this intel?" Silas asked.

"So suspicious." Quinn tsked but her grin was filled with mischief. "Okay, you got me. I do want something."

"Spit it out."

"I want you to work with me," she said. "Give me access to exclusive content so I can break the story, whatever that may be."

Back to that argument again. "It goes against my personal values to make deals with press."

"C'mon, Silas...you can't honestly be this rigid."

"Is this your idea of driving a hard bargain? I've yet to hear why I shouldn't just run with your lead and leave you out."

She stared at him. "Because you have more integrity than that."

"You don't know me."

"It's something I can sense," Quinn said, and this time she wasn't joking or playing around.

This was probably the first time Silas had seen her completely serious. That turn was intensely arousing. It was easy to keep her at arm's length when he saw her as an irritating kid. But when he saw her as an adult...it changed things.

* * *

If you're on Twitter, tell us what you think of Harlequin Romantic Suspense! #harlequinromsuspense

Dear Reader,

As a pantser, it's rare when a story comes to me fully formed and ready to be written, but when it does, the result is simply wonderful.

That's what happened with this book. I knew the characters so well. I knew the town, I knew the victim—I even knew the ending.

Silas is one of those characters that takes on a life of its own, grabbing the muse in a chokehold because it's so strong, and I was happy to let him drive the bus.

Conversely, Quinn is my favorite type of heroine— sassy, classy and a little smart-assy—but her growth arc is huge from the beginning of the book to the end.

I hope you enjoy it as much as I enjoyed writing it.

I love hearing from readers. Connect with me on Facebook, Twitter or drop me an email. Or you can also write me a letter at PO BOX 2210, Oakdale, CA 95361.

Happy reading!

Kimberly

THE KILLER
YOU KNOW

—

Kimberly Van Meter

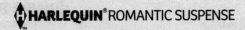

HARLEQUIN® ROMANTIC SUSPENSE

Recycling programs
for this product may
not exist in your area.

ISBN-13: 978-0-373-40199-4

The Killer You Know

Copyright © 2017 by Kimberly Sheetz

This edition published by arrangement with Harlequin Books S.A.

For questions and comments about the quality of this book,
please contact us at CustomerService@Harlequin.com.

Printed in U.S.A.

www.Harlequin.com

Kimberly Van Meter wrote her first book at sixteen and finally achieved publication in December 2006. She writes for the Harlequin Superromance, Blaze and Romantic Suspense lines. She and her husband of seventeen years have three children, three cats, and always a houseful of friends, family and fun.

Books by Kimberly Van Meter

Harlequin Romantic Suspense

The Sniper
The Agent's Surrender
Moving Target
Deep Cover
The Killer You Know

Harlequin Superromance

Family in Paradise

Like One of the Family
Playing the Part
Something to Believe In

The Sinclairs of Alaska

That Reckless Night
A Real Live Hero
A Sinclair Homecoming

Harlequin Blaze

The Hottest Ticket in Town
Sex, Lies and Designer Shoes
A Wrong Bed Christmas
"Ignited"
The Flyboy's Temptation

All backlist available in ebook format.

Visit the Author Profile page at Harlequin.com for more titles.

This book is dedicated to anyone who has ever searched for closure in their life.

May you find it, may it provide solace, may it heal.

Chapter 1

Special Agent Silas Kelly opened the door to the Chicago Bureau office, the biting cold in the air nipping at his freshly shaven jaw. He'd been in Chicago for five years but he still hadn't gotten used to the wind chill of his new city.

A summons to the director's office never boded well. He was still dealing with the aftermath of his latest case—one that he hadn't been able to solve in time, and a kid had died.

As a member of the Child Abduction Unit, it was his job to save kids.

They'd managed to catch the perp but not before the man had slit the boy's throat.

Thomas Fielding, age six, snatched from the park when the babysitter wasn't looking.

Now Thomas's parents were making funeral arrangements.

Maybe that was what the director wanted to talk about, to go over where they'd failed young Thomas so that, hopefully, next time, the news they brought to frightened parents was good.

Silas walked into Director Beatrice Oppenshaw's office and closed the door for privacy. She gestured for him to take a seat.

"I'll get straight to the point," she said, clasping her hands together. "There's been a homicide in Port Orion, Washington, that might catch your attention. I want you to ignore the urge to follow up."

Port Orion, his hometown. Usually the location of his nightmares.

"The body of a sixteen-year-old girl was dumped in Seminole Creek. Based on the marks on her neck, the preliminary cause of death is strangulation, pending the autopsy results."

A shock wave rippled across his body. Seminole Creek.

Flashes of his childhood followed an echo of his little brother's voice.

"There's no reason for the FBI to get involved. Local jurisdiction will handle the case," Oppenshaw said when she saw Silas gearing up to object. "Trust me, I'm doing you a favor."

Silas knew why she was warning him to keep his distance. This new case hit too many triggers. Oppenshaw knew how Silas's little brother Spencer had died.

How his body had been found in that same creek.

And how Spencer's killer had never been found.

"What if there are similarities to my brother's cold case?" he asked, using reason to win his boss over. "This could be a break in a twenty-year-old case."

"A case that just happens to be your youngest brother's," Oppenshaw replied, shaking her head. "It's a conflict of interest. Out of deference to you, if you think there might be some leads, I will send another agent up there to check things out but I don't want you near that case."

"Port Orion is a small town. They won't talk to a stranger. I have an advantage—"

"And a handicap," Oppenshaw countered firmly. "You know you're too emotionally invested to be unbiased. The answer is no."

But Silas's mind was already moving. Oppenshaw could forbid him to go on federal time but she couldn't control his vacation choices.

The Bureau shrink had suggested some R&R—which he'd previously declined—but he suddenly saw the merit.

"I'd like to take Dr. Lyons's suggestion for a little time off."

Oppenshaw's jaw tensed. "Fortuitous timing," she commented drily. "You previously declined therapeutic time off."

"I've changed my mind."

"Bullshit. You want to go chase down this case."

He remained silent, knowing his boss's hands were tied.

The last case had left everyone on the team shaken. And if the Bureau doc had suggested some leave, it was her duty to sign off on it.

It was the kinder, gentler Bureau.

And Silas was going to take full advantage.

Because there was nothing that would keep Silas from investigating that case in Port Orion.

Oppenshaw swore under her breath, conceding the inevitable but she had some stipulations of her own. "You go to Port Orion, you go without your badge. You're not going to use your federal status to open doors. If you go for anything more than a visit home to walk down Memory Lane, then you're doing it completely off-books."

Silas leaned forward. "My brother's killer went free. His death shattered my family. The strain of a failed investigation ruined my parents' marriage. If there's even a slim chance that this case is connected, I'll do whatever I have to do to chase it down. You're right—I'm biased. No one wants to solve my brother's cold case more than me. I was supposed to be watching him. He died *because* of me. You think that doesn't stick with me every single damn day?"

Oppenshaw held his stare for a long moment then exhaled in irritation. She wasn't known for being a pushover but Silas was one of her best team members.

"All right. I'll give you a few days to go up there, check things out. You can take your credentials *but* you're not to step on the local investigation unless you find something that warrants federal jurisdiction. If you don't find anything, you come home. Got it?"

Silas nodded, knowing that was the best offer he was going to get. "I'm taking the first flight out."

"Keep me informed. I want to know every move you make. This has the potential to blow up in our faces. You know local authorities don't take kindly to the FBI poking their nose where it's not justified and I don't need that kind of grief right now."

Silas agreed, thanked Oppenshaw and left.

His mind was already moving, already preparing to face his childhood home. Unlike his brothers, he hadn't been back. Although no one blamed him for Spencer's death, Silas blamed himself.

And the guilt was a familiar weight on his shoulders.

If he could finally find justice for Spencer, nothing would stop him.

He owed Spencer that.

Solving his brother's murder wasn't going to bring Spencer back...but it might make it easier for Silas to look in the mirror every day.

At least he hoped.

Silas's worst fear was that, win or lose, he would carry his little brother on his back until the day he died.

Because nothing could erase the shame of letting your family down in such a grievous way.

There was no "I'm sorry" deep enough to change the fact that Spencer was dead because Silas had ditched him that summer day twenty years ago.

Quinn Jackson held her notebook and clutched her pen tightly so as not to betray the shaking in her fingers.

This was her big break.

Finally.

This was the kind of story that she'd dreamed about, the kind that made careers, with the potential to take her away from Point Orion and on to something bigger. Maybe even out of Washington State altogether.

The *New York Times* was probably a stretch but she liked to aim big.

But the pressure to make something happen—and keep the story fresh without the bigger news outlets scooping her—was immense.

"Can you tell us about the victim?" Quinn asked, angling for a better spot in front of the sheriff as he addressed the throng of reporters crowding the station. "How did she die? Preliminary reports say that the victim is Rhia Daniels, a junior at Point Orion High. Can you confirm this information?"

Sheriff Lester Mankins scowled at Quinn's question but read from a prepared statement. "At 0600 hours this morning, the body of a young girl was found in Seminole Creek. Cause of death has not been determined. We will release the identity of the victim after the next of kin has been notified. That'll be all."

Quinn frowned at the sparse information but waited for the television reporters to file out before chasing after the sheriff, catching him before he disappeared behind the security door.

He started talking before she could. "Don't give me those puppy dog eyes, Quinn Jackson. I gave you all the information I'm going to."

"C'mon, Lester, you have to give me something that the others don't have. I'm trying to make a career move here. Bigger news outlets don't want to see a portfolio filled with potluck dinners, Little League pictures and city council squabbles about cobblestones. I need something big and this is the biggest thing since...well, in a very long time and you know it."

Lester had known her her entire life. He was a good friend of her uncle Leo's and, thus, a frequent visitor to her uncle's place.

And right now that connection was her ticket to information no one else had.

Unless Lester continued to be a stick in the mud.

Lester fixed a stern stare on her. "Quinn...a girl is dead. As much as I want to help you find your way to bigger and better things, we have to remain cognizant of the fact that a young lady isn't going home to her family. Forgive me if your ambition is going to have to take a backseat."

Okay, so that wasn't entirely out of line but Quinn couldn't let a setback derail her. That was not what the professionals did.

"I'm sorry, that was terrible of me. I really want justice for this poor girl. I mean, someone snuffed out her life and the *local* press can help put some pressure on. Just one nugget, Lester. *Please*? Just one."

"No," he answered before closing the door behind him.

She stared, unable to believe that Lester had stonewalled her like that. Quinn chewed the inside of her cheek, a habit she'd picked up in grade school when she was confounded, and wondered what was so special about this case that Lester couldn't give her a tiny tidbit of information, separate from the boilerplate he was giving everyone else.

Well, he hadn't denied that it was Rhia Daniels. So she'd start there. But first…she wanted to see the crime scene.

Seminole Creek was a tributary to the inlet and a popular swimming hole with the locals—in the summer.

It wasn't exactly swimming weather right now.

Quinn wound her scarf more snugly around her neck and burrowed into it. The wind pushing off the water of Puget Sound made for some brisk air. It was the kind of damp that dug into your bones and stayed there.

The weather was one reason Quinn was ready for a change of scenery. Washington was so wet and melancholy. Sure, it was green and "pretty" but for people with Seasonal Affective Disorder, it was the pits.

Quinn didn't have SAD, but that was beside the point. It was a real problem for some people. And just because she didn't have SAD, didn't mean she enjoyed the constant rain. There was more to life than galoshes and rain jackets.

And the smell of fish…yuck. Not a fan.

I know, I know, how can I live on the coast and gag at the smell of fish?

Because Quinn suspected, in a past life, she'd been more of an arid desert kind of dweller because a dry heat didn't bother her at all.

However, high humidity…made her lungs seize.

She climbed into her Jeep and made her way to Seminole Creek. News vans passed her on the road going the opposite direction and she was glad. She didn't want to share any clues she might pick up with the bigger outlets.

It did feel odd to see strangers trampling all over Port Orion, almost as if they were trespassing.

Port Orion was small—a mere blip on the map—and most people completely bypassed it for more interesting places, such as Spokane or Tacoma.

Who wanted to visit a dinky little seaside town with all of its 8,500 people and with a lighthouse as its biggest tourist attraction when they could visit Seattle in all its grungy glory?

Yeah, not me.

So, having people in town who were clearly not local... made for some discomfited feelings.

But she'd been waiting for something big, something worth writing about that would make people sit up and notice. Let's get real, writing about bake sales and fund-raising efforts weren't going to further her career. Sure, currently she worked for the *Port Orion Tribune* but that was just to build her résumé. Not that the *Tribune* was sending her on ground-breaking news leads but opportunity was what one made of it, so Quinn never treated one story above another.

Which, she'd admit, wasn't easy when she was tempted to "forget" the deadline for a fluff piece on the church Sunday school daycare when she really wanted to focus on something that could actually make a difference, such as the time she discovered the school district central kitchen had been using food stuffs that were past their expiration.

Maybe the threat of a little soured milk wasn't all that dire in the big scheme of things but Quinn liked to think that stories like that helped build her foundation for later.

For example, if she hadn't followed up on the expired foods, she wouldn't have been able to put the dots together when a rash of kindergartners caught a whiff of food poisoning and ended up in the hospital after a *vomit-fest* had followed afternoon snack.

The school was lucky the parents didn't sue.

But *if* they had, Quinn would've been right there to catch the story, which given the fact that she'd discovered the misdeed in the first place, would've been a huge feather in her cap.

However, no one sued.

The school called it an "oversight" and in response,

put a new committee in place to ensure it never happened again.

They also fired the head cook, although not because of the food situation but because it was discovered that he had been going up to Seattle on weekends to do things best left unsaid, and the district didn't think it was prudent to keep him on staff.

Another story that fizzled to nothing under the suffocating veil of a "confidential personnel issue."

And Quinn was tired of her hard work going down the tubes.

This story was the one that was going to change everything. She could feel it in her bones.

Nothing was going to stand in her way.

Chapter 2

Silas pulled into the sleepy coastal town of his birth and took a moment to adjust. A barrage of memories assailed him as he maneuvered the rental car through the tiny downtown, the storefronts nearly the same as the day he'd left, and swallowed against the continuing echo of his brother's voice.

The chill in the air was damp. This was the kind of weather that got stuck in your lungs and stayed there throughout the winter, as storms lashed the seas and battered the coast.

He parked outside the sheriff's department, choosing to go straight to the authorities before checking into his hotel.

A lone seagull screeched and he glanced at the bird. After losing Spencer, the sound had always creeped him out.

Silas walked over to where the dispatcher sat behind a heavy glass window and flashed his credentials.

"Special Agent Silas Kelly here to see the sheriff about the recent Seminole Creek murder investigation."

The woman behind the glass gave Silas a once-over but buzzed the sheriff.

Moments later Sheriff Lester Mankins appeared, looking older, grayer, with more lines on his face, but certainly the same guy he remembered from when he'd been a misguided teen, acting out from grief.

He would've thought that Mankins would've retired by now.

"As I live and breathe… Silas Kelly, the most stubborn, angry cuss that I'd ever dragged by the scruff of the neck down these halls. How are you, son?"

And just like that he was fourteen again. Silas struggled against the pinch in his sternum and extended a hand. "Can't complain, Sheriff. How about you? Why haven't you retired yet? Isn't there some fish out there with your name on it?"

"Every damn weekend," he joked, patting Silas heartily on the back. "C'mon back. Let's talk in my office."

Silas followed Mankins and took a seat once the office door was shut behind them.

Mankins spoke first. "I can only imagine that you're here because of that poor girl we fished out of Seminole Creek early this morning. Bad news surely does travel fast."

Silas confirmed with a nod.

Mankins sighed. "I figured. But I gotta say, seems a little out of federal jurisdiction. Tragic as it is, the case is likely just a grim statistic. Girls find themselves in bad situations and things get out of hand."

"Is that what you think happened?"

The sheriff shrugged, spreading his hands. "Well, it's how the case presents at first blush."

"I'd like to see the case file."

"Hold on, hold on, big shot. My investigating officer hasn't even had time to put thought to paper. Have you checked into your hotel yet?" At Silas's head shake, he said, "Well, how about you get checked in, go eat some chowder, warm up your bones and then tomorrow morning we'll see how things look."

Silas hated waiting. "I'd like to pull my brother's cold case."

That caused Mankins to do a double take. "Whatever for, son? Let the boy rest in peace. There's no sense in dredging up painful memories."

"I can appreciate that, Sheriff. But I think the two cases might be linked."

"And why would you think that?" Mankins asked. "Your brother disappeared almost twenty years ago and there's been nothing like that since. This girl has nothing in common with your little brother. Whoever did that terrible thing to Spencer…they're long gone. I can almost guarantee it."

Silas didn't believe that, no matter how many people had suggested the same theory.

It was too random.

Most murders were rarely random.

"If it's all the same…I'd like to pull the files."

Mankins heaved a sigh as if Silas were chasing ghosts and wasting his time but he pressed a button on his phone, saying, "Janice, can you get Hanford to go into the archive and pull all the files pertaining to Spencer Kelly? He's likely gonna have to go to storage. I don't think they're still in the building."

"Yes, Sheriff."

Mankins leaned back. "Satisfied?"

"Thank you."

"Look, those files aren't going to be ready until tomorrow, either. So either way, you're going to have to cool your jets, get settled in and try to enjoy the salty air. Does wonders for the soul."

Silas had no plans to wander the streets, drinking in the sights or the ambience. He was here for one purpose—to determine if this girl's case had any connection to Spencer's.

"What can you tell me about the victim?"

"It's the damnedest thing. Good kid. Comes from a great family. Her name is Rhia Daniels, sixteen, popular, pretty. Cheerleader, academic scholar, volunteers at the animal shelter, hell, she's the poster child for the all-American teenager. We're running into a brick wall as to who might want to hurt the poor girl."

"Looks can be deceiving," Silas murmured. "What do you know about the family?"

"Solid. Good people. They didn't deserve something like this."

How many times had he thought the very same thing when delivering bad news to grieving parents?

No one deserved to lose a child.

Mankins switched gears. "How's your mama? She still in Florida?"

"Yes, sir. Loves the sun, sand and the fact that when it rains, it's sunny five minutes later."

"And your dad?"

"He passed a few years ago."

"I'm sorry to hear that. He was a good man. How about your brothers?"

Silas knew polite conversation was expected but he had little interest in chewing the fat. He kept his answers short. "All well. Thank you."

"It's a damn shame your family didn't stay local. The Kellys are good folk."

Port Orion had lost its charm after Spencer died. His parents split and soon as the boys were done with school, the Kellys put Port Orion in their rearview.

Too many memories.

Too many unanswered questions.

He rose. "Thank you for your indulgence. I'll try to stay on the peripheral. When is the autopsy scheduled?"

"Tomorrow morning."

"I'll check in afterward."

"I wish it were under better circumstances, but it's good to see you again," Mankins said. "You turned out pretty good."

Silas accepted the comment with a subtle nod and a definite burn in his cheeks. Sheriff Mankins had been one of the people who'd seen a kid eaten by grief and guilt instead of the little shit that everyone else thought he was.

And now, seeing Mankins again, brought back all those feelings he'd long since put to bed.

He'd never properly thanked Mankins for his help. But now wasn't the time. Silas wanted to keep things professional.

"It's good to see you," Silas offered by way of goodbye then saw himself out.

He drew a deep breath once outside the station. It felt as if an elephant was sitting on his chest.

Silas hadn't expected to see Mankins still serving as sheriff. But hell, nothing changed in Port Orion it seemed, so why would he assume that Mankins would be retired?

Port Orion wasn't exactly a hotbed of crime. Aside from Spencer's abduction and murder and now this young girl, Port Orion was the picture of tranquility.

But what Silas had learned through his investigations with the FBI was that nothing was perfect. There was no perfect family, no perfect town.

Everyone had secrets they didn't want to share.

Every place had dark shadows.

So Silas was going to do what he hadn't been able to do back when he was thirteen—throw some light on the shadows…and rattle some closets to see what skeletons fell out.

Port Orion was about to have its bloomers blown up.

* * *

Quinn arose early, as she always did, and hustled down to Reba's, her favorite diner, for breakfast. She had a standing order of coffee and Reba's bestselling zucchini bread. Quinn liked to tell herself that she was getting her greens by eating zucchini bread for breakfast but deep down, she knew it was just delicious cake.

And she was okay with that.

She walked into the cozy diner and smiled at the waitresses, noting every familiar face that was always in the diner at this hour—Bill, Nancy, Georgia, Edwin—but her gaze skidded to a stop at one particular person who was certainly not local. Talk about tall, dark and mysterious.

And easy on the eyes—in an intense sort of way.

Black, austere wool coat, slicked back dark hair and an air about him that said, *I'm not friendly so don't even try*, which pricked Quinn's need to know more.

Either he was part of the Trenchcoat Mafia or he was a Fed.

Quinn was putting her money on a Fed.

And what exactly was a Fed doing here in Port Orion? Well, there was one way to find out.

She scooped up her order and went straight to his booth, sliding in on the opposite side with a smile.

"You're not from around here," she said, going straight for the obvious. "So who are you?"

He looked up and she was hit with stormy gray eyes that mirrored the skies when it was about to drop a bucket of water on the land. Her usual witty comebacks died on her tongue as she was momentarily stunned by the energy coming off him in waves.

"You first," he countered, holding her gaze, taking her measure as surely as she'd *tried* to take his.

Remembering herself, she smiled brightly and extended a hand across the table, which he accepted briefly then released quickly. "Quinn Jackson. Reporter for the *Port Orion Tribune* and my Spidey-sense is telling me that you are a federal agent."

"Your Spidey-sense is not wrong," he answered, though his gaze had narrowed a bit. "And to what do I owe the pleasure? Are you part of the welcoming committee?"

"Not at all. I'm curious as to why a federal agent is in town, right when our poor town is being overrun by strangers because of the recent murder of Rhia Daniels, a pretty, little cheerleader girl, who, at first glance, was universally loved. Seems highly coincidental, right? I mean, what does the FBI care about a murder in a small town?"

He took a slow, measured sip of his black coffee. Quinn grabbed six tiny cream buckets and dumped them into her own coffee, adding about five packets of sugar.

She liked her coffee…less like coffee.

"What did you say your name was?" Quinn asked, blowing on her coffee.

"I didn't."

"Ah, that would explain why I still have no clue as to who you are. Are you going to tell me or do I have to guess?"

A brief smile lit up his mouth before he answered. "Special Agent Silas Kelly, FBI."

Triumph at being right sang in her voice. "See? I knew it. Now my next question…what the hell are you doing here?"

"I used to live here."

"Yeah? When?"

"My entire family was born here."

"Hmmm, I'll have to verify that statement from different sources. Back to my original question…what are you doing here? It has something to do with Rhia's death, doesn't it?"

"Perhaps."

"Cryptic," Quinn stated with a frown. "Okay, I'm going to assume that you're here because of Rhia's murder. So what's so special that the FBI is getting involved? Government conspiracy? Not likely. Aliens? Probably not. Some connection to a different case? I can't imagine. So you've got me stumped. Help a girl out and give me a hint."

"I'm not here to give interviews, Miss Jackson."

"What are you here for?"

"That would be my business."

"So this is a personal trip, not official?"

He hesitated and she capitalized on his minute pause. "Aha! Let me guess…you are here on semi-official business but you're not taking over the investigation, which means you're here on a fact-finding mission," she finished, pleased with herself. "Tell me I'm not wrong."

But he couldn't. All he would say was, "You can believe what you wish."

Well, this was going nowhere.

"Let me tell you what I think… I think—" she began, fishing a little "—that Rhia Daniels was killed by someone that the FBI is interested in."

"Everyone is entitled to their opinion…or speculation."

"So you're really not going to tell me anything, are you?" When he graced her with a sardonic expression, she said, "All right. Fine. Play it your way. I mean, we could work together and help each other out, but if you'd like to go it alone in a small town where the locals are wary of strangers…then I guess that's your choice. But don't come crawling to me when you get stonewalled at every turn."

"I'm not a stranger."

"Yeah, but how long has it been since you've been gone?"

"Fifteen years."

"A lot can change in fifteen years."

She left him with that thought.

And a smile.

With any luck, that seed she'd just planted would sprout and grow wild.

Chapter 3

Pastor Forrest Simms was in his office when two members of his flock came in, eyes and noses red from uncontrollable weeping.

Violet and Oliver Daniels, Rhia's parents.

"Pastor," Violet started, turning to her husband and clutching at his jacket. "I can't tell him. You do it."

Oliver nodded gravely and swallowed before saying, "We wanted to tell you before you heard through the grapevine… Rhia is dead."

Forrest felt the blood drain from his cheeks. "How?"

"She was murdered. Someone took our Rhia away. Who could do such a thing?" Violet was seeking answers that Forrest couldn't give her.

His gut churned as he searched for something to ease their heartache but his thoughts were crashing into each other. He leaned on platitudes to get him through. "She's in a better place. She's with Our Father. Take comfort in that where Rhia is, she is loved by the Almighty and knows only peace."

"I want her back," Violet wailed, sobbing against her husband's chest. "She was my baby. My miracle baby. And now she's gone. Who would do such a terrible thing to such a sweet girl?"

Oliver tried to hush his wife but he was barely hanging on himself. He looked to Forrest with an apology. "We're sorry for interrupting your private time, Pastor. We just wanted to share the news personally, on account of how close you and Rhia were. She really looked to you for spiritual guidance and we will always keep you in our hearts for that."

Forrest nodded, his discomfort making his skin itch as if a thousand fire ants were biting him. "She was a lovely girl."

Violet nodded and Oliver walked with his bereft wife out of the office, leaving Forrest alone for a brief moment before Gladys, his secretary came in, her expression one of shock.

"Rhia Daniels? Did I hear that correctly?"

"Yes."

Gladys fluttered her hands like a bird trying to take flight and then pressed her hands to her chest as if she was going to faint. "What is this town coming to? The wickedness is overwhelming. I mean, just the other day I was at the grocery store and someone stole cash right out of my purse when I had my back turned. The nerve! And now a murder?" She shuddered, adding, "This brings up so many bad memories. Hasn't this town suffered enough?"

Forrest nodded, knowing that Gladys was referencing the death of Spencer Kelly almost twenty years ago. He and Spencer had been in the same grade. His death had been a major blow to the community.

Then Gladys thought of something. "Oh goodness, that

must be why I saw all those news vans milling around downtown. That means the restaurants are going to be full. Darn if I'm going to get a table tonight now."

"Gladys," he admonished and she was immediately contrite.

"Excuse me, Pastor. Where is my head? I don't know what's wrong with me. We should host a gathering so people can come and grieve for poor Rhia."

Forrest knew that was the right thing to do. But he struggled to say the words. Rhia was, indeed, a special girl. He didn't know if he was ready to face all the grieving friends and family.

But he also knew with everyone in a lather about a potential murderer in their midst, he had to tread cautiously.

"That's a beautiful idea, Gladys," he finally murmured with a faint smile. "Please make the necessary arrangements. Now, if you'll excuse me, I feel the need to pray. My heart is heavy."

"Yes, of course." Gladys quickly left the room and Forrest exhaled a shaky breath.

Rhia.

No more flirty smiles from across the pew.

No more struggling with his guilt.

His hands were still shaking.

He just had to get through the next few weeks.

God would provide solace and understanding.

Please, forgive me.

Silas checked into the hotel and, after making quick work of hanging his clothes and setting up his toiletries, he loosened his tie and sank into the small chair by the window.

Condensation gathered between the window panes from the damp air. Silas could already feel the cold creeping into his bones.

You're tired, he rationalized. He wasn't about to let his imagination start messing with him.

There was still time to head out to the scene.

Doing something was preferable to staring at the peeling wallpaper while he waited for his brother's case file.

Grabbing his coat, he scooped up his keys and headed for Seminole Creek.

The road was bumpy just as he remembered. Only the locals swam in Seminole. It was difficult to find and easy to miss.

But in the summer it was the best place to hole up, drink a few beers and make out with your girlfriend away from prying eyes.

Except Silas had never much cared for the place after Spencer had been found there.

None of the Kelly boys hung out at Seminole after that.

The fact that he could still remember the way was a testament to how it was burned into his memory for all the wrong reasons.

You had to climb down to the actual creek from a short embankment, which was something someone else had known, too.

A Jeep was parked on the shoulder.

Silas pulled up behind the vehicle and climbed out, his gaze sharp.

Woodland creatures skittered behind ferns and tall trees flanking the wide creek bed. His breath plumed in frosty clouds as he surveyed the area.

Nothing had changed.

But then nothing changed in Port Orion it seemed.

It was as if the town had been caught in a time loop. Nothing moved forward or behind—everything was static.

He climbed to the top and looked down.

A huge rock jutted out across the water, a popular jumping point above a deep spot on the creek bed.

Spencer's voice echoed in his mind.

"Silas, watch me!"

Spencer, the precocious shit, had wanted to prove himself. He was going to jump from the high rock, like the rest of them.

Their oldest brother Sawyer didn't approve. "It's too high for him."

"Stop babying him," Silas had shot back. "You practically pushed me off this rock when I was his age."

"I can do it," Spencer boasted to Sawyer with a tiny amount of pleading. "C'mon, let me try."

Silas wanted to see Spencer jump. Everyone babied Spencer and he was sick of it. Why were the rules always different for Spence? "Go on, I dare you, you little mama's boy," Silas had taunted with a grin. "You're too chicken to do it."

Before Sawyer could tell him not to, Spencer flipped Silas off and then leaped from the rock, screeching like a little girl the entire way down.

Silas had laughed until Sawyer had picked him up and tossed him off the rock to join Spencer, saying, "You made him jump. You can make sure he's okay."

Silas's balls still ached from the awkward way he'd landed in the water.

Yeah, his brothers had thought that was hilarious.

The memory of that day faded and Silas returned to the present only to see that aggressive reporter, Quinn Jackson, nosing around the crime scene.

"Hey," he called out. "What the hell do you think you're doing? This is an active crime scene."

Quinn looked up, caught, and tried blinding him with a bright smile as if that was going to work.

The young woman was nice to look at. In another time, another place, he might even be tempted to get her number, but in this current circumstance, he had zero interest so that pretty smile was wasted on him.

"You can't be down here," Silas told her sternly as he joined her. "Exactly what do you hope to accomplish aside from contaminating a crime scene?"

"Hold on, there, Mr. Grumpy Pants, I'm not stupid. I'm not touching anything on the other side of the tape, I'm just trying to get a feel for the scene. It helps for my story."

Silas narrowed his gaze, seeing her for what she was—a soulless shell of a person who only cared about her story.

Much like the reporters who'd ruined Spencer's case.

Over-eager, aggressive and completely disinterested in how their meddling affected the outcome of a case.

"Get out of here before I call your boss," Silas growled. "Try to show some respect for the girl who died."

Quinn stiffened, taking immediate offense. "Excuse me? I *knew* that girl. I took her picture plenty of times for the paper so don't lecture me on something you have no moral ground to stand on. *You* are the trespasser here. Try to remember that."

"Her family is grieving," Silas returned, disgusted with all press. "The last thing they need is some nosey reporter digging around, contaminating the case. Now, get out of here."

"This is public land," Quinn said, lifting her chin, her eyes flashing. "I can be here all I want as long as I don't cross the tape. So deal with it."

Silas shook his head. Reporters were all alike. Intent on their own purposes, and damn anyone else.

"What are you here for?" Quinn asked.

But Silas disregarded her question and walked away, prepared to tune her out. If she refused to leave he couldn't make her, but he didn't have to be polite and suffer idle chatter.

Quinn took the hint but he sensed she was put out.

Small town—she wasn't used to being on the outside of a local issue. She probably got what she wanted by using charm and sweetness but he got the feeling Quinn was more than she seemed.

Quinn's surface was a cultivated act that she'd honed over the years but past the superficial layer of candy was nothing but rock.

He'd have to watch out for her. She was going to be trouble.

Silas gave her a covert glance, catching her scribbling notes in her notepad, her nose pinking from the chill.

What was she writing?

The creek, high for this time of year, rushed over rocks, creating small whitecaps. Although Seminole was technically a creek, it was quite wide and deep in some areas.

The gurgle of the water as it traveled was soothing to some—but Silas didn't care for it.

Rushing water reminded him of Spencer's murder.

Swearing mentally at his inability to stop his brain from throwing too many pieces from his childhood into his way, he realized without the report, he was wasting his time at the crime scene.

Maybe he'd already known that at a core level but he had to come to test himself.

He didn't see the raw, lush beauty of Seminole Creek—he saw the place someone had dumped his brother's body.

Oppenshaw had probably been right; his thought process was too cluttered with shit from the past to be of any use here.

But he wasn't leaving.

Hell, he couldn't if he tried.

The pull to remain was too strong.

Without another word, he left Quinn behind at the scene. It was getting dark, anyway. If she wanted to stumble around without any light that was her business.

He needed food, a shower and bed.

In that order.

Tomorrow he was attacking this case with his head on straight.

Chapter 4

Quinn knew when the FBI agent, Silas Kelly, had left the scene, because she found herself releasing the breath that must've been pent up inside.

There was something about the austere man that troubled her.

He wasn't friendly in the least.

But that wasn't it.

Okay, so he was good-looking. Older than her by close to ten years, but he wore his age well.

His skin was clear, his eyes sharp.

If she was being honest, he probably could double as a model or something.

But that wasn't what was pulling at her, either.

Quinn sensed something beyond the stoic face, the stern glance.

Pain.

The man was hiding something really painful, something that he preferred to keep private.

Which, of course, only pricked at her need to know more.

Her uncle Leo was always telling her that she was the cat that curiosity eventually killed.

A little morbid but probably true.

What could she say? She loved uncovering details that others would rather hide.

Such as…why was an FBI agent poking his nose into a local case that, on the surface, had absolutely no connection to anything with federal jurisdiction?

Time for a little fieldwork. Someone in town had to know more about Silas Kelly.

Seeing as the sheriff was being unaccountably mum on the subject of this recent murder, she'd just have to go to a different source.

The one man she knew who knew everything about Port Orion was right under her nose.

Uncle Leo.

Pocketing her pen and pad, she wandered a few more times up and down the bank, steering clear of the tape, and when she found nothing that stood out, she followed Silas's lead and left the scene.

Just in time, too. Her nose felt ready to fall off.

Quinn popped into the diner to grab some soup—minestrone for her and chowder for Uncle Leo—and went home.

The best way to get her uncle to start talking was to ply him with his favorite foods.

Chowder was his weakness.

"I'm home," she called out, carrying her bags of goodies. "And I've brought something yummy."

Leo hollered from his office. "I'll be right there. I can smell the chowder already!"

Quinn chuckled and found some bowls to ladle up their portions. She broke off some sourdough bread and liberally buttered it so by the time Uncle Leo appeared she had everything ready to go.

"You are an angel from heaven," he said, sinking into the chair at the table, his eyes as round as the soup bowl. "How did you know that I was craving chowder?"

Quinn pretended to think then answered, "Because it's a day that ends in Y."

"Clever girl," Leo quipped before dipping in, his expression of glee tickling her.

Uncle Leo was like a father to her but cool like an uncle. She liked to call him her *funcle.*

After a few bites, Leo leaned back and eyed Quinn with suspicion. "All right, out with it, missy...what's on your mind? You always bring me chowder when you want something."

"Not true," she protested but she couldn't help the smile because it was true. "Maybe I just love seeing you happy and I know chowder is the way to your heart."

"Exactly," he returned drily. "What do you need?"

Since there was no further point in denying it, Quinn said, "Okay, since you asked... I need information."

"Is this on the record?" he said semi-seriously. "Because I don't need to be quoted on nothing."

"Off the record," she assured him. "I just need to know some Port Orion history."

Leo lost his seriousness. "Oh, then. That's easy. What do you need to know?"

Quinn jumped right in. "So, there's an FBI agent in town, seemingly interested in the murder of Rhia Daniels, and he says he's from here but I don't know him. I mean, he's older than me, but I thought you might have some insight."

"What's the name?"

"Silas Kelly."

At the mention of the name, Leo's gaze shuttered and

he shook his head. "Sad story there. Hard to believe he came back."

"What do you mean?"

"What's an FBI agent interested in the Daniels case for?"

"I don't know," she admitted. "I was hoping I could find out by learning who he is to this town. Can you help me?"

"I don't know much more than what was told in the papers," Leo said, tearing off a chunk of bread to dunk in the chowder.

"Yeah, but surely there must've been chatter. Just tell me what you remember."

Leo fidgeted, seeming lost for a minute. Finally, he roused himself when he realized Quinn was still waiting.

"Sure, sure. Okay, well, it's a terrible story. Here's what I remember. The Kelly family used to live here. Good family. Good people. But then something bad happened to the youngest Kelly boy and nothing was ever the same again."

"What do you mean?"

"Well, when you live in a small town, where everyone knows everyone else, you feel insulated against the troubles of the world. So when something real bad happens, it shakes people up, makes them realize that they're not immune to the dangers everyone else faces. Losing that Kelly boy...and never finding the killer...well, it was just too much."

"His brother was murdered?" Quinn's eyes bugged. "How awful."

"And the family picked up and left town as soon as Silas graduated from high school. I heard the family broke up, went in separate directions."

Quinn thought of the austere air about Silas and pitied the young kid he'd been. That was some rough stuff.

"Do you think there could be any connection between Spencer Kelly's murder and Rhia Daniels?"

"No, I really doubt it," Leo answered with conviction.

"Whoever did that terrible thing is probably long gone but people who crave closure will grasp at any straw. I can't blame the man for trying."

She couldn't, either.

The gears in her mind were moving quickly, testing out theories and possibilities.

"I imagine if, by some incredible chance, the cases are connected...that would be a pretty amazing coup to solve them both."

Leo shrugged as if he thought the possibility was far too remote to contemplate and returned to his chowder, pausing to ask, "What's with all the curiosity? You think you're going to bust this case wide open and report on it?"

"And if I did?"

"I'd say that's a helluva long shot."

Quinn smiled. "That's okay. I like a challenge."

Leo's brief smile felt vaguely patronizing but Quinn let it slide. Everyone was allowed an off day.

Besides, she had bigger fish to fry.

First and foremost...she needed to find a way to get Silas Kelly to trust her.

Given the fact that he seemed to have little respect for the press that would be a challenge indeed.

Silas felt it prudent to let his brothers know that he was in Port Orion. His call to Shaine went to voice mail—not surprising, Shaine was always undercover somewhere—so he left a brief message and called Sawyer.

Sawyer picked up on the first ring.

"You're up late," Silas said, checking his watch. "Working a case?"

"Yeah, possible fiduciary elder abuse case in Wyoming. Pretty sophisticated operation, too. What's up?"

Silas decided to go straight for the meat. "I'm in Port Orion, working a murder case."

A beat of silence followed before Sawyer said, "Why? Is it related to Spencer's case?"

"I don't know, but the victim was found in Seminole Creek around the same time as the anniversary of Spencer's murder. Seemed like a good idea to follow up."

Silas could feel the weight of his brother's concern from across the line. "You know the likelihood that the two cases are related is very slim," Sawyer said carefully. "I just don't want you chasing after a ghost."

"I'm only here for a few days to sniff things out. If it looks like the cases aren't connected, I'll leave."

"Will you?" Sawyer didn't sound convinced.

"Of course."

"Good. Nothing but sadness left in that place. You need to give yourself some closure."

"That's what I'm trying to do."

"No, you're trying to find forgiveness. No one blames you for what happened to Spence."

Silas struggled for a minute. That familiar choking sensation pressed on his windpipe. He was to blame. It was his fault. "I shouldn't have left him."

"You were a kid," Sawyer said. "Spence should've gone home like he was supposed to. No one could've known what was going to happen that day."

Silas knew all the rational arguments—didn't matter. His guilt still crushed him every day.

And returning to Port Orion had only dredged up those buried feelings.

As if reading his mind, Sawyer asked, "How's it being back?"

"Weird. Uncomfortable. Sad."

"Seems about right."

"Nothing has changed. Everything is as it was. Time doesn't exist here. Mankins is still the sheriff. He should've retired a long time ago."

Sawyer chuckled. "If it weren't for Mankins, your ass

would've landed in jail. He saved your skin more times than I can count."

That much was true. After Spencer's death...well, let's just say that being a good kid hadn't been big on Silas's list.

"I went to the crime scene. You know that big rock that we used to jump off from?"

"Yeah."

"Looks the same. Reminded me of the time Spencer wanted to jump and you didn't think it was safe, but he did it anyway and then you pushed me off to make sure Spencer was all right."

Sawyer chuckled at the memory. "Racked your nuts if I recall correctly."

"Hell, yes. It'll be a miracle if I can have kids."

"Well, we all babied Spencer."

Everyone but Silas. "Yeah, made me jealous. Why did he get special treatment?" he said, half joking but it was difficult to talk about Spencer without sinking into the tar pit of banked grief. Silas returned to the reason he called. "Look, if there's a chance to solve his murder, I have to take it. My boss thinks I'm chasing after a ghost, too. But I don't care. My intuition says I have to be here. For whatever reason that may be. But I can't leave."

"So tell me about the recent case," Sawyer said, resigned. "What are the details?"

"Sixteen-year-old girl, popular, pretty. Dumped into Seminole Creek two nights ago. I'm waiting on the autopsy report to see if there were any trace forensics that I can compare to Spencer's case."

"No preliminary cause of death?"

"Hand marks on the neck suggest strangulation."

"Similar to Spencer. But choking a victim out isn't unique," Sawyer pointed out.

"True. That's why I'm pulling Spencer's case file to refresh my memory."

"I would've thought you had that case file memorized by now," Sawyer said.

Truth was, Silas had put Spencer's case far out of his mind so he could focus on the cases that landed on his desk today. "I could use a refresher. I know the basics but I don't want any detail left on the table."

"I don't know, Silas. Refreshing the details of Spencer's case seems like an unnecessary agony."

Silas knew that it was different for his older brothers. They'd mourned Spencer's death like any sibling would, but they would never understand Silas's driving need to find who had killed the youngest Kelly.

A beat of silence passed between them and then Sawyer exhaled, knowing Silas wouldn't be deterred. The Kelly men were known for being stubborn.

"I know you're going to do whatever you feel is necessary. Be careful and keep me updated."

"I will," Silas agreed.

"All right. It's late. Be safe, brother."

Sawyer clicked off and Silas plugged his cell in to charge for the night. It felt good to talk with Sawyer. Even though they were all adults, the Kelly brothers had a special bond.

Spencer's death had drawn them together in a way that he would never wish on anyone but he was thankful for their support.

He couldn't say the same for his dad.

Silas was the only Kelly boy who hadn't attended the funeral.

Dad never forgave Silas for what'd happened to Spencer. Messed up, yeah, he knew. But even though he could rationalize his father's feelings, the kid inside him still hurt for the rejection.

And he'd never get closure from his father.

Dad had died a handful of years ago with harsh words lodged between him and Silas.

He stiffened his backbone as a shock of pain jolted him.

Even if Silas had been willing to patch things up, his dad couldn't.

Just…couldn't. Each time his dad had looked at Silas, the corners of his mouth would pull as if he was being reminded all over again that it was because of Silas that Spencer was gone.

Thankfully, his mother hadn't drawn such a harsh line. Though there were times Silas wondered if deep down, she harbored a secret resentment against him. Maybe it was his guilty conscience, but it was hard to ignore just the same.

Climbing into bed, he closed his eyes, willing himself to sleep. His alarm was set for five a.m. and seeing as it was past midnight already, that didn't leave much time for shut-eye.

But as he was drifting, Quinn Jackson popped into his last conscious thought and he was left with a feeling that he hadn't seen the last of the redhead.

Silas frowned, irritated at himself that his thoughts kept gravitating toward Quinn.

What was it about her that his brain stubbornly refused to latch loose?

The easy answer—her looks.

But that wasn't it.

Silas was old enough to recognize the pitfall of chasing after a pretty face and perfect figure.

She had a sense about her that made people stare.

Including him.

Raw, boundless energy crackled around her.

Like a…kitten.

No, not a kitten.

Like something wild.

Untamed.

And completely dangerous.

If he were smart, he'd steer clear.

Chapter 5

"Please, Lester," Quinn pleaded. "What's the point of being local if I can't even get some kind of exclusive content?"

"Isn't there some environmental catastrophe you could report on? Maybe go piss off some timber company and leave this case alone."

"Why are you so intent on pushing me away from this case?" she asked. "If I didn't know better I'd say you're afraid I'm going to uncover something you'd rather keep hidden."

Oops. Too far.

Lester narrowed his gaze at her. "Watch it," he growled and she immediately changed her tactic.

"I just want justice for this poor girl. I mean, the whole school is grieving right now. The town is hungry to know what happened. We need to be able to give them the answers they seek in the most responsible manner possible. Do you really think that the big presses are going to care if the case is handled sensitively? Hell, Lester, I saw news vans camped out in front of the Danielses' family house yesterday! How awful, right? You don't see me doing that, but if you don't give me something I can work with, I might have to."

Lester appeared to take her point under consideration. After a long pause he said, "All right. You're worse than a damn bloodhound. The autopsy is scheduled for this morning. If you want, you can sit in and watch."

Watch an autopsy? That wasn't exactly what she had in mind but she'd take it. "Perfect! Am I allowed to ask the coroner questions?"

"No. Keep your lip zipped."

"Then why am I watching?" she said, frustrated. "C'mon, Lester, you're tying my hands at every turn. Don't you love me?"

At that Lester softened. "Of course I do. I just think this case is above your pay grade, sweetheart."

That really stung. Quinn tried not to let her bruised pride overrun her mouth but it was hard. "I'm trying to elevate my pay grade," she replied with quiet dignity. "I need a case like this to do it."

"What does your uncle think of you poking around on this case?"

"He doesn't have an opinion," she answered, frowning at the odd question. "Why would he? It's my job."

Lester nodded, conceding the point but not before adding a few stipulations. "You are to be quiet so the doc can do his work. The only reason I'm letting you do this is because you need to see the ugly side of the work you want to do. Rhia Daniels is more than just a story angle for your career. She was someone's daughter, and her parents are grief-stricken."

"Of course," Quinn said quickly. "I'll be very respectful."

"See that you are. Or else this will be the last time your pretty pleas will work on me."

"Is that it?"

"No. I want you to steer clear of Silas Kelly, too."

"Why?"

"Because his agenda has nothing to do with yours."

That stipulation put her in direct opposition with her plans. She needed Silas. Seems out of everyone, Silas was her best bet to get solid leads.

The irony was not lost on her.

"Sure," she lied. "I mean, it's a small town so we're bound to run into each other but I won't go out of my way to spend time with him."

"Fair enough." Lester leaned back in his chair, looking suddenly very weary as he gestured for her to go. "You've got your marching orders, now go on."

"Thank you, Lester," Quinn said, pleased with her victory. "You're the best."

Lester snorted at her flattery and she left with a smile.

Her first autopsy. Should be…fun.

It might be disgusting, but at least she could get a look at the condition of the body, which might turn out to be good color for her story.

Quinn pulled her hair into a messy bun on top of her head, wound her scarf around her neck and headed for the morgue.

The tiny flutter in her nerves betrayed her nervousness. Even if she didn't want to admit it, she wasn't entirely sure how her stomach was going to react to seeing a dead body.

What if she puked?

She liked to think she was tougher than that but the only way to know was to go through with it.

Quinn pushed open the double doors of the morgue and shivered at the icy chill in the sterile room. She found Silas already there, looking austere and unapproachable. Maybe if he smiled more…*no, don't go there*. Even when he was looking as if a giant stick was wedged up his behind, he was still pretty handsome.

So…no smiles necessary.

"What are you doing here?" Silas asked.

"I have permission to be here," Quinn answered, lifting her chin. To the coroner, she assured him, "I promise I won't get in your way."

Quinn didn't know the doctor, and she didn't usually make a habit of rubbing elbows with the man who poked and prodded the dead, but he didn't give off the impression that he was open to making friends either.

With a faint scowl, the coroner nodded and motioned for them to come over to the table where the body of Rhia Daniels lay beneath a white sheet.

"Is this really necessary?" Silas asked her in a low tone. "What can you possibly hope to put in your story from this angle? Try to remember her grieving family."

"Why does everyone assume that I don't?" Quinn shot back, irritated. "Maybe her family would like some closure. I imagine your family would've liked to know who killed your brother."

A flash of heat in his eyes warned her to tread carefully. Maybe that comment was a little too much. "I'm sorry. I didn't mean to be hurtful. I'm just trying to put things in perspective."

"Perspective for whom?"

"You, of course," Quinn answered. "You seem to have something against me and you don't even know me."

"You're press. That's all I need to know," he said.

"Well, that's painting with a wide brush. Not all press are the same."

"In my experience, they are. The story is always more important than the feelings of the people involved. I've watched reporters step all over people to get their story, no matter who was standing in their way. Reporters are worse than ambulance-chasing lawyers."

The coroner looked up, annoyed. "If you'd like to continue your conversation elsewhere, that would be appreciated. I'm trying to do my job."

"My apologies," Silas said, shooting Quinn a look as if she was the problem and not him.

Quinn chose to ignore Silas for the moment and concentrate on taking in every detail she could without losing her breakfast.

Rhia Daniels, young, beautiful and dead.

Black-and-blue smudges betrayed where fingers had gripped her slender neck, squeezing the life out of her.

The hands looked large on her small body. Quinn struggled with the little voice inside her head that disapproved of being there.

It seemed…disrespectful.

Silas's expression remained stony, stoic—devoid of emotion as the doctor went about his exam, speaking his notes out loud to his digital recorder.

"Victim is female, age sixteen, healthy, with visible defensive wounds on her arms and legs. Bruising around the neck that suggests strangulation."

Quinn couldn't imagine how terrified the girl must've been. Had a stranger done this to her? Or was it someone she'd known?

A jealous boyfriend, perhaps?

"A sexual assault exam, as well, Doctor," Silas reminded the coroner, which was not appreciated as the older man cast Silas a dour look.

"You do your job; I'll do mine."

Silas didn't bristle at the rebuke.

Probably because the man was made from stone.

He wouldn't know a genuine emotion if it was dumped on him.

Harsh, Quinn. Don't play into the stereotype of a heart-less journalist.

Quinn managed to hold herself together until the doc started the incisions, then she had to excuse herself.

Quickly.

Gulping big breaths of fresh air, Quinn struggled to keep from upchucking her breakfast burrito.

Moments later Silas joined her, a small smirk on his chiseled face.

"Maybe you could do a narrative piece on your first autopsy."

"What makes you think it was my first?" Quinn bluffed, still feeling hot and shaky. She pressed a cool hand against her cheek, fishing a bottled water from her purse.

"Because you look green, which surprisingly isn't a good look with your red hair."

"Okay, it was my first," she said, blowing out a breath before guzzling the water. Quinn wiped her mouth. "I take it you watch autopsies in your spare time?"

"I've seen my share—and it's never something I take lightly."

Darkness rippled around Silas like an aura, emanating mystery.

There was something primal about Silas, something alluring. She caught herself when she realized she was leaning toward him, trying to catch a whiff of whatever spicy, manly cologne he was wearing.

"Eau de FBI," she murmured, mostly to herself but Silas caught it.

"Excuse me?"

Heat flushed her cheeks and she shook her head, saying quickly, "Nothing," before adding, "Sheriff Mankins says I should steer clear of you. Says you have your own agenda. What would that be, I wonder?"

Instead of denying the claim, Silas just shrugged and said, "You ought to listen to your sheriff."

"Why?"

"Because maybe he's right."

"So what is your agenda?" Quinn asked boldly.

Silas regarded her with a quiet intensity that she felt like a physical thing as he replied with a faint smile, "That would be my business, now, wouldn't it?"

And then he left her standing there, looking like a dope.

Quinn groused to no one. "Well, that went swimmingly," and tossed her empty water bottle in the trash before heading to her car.

She wasn't sure what she could use from the autopsy and she'd learned less than nothing from Silas.

Time to do some more digging on her own.

Silas left the autopsy and headed for the sheriff's office. Spencer's case file should be ready as well as the preliminary report from the investigating officer on the Daniels case.

He entered the building and went straight to the receiving window where a woman sat behind thick glass.

He flashed his credentials. "I'm here to pick up the case files on Spencer Kelly and Rhia Daniels."

The woman nodded and pulled two manila envelopes then pushed a log book under the window opening. "Just sign here."

Silas scrawled his name across the book and accepted the envelopes, tucking them into his jacket to protect them from the weather.

It wasn't raining yet but the dark clouds signaled that a deluge was imminent.

He was nearly to his car when he ran into someone he would've been content to avoid while in Port Orion.

"Well, look who's gracing Port Orion with his presence. Big shot Silas Kelly…what are you doing around here?"

Marc Boggs, former friend turned adversary, still wearing his jealousy over Silas's accomplishments like part of his uniform, eyed him with banked dislike.

"Marc," Silas acknowledged with a small nod. "Just doing legwork on a case."

"Here? In Port Orion? It's gotta be that young girl we fished out of Seminole Creek." Marc didn't wait for Silas to confirm or deny. "Hell, that girl is giving our little town as much publicity as the last time a kid was found in that place."

Silas narrowed his gaze at Marc. "Yeah, it would seem."

Marc sighed as if he felt some kind of empathy for Silas but Silas knew better. Marc only cared about Marc. But it seemed he was interested in playing the part of "long-lost friend" and threw out an offer to get a beer. "Me and a few buddies, you know those of us who chose to stick around, we get together on Saturday nights to blow off some steam down at The Pier. You're welcome to come by and join us."

"Sorry, another time. I'm on the clock."

Marc chuckled. "Damn, Silas, loosen up. Big shot now, can't hang with the lowly peasants, right?"

"Not here for a good time," Silas said.

The subtle downturn of Marc's mouth gave away his displeasure at being rebuffed. Likely the scenario that played out in Marc's head was a night of getting under Silas's skin with veiled insults and condescending jokes.

Yeah, no thanks, Silas thought.

"Catch you later, Marc."

He didn't wait for Marc's reply.

Silas sat in his rental car, wondering how many sour apples he'd run into while in town.

Damn this place. Same people, same buildings. Same bullshit small-town politics.

Everybody talking about everyone else's business with little regard for how their tongue-wagging might hurt someone else.

He preferred the anonymity of a large city. His neighbors didn't bother him or poke their noses where they didn't belong.

Quinn came to mind and he grimaced, though not entirely for the same reasons as he would've liked.

That red hair...it was like a halo of fire around her head, which only accentuated the green of her eyes.

She looked out of place in Port Orion but she'd fit right in walking the shores of Ireland.

An odd moment of whimsy struck him. Ireland with Quinn.

The discordant thought twanged like an out-of-tune guitar string.

Shake that shit off. What was he doing thinking of Quinn in any way aside from professional?

It was the strain of being here, he rationalized. His brain was clawing at any possible way of providing relief, a distraction from the bone-deep grief that remained lodged in spite of how many years had passed.

Quinn was annoying, a pest. And way too young. He preferred women with more seasoning.

But that hair was distracting.

Flowing down her back in wavy ripples, curling at the ends.

The stubborn cowlick near her forehead probably gave her fits.

Silas shut his eyes, trying to push Quinn from his mind.

But all that did was provide a rich curtain for thoughts that immediately caused him to shift inside his trousers.

Damn it. He needed release. All the tension from arriving in Port Orion, memories jamming his brain, were causing his impulses to come out sidewise.

He didn't want anything to do with Quinn.

He didn't want to work with her and he certainly didn't want to bed her.

Focus on the case.

He breathed deeply as he willed his stubborn erection to fade.

Maybe later he'd take care of himself. Release that tension. Quick and efficient.

In the meantime, it was time to get to work.

That was a better distraction anyway.

Chapter 6

Quinn pulled up to the Daniels home and frowned when she saw news vans still camped out in the street.

That's not very classy, Quinn thought with a sniff, even though she was there for the same reason.

But it was different for her. She actually cared about the family.

She started up the steps when a car door closed behind her.

"You're like an unlucky penny."

Quinn bit her lip and swore mentally before turning to face Silas.

"What are you doing here?"

"Looking for answers. The question is…what are you doing here? I would've thought that picking at the family during their time of grief was going too far for a *local* who supposedly cares about them."

Quinn seamed her mouth shut. The man had a comeback for everything. "I do care about the family. I wrote a story about Rhia's award-winning photography in the amateur division at the state fair level. It was a big deal around here. And the story was very well received."

"Something tells me the family isn't going to embrace you with open arms to chat about their dead daughter, no matter how many fluff stories you wrote about her."

"Feature stories are not fluff," Quinn retorted, freshly irritated. "But what would you know about journalism? Nothing. I won't tell you how to do your job and you won't tell me how to do mine."

"Well, the press's place is over there." Silas pointed to the row of vans lining the street. "I've got work to do."

Quinn knew that if Silas gained access to the Daniels family before her, he'd find a way to shut her out. Swallowing her pride, she hustled after Silas with a quick proposition. "Look, we both have jobs to do and we are both at a bit of a disadvantage. I say we help each other. We don't have to be enemies."

"I don't work with press," Silas said, climbing the steps and knocking on the door. "Now, get out of here before you upset people."

Before Quinn could counter, the front door opened and a haggard Mrs. Daniels answered.

Silas produced his credentials. "I'm Special Agent Kelly. May I take a few moments of your time to talk to you about your daughter's case?"

Mrs. Daniels swung red-rimmed eyes toward Quinn and recognition broke. "Are you…with him?" she asked.

"God no," Quinn answered quickly, actually stepping forward to put some distance between them. "We just happened to have the misfortune of arriving at the same time."

"Why is the FBI interested in Rhia's case?" Mrs. Daniels asked, her fingers clutching at her necklace.

"May I come in so we can discuss the case?"

"I…" Mrs. Daniels's gaze darted again and Quinn took the opportunity to insert herself.

"Mrs. Daniels, if you'd be more comfortable… I'd be happy to sit with you. I can only imagine the pain you're going through. Rhia was an amazing and talented girl. The story I wrote on her photography has always been my favorite."

Mrs. Daniels nodded, tears brimming. "Yes, she was." Then she gestured for Quinn to come in as she said to Silas, "I suppose I can answer a few questions if it would help Rhia's case."

If Silas was pissed that Quinn had outmaneuvered him, he didn't show it. Quinn had come to the conclusion that Silas was built from ice.

The man was as stoic as they came.

Did he ever smile? What did his laugh sound like?

Quinn couldn't even imagine his face allowing a smile to happen.

But if it did…man, he was probably devastating.

Again with the smile. She was annoyed at the broken record of her thoughts. *Give it a rest already.*

Quinn shoved aside the unwelcome meandering thought and smiled for Mrs. Daniels as they each took a seat in the family room.

It was as Quinn remembered.

Several clocks interrupted the silence with soft ticks while the house seemed to sigh with grief.

Quinn wasn't one to entertain woo-woo stuff but the sadness in the air was almost a physical thing, and not even Mrs. Daniels's fondness for crocheted doilies could lighten the mood.

She fingered one of the delicate lace creations draped across the arm of the sofa like a frozen lily pad, murmuring, "So pretty," for Mrs. Daniels's benefit.

The grieving mother accepted the compliment with a

nod. "My grandmother always said, 'A bit of lace will brighten any room.'"

"So true," Quinn agreed, wondering when Silas was going to pounce. She'd prefer that he be the bad guy in this scenario but she desperately wanted any information that could help her story.

Quinn already knew Rhia's backstory—miracle child, beloved darling of much older parents, indulged and pampered—but in spite of all this, Rhia had been a decent kid.

At least what Quinn could remember of her.

Who knew what kids were really like when their parents weren't around?

"Is there any reason you can think of why Rhia would be around Seminole Creek at this time of year?" Silas asked, going straight to the hard questions.

Sheesh, man, way to go for the soft spots right away.

Quinn took a different approach. Sidestepping Silas's brutal question, Quinn interjected with kindness.

"How are you holding up, Mrs. Daniels? I can only imagine the hell you're in right now. Is there anything I can do to help?"

Mrs. Daniels sniffed back tears but cast a grateful smile Quinn's way. "You're such a good girl. Thank you." She drew a halting breath to steady her nerves and said to Silas, "I haven't a clue why she was down at the creek. She wasn't the kind of girl who snuck off in the middle of the night."

"Maybe she was meeting with a boyfriend?" Silas suggested.

"Rhia didn't have a boyfriend. She wasn't allowed to date until she was seventeen," Mrs. Daniels said, shaking her head. "Rhia was a very good girl, focused on school. She wanted to go to…Berkeley University in California. It's all she talked about."

Whether Mrs. Daniels wanted to admit it or not, kids often held back information from their parents. Censoring was normal. But Quinn knew they gained nothing by pointing that out to the grieving mother.

Quinn caught the subtle shift in Silas's body posture and she sensed that he was on the same wavelength. She held her breath. Was he going to go there?

But he didn't and she was a little disappointed.

Now you pull back? Go figure.

"Can you lead us through the timeline, Mrs. Daniels?" Silas asked, his voice gentling.

The bereft woman took a moment to collect herself. The pain Mrs. Daniels suffered was almost palpable. Quinn shifted against the pinch of conscience that tempered the hunger she had for a breakout story.

"My husband and I went to dinner that night. Rhia said she had homework and stayed behind. We got home around eleven and went straight to bed." Suddenly, her eyes started to brim. "We didn't think to check if she was in her room. Maybe if we'd checked…"

But Silas shook his head. "Don't go there. I've seen too many parents blame themselves for something that was completely out of their control and it eats them up inside. Please don't do that to yourself."

Quinn was silently in awe of Silas's gentle handling. What happened to Mr. Frosty?

Mrs. Daniels nodded, fresh tears tracking down her face. "That's very kind of you. I can't get it out of my head how she must have suffered. I…I can't sleep or eat. All I think about is that my daughter is gone."

"What happened next, Mrs. Daniels?" Silas asked.

"We got a call from the sheriff saying that Rhia's body had been found by a fisherman the next morning."

Silas nodded, jotting down notes. "Is there anyone you can think of who might want to hurt Rhia?"

"No one," she answered, shaking her head almost desperately. "Everyone loved Rhia. She was kind and considerate to everyone she met. I can't imagine anyone having a problem with her."

Quinn would normally chalk Mrs. Daniels's statement up to a parent's bias but to be honest, Quinn knew that Rhia was well liked.

"How about friends? Who are Rhia's closest friends? Sometimes kids censor themselves around their parents but they're more open with peers."

Mrs. Daniels seemed troubled by that possibility but gave up a few names. "Well, she's very close with Britain Almasey. She's another cheerleader on the squad. They've been best friends since grade school. But Rhia didn't keep secrets from us. We were very close."

"I appreciate that, but I like to cross all the Ts and dot the Is."

Mrs. Daniels nodded, relief coming from understanding. "Of course. I appreciate your diligence, Mr. Kelly."

Silas offered a business card to Mrs. Daniels. "Please feel free to call me anytime. Even if you just need to talk."

Quinn felt foolish trying to follow in Silas's footsteps. Instead, she said, "Rhia was a lovely girl and she will be missed. Your family will be in my prayers."

"Bless you, child."

Silas pocketed his notebook and they rose to leave. Quinn didn't like the way her mind was churning.

Whatever she'd hoped to get by talking with Mrs. Daniels, she'd discarded out of guilt.

It was one thing to chase a story when you weren't staring at the grieving parents of a murdered child, quite another when you could practically feel the grief covering you like a blanket.

Once outside, Silas scrutinized Quinn openly. "Do you pray?"

Quinn scowled. Of course he would ask her that question. "No."

"Then why'd you say that?"

"Because it seemed the right thing to do."

Silas chuckled at her logic. "If you were so concerned with the right thing, you never would've walked inside that poor woman's house."

Quinn stared as Silas drove away.

I kinda hate that man.

Because he was right? A voice questioned.

Her scowl deepened.

Shut up, Inner Voice of Latent Conscience—you're not helping.

Silas returned to his hotel room with takeout Chinese and a plan to reacquaint himself with Spencer's case file, when a knock at his door interrupted his process.

He peered through the peephole and saw Quinn Jackson, of all people, standing outside his door.

What did she want?

For a heartbeat, he was tempted to pretend that he wasn't there.

But clearly she must've tracked him down and she knew he was on the other side of the door so ignoring the woman would just be childish.

Silas exhaled and opened the door. "What can I do for you, Miss Jackson?"

"First, you can call me Quinn. Second, you can admit that if it weren't for me, Mrs. Daniels wouldn't have let you in the front door. And third, you can definitely serve me up a plate of that Chinese food that I can smell because I'm starving."

The girl had balls, he'd give her that. "And why would I want to do any of those things?"

"Because we need to work together, not against one another."

At that he laughed. "That's not going to happen."

"Oh, yes, it is," she disagreed, darting past him and into the room. Quinn did a quick survey and said, "Couldn't the FBI spring for a better room? This place looks like the kind of hotel Dean and Sam Winchester would hole up in because they're trying to catch a wendigo or something."

"Dean and Sam?" Silas asked, confused.

"Do you live under a rock? *Supernatural*, of course. Best show ever. I mean, every season you think they can't outdo themselves and *bam*! They come up with something even more amazing than the last season. That's talent."

"I don't watch a lot of television."

"Your loss. If you want to borrow a few seasons, I have them all on DVD. Or you could stream it from iTunes. Whatever your poison."

"Back to the point. I don't work with reporters."

"You know, you keep saying that but you haven't given me a good reason why. So, what gives? Why don't you work with reporters?"

Her bald question threw him off guard. The woman was as in-your-face as a stereotypical redhead. Or a cartoon character.

"Because I don't," he answered.

"What happened to Mr. Nice Guy? Are you like a Mr. Jekyll and Dr. Hyde kind of person?"

"You have that twisted. It's Dr. Jekyll—"

"Whatever." She waved away his correction. "You get my point. You were, actually, pretty amazing with Mrs. Daniels. I thought maybe you had been possessed by the spirit of someone with an *actual* heartbeat but now I see that was an act for her benefit."

"It wasn't an act," he growled. "And if we're calling people out, what about you? You manipulated that poor woman into letting you in. So what sensational little story are you going to write about the woman's grief?"

"I'm not writing about that," she shot back. "Give me

some credit. Why do you hate reporters so much? I have a job to do, just like you. But you seem to think it's okay to beat me with the guilt hammer because of mine. What gives?"

Quinn settled into the chair and started checking out the contents of his takeout.

"What are you doing?"

"Eating. Duh." She scraped a few pieces of his garlic chicken onto a paper plate and then went for his rice. "I told you…starving. Try to keep up. I thought the FBI were supposed to be the sharpest of the bunch. So far, you seem to have a problem holding on to details."

The woman exasperated him but there was something daring about her that intrigued him, even if begrudgingly. Hell, he wanted to toss her out, but something kept him from doing just that.

Maybe because he didn't trust putting his hands on her. Silas was already suffering the urge to touch that creamy skin. If he accidentally brushed one of those lush, full breasts, hiding his insta-erection would be an embarrassing challenge.

He frowned. Well, if he didn't grab a plate, there'd be nothing left. The girl could put some food away.

Silas took the seat opposite her and made his own plate, watching her enjoy his food without shame.

"Do you always barge into strange men's hotel rooms and eat their food?"

"Only on Tuesdays but for you, I'll make an exception." When he continued to stare, she added, rolling her eyes, "That was a joke. Look, I get it, you don't like me. And maybe I'm not terribly excited about you, either, but the fact is we need each other."

"Yeah, you keep saying that but I don't see it that way."

"Let me break it down for you. You've been gone a long time. Doors are closed. They don't trust you. I, on the other hand, am everyone's trusted local reporter. I'm the one who takes their kids' pictures for Student of the Month and I write about when little Johnny places at the Science Fair. Yes, stupid stuff, but it paves the way to their trust. You, by comparison, are the big bad FBI agent who is, I might add, mysteriously poking around a local case that should have no federal jurisdiction."

Silas offered a cold smile. "Just because I don't share the Bureau's interest, doesn't mean there isn't one."

"Oh, I know your interest. That's pretty easy to figure out. This is all about your little brother. Don't look so shocked. You're not the only one who is capable of poking around. How are you hoping to tie Rhia's murder with a case that happened twenty years ago?"

Silas shifted, fighting against the urge to shut her down for hitting too close to home. But for reasons he couldn't quite fathom, he answered. "Because they were both found in Seminole Creek, both strangled."

"Not to be a buzzkill, but strangulation is a pretty common way to die. I mean, no tools required, you know? What else do you have that might lead you to believe they are connected?"

"Good try," he said, withdrawing as he speared a nugget. "Not interested in sharing."

"You're a stubborn little muskrat, aren't you?"

He nearly choked on garlic chicken. "That's a new one."

"Yeah, well, I like to be original."

"You also like to poke around where you're not wanted."

Quinn didn't take offense. "That's my job," she said simply. "No one wants the press to air their dirty laundry. I hardly think politicians are clamoring for the chance to have their secrets splattered all over the *New York Times*, but that happens and the public is thankful for the information."

"Politicians are fair game. Little kids aren't."

"I'm not trying to capitalize on Rhia's murder—"

"How do you say that with a straight face?"

Frustration laced Quinn's voice as she chewed vigorously. "You are impossible. Let me guess, single? You don't have to confirm. I can tell. You're rigid as a freaking plank."

He was single. The job was his life. But hearing Quinn make such an easy and flippant observation pinched.

"I date."

"Sure you do."

Was he really going to debate his dating habits with a reporter who was at least ten years younger than him? "Shouldn't you be getting home? I'm sure there's a curfew of some sort."

"Ha ha. You're hilarious. Not a kid. I'm actually twenty-four."

"Whoa. Practically an old lady," he retorted. "What about you? Let me take a crack. Also single, because you're too damn pushy for anyone to handle on a daily basis."

He must've hit a nerve. But Quinn wasn't going to give him the satisfaction. "Wrong. I'm single because I choose to be. I don't need a man to validate me. I have big dreams, and getting hitched and popping out kids are not on my agenda."

"What is your agenda?" Silas asked, going straight to the point.

"Getting out of this town."

He saw the hunger, the drive to succeed beyond the borders of her environment, and he recognized that need as something he'd often struggled with in the early days.

"What happened to the Port Orion champion?"

"It's a good town. But I want more."

"And you're going to use the Rhia Daniels case as your stepping stone to bigger and better," Silas guessed with a wry chuckle. "You may think you're an original but that's the tune every reporter has sung in my experience, and they never care about the cases they ruin or the lives they shatter on their way to the top."

"I care about the people here," Quinn replied, stung. "I grew up in this town. I have a vested interest in seeing that this story is handled with sensitivity."

"By the very nature of your job, that's not possible."

"You don't know how to do my job."

"Sure I do. Go for the jugular…*if it bleeds, it leads*."

"Damn, Silas. Who pissed in your cornflakes? Do you hate all reporters, or just me?"

Silas laughed and trashed his empty plate. "Don't take it personal—I hate all reporters. Now, seeing as you've eaten all my garlic chicken, I'm going to have to send you on your way, unless of course, you'd like to finish the fried rice."

This time, there was no negotiating.

Quinn seemed to sense that he wasn't kidding. She rose with an unhappy glare but before she allowed him to send her out the door, she snatched his only fortune cookie.

"That's bad luck, you know," he told her.

Her voice on the other side rang out as she said, "You will work with me, Silas Kelly. You may be a muskrat but I'm a badger!"

A reluctant smile crept onto his lips.

Quinn Jackson was a major pain in his ass but at least she wasn't boring.

Chapter 7

Lester Mankins felt another tension headache coming on. He rubbed at his forehead and the back of his neck, feeling the knots in his shoulders, and wondered if he should've taken his wife's advice and retired.

He took no small amount of pride in knowing that Port Orion was a safe place but this recent event had shaken his foundation.

His buddy, Leo Jackson, Quinn's uncle, was meeting him for lunch, as was their routine each Wednesday, and if there ever was a day that he needed the company of a friend, it was today.

Leo, a man with a whiskered face that never went without a smile, joined him in their booth.

"You look like shit," Leo observed with a grin. "Tell that pretty wife of yours to stop keeping you up at all hours."

"If only that were the reason I haven't slept in three days."

Leo knew what Lester was talking about. Hell, everyone in Port Orion was talking about the Rhia Daniels case. "Any news?"

Lester couldn't discuss the case but the burden of what he'd just discovered this morning from the coroner's report was weighing him down.

Leo sensed he was holding something back. "What's going on? You've got that look on your face."

"Yeah, what look is that?" he asked wearily.

"That look that says you either have really terrible news or you ate bad meatloaf again."

Lester chuckled. "It's not the meatloaf."

"Ah," Leo said, nodding. "So out with it. You'll feel better once you do."

"Rhia was pregnant," Lester said even though he should've kept his mouth shut but he was struggling. "Goddamn, Leo. How am I supposed to break that bombshell to her parents? The sun rose and set in that kid's eyes as far as they were concerned."

"Pregnant?" Leo was just as shocked. "What the hell?"

"Coroner confirmed she was six weeks along. The kid probably didn't even know herself. Hell, I just wish I could go to bed and start the day over without that information."

Leo sighed with a shake of his head. "Kids nowadays… it's a different generation. You never know what they're into."

"This kid was a sweet girl," Lester disagreed. "And her parents were pretty strict. Her daddy watched her like a hawk."

"I hate to point out the obvious but he must not have been watching too carefully if she got herself knocked up."

Lester cut Leo a sharp look. "Careful, you never know who could be listening. I have to find a way to break it to the Danielses and no matter how I've turned it around in my head, it always comes out stinking like a wet pile of crap."

Leo grimaced. "I don't envy you."

"Thanks." Lester grabbed his lager and took a healthy swig. He didn't drink on the job, but a beer seemed in order. "Lately it feels like the job gets harder as I get older."

"Lester, you should've retired five years ago," Leo pointed out gently. "Not sure why you hung on this long. You ought to be spending your golden years chasing a little white ball across a pristine tee or going on a microbrewery tour, not staring down the business end of misery on a case that promises nothing but grief."

Leo's comment roused him from his self-pity party long enough to say, "Hey, hold up there. I've done a pretty fine job of being sheriff of this town. No complaints to this point."

"Calm down. Don't get your panties in a twist, you old fart. I was just saying there are more things to life than just keeping the peace. Time to hand it off to someone else."

"I can't now, not with an active murder investigation. If I retire now people will think I'm running with my tail between my legs, unable to handle this case."

"What do you care what people think? You've earned some R&R."

Lester knew his friend was right but he couldn't in good conscience leave when his town was in crisis.

"I'll see this through. I have to."

"Come with me to Thailand. You'll love the culture."

"They have mosquitos big enough to cart away toddlers. No, thanks. Besides, Thailand is your thing. You know I hate spicy food."

Leo grinned. "You don't know what you're missing."

"I'll take your word for it."

Their food arrived and even though Lester had started out hungry, his appetite had waned. He kept seeing the coroner's report in his mind.

This newest little tidbit was going to throw the town in a tizzy; the tongues were going to be wagging for days.

The town sweetheart…the good girl…maybe wasn't such a good girl after all.

"Didn't you work with Rhia Daniels on some kind of photography project?" Lester recalled, pulling the memory from a foggy place filled with useless data.

Leo cleared his throat, staring down at his plate before answering with a short nod. "Yeah, good kid. Talented, too. Not just a pretty face. Reminded me of Quinn when she was that age. She won some awards for her photography."

Lester grunted an acknowledgment and took a bite of his burger. He chewed, lost in thought, when he realized Silas Kelly had walked into the diner.

Yep, there went the rest of his appetite. Silas was going to take that tiny bit of information and tear into it. He was a bulldog. If only it were possible to bury that damn report and forget he ever saw it.

Silas saw him and headed over. Lester forced a smile, trying to appear as if he wasn't going through the motions.

"That's going to kill you one of these days," Silas said, pointing to the double cheeseburger with avocado and bacon that was Lester's favorite and had been since the beginning of time. "I doubt your arteries are thanking you for that heart attack on a plate."

"Bah! My arteries are just fine. Son, life is about the little things that bring you joy and a fine burger and a glass of lager are about as joyful as they get at my age."

Silas chuckled and looked to Leo, his gaze narrowing with recognition. "Leo… Jackson of Looking Glass Photography Studio?"

"And substitute teacher when the mood strikes me. You must be Silas Kelly, the FBI agent who's come to town to shake things up."

"Not here to disrupt anything," he assured them. "Just trying to lend a hand."

"That's right friendly of you," Leo said, though his smile didn't quite reach his eyes. Lester didn't know if Leo had history with the Kelly family but to his knowledge they only knew each other peripherally.

"I'm glad I ran into you. I was wondering if the coroner's report was ready yet so I can take a look."

"No," Lester lied, shooting Leo a look that said "shut your trap" and returned to his burger, if only to fill his mouth with something. "I'll call as soon as it's ready. Hey, since you're here, get something to eat. Best food is right here in this diner."

"I remember," Silas said, smiling. "Maybe I'll have the heart attack special."

"At least you'd die smiling," Lester joked, relieved when Silas wandered to his own table.

Once they were free and clear, Leo looked at Lester. "Can you tell me what the hell just happened? Why'd you lie?"

"Because I'm not ready for the shit-storm that's coming, that's why," he answered with a bit of an edge. "Look, I don't begrudge Silas coming to see if this case and Spencer's case are connected, but this case is already getting under my skin unlike any before. I just need a breather."

"I don't blame you. No judgment here, my friend. Besides, no offense, but there's no reason Silas Kelly needs to be poking around our business. We have plenty of skilled officers who can figure this mystery out. I say tell him, *thank you but we got this. You can go on home.*"

If only Lester could do that. "I wish it was that simple. I don't want to make waves with the Feds. They saw fit to send him here for a reason. I just hope whatever he's looking for…doesn't tear this town apart."

* * *

"Still nothing?"

Quinn's editor, Mick Creech, was doing that weird frown again, where his forehead crinkled and his bald head started to turn red.

"I'm working on it. These things have to be finessed."

"No, these things have to be pushed along. You need to get more aggressive."

"The family is grieving. I can't just plop down on their sofa and start grilling them about their daughter's death. C'mon, Mick, have some compassion."

"Of course not," Mick said quickly but followed up with, "But we need *something*. We're getting snowed by the competitors and this is our local story."

"I know that," Quinn grumbled, turning to spin slowly in her office chair. She didn't need Mick telling her what she already knew. She'd had a chance to ask some serious questions and she'd passed it up.

Somehow Silas had gotten in her head and made her feel guilty for being there at all.

"I'll have something by Friday," she said to mollify Mick. "You'll have something for the weekend edition. I promise."

"You'd better or I'm putting Gigi on this story instead of you."

Gigi? Was that a serious threat? Gigi was afraid of her own shadow and preferred to write the obituaries.

But she supposed Mick was right to a point. She had to get more aggressive if she wanted to make something of herself.

Quinn popped out of her chair and went to the archives. She was looking for news articles on the youngest Kelly brother.

She pulled the archived news from the year Spencer died and thumbed through it. Quinn found it quickly.

Local Boy Found In Creek
By Sara Westfall
Port Orion Tribune

An 11-year-old boy was fished out of Seminole
Creek, early Sunday morning, dead from apparent
strangulation.

The boy, Spencer Kelly, was found by a fisher-
man looking to catch steelhead in the early morning.

According to the family, the youngest Kelly boy
was on his way home when he disappeared, only to
be found twenty-four hours later, in Seminole Creek.

"We are putting all resources toward finding who
did this terrible thing to one of our own," Sheriff Les-
ter Mankins told press. "Anyone with information is
urged to contact the office."

The story went on with some local color, how the creek
was a tributary to the coastline, but nothing else relevant
about the case.

Sara Westfall.

Quinn didn't recognize the name but sometimes reporters came and went at the local paper.

Not everyone had their sights on bigger things like
Quinn.

She flipped through the following editions, looking for
follow-up but aside from a few blips here and there, as the
months dragged on, so did interest.

Whole lives changed but the world kept spinning.

Quinn returned the volume to the archive and closed
up. The archive room smelled of dust and old books. She
rubbed her nose as a sneeze threatened.

Mystery man, mystery man...why are you stuck in
my head?

More and more, Silas popped into her thoughts and they weren't always work related.

She wasn't blind.

He had a strong, lean build, not that she was surprised. As if Silas would allow an ounce of flab to settle anywhere on his body.

Silas probably had *two* gym memberships because one wasn't enough.

He probably took some weird, off-the-beaten-path exercise discipline that required him to stand on his head and lift weights with his toes.

Because he had a physique that wasn't natural.

Not that she'd been obsessing or anything.

A sigh escaped as she leaned against the archive wall. Silas was a man with his head on straight. She liked that about him.

Even if he didn't feel the same about her.

What kind of woman would turn his head? It was idle curiosity, not genuine wonder, but she pictured a woman with diamond-cut abs, a short, efficient haircut and combat boots.

Silas wasn't the type to seek out a woman to serve as an accessory. He was all about purpose.

She liked that about him, too.

What she *didn't* like about him was his rigid refusal to play nice in the sandbox. He didn't want to share any of his toys and he suffered no shame in admitting it.

Silas had been pretty clear that he wasn't willing to work together.

Fine.

She didn't need him to hold her hand.

It was time to start digging around on her own to see what she could scare up.

Maybe then Silas would see that she could be an asset.

Chapter 8

Silas sensed Lester wasn't up to this investigation. He seemed haggard, as if he were aging by the day.

The Port Orion Sheriff's Department was small by most city standards but then it wasn't really a hotbed of crime, either.

The usual crime feed was filled with a host of nuisance crimes such as vandalism, petty theft, and the occasional pervert flashing his genitals.

Big crime had always seemed to bypass Port Orion for juicier targets. Well, except for the murders of Spencer and Rhia Daniels.

But the lack of crime meant the law enforcement didn't have a lot of experience in closing serious cases.

Oppenshaw had given him strict instructions to avoid stepping on local law enforcement toes but Silas couldn't help but worry that the locals weren't up to the task.

So what did that mean?

Was he ready to insert himself into the equation in a less than peripheral manner?

It would ruffle feathers.

Did he care?

Again, his thoughts bumped into Quinn. The unerring direction his thoughts seemed intent on going was disturbing.

She was not his type.

One, she was too young. The generation gap was more than he could stomach. He preferred older women when he took time to date. More mature, less interested in games and they didn't cry and carry on when the relationship had run its course.

Two, she annoyed the hell out of him. That persistent tenacity to dig until she found her prize was a thorn in his side.

Three, he hated reporters. That wass all that needed to be said on that score.

Three excellent reasons why thinking of Quinn in *any* capacity was ill-advised.

And yet…he wondered what the texture of her hair would feel like between his fingertips.

Wondered if she was a wildcat in bed.

Heat crept into his cheeks.

What the hell, Silas? Try digging a deeper pit to climb into, why don't you?

But Quinn had the body type that usually turned his head—strong, athletic, with curves in all the right places—and his best efforts to shut down that kind of interest didn't seem to be working.

And the way she looked at the world, inquisitive, tenacious, wondrous…that quality intrigued him.

He couldn't remember the last time he'd felt any of those things.

The nature of his profession had a tendency to jade even

the best, but circumstance had blunted Silas's edges way before joining the Bureau.

Quinn seemed to kindle that dying spark he'd long since forgotten could burn.

Like you need that kind of distraction.

Being in Port Orion already had him edgy as a long-tailed cat in a roomful of rockers.

He was off his game when he needed to be razor sharp.

Spencer haunted this place. Silas saw his little brother everywhere.

That was the trouble with going back to his home-town...there was the potential threat of mental contamination everywhere.

He pulled up to his hotel room and saw Quinn sitting out front, waiting.

Swearing under his breath, he exited the car and went to Quinn. "What are you doing?"

"Stalking you?" she supplied as if that was obvious. "But I think you're going to want to hear what I have to say."

Silas didn't have the mental energy to play games. "Yeah? And why is that?"

"Because I have something big. Something I shouldn't have. And you want it."

He narrowed his gaze at Quinn, trying to discern her angle, but the sky suddenly opened up and buckets of water began to fall, pelting them both.

Quinn shrieked, covering her head as Silas opened the door and they both rushed in.

"Man, that came quick," Quinn said, grinning as water dripped down her hair and into her eyes. "Got a towel I can borrow?"

Silas grabbed two towels and they wiped down quickly.

The way the light in Quinn's eyes danced with an inner joy briefly caught him off guard. If she had half a mind to, Quinn could make men crawl after her, hoping for a crumb of affection.

But Quinn seemed oblivious to her own reflection.

Which was probably a good thing.

Silas roused himself to fix a stern look her way. "All right. Spit it out. What's so important that you had to stalk my hotel room?"

"Well, I don't have your phone number so I really had no choice," she said as if that made perfect sense. "But I agree that it's really not efficient to stalk you when I need to talk so we should exchange phone numbers."

Silas hesitated. Did he want Quinn having the ability to call him at all hours? Yeah, he kinda did. He'd examine that motivation later.

"Fine. But this is just for business. Don't go calling me to chat."

Quinn fixed him with an incredulous look. "Like I would call you for some scintillating conversation. You, my friend, are the poster boy for dull."

Dull? He was a Kelly. *Dull* was not a word used to describe them.

"I'll try to be more entertaining," he retorted. "Now, out with the intel or you're back in the rain."

"Right," she said, excited. "Get ready for a doozy... I can barely keep this to myself."

Silas gestured impatiently.

"Rhia was pregnant."

Silas regarded Quinn with a frown. "How do you know this?"

"I am not at liberty to reveal my sources, but let's just say that the person who may have *inadvertently* revealed this information may not have known that I gained access to it."

"You stole it."

"When something is lying in plain sight on someone's desk, it's not stealing."

"It's a credible source?"

"If you consider the coroner's office a credible source."

Yeah, that was pretty credible.

He had to admit, this was good intel.

"You can bet her parents didn't know." A thought occurred to Quinn. "What if the father is some bigwig in town and he murdered Rhia because he didn't want to get caught?"

"Or maybe she just had a boyfriend on the side," Silas countered, playing devil's advocate. "But I agree it warrants a second look."

Her pleased smile played with his insides. A flutter of unwanted pleasure danced through him. Her smile could light up Martin stadium.

"Don't get too excited. It could lead nowhere," Silas said, trying to remain realistic. "So what's your agenda for bringing me this intel?"

"So suspicious," she said but her grin was filled with mischief. "Okay, you got me. I do want something."

"Spit it out."

"I want you to work with me. Give me access to exclusive content so I can break the story, whatever that may be."

Back to that argument again. "It goes against my personal values to make deals with press."

"C'mon, Silas. You can't honestly be this rigid. If you pull that stick out of your ass for just a minute, you might find you can relax a little."

"Is this your idea of driving a hard bargain? I've yet to hear why I shouldn't just run with your lead and leave you out."

"Because you have more integrity than that."

"You don't know me."

"It's something I can sense," Quinn said. This time she wasn't joking or playing around. This was probably the first time Silas had seen her completely serious. That turn was intensely arousing. It was easy to keep her at arm's length when he saw her as an irritating kid. But when he saw her as an adult…it changed things.

"You could get hurt. The person who did this could be hiding in plain sight and we wouldn't know if you were in danger until it was too late. I don't want to take that chance."

"I'm not asking you to be my bodyguard," she said, stubbornly refusing to back down. "I'm asking you to stop stonewalling me. We can help each other. It's no secret I want out of this town. I want to make something of myself. I want to be more than just Quinn Jackson, that spunky niece of Leo Jackson, the town photographer. I want my life to be more than what others think it should be. I won't be able to do that until I leave this place."

"What makes you think that writing about this tragedy is going to do that?"

"Maybe it won't. But it's the best shot I have of writing something that matters. Something I can send to other newspapers for writing samples. I have to try."

Silas could respect her ambition, even if she got in his way at times.

"Look, I can appreciate your desire to make more of yourself—and hell, I can even respect your tenacity—but I can't willingly do something that could put a civilian in danger. I could lose my job."

"I'm not asking you to break rules…just don't deliberately keep me out. I wouldn't reveal that you were my source anyway."

"That's not how I operate."

"C'mon, Silas…you can't tell me you've never bent the

rules before. We can help each other. I can get access to things that you might need a warrant for otherwise."

"True, but the problem with unlawfully gained evidence is that it's inadmissible in court. I'd rather go the legal route for a better outcome."

She stomped her foot in frustration, an action that should've been annoying but he found ridiculously endearing. The urge to smile took him by surprise. He was slipping further and further down a wet slope, which wasn't like him.

"Sorry. I can't help you. But I appreciate the intel on Rhia."

"That's it? Wham-bam, thank you, ma'am?" Quinn asked, frowning. "You're willing to chase down my lead but you're not willing to give me something in return. Real classy, Silas. Real classy."

"I never asked you to bring me leads. I would've found out about Rhia tomorrow but I do appreciate the heads-up."

Quinn huffed, casting Silas a sour look. "I'll remember this when you're looking for help and I give you the cold shoulder. Quid pro quo and all that."

Silas walked Quinn to the door and once she was safely on the other side he gratefully closed and locked it.

There were too many things going around in his mind at once.

Quinn had undoubtedly dropped some good intel in his lap. It was true that the coroner would probably share the same information tomorrow but it helped to have a heads-up.

Of course, the biggest question was, who was the father? Was Quinn correct in her assumption that Rhia had been killed by a man trying to keep a secret?

It also opened up a whole new can of worms. Rhia's family thought their daughter had been a saint. It was going to break their hearts even further to find out that Rhia had bigger secrets than they could've imagined.

Silas was accustomed to being the bearer of bad tidings; it was a role he knew well.

But it never got any easier.

Unbelievable. What a jerk.

Quinn had gambled giving Silas that information. She'd been pretty sure that if she could prove that she was useful he would've had no choice but to include her in his investigation.

The joke was on her, because Silas obviously had no integrity.

Okay, maybe he had *integrity*. The reason he wasn't letting her into the investigation, or so he said, was to protect her but she sensed that wasn't the only reason.

And, maybe she was crazy, but there may have been a brief moment when she thought for sure she saw a spark in Silas's gaze that suggested something far more personal was going on behind those dark eyes.

How did she feel about that?

She wasn't sure.

The thing was, she didn't have the option of getting involved with someone like Silas. She had goals, dreams, huge ambition, all of which did not include hooking up with a rigid FBI agent.

But then sometimes things happened without our express intention, right?

Maybe she was trying to justify the fact that when she saw him, there was a faint tickle in the pit of her belly.

So sue me, he's cute.

Cute in a stiff I-always-play-by-the-rules, I-probably-report-pennies-picked-up-on-the-sidewalk-on-my-taxes kind of way.

And just as she'd feared, in the brief moments when he smiled, he was actually quite handsome.

Pearl-white teeth, the sensual smile, the shock of dark hair that made Quinn want to run her fingers through it—yeah, he was good-looking.

But that's beside the point.

Silas had punted her idea of working together so far across the field, it was in another stadium.

And that'd hurt her feelings, pricked her pride and pissed her off.

What was his deal with reporters? Everyone had to make a living, right?

What made him so hateful?

Quinn walked into the house and found her uncle Leo sitting in his recliner quietly working on a crossword by the light of his small lamp and firelight.

She dutifully kissed him on the cheek and then flopped into the chair beside him. "I don't understand men," she said without preamble then immediately clarified perhaps for her own benefit, saying, "No, I don't understand men like Silas Kelly."

Quinn wasn't sure if she was asking for advice, per se, but her uncle had always been good for a listen at the very least and she needed to vent.

Usually Leo just nodded and let her blow steam but tonight he seemed of a mind to offer his own brand of wisdom. "What do you care what Silas Kelly is all about?" Leo asked with a frown. "He's much too old for you anyway."

"He's not that much older. A handful of years," she disagreed, but that wasn't the point and said as much. "Besides, I'm not looking to date him. I just don't understand why he hates reporters so much. I mean, he looks at me like I'm vermin."

Well, not every time. Sometimes Quinn caught him looking at her in a way that made the butterflies in her stomach triple in count. But the moments were brief—so brief that sometimes that she wondered if she'd imagined them.

"I mean, I know it probably has something to do with his brother's death but why does he take it out on me? I wasn't a reporter when Spencer died."

Leo sighed, placing his crossword on the small nightstand beside his chair. "I wouldn't worry yourself about Silas Kelly. Soon enough he'll leave again and everything will go back to normal."

That's exactly what she *didn't* want. She didn't want normal. She wanted something new, something that challenged the status quo.

Leo continued, "As far as I'm concerned, I think it's an insult to our officers that he's here poking around at all."

"An insult? Only an idiot would pass up the opportunity to work with someone with Silas's experience," she disagreed.

"Honey, all he's doing is stirring up trouble. Look how he's ruffled your feathers," he teased.

But Quinn wasn't in the mood to be placated. "Even if Silas leaves, it doesn't erase the fact that a young girl was murdered. Rhia deserves justice."

"Of course, of course," Leo agreed quickly. "And I'm sure Lester will do his best to solve this terrible crime. But the fact is bad things happen to good people and sometimes we never know why. There's no rhyme or reason as to why it happens. We just have to trust that we are living our lives in the best way possible and pray for the families involved."

Prayer? Yeah, that worked. "Sorry, not a huge fan of 'prayer is the only answer.' Prayer isn't going to bring Rhia back."

Leo leveled a look her way that he reserved for when

she was being a pill. "You're in a fine mood. Have you eaten? You always get crotchety when you haven't eaten."

It was true; she tended to get "hangry." But she didn't want to eat. She wanted people to stop looking at her like she was still a kid. She wanted Silas to treat her like a peer. She wanted everyone else in this town to realize that she was meant for bigger things and stop stonewalling her.

The worst part was that she had no freaking clue how to make any of those things happen. It was as if she didn't know the secret handshake and everyone else was determined to keep that information from her.

"I think I'll just go to bed."

"It breaks my heart that you're taking this case so hard," Leo said. "I know you want to be this big shot reporter and I think you have the writing chops to do it. However, maybe you should think about what the cost of your ambition could be."

"What do you mean?"

"Sweetheart, you're a nice girl. Investigative reporting takes a certain type of personality and I just don't think you have it. You're charming and sweet and kind and generous. None of those qualities lend themselves to the career that you're chasing. And frankly, it worries me when I think of you putting yourself in dangerous positions just to get a story. Let someone else do that kind of work."

Quinn didn't know whether to be angry or understanding. On one hand she knew that her uncle's words came from the heart. On the other, he was the one person she'd expected to understand and support her no matter what.

A bubble of hot words danced on her tongue as frustration welled under her breastbone.

Her uncle Leo was a good man and had always been in her corner but right now she wanted to tell him to shove his poor opinion.

Instead, she managed a curt, "I think I'll just go to bed. I'll see you in the morning."

Before Leo could say anything else, Quinn escaped.

She leaned against her bedroom door, allowing a moment to wallow in her own pity party created by the day's turn of events. She'd been on a high when she'd discovered the coroner's report.

But when Silas hadn't reacted the way that she thought he would, followed by her uncle's opinion on her career choice, she just wanted the day to end.

Tomorrow was a new day.

She'd think of a solution.

I'll find a way to get Silas to trust me, she vowed to herself.

And if she couldn't do that, she would find a different way to break the case open because it was her ticket out.

Anyone who thought otherwise could stick their opinion where the sun didn't shine.

Including Uncle Leo.

Tomorrow she would do whatever it took to put herself back on track.

Quinn crawled into her bed and pulled the covers over her head.

Chapter 9

Silas walked into Sheriff Mankins's office to find the man sitting at his desk, staring at his wall of accomplishments, his expression weary and bleak.

Lester acknowledged Silas with a subtle grunt but didn't seem ready for a full conversation.

"You've read the coroner's report," Silas guessed.

Lester exhaled as he swore softly under his breath. "Yeah," he answered, his tone heavy. "What the hell am I going to tell those grieving parents? This is going to destroy them. They're barely hanging on as it is."

"May I speak frankly?"

"Nothing is stopping you."

Silas took a breath. "Let me help you with this investigation. Let's be honest. Your staff isn't trained for something like this. I can help you catch whoever did this."

That seemed to rouse the sheriff. "My staff can handle this case just fine," he disagreed with a little salt in his tone. "Just because you're FBI doesn't mean you're any more qualified than my deputies to solve this case."

"I don't want to step on toes. But you're already overwhelmed by this case. The truth is…you and I both know that you should've retired a while ago."

"You always were a little shit," Lester said, shaking his head as if amazed not much had changed. "So what do you think you can do better than we can?"

Silas had to tread cautiously. He was going directly against Oppenshaw's instructions but he couldn't stop himself. He wasn't going to take the chance that Rhia's case was bungled like Spencer's.

Especially seeing as if there was even a remote possibility that the two cases were related, he wasn't going to lose this opportunity to finally get justice for his brother.

"I handle cases like this every day. It's what I do. I don't have the personal connections that you do to this town. You're going to hesitate to ask the hard questions. I can be the bad guy and you've got no blood on your hands. I'll shoulder that burden for you."

Lester narrowed his gaze but didn't shut Silas down, which seemed like a good sign.

"You and I both know that we're going to have to find the baby's father to see if he had motive to kill Rhia. In order to do that, we need to start poking a little harder at soft spots. You want to do that?"

"God, no," Lester admitted.

"Then let me. I don't care if no one wants me on their Christmas list. What matters is finding this son of a bitch before he can do this to someone else's child."

"Do you really think it could be someone here?"

"Statistically…the numbers say yes. Emotionally, I would love to be able to tell you it was a stranger passing through. But nine times out of ten…the victim knew their attacker."

Lester rubbed at his forehead as if trying to massage away the pain squeezing his brain. "What's happening to my little town?"

"What happens everywhere eventually," Silas answered. "Port Orion had a good run but there's a killer hiding in this town and I aim to catch him."

"It used to be that you could sleep with your doors unlocked and not waste a minute worrying that someone might walk in uninvited. Now…that's not the case."

"Times have changed," Silas agreed, sensing that Lester's nostalgia was a sign that he was ready to let Silas in. A beat of heavy silence passed between them until Lester drew himself up to meet Silas's gaze.

"You think you can catch this bastard?"

"I do," Silas answered without hesitation. He'd been waiting a lifetime to do this—he wouldn't fail. "I won't let you down."

Lester nodded but Silas knew the old man's pride was a bit bruised. However, Lester, at his heart, was a good cop and he'd do what needed to be done to get results.

"I'll let the department know that you have full run of our resources. No one will get in your way."

"Thank you, Lester. You won't regret it."

"That remains to be seen."

Silas understood Lester's cryptic answer. They both knew that it was possible the killer was someone he saw every day, smiled at, chatted with, shared coffee with… hell, it could be anyone at all.

Because the one thing that Silas had learned in his career was that people with secrets to hide became experts at hiding their secrets.

Quinn sat with her best friend Johnna Silverton at the bar. She hadn't wanted to come but Johnna had played the guilt card, saying Quinn had been dodging her calls since this case had blown up and because it was true, Quinn had no defense.

"Okay, the word on the street is that an ultra-hot detective guy is in town working this case. What do you know about him?" Johnna asked, hungry for details.

"He's not a detective, he's FBI," Quinn clarified, toying with the tiny straw in her gin and tonic. "His name is Silas Kelly and I guess his family used to live here."

"Kelly… I know that name…wait a minute…wasn't there a kid who died years ago named Kelly?"

"Yeah, it was his little brother, Spencer. I guess the murder was never solved, either. Tore the family apart. They moved after Silas graduated high school."

"I thought I recognized the name. How scandalous. So, what's he doing here?"

"He's trying to see if there are any connections to his brother's case."

"That's a stretch, don't you think?"

Quinn shrugged. "It's his dime, not mine."

"Well, from what I hear…he's a hottie. So you've seen him?"

"Of course," Quinn said, mildly annoyed at how interested Johnna was in Silas. But then Johnna loved a fresh challenge when it came to men. The minute Quinn thought of Johnna setting her sights on Silas, her hackles rose. Not a good sign. "He's all right," she lied, trying to throw Johnna off the scent. "I mean, he's pretty stiff. The man doesn't have a funny bone in his body. He's one hundred percent the job. He probably sleeps in his suit."

Johnna frowned at first but then her expression turned sly. "Maybe he just needs someone to show him how to loosen up?"

"Do yourself a favor and steer clear. He's no fun at all. I brought him good intel and did he thank me for my troubles? No. He took the information and then shoved me out the door. I'm telling you, he has zero manners."

"What intel did you give him?"

Quinn hesitated. "I really shouldn't say. It's not common knowledge and it's kind of a big deal to this case."

"And how did you get it?"

Quinn smiled angelically. "I can't reveal my sources."

Johnna rolled her eyes. "Talk about someone who takes herself too seriously. I mean, c'mon, Quinn…this is the hometown rag we're talking about. We're not talking the *New York Times*."

That stung. She hated when people said things like that. Quinn took pride in her job and it pinched when her hard work was so easily dismissed.

"Well, that's why I'm trying to build a good portfolio so I can go somewhere where my work will matter."

Johnna winced, immediately contrite. "I'm sorry, Quinnie. I didn't mean it like that. I just… I don't know, I guess I never really thought you were serious about this whole reporter gig."

"I'm very serious."

"Oh."

Man, she was in a cranky mood. Her conversation with Silas was still sitting wrong. Not to mention the comments her Uncle Leo had said and now her best friend. Did the entire town think she was a joke?

"Did you know Rhia?" Quinn asked, switching tracks.

Relieved to change the subject, Johnna answered, "Not really. I mean, just from what I read in the media. She seemed like a good kid. I can't imagine why anyone would want to hurt her."

"What if she wasn't as good as people thought?"

"What do you mean?"

"I mean, what if she had some dark secrets?"

Johnna frowned. "She was a kid. How dark could her secrets be?"

"Maybe she was like Laura Palmer."

"Who?"

"You know, Laura Palmer from that show *Twin Peaks*."

Johnna rolled her eyes in annoyance. "You and the obscure television references. Okay, I'll bite. What was Laura Palmer like?"

"She seemed this Goody Two-shoes. Everyone liked her. The town darling. But as it turned out, she was sleeping with everyone under the sun, including her own father. But to be fair, when she was sleeping with her father he was actually some kind of other dimensional demon or something, I don't know. It gets fuzzy after that. But the point being…not everyone is as they seem."

"Are you saying that you think Rhia was sleeping with her own father?"

"God, no. At least I hope not. But strange crap happens. The fact remains that she wasn't as innocent as everyone thought. I think it's safe to say that we have to open any door that might lead to her killer."

"Who is this 'we?'" Johnna asked with concern. "What are you up to?"

"I told you I was serious about breaking open this case. It's my ticket out of here and I'm not going to waste it."

"Whoa, whoa. Hold on. How are *you* supposed to break this case? For goodness' sake, Quinn…you're a small-town reporter. Don't you think you ought to let the professionals deal with this?"

"I *am* a professional. And you know what? I'm the only one not afraid to peek into dark corners. No one wants to accept that Rhia wasn't the perfect princess because it'll shed light on the dirt people in this town have been sweeping under the rug for decades."

Johnna wasn't convinced but Quinn wasn't looking for validation.

"Doesn't it bother you that a killer is walking the streets of Port Orion?"

"Of course it does. But there's also the likely possibility that it was a drifter who is long gone by now."

"That's the easy answer, but my gut says…the killer is someone we all know. And I want justice for Rhia."

"Do you really want justice or do you just want to use the situation to your advantage?"

"Why can't I want both?"

Johnna sighed. "I don't want to be a jerk but I'm kinda worried about your decision-making skills right now. I've never seen you so obsessed with something."

"I'm not obsessed—I'm focused on a goal. There's a difference."

"Not from where I'm standing."

Quinn was getting nowhere with Johnna. Why was everyone so stuck in their small-town narrow-minded thought process? Didn't anyone see what Quinn did?

She didn't want to be there. Her heart was elsewhere but she couldn't bail on Johnna now even as she wanted to pay the tab and go home.

Already moving on, Johnna was ready to hit the dance floor. In that moment she realized how much she and Johnna had changed in the last year. Whereas Quinn had been focused on building a good portfolio, Johnna had focused on a good time, wherever that may be.

Johnna had simple goals in life. Meet a guy, settle down, have a few kids.

Quinn couldn't imagine falling into that pattern.

She thought of Silas, how he was a top agent in the FBI and stoic as hell even in the face of terrible circumstances. Even if he hadn't been a "hottie" as Johnna called him, Quinn would've been drawn to Silas's shrewd intelligence.

It was arousing to be around someone whose mind wasn't caged by their environment.

Maybe she ought to stop denying that she was attracted to him.

It took too much energy to fight what was growing between them when they could be spending that precious energy on finding the killer.

And if her instincts were correct, Silas was attracted to her, too.

She sensed his interest, even if he was in denial.

As if summoned by her inner demons, Silas walked into the bar. He was out of his austere FBI garb and dressed like a local—worn jeans, a flannel shirt over a T-shirt and he was looking like fresh meat to every sharp-eyed woman over the age of twenty-one.

"Oh my God, is that him?" Johnna squealed, gripping Quinn's arm painfully. "He is gorgeous."

"He's off-limits," Quinn said a little too sharply.

Johnna caught the snip in Quinn's tone and gave her a quizzical look. "Is there something between you two?"

"No, of course not," Quinn said, freshly irritated by the turn of events. "I just don't want my best friend mucking with the one person in this town capable of helping me break this case."

Johnna pouted but agreed to keep her distance. "Oh, fine. Donnie is here anyway. He's always available for a few drinks and a good time. Are you okay?"

"Yeah, go ahead. I'll probably head home early."

"Okay." Johnna was disappointed but good ol' Donnie was already front and center in Johnna's sights and Quinn was glad. Likely those two would eventually marry but for the time being Johnna enjoyed stringing Donnie along, flitting from one good time to another.

Quinn loved Johnna but they were on two separate paths and that had never been more apparent than tonight.

Winding her way past the clot of people, she found Silas drinking a beer by himself, reading a report.

"You bring your work to the bar."

Silas looked up and offered a small smile. "Helps me think. The silence of a hotel room is distracting."

She gestured to the seat next to him. "May I?"

"Are you sure that's a good idea?"

"Why wouldn't it be?"

"People might get the wrong impression. You know how small towns are."

"I don't care what people think."

That seemed to impress him. Maybe the key to Silas wasn't her usual schtick. Flirting and being charming had always opened doors for her. Silas was a different breed. She respected that about him.

Silas scooted over and made room for her. Quinn waved over the waitress and ordered a beer, as well. "I like to work at the diner. The white noise of people is relaxing to me," she shared.

"You here with friends?"

"My best friend, Johnna." Quinn pointed discreetly toward Johnna slow-dancing with Donnie, all cuddled up and looking happy. "But I think she's going to go home with her dance partner."

"Did you come together?"

"Yeah," Quinn answered but shrugged it off. "I can get a ride home. It's not a big deal."

But Silas didn't seem satisfied with that answer. "Need I remind you there's a killer on the loose?"

"I'm hardly his demographic," Quinn returned drily. "Besides, I'm not worried. I'll be fine. It's not the first time Johnna has ditched me and left me to find a way home."

"She doesn't sound like a very good friend."

"Oh, don't get me wrong, she's an awesome person but she knows I'm safe. She would never leave me someplace dangerous." Quinn paused a minute then ventured, "Are you working the case?"

"Brushing up on my brother's case."

"Doesn't that…hurt?"

"It would if I didn't shut off that part of my brain. I look at the case notes clinically. If I let emotion cloud my judgment I might miss something important."

"How do you do that? Just shut off your emotions like a robot?"

"A defense mechanism, I suppose. If I didn't shut off certain parts of my brain, I'd lose my mind with all the terrible things I see every day. The world is a dangerous place, filled with nut jobs."

"You ought to write travel brochures because that's pretty catchy."

Quinn caught a rare smile, sending a flutter of butterfly wings to tickle her stomach.

"You're unlike anyone I've ever met," she ventured, trying for a bit of honesty between them.

"I would say the same for you."

This time she smiled. Maybe she'd been going about this situation all wrong with Silas. He didn't respond to flattery or flirty behavior, which only made her respect him more. Silas was the kind of person who appreciated someone who worked as hard as him and didn't mess around.

And that was an incredible turn-on.

Chapter 10

Silas knew he should've packed up and left the moment he saw Quinn from across the bar.

He'd seen her before she'd seen him.

Wearing tight jeans and a light, form-fitting blouse with boots, she looked far different than he was used to seeing her.

He'd like to say he was immune to the charms of a beautiful woman but Quinn was something else entirely.

Beyond beautiful. Hell, that word seemed inadequate when used to describe the redhead.

And he had no business looking twice.

So when he remained where he was and allowed her to sit beside him, he knew he was screwing up.

Big time.

But that didn't stop him.

Quinn smelled like the outdoors after a hard rain—wild and untamed.

Clean.

He liked that she didn't drown herself in perfumes that always made him sneeze.

Silas also liked the fact that she wore very little makeup. A light application of mascara and a dab of lip gloss was all she needed.

"So do you come here often?" he asked then chuckled when he realized how cheesy his comment had sounded.

She laughed and took a swig of her beer. "Not so often. But it's really the only place to come and blow off steam. The town doesn't have much in the way of entertainment, as well you probably remember."

"I remember."

He remembered prowling the streets, pissed off at the world, too young to drink legally, and nowhere near mature enough to handle the grief and guilt that fueled him those days. His brothers had moved as soon as they graduated.

He'd wanted to move, too, but his parents had felt it important for him to finish high school in Port Orion, a closing of a chapter.

Silas hadn't agreed. He'd been ready to bail the moment his brothers had announced they were going away for college.

His parents' marriage was already falling apart, being held together by duct tape and financial commitments. Silas hadn't seen the point of dragging out the inevitable.

But then Lester got a hold of him. Showed him how to channel his grief into something constructive.

So that he could get through his high school years without committing a felony.

Otherwise... Silas didn't know where he'd be at today.

"I know you said you're not interested in working together and I respect your decision. However, I'm not going to stop looking on my own."

"This case is dangerous," Silas warned, not liking the idea of Quinn going off on her own, poking around without any clue as to how she might be putting herself at risk. "Why are you so determined to put yourself in harm's way?"

"I'm not, but I am determined to see this through. You have to understand...no one takes me serious here. Not even my closest friend and my only living relative. Until I get out of Port Orion, I'll always be that kid with impossibly big dreams and no sense of reality. I'm more than that and I'm going to prove it."

Silas could respect her position. Hell, he knew the frustration of being crammed into someone else's perception. He couldn't fault her for aggressively going after what she needed to excel.

He grudgingly found her grit compelling.

"You realize that breaking open this case will blow apart lives," he told her. "No matter what, when this ends, Port Orion will never be the same."

"Maybe that's a good thing."

He regarded her intently. "You sure about that?"

Quinn shrugged. "Only one way to find out."

He chuckled at her steadfast answer. "True enough, but are you ready for what might shake out? It might not be pretty."

"Yeah," she said with a slow nod and he believed her. Quinn wasn't backing down. "So...are you going to work with me or not?"

Silas's position hadn't changed but there was a subtle shift in his opinion about Quinn. He didn't want her poking around and putting herself in unnecessary danger but then he didn't want to handfeed the press juicy tidbits about the case, either.

"You put me in a difficult position," he said.

"That's life, right?"

He appraised her openly. "Where was this woman when we first met?"

"I'll be honest, I use my charm to get my way. When I realized you don't respond to charm, I went with brutal honesty. If I'm reading you right…that was a good call."

Silas smiled. "You're good at reading people." A skill that could be honed with the right training. "All right, here's the deal—you can tag along, but before you publish anything, I need to see what you're writing first."

Quinn laughed as if his request was absurd. "Would you ask a *New York Times* reporter to do that? And the answer is no. You'll have to trust that I won't release sensitive information."

Trust a reporter? "You might as well ask me to rope the moon. I don't trust any reporter."

"And why is that?"

"Because reporters, in my experience, don't give a shit about anything but their story."

"Not all reporters are like that."

"But most are."

"We'll agree to disagree. But even if that's the case, I'm not asking you to trust all the reporters in the world… I'm asking you to trust me."

"I don't know you. Why should I trust you?"

"Because like me, I suspect you're a good judge of character and you can read people. Look me in the eye and tell me whether or not I'm a trustworthy person."

Silas didn't want to stare into her eyes. He was afraid of what else he'd feel. Quinn was quickly getting under his skin and the sensation wasn't entirely unwelcome, but it was certainly ill-advised.

But she made a good point. He was painting with a wide brush.

"The reporter who wrote about Spencer's case…she revealed information that collapsed the case. Any chance investigators might've had to catch who had killed my brother was destroyed."

"How so? I've read the archived articles. The stories were pretty bland."

"It wasn't in the official newspaper. At the time the reporter had a personal blog. She inserted her opinions on what had happened, but revealed sensitive case information to bolster her claims."

"That's unprofessional," Quinn murmured with disappointment. "I can see how you would hate reporters after that."

"Yeah, it wasn't easy to deal with. But honestly, from my experience reporters are usually cut from the same cloth. They all trample over whoever they need to to get the story."

"That's not exactly true, but if that's all you've been exposed to, then I guess in your world, it is true."

It was a surprisingly mature statement from one so young. He wasn't ready to hand her the keys to the castle, but he realized that he might've judged quickly and harshly.

"Do you have any insight as to who might've gotten Rhia Daniels pregnant?" he asked.

"I don't. But I aim to find out."

"And by that statement, you're implying with or without my help," he said, to which Quinn nodded. He exhaled a short breath, impressed by her chutzpah even if it did put him in a difficult spot. "All right. We'll do this on a trial basis, only because I don't want you getting yourself into a mess. Whoever did this…they aren't going to welcome the two of us poking around."

"Fair enough," Quinn said with a bright grin that smacked of victory. "Let's head back to your hotel. We need a game plan."

Silas knew better than to agree to that plan.

Strange things were afoot. Had he just agreed to work

with a reporter? And now he was contemplating letting her into his hotel room to discuss confidential materials?

Best to decline.

Be smart.

But for reasons he chose not to examine...he ignored his better judgment, grabbed his jacket and said, "Let's get out of here, then."

Quinn felt giddy. Getting Silas to agree to work with her was a huge win and even though she tried to keep her joy under wraps, it seeped out in the form of a silly smile.

Silas opened his hotel room and flicked the lights as he removed his jacket. "Are you going to smile at me all night like that? It's distracting."

Quinn pressed her lips together but then decided against smothering her smile. "Deal with it. It's not every day I managed to convince a hardened FBI agent to listen to reason."

He surprised her with a laugh. "Hardened? I wouldn't say I'm hardened."

"No? Well, you do a pretty fair impression."

"Just because I don't try charming information out of people doesn't mean I'm not a nice person."

"Oh, I don't mean to imply that you're not nice. You're just...stoic. That's the word I would use to describe you. Everything about you is hard and unyielding. Like a giant oak tree."

"A tree."

"Yeah. But that's not a bad thing. Trees are strong. I like that about you."

It was a small admission but it seemed to suck the air from the room. She swallowed and risked a nervous laugh to dispel the sudden tension. "Anyway...so should we talk about the case?"

Silas seemed slow to respond but when he did, he shook

his head as if clearing cobwebs. "Yeah, the case." He gestured to the small table and they both took seats opposite each other but because the table was short on real estate, they were practically in each other's bubble.

As in...she could smell his skin beneath his T-shirt, could see the dark hairs along his forearm, which made her wonder...was his chest full of dark, wiry hair or was it smooth as a baby's behind?

Quinn's breath shortened and she pulled back to put some space between them.

"Okay, so here's what I'm thinking...we need to talk to Rhia's friends. Teenagers rarely tell their parents anything that's going on and given how conservative Rhia's parents are, it's a safe bet that they didn't have a clue as to who their daughter really was. That leaves the friends and frenemies."

"Frenemies?"

"Oh yeah, people who are surface friends but behind your back they talk shit about you."

"Why would anyone want a frenemy?" Silas asked, perplexed.

Quinn shrugged. "Women are complex. But I will say, we will probably get better intel from the frenemy than the actual friends because the friends will try to protect whatever secrets Rhia was hiding."

"I have to talk to the parents tomorrow morning. Give them the news about Rhia's pregnancy. Chances are they were clueless but sometimes parents know more than they let on."

"Okay, you talk to the parents. I'll find the friends and frenemies. We'll report back here to share our findings."

"And what will you do with that information?" he asked.

"That's for me to decide."

"I'm not comfortable with this."

She thought to reassure him but when she impulsively

placed her hand on his, the electricity that snapped between them had her jerk away as if she'd been scalded.

"I'm sorry... I'm a touchy-feely person," Quinn mumbled, biting her lip, embarrassed by her reaction. "I didn't mean to invade your space."

She expected him to shrug it off so they could move away from the awkward exchange but when he simply said, "I wasn't complaining," her pulse jumped a little.

The tension between them was growing by the second. She was aware of his body in ways that engulfed her ability to stay focused.

Quinn searched desperately for something to put her back on track before she did something incredibly stupid such as close the short distance between them and kiss the man.

"Maybe we could find Sara Westfall and ask her some questions about her theories on your brother's case," she suggested.

But Silas shut that idea down quickly. "She died six months after Spencer."

"What?"

"It was a freak accident. She was driving late one night, overcorrected on a turn, hit the guardrail and went over the side. She was killed instantly."

"That's crazy. What bad luck," Quinn said, thinking. Something about that tidbit of info sat wrong. "You don't think it's a little suspicious that the reporter who was writing independently about Spencer's murder conveniently died a few months later?"

"Coincidence, probably."

"Or...what if it wasn't?"

"Your little mind is full of conspiracy theories, isn't it?" he teased, but Quinn could tell his mind was working all the angles just as quickly as her own. "Let's just say for argument's sake, Sara Westfall had inadvertently stumbled on something...it would be in her blog. But that was years ago. Likely the blog has been taken down by now."

"Right. But nothing is truly gone on the internet. However, let's go the easiest route first. Talk to her family. Maybe they still have the original computer and if that's the case...all it'll take is some forensic computer work to recover the files."

"And do you know someone who could recover files? Because if I send a computer back to the Bureau for analysis, it'll take weeks before we get an answer."

"Actually, I can do it myself. Amateur hacking was a hobby of mine until I discovered the bug for writing. So be thankful I didn't go the criminal route because I was pretty good."

Silas laughed. "You constantly shock me. Next are you going to tell me you're secretly part of a hush-hush government group that flies under the radar looking for aliens?"

"Please. Like I would work for the government."

Laughing with Silas came easily. He enjoyed her dry wit and she got a tickle each time he dropped his guard a little further.

Silas was the challenge she'd been craving but Quinn knew better than to cross the line.

Even as much as she wanted to.

"Are you single?" Quinn asked abruptly. She hadn't meant to go there but the words had jumped from her mouth and now it was too late to reel them back.

"Yes."

I knew it! Score one for female intuition. Now for the bigger question...

"Why?"

Silas leaned forward. "Why do you want to know?"

"Because I'm attracted to you," she answered bluntly. Why lie? He seemed to appreciate her honesty thus far. "And I don't mess around with people in relationships."

"Very single," he said, his gaze drifting to her parted lips. "And not looking to be in a relationship."

"Good. Neither am I." And then she threw caution to the wind and kissed him.

Because life was short and Johnna was right—Silas was hot.

Chapter 11

Bells and whistles warned him to pull away, to put some distance between his lips and Quinn's but damn, it would've taken more strength than he possessed at the moment to make that happen.

Kissing Quinn was like being zapped with a million tiny electrical impulses at once. His heart raced and his hands itched to slide up her arms to cup her face.

But he broke the kiss, drawing away with Herculean effort. Both their breaths were shallow; Quinn's pupils were dilated with desire, which probably mirrored his own but he couldn't let something as ephemeral as lust to get in the way.

"Quinn…"

"No, good call," she agreed breathlessly as she stood. "I don't know what I was thinking. Feel free to forget this ever happened. I'll see you tomorrow."

She was running away from her embarrassment. Silas caught Quinn before she opened the door and pulled her close. "It's not because I'm not interested," he clarified in a low tone, fighting the urge to explore every inch of that strong, vibrant body. "It's because this case is too important to screw up with rookie mistakes."

"Is it because I'm younger than you?" Quinn asked, her tone vulnerable.

"In the beginning…yes. But not now. Hell, Quinn, it's taking everything in me to be the better person and let you walk out that door without my hands all over your body. Does that sound like someone who isn't interested?"

Quinn worried her bottom lip with her teeth, her tongue darting. Silas suppressed a groan as his pants tightened.

"Everything about you excites me," she admitted. "You're unlike anyone I've ever met and it turns me on. I mean, I'm not stupid. I know it's not a good idea to mess around with you but you have no idea what it's like to be in a town where no one walks to the same beat as you. I sense we hear the same drum and that's hard to ignore."

"Do you always say what you mean?"

"With the right people."

He allowed a smile. "I like that."

"Good."

Silas's hands found her rounded ass. Pert and firm, he squeezed and drew her against his erection so she would suffer no doubt as to how much she turned him on, too.

"And what if I told you we both know this is a bad idea?"

"You think I can't be professional if we sleep together?" she parried, angling her head to give him better access to her pouting lips. "What if it's just about scratching an itch?"

"No-strings-attached sex?" he murmured, traveling along the column of her neck with tiny nips and kisses, causing her to shiver in his arms. "Are you capable of separating the physical from the emotional?"

Quinn gave a throaty laugh. "What makes you think I'll be the one with the problem? I should probably warn you…my lovers rarely tire of me first."

Ohhhh, a challenge he couldn't resist.

Silas kissed her hard, lifting her onto her toes, grinding the hard shaft in his jeans against her. Quinn clung to him, hopping into his arms to wrap her legs around his waist.

He dropped her to the bed and started to strip. The hungry light in her eyes as she unabashedly enjoyed the show was intensely sexy.

When he stepped out of his underwear, Quinn's gaze widened with open appreciation, which only made him swell harder.

Quinn shimmied out of her jeans and within seconds, they were both naked, skin against skin, forgetting about all the reasons why it was a bad idea to throw sex in the mix.

Silas sheathed himself in a condom—he never took chances—and Quinn took over from there, riding him with a skill that came from knowing how she liked to be touched.

Sweat beaded his brow as he neared his climax, even as he tried to hold back. But Quinn was merciless in her pursuit of her own pleasure. She was a wild thing, her moans filling the small room as she writhed against him.

Good God. Silas grit his teeth as he began to shake, the need to explode more than he could hold back.

But Quinn found her release as she stiffened, releasing her pent-up breath in a long exhale as she slumped forward over his chest, his name a sultry cry on her lips as she jerked with each wave of pleasure.

Silas gripped her hips and pumped hard into her clenching core, finding his own release in a wild explosion that stole his breath and stopped his heart for a brief moment.

He gasped as his pulse thundered, blood rushing to his ears.

Quinn slowly sat up, his shaft still firmly embedded in her hot folds, and smiled like a sated cat. "That itch has definitely been scratched," she said with a contented sigh.

And then she climbed off, stretching with a dainty moan as she pulled her panties back on and scooped up her bra.

Silas disposed of the condom and tossed the sheet over his exposed parts. He expected her to try and cuddle with him but when she seemed completely happy to dress and go, he sat a little straighter.

"Do you want to talk?" he ventured.

"About what? The case?"

"No...about what just happened."

She answered with an amused chuckle as she swung her purse over her shoulder, pausing at the door.

"I'll see you tomorrow morning. I'll bring a protein bar and smoothies."

And then she was gone.

Silas leaned against the headboard. That was...unexpected.

But not unwelcome.

The tension that'd been bunching his shoulders since stepping foot in Port Orion was gone.

Silas grabbed the blanket, plumped his pillow and closed his eyes.

His last thought before drifting off...he would've been down for just a little snuggling.

Quinn awoke the following morning and bounded from the bed. Too many thoughts crammed in her brain made it impossible to remain still.

She passed Uncle Leo in the kitchen as she wolfed down a bagel and cream cheese.

"There's a speed limit in here," Leo teased as he poured

himself some coffee. "Where are you going in such a hurry?"

"Just excited to go to work," Quinn answered, smiling. Leo's chagrined expression caused her to falter. "What's wrong?"

"I've been thinking about what I said the other day and I feel really bad for being a Debbie Downer. You should chase any dream that you see fit. It's not my place to suggest otherwise. I guess I just worry too much."

Leo's apology sparked immediate tears. Her uncle was her Achilles' heel. Although she tried to hide it, his opinion mattered.

"Uncle Leo, you don't need to apologize for caring too much," Quinn assured him, pushing back the tears. "I love that you care."

He smiled. "Well, thank you for indulging an old man. You're a good girl."

It was a simple, endearing statement but Quinn struggled with the implication. The thing was, as much as she adored her uncle, she was prepared to go to any length to get this story. She wasn't content to mimic what other reporters had figured out—Quinn wanted to break open this story and expose its guts.

And with that decision came the realization that her uncle Leo's view of her might change.

God, that hurt.

But she wasn't going to think about that right now.

"Love you." Quinn pressed a kiss to Leo's cheek and walked to her car, winding the scarf more tightly around her neck as a stiff wind picked up. A glance at the sky told her rain was coming, which meant if she didn't want to drown, she needed to get moving.

True to her word, she picked up smoothies and protein bars and then swung by Silas's hotel.

An immediate smile followed as she approached his

door, memories of last night fresh and vibrant. She could almost still smell him on her skin.

It was a scent she could get used to.

There was something so intensely virile and primal about Silas Kelly that made every other man seem lacking.

She took a moment to compose herself so she didn't walk into his room acting like a silly girl with a crush. Blowing out a quick breath, she squared her shoulders and knocked.

Silas opened the door, dressed and looking like the same stoic man who'd first brushed her off when he came to town, which worked for her.

If he'd opened the door, barely dressed, sporting a bedhead, she might've weakened and suggested another itch-scratching session.

But as it was, Silas seemed on the same page as her—which was a relief.

Quinn tossed the protein bar, which he caught handily. "Breakfast of champions," he said, ripping into the bar. "Is there kale in that smoothie?"

"Of course. And wheatgrass. There's enough greens in this smoothie to satisfy a horse."

"Excellent." Silas chugged his smoothie as efficiently as he did everything. He paused a minute to regard her with speculation. "Do we need to talk about…"

"Nope."

Silas jerked a short nod. "Good. Let's make a game plan, then. I think you ought to come with me to the parents' house. They seemed to relax more around you than me. Delivering bad news is never pleasant but sometimes you can soften the blow with support."

Quinn nodded, though the idea of being there when Silas informed Rhia's parents that their perfect daughter had been pregnant? Her skin crawled with anxiety but she'd do it, nonetheless.

"Afterward, we'll break off and you can talk to the friends and I'll swing by the coroner's office to see if there's any DNA evidence that might lead us to the father's identity."

"At six weeks along...it's possible Rhia didn't even know she was pregnant."

"Maybe. But doesn't change the fact that it could be motive."

Quinn agreed, a chill popping along her forearms. She rubbed at the gooseflesh, saying, "It's bad enough that a sixteen-year-old girl died, but knowing that she was pregnant...somehow makes it so much worse."

"It's the innocence of the unborn child," Silas said then grabbed his keys, ready to leave. "Let's go. Time is wasting."

Quinn and Silas broke off, agreeing to meet at the Danielses' home. Butterflies erupted in her stomach as she pulled into the driveway. There was no way this meeting was going to go well. Rhia's parents were ultra-conservative. Chances were they weren't going to believe the coroner's report because to acknowledge the facts was to admit that they hadn't known their daughter at all.

Be supportive, she reminded herself. That was her role right now. Silas would play bad cop, Quinn would be the gentle hand guiding them.

Silas shared a look with Quinn before they climbed the steps and rang the doorbell.

A moment later a worn and grief-stricken Mrs. Daniels opened the door, her eyes red-rimmed and swollen from, what Quinn would assume, was nights of crying.

"Yes?" Mrs. Daniels ventured, her voice hoarse.

"May we come in? We have some sensitive information about the case to share," Silas said.

The solemn tone of Silas's voice seemed to penetrate through the woman's haze and she slowly moved aside, clutching at her cardigan nervously. "Of course," she said, leading them into the drawing room where they'd talked previously.

"Is your husband here?" Silas asked gently. "He might want to be here, as well."

"Yes, yes, of course, I'll get him. Would you like something to drink?"

The woman was on autopilot. Quinn and Silas both declined and she shuffled from the room.

The couple returned and sat opposite Silas and Quinn, awaiting the news like the condemned awaited the executioner's ax.

Silas went first. "Mr. and Mrs. Daniels…was your daughter involved with anyone romantically?"

"We did not feel she was old enough to date," Mrs. Daniels answered staunchly. "And Rhia agreed. She wanted to focus on her studies."

Mr. Daniels's mouth tightened but he remained silent.

Quinn cringed privately. The news was going to go down like a cactus ball lozenge.

"The coroner's report came back with preliminary results. Although DNA won't be in for a few more days, the coroner has determined that Rhia was six weeks pregnant."

Violet Daniels blanched as her mouth worked without sound. Her husband's complexion turned as red as his wife's turned white. "What the hell are you talking about?" he demanded, his voice shaking. "Someone is wrong. The report is wrong. My girl wasn't loose."

Quinn tried not to take offense on Rhia's behalf. Just because the teen hadn't been a virgin didn't mean she was a slut. "Mr. Daniels, no one is implying that your daughter was…*promiscuous*. But it takes two to tango," she pointed out. "Rhia didn't get pregnant on her own."

Something that looked like possession flashed in Mr. Daniels's eyes, taking Quinn by surprise. What the hell?

Was she imagining what she'd seen? If Rhia's father was... *ewww*. She couldn't even finish the thought without bile rising in her throat.

Silas jumped in firmly. "The results aren't wrong. The remains of a pregnancy were evident in her womb. Your daughter was, indeed, pregnant."

"It doesn't mean she wasn't a good girl." Quinn tried offering a different perspective. "Maybe she fell in love and—"

"If Rhia was pregnant, someone did this to her against her will," Oliver Daniels said stiffly. "You don't know my daughter. She would never...she was very modest."

Violet moaned and collapsed against her husband, burying her face against his shoulder. "What is happening?" she cried and Quinn knew the poor woman's world was crumbling. "Our daughter...*pregnant*?"

"I want to know who is responsible and I want them to pay for what they've done," Oliver said, his voice trembling. "Someone is going to pay for sullying our girl."

"Mr. Daniels, we don't know that the father is to blame for her death but it's a good place to start asking questions. To your knowledge, was there anyone Rhia was close to? Anyone who might know who Rhia was seeing?"

"We already told you. Rhia wasn't old enough to date," the father answered bitterly. "Boys weren't even allowed at the house."

Quinn was starting to get a dour view of the Danielses' everyday living. In Quinn's experience, kids who were caged often went wild without their parents' knowledge.

Which seemed the case with Rhia.

"I thought Rhia told me everything," Violet mourned. "I feel as if you're speaking about a total stranger. Rhia was very close to her faith. She was a good girl who valued her relationship with God. She even took a purity vow.

How can I reconcile what you're saying with what I knew about my own daughter?"

Silas seemed to understand Violet's confusion, even sympathize, which privately awed Quinn with how gentle he became with grieving parents.

"Everyone has secrets," Quinn offered softly. "But Rhia loved you. Maybe she didn't want to disappoint you. And maybe she didn't even know herself that she was pregnant. It was very early in the pregnancy. Had Rhia seemed under the weather lately?"

Violet shook her head. "No. She seemed no different than she ever was. Bright, bubbly, smiling…" The woman choked up a bit before continuing, "Just a ray of sunshine wherever she went." Violet reached for her husband's hand. "And such a Daddy's girl. They were so close."

That icky feeling returned. Quinn fell silent, unable to manage a suitable response when her brain was throwing gross scenarios at her.

The fact was no kid was as perfect as Rhia Daniels seemed. The tragedy was that the more they learned about Rhia, the more Quinn got the feeling Rhia was hiding a lot more than an unexpected pregnancy.

A stone felt lodged in her gut for what she had to do next. Drawing a deep breath, Quinn said, "Mrs. Daniels, you know I have to write about this new discovery."

Violet's head snapped up with horror. "You can't write that. No. I forbid it."

Quinn wasn't going to point out that she didn't need Violet's permission to print the truth but she tried to soften the blow. "I can only imagine the pain you're going through but the news isn't going to stay quiet for long. I'd rather write the story and give Rhia some dignity than let an outsider splash the news all over without an ounce of sensitivity."

Violet's lip trembled. "What will people think if they find out...?"

"Hopefully, they'll be kind and be thankful that it wasn't their child who was found murdered," Silas answered firmly. "We want to find out what happened to Rhia but we can't do that if we shy away from potential leads that may make us uncomfortable. I'm asking you to be brave for Rhia's sake so we can get her the justice she deserves."

Oliver didn't seem ready to hear such a stark truth but Violet was wavering. In her eyes burned the light of a grieving mother who would do anything to find answers.

Quinn had never seen Violet Daniels in such a way. She'd always written her off as stuck in a time warp where women vacuumed in heels and had a martini at the ready for when the man of the house returned from work. Now Quinn wasn't so sure that she hadn't misjudged the woman's grit.

"I would start with Britain Almasey. She was Rhia's closest friend. If she was keeping any secrets, Britain probably knows."

Violet's information confirmed what Quinn had already supposed. She shared a look with Silas and they both knew it was best to let the Danielses process this new information privately.

Silas rose and Quinn followed his lead. "Thank you for your time. We'll be in touch," he said to the couple. Oliver barely registered Silas's comment but Violet nodded.

Once they were outside Quinn said, "I don't think Mr. Daniels is ready to face the music about Rhia but his wife seems to realize what's at stake."

"Fathers are usually the last to come around." Silas paused at his car to say, "You did pretty good in there. You continue to surprise me."

Quinn smothered the pleased smile that his praise

sparked. Instead, she said, "I'll see what I can shake out of Britain. Let me know if you find anything new from the DNA samples."

"Meet back at my hotel later?" he asked.

"Depends on what I find out from Britain."

Quinn left Silas to chew on that as she climbed into her own vehicle. Only until she was free and clear did she allow the smile to break free.

Was it a victory?

Of sorts.

But she wasn't sure if this was a game she ought to be playing.

Especially with Silas Kelly.

Chapter 12

It never got easier, telling parents bad news. But there was something about talking to the Danielses that made him flash back to when his parents had gotten the news about Spencer.

The tension in the house had been enough to choke a horse.

The tight expression on his dad's face mirrored the anxiety in his mom's. His parents were handfasted in their joint fear that the worst had happened to the baby in the family.

The subdued rap on the front door might as well have been a thunderous clap for the collective jump in the living room by every Kelly.

His dad opened the door and a deputy came in, immediately doffing his hat. The somber expression told the story.

His mom started crying right away and would've collapsed if it hadn't been for Sawyer being there to catch her.

Silas only caught bits and pieces of the conversation.

"A body's been found matching the description…" Which was followed by "…come down to the station to identify…" and Silas had heard enough.

Bolting from the living room, Silas ran to the bedroom he shared with Spencer and stared with growing horror at the realization that his annoying little brother was never going to walk through that door again.

Never bug Silas to let him play with his LEGOs.

Never whine to Mom that Silas was being mean.

Never look at Silas like he was a hero, in spite of the way Silas was always trying to ditch him.

In that moment he hadn't felt eleven—Silas had felt the burden of adulthood.

Tears burned behind his eyes at the painful memory. Jerking the wheel, he chewed up the shoulder and shoved the car in Park before grinding his fists into his eyeballs.

What had happened? Why hadn't Spencer made it home?

Why the hell hadn't he just let Spencer come with him?

The passage of time didn't dull the cut of unanswered questions. Silas kept those memories at bay for a reason. His stomach clenched as another wave of grief rolled over him, pressing him down as he gulped for air.

It didn't matter how many people tried telling him that Spencer's death wasn't his fault—he knew that to be false.

Spencer would be alive today if Silas hadn't been such a prick to him.

Silas often counseled parents to avoid dwelling on how their lost children may have suffered because it wouldn't bring them back.

But Silas never admitted that the nightmares would continue because he didn't know how to burden the already grieving parents with more reality.

Spencer haunted him and probably always would until he managed to find who had stubbed out his young life.

The crash of the ocean against the shore drew his gaze. Turbulent waters churned the surf as dark clouds crouched on the horizon, growing and spreading like a malevolent force aimed at destruction.

A drizzle had already started to pelt the car, sounding like tiny fingertips drumming on the roof.

His mother had turned to prayer when she'd been too lost to find herself but Silas knew there was no comfort waiting for him in the power of words.

Maybe he was still that pissed off eleven-year-old, angry at God for taking his little brother.

Maybe he always would be.

People don't realize that the hits keep coming when you lose someone. First, it's the initial shock of loss. Then it's the lingering pain of facing the practical concerns—the burial, the sifting through the personal items—that are worse.

His dad had handled packing up Spencer's things.

Quietly, efficiently...like a robot. The dull stare as Spencer's prized possessions were stuffed into a trash bag was more than Silas could bear.

And maybe it was his guilt but Silas felt his father's condemnation in every shuttered expression, every word not said.

Silas and his father had never recovered.

Sawyer's voice cut through his memories.

Sawyer had found him crying alone at his favorite hide-out, a tree deep in the woods behind their house.

Maybe Silas had planned to run away.

Maybe he just wanted someone to notice that he was gone, that he was dying inside but didn't dare share that pain because it was too damn selfish and even he knew it.

Sawyer didn't rip into him as Silas expected.

Instead, he climbed into the tree to perch beside him, their feet dangling.

"You got a plan?" he asked.

Sniffling, Silas shook his head.

"You always gotta have a plan, Silas."

It was sound advice.

"Do you hate me, too?" he choked out, miserable.

"Why would I hate you?"

He could barely get the words out. "Because it's my f-fault Spencer is g-gone."

"Don't be stupid, Silas. It's not your fault. It's—" he exhaled a deep breath "—it's just dumb bad luck. Spencer was at the wrong place at the right time. That's it. You had nothing to do with it."

"I should've stayed with h-him."

"True. But you didn't. How many times have me or Shaine shined you like you shined Spence? It's a brother thing. It's not your fault, do you hear me?"

Silas squeezed his eyes shut, his heart caving in but he jerked a short nod.

"C'mon, you're going to freeze out here." Sawyer jumped down and Silas followed.

Then Sawyer pulled him into his arms for a rough but tight embrace—something Sawyer had never done.

"I won't lose another brother," Sawyer said roughly against Silas's damp crown. "So stop being an idiot and come home. It's not safe anymore."

And that was the damn truth.

Nothing felt safe anymore.

Especially not the sleepy little town where nothing bad had ever happened.

Until now.

Silas roused himself from that long-ago moment, shaking off the pull of those awful memories, and wiped at his nose.

It didn't matter that everyone else thought Rhia's case was unrelated to Spencer's.

Silas knew in his gut they were connected.

And nothing was going to stop him from finding out how.

Quinn knew she couldn't approach Britain on school grounds, so to kill time before school let out, she tried doing a little more research into Sara Westfall, which meant talking to her editor.

Popping into the office, she spent about a half hour tying in a rough outline of the story she was planning to release about Rhia's pregnancy, leaving some gaps that hopefully Britain would be able to fill in, and then found her editor, Mick.

"I told you I would deliver," she said, leaning against the doorjamb with a triumphant smile. "I have a juicy lead that no one else has."

Mick eyed her with interest. "Yeah? Such as?"

"And spoil the surprise?"

Mick gestured impatiently. "Out with it."

"Fine. Rhia was six weeks pregnant."

"That's interesting," Mick agreed, steepling his fingers for a moment. "Who's the father?"

"Don't know yet. But I'm working on it."

"Murdered Teen Girl Pregnant." Mick nodded. "I like it. Catchy."

"Maybe the father is our killer."

Mick shrugged. "Possibly. What else you got?"

"Well, I have some leads to chase down but I'll have something filed by tonight. I'll email you the story but it might be late so watch for it."

"How'd you get this information?"

Quinn scoffed. "As if I would reveal my sources. Trust me when I say it's legit."

"It better be. I don't need a lawsuit slapped on our ass because you were sloppy with your sources."

"That's offensive," Quinn grumbled but took the point. "I will be thorough."

"Good."

But now that she'd shared a tasty tidbit for him to gnaw on, she needed to ask about Sara.

"Do you remember a reporter named Sara Westfall? She wrote the story on the Kelly boy's murder."

Mick shifted his gaze. "Vaguely. Why?"

"I heard she had a personal blog. I'm trying to find a copy of it."

"It wasn't written here," he said gruffly, as though putting an end to the conversation, but Quinn wasn't ready to let it go.

"Yes, I'm aware of that. I also heard that she died about six months after the story broke about Spencer's murder."

"Ever since that FBI agent started poking around you're seeing conspiracies everywhere. Look, it was tragic but Sara had her own demons. I'm not one to speak ill of the dead, but let's just say Sara liked her nightcaps and leave it at that."

"She was drunk driving? If that's the case, there was a report made."

"Hold on there., Where are you going with this?"

"I'm not sure. I just feel there's something to the fact that Sara had a blog where she posted her theories on Spencer's death and then she died about six months later. Seems suspect."

Mick heaved an agitated breath. "Stick to what you know. Sara is long gone. The story for today is about Rhia Daniels. Spend your energy there, not chasing after ghosts."

Was Mick deliberately shutting her down for a reason or was his reporter's nose so dulled from being behind a desk for so long that he couldn't tell a fresh scent when it was waved beneath him?

Either way Mick wasn't in the mood to continue sharing.

And no one else had been around when Sara worked for the paper.

Except… Ruth, the ages-old woman in billing. Quinn called her the Crypt Keeper—in her mind, not to her face, of course—because the woman was practically a fossil, and a little bit scary.

She also hung out in the oldest part of the building, which by its very nature gave Quinn the creeps.

Drawing a deep breath, Quinn grabbed a pocket notebook and headed to the billing department.

A small-town newspaper only needed a skeleton crew to handle the billing, and Ruth was a one-woman army. She knew too much to replace and the company was content to just let her do her thing until she croaked at her desk.

Harsh truth, but accurate.

Forcing an engaging smile, she entered Ruth's domain and found her behind her desk, her glasses perched on her nose like an old, disapproving matriarch from the 1800s.

"Hi, Ruth, how are you?" she asked.

"What do you want?" Ruth cut to the chase, annoyed at being interrupted.

Quinn swallowed and dropped the fake smile. "I need to ask you something." Ruth waited in dour silence and Quinn told herself to get over her irrational fear of the old woman. "You are the only person aside from Mick who was around when Sara Westfall was a reporter here. I wondered if you knew her and if you did, I wondered if you might share what you knew about her."

"I didn't know her."

Quinn's hopes fell and she seamed her lips against the disappointment. "Okay, sorry to have bothered you," she said and turned to leave, but Ruth's voice at her back turned her around.

"Some reporter you are. Are you always this soft and weak?"

Quinn straightened. "Excuse me?"

"You heard me just fine. You want to know what I know about Sara, you have to ask the right questions."

Irritated at being judged, Quinn retorted, "You already told me you didn't know her."

"I signed her paychecks."

"You sign everyone's paychecks," Quinn said, confused and annoyed by the woman's coy act. "So what?"

"Maybe I also signed advances on her checks and by the time she died, she owed the company about three months' wages."

"Are you kidding me?" Quinn breathed, not quite sure what to do with the information. It was certainly juicy but was it relevant? "Why did she need advances on her checks?"

Ruth shrugged as if that wasn't her concern.

"Was she an alcoholic? Mick said she liked to drink and implied that she'd died in a drunk-driving accident."

An indelicate snort followed and Quinn drew back.

"Are you saying Mick lied to me?"

"A lie is simply someone else's interpretation of an event."

There was a reason Ruth was stuck in this section of the building—she was probably a bit batty.

Or maybe the woman was smarter than she appeared.

"Why would he twist the facts?" Quinn asked.

"Maybe he doesn't want people poking around in his business. Questions he doesn't want to answer."

Oh, this was getting seven levels of weird. "Was Mick... involved with Sara?"

"How should I know? I only sign the checks and send out the bills."

The woman was impossible but her information had created a queasy feeling in Quinn's gut.

Why would Mick lie about Sara? If he was involved with her, why would he want to smear her reputation by implying that she was an alcoholic?

Sara died in a car accident. There would have to be a paper trail somewhere.

Should she share this information with Silas? Quinn wrestled with the fear that it was simply extraneous information and not a true lead at all.

She didn't want to waste time on wild goose chases.

But what if this obscure bit of information was the key to unlocking a bigger puzzle?

"Thanks for your help," she said, hustling out of there, feeling as if something was chasing her.

Once free of that section, she breathed a little easier, laughing even at how ridiculous she was being.

There was no boogey-monster waiting in the closet.

The real monsters hid in plain sight behind smiles meant to lower your guard.

She would decide after she talked to Britain if she was going to share the information about Sara.

Maybe by that time, she'd be able to figure out whether or not it was a lead worth chasing.

Chapter 13

Leo enjoyed the security of being the only photographer in town people trusted with their family pictures, senior portraits and bar mitzvahs but the best perk, by far, was being able to spearhead the Photography Club at the high school.

Young talent always fired him up, reminded him of why he got into this business in the first place—the thrill of discovery, the creation of art in its most raw form, which was why he decided to substitute-teach, as well.

The money was a nice supplement and being around kids kept him young.

"Is it good?" Joshua asked, his expression filled with doubt. "I mean, I was worried the light was too hot."

"I think it's great. Sometimes what makes a photo extraordinary are its flaws. Your character comes through the lens. I like it," he announced, giving it his seal of approval.

Joshua, such a good kid. Too bad his parents were numbskulls.

Leo went to pat the kid on the head when a girl interrupted them.

"You have Rhia's photography still?"

"I have her unfinished work," Leo answered with a frown. "And you are?"

Joshua, sensing the tension, slipped out of the shop.

"Britain Almasey. Rhia was my best friend. I want to see what she was working on before she died."

Leo graced the girl with an indulgent smile, forgiving her rudeness. "Ah, I see. Unfortunately, the unfinished photos belong to me per the guidelines of the club."

"Why would you keep them?"

"She was very talented. I was proud of her work. I'd like something to remember her by."

Britain narrowed her gaze, her mouth tightening as if she wanted to say something but was too afraid.

"I understand your grief, I do," he assured her. "But I can't give you those photos. Besides, half of them are still negatives."

"Negatives? As in, like, real film? Why don't you use digital?"

"There's no soul in digital," he answered with an indulgent smile. He might be the last of the great dinosaurs still using film but digital would never replace the integrity of celluloid.

"You should give them to the police."

"I hardly think the police are interested in wildflower shots," Leo chuckled.

"She was working on other things."

Leo sobered, the smile dying. "Other things?"

"That's why you ought to give them to the police. Maybe her killer left behind a clue."

"Maybe. I hadn't thought of it that way," Leo said. "I'll get in touch with the sheriff and see if he thinks the same. If so, I'll happily hand them over to the authorities."

He got the impression she didn't believe him. "Have I offended you in some way?" Leo asked. "We seem to be at odds but I can't for the life of me figure out why."

"Just see that you turn in those photos," she said before leaving abruptly.

Leo sat in concerned silence for a long moment. Was there something in her films that he'd missed?

Was it true that Rhia had left something behind that might help close the case?

Of course not, a voice scoffed. Britain was a child and reacting as such.

Leo paused a minute to allow his thoughts to drift to Rhia. So much talent. Too bad her talent was wasted.

The girl had been too interested in things she should've left alone.

A sigh rattled out of Leo and he returned to the negatives from the club.

He pulled Joshua's newly processed black-and-whites. Potential.

Perhaps with a guiding hand, a mentor…

Leo discarded the thought as quickly as it occurred.

He didn't need to touch a stove twice to know that it was hot.

Quinn waited for cheer practice to let out and caught up with Britain as she was walking to her car.

"Britain Almasey?" Quinn called after her, causing Britain to turn.

"Yeah? Who's asking?"

Quinn flashed her credentials, wishing they said something more impressive than the local rag but that was all she had to work with. "Can I talk to you for a minute?"

"About what?" Britain regarded her warily.

"You were good friends with Rhia Daniels, right?"

"Yeah."

Quinn glanced around, noting the curious looks they were getting. "Mind if we go somewhere and chat?"

"Like where?"

"How about Gilbert Park? It's just around the corner."

"I'm supposed to be home by five." Britain retreated, unlocking her car, ready to leave.

Quinn blurted out. "It's about Rhia. She was pregnant."

Britain stopped and cast a sharp look at Quinn. "How do you know?"

"Did you?"

Britain held Quinn's gaze for a long moment, caught between being loyal and needing to share. Finally, she said, "I'll be at Gilbert Park in five minutes. I don't want to talk about it here."

Quinn agreed quickly and sprinted to her own car. Her hands were trembling as she fought to catch her breath.

Britain knew something. And she wanted to share.

It must be something bad; the kid seemed burdened by whatever knowledge she was holding on to.

The park came into view and Quinn chose an inconspicuous spot away from the road to wait.

Britain showed up a few minutes later, pulling alongside Quinn's car but before Quinn could exit, Britain told her to stay there.

"I'm not staying long," Britain said, talking through her window to Quinn. "How did you know Rhia was pregnant?"

"The coroner report. Do you know who the father was?"

Britain shook her head. "Rhia wouldn't tell me. She was so freaked out."

"Was she planning to keep the baby?"

"I don't know. I mean, she was barely pregnant. I told her if she was lucky, she would lose it. I know that sounds harsh but I mean, c'mon, she was sixteen years old and definitely not ready to be a mom."

YOUR PARTICIPATION IS REQUESTED!

Dear Reader,

Since you are a lover of our books – we would like to get to know you!

Inside you will find a short Reader's Survey. Sharing your answers with us will help our editorial staff understand who you are and what activities you enjoy.

To thank you for your participation, we would like to send you 2 books and 2 gifts – **ABSOLUTELY FREE!**

Enjoy your gifts with our appreciation,

Pam Powers

SEE INSIDE FOR READER'S SURVEY

For Your Reading Pleasure...

We'll send you 2 books and 2 gifts
ABSOLUTELY FREE
just for completing our Reader's Survey!

YOUR READER'S SURVEY
"THANK YOU" FREE GIFTS INCLUDE:
▶ **2 FREE books**
▶ **2 lovely surprise gifts**

PLEASE FILL IN THE CIRCLES COMPLETELY TO RESPOND

1) What type of fiction books do you enjoy reading? (Check all that apply)
- ○ Suspense/Thrillers
- ○ Action/Adventure
- ○ Modern-day Romances
- ○ Historical Romance
- ○ Humor
- ○ Paranormal Romance

2) What attracted you most to the last fiction book you purchased on impulse?
- ○ The Title
- ○ The Cover
- ○ The Author
- ○ The Story

3) What is usually the greatest influencer when you <u>plan</u> to buy a book?
- ○ Advertising
- ○ Referral
- ○ Book Review

4) How often do you access the internet?
- ○ Daily ○ Weekly ○ Monthly ○ Rarely or never

5) How many NEW paperback fiction novels have you purchased in the past 3 months?
- ○ 0 - 2
- ○ 3 - 6
- ○ 7 or more

YES! I have completed the Reader's Survey. Please send me the 2 FREE books and 2 FREE gifts (gifts are worth about $10 retail) for which I qualify. I understand that I am under no obligation to purchase any books, as explained on the back of this card.

240/340 HDL GLN6

FIRST NAME

LAST NAME

ADDRESS

APT.#

CITY

STATE/PROV.

ZIP/POSTAL CODE

RS-217-SUR17

Quinn didn't judge. "I don't know that anyone is ready to be a mother at that age," Quinn murmured. "So I'm guessing the father wasn't someone at school?"

"Why do you say that?"

Quinn backtracked quickly. "I just assumed because her parents said she didn't have a boyfriend."

"Well, not to their knowledge, of course. Her parents were so strict. I mean, like, Amish-strict. Rhia wasn't allowed to date, curfew was at 9 and she had to go to church every Sunday with Bible study on Tuesdays. I would've died if my parents had been so medieval-times-old-fashioned."

"Mrs. Daniels said Rhia was close to her faith. Do you think that was true?"

Britain considered Quinn's question then answered with a baffled, "Yeah, I guess so. She didn't seem to mind spending so much time with the pastor. Don't get me wrong, he was kinda cute in an old guy sort of way but, you know, he's like married to God or something."

"I think you're thinking of nuns," Quinn said, biting back a short laugh. "So...did Rhia have a boyfriend at school?"

Britain nodded. "Brock Teichert. He's like, a total D-bag but he's the most popular guy in school so, of course, Rhia had to have him. I think he was going to break up with her, though. That was the word around the lockers anyway."

"And you think she was pregnant with his baby?"

"Who else could it be? I never saw her with anyone else."

"How do you think Brock was going to take the news?"

Britain's eyes widened. "I doubt he'd take the news very well. He's got his eye on a scholarship to Washington State University and I'm sure a kid would mess that up."

"Do you think that Brock could hurt Rhia in order to protect his scholarship chances?"

"I don't know but...he's got a wicked temper. He and

Rhia got into a huge fight last weekend at the bonfire. I don't know what they were fighting over but he was pretty pissed."

Quinn tried to contain her excitement. "Thank you, Britain. I appreciate you talking to me."

"Are you going to quote me in the paper? I don't want anyone to know I said those things. You know, 'cause people might think I was talking trash behind my best friend's back and that's not true. I loved her. Rhia could be a bitch but she was my girl, you know? We've been cheering together since we were kids. We even talked about going to college together."

"You were interested in Berkeley?"

"Maybe. I don't know. I figured we had more time to figure it out."

Quinn commiserated quietly.

Britain wiped at her eyes, sniffing a little. "I still can't believe she's gone. I keep thinking I'm going to wake up and this will all be a terrible dream."

"Not a dream," Quinn said quietly. Genuine grief rippled around the girl and Quinn felt the burden of her job for the first time. The thrill of the chase clanged at odds with the natural urge to be supportive. But she wasn't going to get anywhere by hesitating to go for the jugular. "Britain… was Rhia a secretive girl? Did she like to hide things?"

Britain sniffed. "What do you mean?"

"We all have things we keep to ourselves and that's normal, but it's really shocking to find out the things Rhia was keeping under wraps. It makes me wonder…what else was she hiding?" A flash of guilt in Britain's expression had Quinn press a little harder. "I'm not talking about the occasional party that we don't tell our parents about or the time we experimented with drugs or alcohol. I'm talking about bigger secrets."

Britain quieted, chewing on her bottom lip as she considered her answer. "I don't think so. But... I don't know... Rhia was private."

Quinn went out on a limb and threw out her suspicion. "Was...Rhia's father...I don't know how to say this delicately but if anyone would know, it would be you." She paused a beat then dropped the question. "Was Rhia's father messing around with her?"

Britain paled and gave a subtle shake of her head. "I don't know," she whispered. "But he was always looking at her weird. Gave me the creeps. I mean, it was just... I don't know."

"What do you mean? Can you give me some examples?"

Britain licked her lips. "Well, last year he found text messages on her cell phone from this boy who liked her. Mr. Daniels freaked out on Rhia, like totally, crazy, possessive-boyfriend kind of freak-out. It was gross. Like he was jealous or something. What kind of dad reacts like that?"

"What did Rhia say about it?"

"She said he's just really overprotective and then we dropped it because it was uncomfortable to talk about. Neither of us brought it up again."

If Britain knew anything else, she wasn't sharing.

Quinn understood. Britain was trying to remain loyal to her dead friend. Whatever true secrets Rhia was keeping, the girl took them to the grave.

"Thank you, Britain," Quinn said, ending the conversation. "Are you going to be okay?"

Britain nodded. "I just need a minute. I don't want anyone to see me like this." To prove her point, she pulled her visor down to check her mirror and groaned as she wiped away smeared mascara. "Ugh. That's all I need, my mom grilling me about why I was crying. She already wants to send me to therapy because of what happened to Rhia."

"I hate to side with an adult but that might not be a bad idea. Sometimes talking to someone…it helps."

That was Quinn's contribution. Grief could twist a person until they broke. She didn't want to see that happen to the girl.

Quinn waved and slowly pulled away, her thoughts moving too quickly to process all at once.

Weird, creepy dad lusting after his own daughter?

A secret boyfriend with a temper and big dreams?

Either one sounded like they had a solid motive for murder to Quinn.

But if that was true and it really did turn out to be the boyfriend or Mr. Daniels who snuffed out Rhia's life… that meant Silas was wrong.

The two cases weren't related at all.

Her shoulders ached with the sudden tension she was holding.

Had she wanted the cases to be related—not for the potential story—but for Silas to have closure?

The answer to the rhetorical question mocked her.

Yeah, she wanted closure for Silas's family.

And for Silas.

Chapter 14

Silas took the liberty of ordering a pizza for him and Quinn, though as he waited for her to show up at the hotel, the awkwardness of the situation hit him.

He was actively working with a reporter.

He'd slept with that reporter.

Now he was eager to share a pizza and beer with that reporter.

He should've kept things professional.

Never in his entire career had he done something so reckless and out of character.

His actions worried him.

What if his biggest strength—his instincts—were completely off base with Quinn?

What if she screwed him over and stole his shot at finding Spencer's killer?

There was an earnestness to Quinn that vied with the hunger he saw in her eyes.

She wanted to do the right thing but she was torn by her ambition to get the job done any way possible.

In the end, would that ambition win out?

No matter the cost?

An urgent knock interrupted his thoughts. Silas opened the door and Quinn strode in, her expression teeming with activity. She was onto something.

The excitement of new information eclipsed his previous misgivings.

"I'm starting to know that look. What do you got?"

Quinn unwound her scarf and tossed it on the chair, grinning. "I got something good. Possibly something big enough to bust this case open."

Pizza forgotten, Silas was all ears but Quinn had spied the food and went straight for a slice with a happy groan. "Thank God. I'm starved." Without missing a beat, she grabbed a piece, tore off a bite and kept talking. "Okay, I managed to meet with Britain Almasey, Rhia's best friend. Turns out… Rhia had a boyfriend, but that's not all."

Mildly amused by how Quinn could devour her pizza and keep talking between swallows, he said, "Okay, not a huge surprise. The girl didn't get pregnant by herself."

"True. But this boyfriend may have motive to kill."

Silas lost his amusement and sank into the chair. "How so?"

"Apparently, he's got his eye on a football scholarship to Washington State University, and having a baby could screw all that up."

"Most boys don't turn into murderers over a lost scholarship."

"Britain said the boy was a real D-bag with a temper. Something tells me becoming a father wasn't high on his to-do list before skipping off to college."

Quinn was right—the lead had potential. And if it was true…a stone landed in his gut, killing his appetite.

"You said there was something else?" he reminded Quinn.

"Yes." She nodded, wiping her mouth. "Britain said there was something weird going on with Mr. Daniels. Said he freaked out when he discovered text messages on Rhia's phone from a boy."

"He is strict," Silas said, thinking. "But you're thinking it's something else?"

"Well, I don't know if you caught this but he seemed more possessive than fatherly when we talked to him. It gave me an icky vibe."

"I caught it, as well," Silas said, impressed with her keen eye. "It wouldn't be the first time a father has had an incestuous relationship with his daughter. A DNA test will either rule him out or point the finger."

Quinn wiped her mouth. "I think that news would pretty much put Mrs. Daniels in her grave."

Silas agreed. The poor woman was hanging on by a thread.

"Did you learn anything at the lab?" Quinn asked.

"The DNA didn't match anyone in the database, but that's not surprising if the child turned out to be the boy's or Mr. Daniels's. All it will take is a cheek swab to confirm paternity and if that's the case…"

Quinn nodded. "Then Brock Teichert better have a really solid alibi for the night of Rhia's death."

"Or Oliver Daniels better have a damn good lawyer."

Silas nodded. *Damn it.* The connection to Spencer was becoming more tenuous with each developing lead.

"Are you okay?" Quinn ventured, her knowing expression cutting at him. "It's good news but not so good news, right?"

"Yeah. If it turns out either killed Rhia…there's no way they had anything to do with Spencer's death," he said with a heavy sigh.

"I'm sorry, Silas."

Silas shook his head. "Don't be. Rhia deserves justice. That's what's important right now."

"So does Spencer."

Silas blinked back the rush of emotion that Quinn's simple show of support caused. He took a minute to collect himself then said, "Thanks. I appreciate that."

A beat of silence passed between them, then Quinn changed subjects with a mild frown. "I asked around about Sara Westfall…"

"And?"

"And I have no idea what to do with the crumb of information that I got. It could be nothing or it could be that insignificant side note that ultimately breaks the case."

"That's cryptic."

"Wait until I tell you what I found out." Quinn chuckled, shaking her head as she drew a deep breath. "Okay, here it is—apologies if this turns out to be nothing—Sara Westfall was taking advances against her checks. By the time she died she was in the hole by three months."

"Sounds like bad business, but I don't see how that could be related to either case."

"I thought that, too, at first," Quinn agreed. "But there's more. My source implied that Sara and my editor were having an affair and that Sara was an alcoholic. Now, on the surface, that sounds like average fodder for a police drama but here's the thing… Sara died six months after Spencer, and my editor was quite adamant that I drop the topic altogether."

"Could be guilt. Is your editor married?"

"Yes."

"Sara was probably his side piece and he doesn't want to dredge up a potential land mine to his marriage."

"Makes sense. I don't know why it's bugging me. If Sara died in a drunk-driving accident, there should be a report. I think I'm going to do a little more digging, just to satisfy that little voice in my head so I can move on."

Silas smiled with respect. "Always follow your instincts. If something is telling you to keep digging, then don't ignore it."

Quinn graced him with a matching smile that caught his breath. He covered by rising abruptly to grab two beers.

"Pizza and beer. Are you my soul mate?" Quinn teased, cracking hers open for a healthy swig. She sighed with happiness, declaring, "Today was a good day."

Quinn popped her boots off and propped her feet in Silas's lap. "Feel free to do whatever comes to mind," she suggested, wiggling her socked toes. "I mean, if you wanted to rub my tootsies, I wouldn't complain."

In spite of his sharp disappointment over the new direction of the case, Silas laughed, taking the hint. "Is that so? You're a bold one, Quinn Jackson."

"Yes, I am."

Silas removed her socks and slowly began rubbing her feet, gently massaging the soles. Quinn's breathy sigh went straight to his groin. Damn, the girl was the freshest kind of sexy. It was going to be a challenge to keep his hands focused on her feet.

But as luck would have it, Quinn had other plans.

"I barely know you but there's something about you that I'm drawn to. Am I wrong that feeling this way is a bad idea?"

"Depends on your perspective," he murmured, struggling with his own misgivings. The simple, unadorned truth was that Silas and Quinn didn't make sense, and trying to make heads or tails of their wild, inappropriate attraction was a futile task because it would never make sense. "But yeah, I see where you're coming from."

"You think I'm too young."

"Among other things."

"You hate reporters."

"There is that, too."

Quinn sat in reflective silence then said, "For the first time today I understood why you don't like reporters. I mean, I know you told me the surface reason but I really didn't 'get it' until today."

"Oh?"

"Talking to Britain, I struggled with the knowledge that gaining valuable information from a source meant I had to press on an open wound to see what would spill out. She's just a kid herself, dealing with unimaginable grief. For a split second... I didn't like what I had to do."

Silas paused in his ministrations, a subtle smile twisting his lips. "A conscience could be a liability in your chosen career."

Quinn pulled her feet free and straightened. "You have to press on people to get information, too. Sometimes the greater good outweighs the suffering of the few."

"True."

"But in my case...it's not okay?"

She had a point. "I guess at the end of the day, we all have jobs to do. How we do them...that's up to the individual."

Quinn nodded. "I can be a reporter with integrity."

Maybe she could. Silas would have to wait and see. The game was much too early to put bets on the outcome just yet.

Quinn rose and began pulling her sweater free, tossing it to the floor as she beckoned to him.

"What are you doing?" he asked, trying to keep a level head.

"I have another itch that needs scratching."

He shouldn't.

The smart decision would be to gently decline, to be the bigger man and send her on her way.

The last thing he needed was to entangle himself further with Quinn.

But he rose and began unbuttoning his shirt.

Actually, in this moment, being tangled up with Quinn seemed like the best idea ever.

Quinn shuddered at Silas's touch, the way he made her body shake with an expert hand could become an addiction if she wasn't careful.

His body, strong and masculine, covered hers, pressing her into the mattress as he slowly breached her, entering with exquisite precision, teasing her with each deliberate inch until he was seated to the hilt inside her.

Quinn cried out, clutching at his back, wrapping her legs around his torso as he lifted her up, impaling her on his length.

He held her as if she weighed nothing. She clung to him as he thrust into her, the sweat between them drenching their bodies.

"Silas," she cried, nearly unable to stand the sweet torture. Everything about him fit perfectly against her—inside her. They were puzzle pieces, interlocking. It was all she could do to hold on as Silas took over, forcing her to be present for every shuddering thrust, every ripple of building pleasure.

"God, you're perfect," he growled as he rolled to his back, giving him an unobstructed view. She felt powerful perched on Silas, riding him as his hazed eyes locked with fever on her body.

His hands filled with her breasts but soon that wasn't enough. He needed them in his mouth. Silas sat up, wrapping her legs around him as he took her nipple in his mouth, sucking and teasing, until she was writhing against him, grinding on his length like a cat in heat.

Quinn's mouth popped open on a rigid cry as every

muscle clenched in concert. *"Yes, Silas!"* she cried, quivering as her release crashed into her, blacking out everything around her until all she could fathom was the pleasure rocking her world.

Nearly limp from the force of her climax, she gasped as Silas rolled her to her back, throwing her legs over his shoulders. He loomed over her like a dark god, the sheen of their sweat gleaming in the soft light, the scent of their lovemaking a thick perfume in the room. As he went deeper than before, Quinn squeezed her eyes shut as another unexpected arrow of pleasure punctured her core.

Silas showed no mercy, driving her toward yet another orgasm. Bent in half, she had no choice but to accept the sensual invasion. The knowledge she was powerless to stop whatever Silas wanted took her breath away with fresh arousal.

She knew he wouldn't hurt her but he would push the limits—that was sexy as hell.

This time when Quinn tumbled into that abyss, Silas was right there beside her, shouting as he came, his thrusts hard and erratic as if he'd lost all control as well.

She was alive with tiny pulses even as she struggled to catch her breath.

Silas rose unsteadily, still buried deep inside her, the vision of their connection a heady thing. This was a mental snapshot she would keep for eternity.

In all the world, there would be nothing sexier than this moment.

Quinn swallowed, her mouth dry as Silas carefully withdrew, taking the briefest second to discard the condom before falling back to the bed beside her, his arm flung over his eyes as he recovered.

It felt wrong to toss out a flippant comment and bounce like she normally would in light of what they'd just shared.

But she couldn't stay, either.

Even though she wanted to.

The idea of falling asleep just as they were, side by side, naked and spent, seemed the perfect end to the day.

But even as the silly thought flitted across her brain, her eyes popped open on a frown.

What was she thinking?

Spend the night with Silas?

Was she mental?

If you want everyone to take you seriously, you have to start taking yourself seriously.

Quinn rose abruptly and started to dress with the intent to leave when Silas said, "Stay."

A sharp pang of want and need nearly made her jump back to the bed but another part of her—the smarter part—stayed the course.

She turned with a chagrined smile. "Sorry. Things get muddled when, you know, lines blur too much."

"How much more muddled could they get?" Silas challenged with a wry twist of his lips. "In case you missed that memo, I don't tango with reporters…in any fashion. But you're different."

"I am different," Quinn agreed but she also set him straight. "But I'm going to do my job. Even if at the end of the day, what I need to do is in direct opposition to what you want me to do. And I don't want anything to get in the way of that. If I stay the night with you, I might catch a case of the feels and I can't afford that. And neither can you." Damn, her heart ached delivering that message but it was for the best. "Sex with no strings attached. That was the deal. I'll see you tomorrow." Silas didn't argue or try to persuade her differently and she was grateful. Quinn forced a bright smile, ending with, "You're in charge of breakfast. Anything with cheese is good with me."

And then she left him there, lying naked in the bed

they'd just completely destroyed, telling herself she was doing the right thing.

Too bad, as victories went, the feeling was as flat and unsatisfying as day-old soda.

But the climb to the top was lonely.

She might as well get used to it.

Chapter 15

Lester wasn't surprised when his lead detective—basically, his only detective—Harrison Dex walked into his office all full of piss and vinegar.

"Since when do we need Feds to do our work?" he asked with a scowl. "That's a fine howdy-do when I get to the office after a short three-day vacation to find that the biggest case Port Orion has ever seen has been handed off to a Fed for no good goddamn reason."

"Hold up, son. Watch yourself. I'm still your boss," Lester reminded him, taking a moment to sip his coffee. "And the Fed used to be local. He's just here to lend a hand."

"We don't need him," Harrison scoffed, openly offended. "You made me detective for a reason—my skill set. By right, this is my case."

"You sound like a spoiled teenage girl," Lester grumbled. It was too early for this crap. "I made you detective because my choices were slim and frankly, Port Orion isn't exactly a hotbed of crime. I wasn't worried."

"That's bullshit. You made me detective because I'm suited for the job. Don't try to downplay my work history just because you're dazzled by some Fed's bullshit."

Lester wasn't in the mood to placate the young man's ego. His town was on the edge of falling apart and he was dealing with a serious case of regret for not retiring gracefully when he'd had the chance.

"Are you finished?"

"I want this case."

"No."

"No?"

"You heard me. Last time I checked, I was still sheriff so check your attitude before you find yourself demoted to something less...illustrious."

"So what am I supposed to do while this Fed is out there doing my job?"

"We have other crimes, maybe not as horrible as a young girl's tragic death, but crimes that need solving nonetheless."

Fate must've been PMSing, because right at that moment, the Fed in question strode in, looking the picture of quiet confidence, which only made Harrison look like a whiny bitch in comparison.

"Do you have a minute?" Silas asked, bypassing Harrison, which only pissed off the man even more.

"Yeah, sure," Lester answered, gesturing for Harrison to take himself out. "Close the door, too."

Harrison shook his head as he muttered under his breath and then slammed the door behind him.

"Was I interrupting something?" Silas asked.

"Just a temper tantrum by a man old enough to know better. That was Harrison Dex, my detective. He just returned from vacation and found out that I'd given you lead on the case."

Silas nodded. "Sorry for the trouble I've caused."

Lester waved away Silas's apology. "Don't worry about him. Harrison is my problem. Tell me what you came to say. Something tells me it's going to make the coffee curdle in my gut."

"I'd like to bring Brock Teichert in for questioning. I'll also need a warrant for a cheek swab."

"Brock? The football player?"

"Yeah, apparently, he was Rhia's secret boyfriend and they had a major fight last weekend in front of a bunch of kids at a bonfire. He also has a rep for having a temper."

Lester rubbed the back of his neck. "He's a good kid," he said, hoping it was true. "I mean, helluva football player. That kid's going places if he plays his cards right."

"Rhia's pregnancy gives him motive."

"Ahh hell, Silas, he's just a kid. There's no way he did what someone did to Rhia. That poor girl's neck was crushed."

"You know I have to bring him in. I'd like to use your interrogation room for the questioning."

Lester agreed wearily. What could he say? Silas was right. All leads had to be followed and even if he didn't like to think that a star Port Orion football player had the stones to do something so awful to his own girlfriend, he couldn't ignore the possibility.

"So you're thinking that he might be the father of Rhia's baby," Lester guessed, to which Silas shrugged. "Yeah, gotta rule him out if nothing else."

"We also need a warrant for Oliver Daniels."

Lester stared, uncomprehending. "Whatever for?"

"There's no way to say this delicately...we need to rule him out as a suspect."

"Her father?" Lester repeated, dumbfounded. "What the hell are you saying?"

"I'm not saying anything. It's just a precaution."

But Lester knew Silas was lying. "Out with it, Kelly," he growled.

"Rhia's best friend Britain said the dad was weird, as in possessive over Rhia. You and I both know that kind of behavior is a red flag. We can get probable cause. Fathers aren't supposed to see their daughters in that way. I hope I'm wrong. A DNA test will at least rule Mr. Daniels out as the father but if he was molesting Rhia, there's no way we'll ever know unless someone comes forward."

"Ah hell," Lester exhaled, his acid reflux kicking up. "That's just great."

"All we know at this point is that whoever fathered Rhia's baby, their DNA was not in the database. A cheek swab will either confirm or deny paternity. We'll go from there once we get the results."

"I don't know which outcome I'm hoping for," Lester admitted. "If either comes back positive, we'll have a direction to head in but it makes me sick to think of it. If they come back negative, hell, we're back to square one."

"It's a difficult spot," Silas agreed. "I wish there were easier answers."

Lester grimaced as a splash of stomach acid burned his throat. "There goes my coffee. Damn it all to hell." He reached into his desk and shook out a handful of antacids, crunching them as he said, "Look, I want you to handle this with some delicacy. People are scared. I don't want you to drag the kid into the station. Do it nice-like. He's still a kid and his parents are good people. Hopefully, he'll volunteer his DNA in an effort to help the investigation. As far as Oliver goes, I'll have Dex go ask for the DNA so he can do it at home. No need in causing more suffering if it turns out the poor man is innocent."

"Thanks, Sheriff." Silas went to leave but paused when he saw the newspaper on the edge of the desk. Lester hadn't had a chance to open it yet.

"May I?" Silas gestured with a mild frown.

"Be my guest."

Silas grabbed the newspaper and his frown deepened. "Damn it."

That didn't bode well. "What's wrong?"

Silas turned the front page toward Lester so he could see the main story.

Murdered Teen Girl Pregnant.

"Why'd she have to go and print that?" Lester groaned, freshly irritated. So far, his morning had been crap. This newest shock was just a steaming fresh pile. "What's it say? I can't read the tiny print that good anymore."

Silas read, "Recent forensic evidence has determined sixteen-year-old Rhia Daniels of Port Orion was pregnant when she was strangled to death. The paternity of the father has not been revealed. The investigation is ongoing. Anyone with information in regards to the young teen's murder is urged to call the Port Orion tipline." He paused to regard Lester. "Do you want me to keep reading? She goes on with some quotes from locals about Rhia, including a few from an unidentified teen."

Lester didn't need to hear the rest. "Forget it. I can use my imagination. That girl is more trouble than she's worth these days."

Silas folded the paper and returned it to Lester's desk. "She's doing her job," he said, although Lester would've never expected Silas Kelly to be any reporter's champion after what'd happened with Spencer.

A germ of a thought came to Lester and he stared with suspicion at Silas. "Stay away from her. She's just a kid," he warned.

"She's not a kid. She's an adult," Silas disagreed, which didn't sit well with Lester at all.

"Look here, I gave you leave to help with this investigation but I won't have you breaking hearts of good girls who've gotten in over their heads."

Silas chuckled. "I think you ought to let Miss Jackson figure out what she wants instead of trying to micromanage her life. But before you give yourself a coronary, calm down. I'm not breaking anyone's heart."

Lester figured that was as much as he could hope for but a part of him knew Silas was right. Quinn had grown up at some point and she was itching to get out of this town.

He grunted in agreement and motioned for Silas to get out.

He'd had enough of everyone.

And it wasn't even 8 a.m. yet.

Silas found Quinn at Reba's Diner waiting for him. He slid into the booth, his gaze lingering too long on the brightness of her eyes and the memory of her soft skin.

It only took a second to realize he was stumbling down a dark road and pulled back.

"Catchy headline. When'd you write that?"

"The headline was Mick's idea. I wrote the story after I left your hotel last night and emailed it just in time to make the morning print."

"Busy bee," he murmured as he sipped his coffee, leaving his opinion at that. He wasn't going to grab for the low-hanging fruit and jab at her for doing her job.

"Got any opinions?"

"Nope."

"Good." The waitress came and took their order. When Quinn ordered a cheese omelet with extra cheese, his quizzical look was met with a flip, "What? I told you I liked cheese."

"That's a serious commitment to cheese," he said, smothering a smile.

"This breakfast is on you. I paid for the protein bars and

smoothies," she told him with a cheeky smile that made him want to reach over and kiss her good morning.

But he didn't do anything of the sort and simply accepted her terms. He didn't mind picking up the tab for breakfast.

"So when are you bringing Brock in for questioning? I want to be there behind the glass when you do."

"For what purpose? You can't write about anything that's said. Besides, his parents might lawyer up and we could get nothing out of the boy aside from the cheek swab."

"I promise I won't write about the interview. I just want to get a look at the kid while you question him. I want to see what my instincts tell me."

"Lester says the boy is a star athlete."

"Yeah, I guess so. Not a huge football fan. Jocks were never my thing."

"No?"

"Hell, no. I was in the yearbook club, journalism club, the French Club, and for a brief, excruciating time, in the photography club. No time for jocks or the silly politics of high school."

"Your uncle runs the photography club, doesn't he?"

"Exactly. I love my uncle Leo to death but I was being crushed by the weight of his expectations. He sucked the joy out of learning. I got out as soon as I could and nothing could've persuaded me to return. I love my uncle too much to destroy our relationship like that."

He chuckled softly then remembered. "He worked with Rhia, too."

"Yeah, so? He works with a lot of kids from the high school. Especially after he started subbing. For the life of me I have no idea why he'd want to be a substitute teacher. High school kids are the worst."

"He said she had real talent…that she reminded him of you."

"Really? He never mentioned it." Quinn shrugged. "He doesn't tell me everything. Thank God. Sometimes he can go on forever about composition and lighting. Not exactly scintillating conversation for someone who identifies as a lukewarm hobbyist."

Silas nodded, pausing while the waitress delivered their plates. Quinn wasted no time tucking into her omelet.

"I'm starved today," she said with a happy groan. "This hits the spot."

Then it was as if she recalled why her appetite was revved and her cheeks pinked.

Silas nearly choked on his bacon. He cleared his throat with the intent of returning to the case, if only to save each other from an awkward silence but he took a detour instead. "Lester doesn't want me to break your heart."

Quinn surprised Silas with an amused chuckle. "As if I would let anyone break my heart. That man is so protective. It's like having two mother hens, except they're both male instead of female."

"They're pretty protective of you. Lester told me to keep my distance. I think he's afraid I might steal your virtue or something."

Her cheeks pinked again and she bit her lip, a tiny action with the power to devastate his resolve. He wanted to kiss her. Instead, he returned to his breakfast, shoveling a few bites into his mouth before he could do or say something stupid.

"What time are you bringing Brock in?" Quinn asked without missing a beat. "And what's happening with Mr. Daniels? Are you going to get his DNA?"

"We're bringing Brock in after school. Lester wants this done quietly. Lester is going to send a deputy over to the Danielses to collect DNA privately to spare them any further pain."

"Of course he does," Quinn murmured with disappointment. "Lester doesn't want to upset the status quo. He's not ready to accept that the town isn't the same as it used to be."

"It's a hard thing to accept," Silas said in Lester's defense. "When something shakes your foundation…it's hard to feel safe anywhere. Everyone looks suspect and no place is secure enough."

Quinn regarded him keenly. "Is that how you felt after Spencer died?"

He saw no reason to lie. "Yes."

"So you went into law enforcement to help make the world a safer place," she supposed.

"I guess. All my brothers went into law enforcement."

"That's quite an impact. Are they all in violent crimes?"

"Sawyer does white-collar crime but Shaine does undercover stuff in narcotics. Shaine was always an adrenaline junkie. He gets off on the danger."

"What do you get off on?"

That wasn't an innocent question. Or maybe he was reading into it but his pants immediately felt tight. He held her gaze. "Careful," he warned softly. Her pupils dilated and he knew the question hadn't been innocent at all. "What are you doing?"

"Hopefully, you in about ten minutes." She rose and grabbed her purse and jacket. "I'll see you back at your hotel for a *debrief.*"

And then Quinn left the diner. Silas took all of five seconds to throw a wad of cash on the table—leaving what was probably a monster tip—and followed.

Even as he told himself to put a stop to what was happening between him and Quinn, it was just lip service.

He didn't want to stop.

He wanted more.

Hell, he was practically free-falling into a morass of bad, career-wrecking decisions and yet...he couldn't get to his hotel fast enough.

Chapter 16

Quinn left Silas's hotel room later that morning, sated and sleepy, but since she had time to kill before Silas picked up Brock after school for questioning, she returned home to quickly shower to perk up.

She was surprised to see Uncle Leo still at home but judging by the glower on his face, he wasn't happy about something.

"What's wrong?" she asked, pausing in the doorway of the living room.

"We need to talk, young lady."

"Well, that sounds ominous," Quinn joked, stepping out of the hall and into the room. "What's up?"

"Lester just told me you've been spending quite a lot of time with Silas Kelly and I don't like it."

Quinn's first inclination at Uncle Leo's gruff over-protectiveness was to laugh but there was an edge to Uncle Leo that told her laughing wouldn't go over well.

"We're working together," she started but Leo cut her off.

"Feds don't work with reporters. It's like asking me to believe that a hungry bear just wants to be friends with the fish he just caught."

"That's a terrible analogy," Quinn said, trying to smile but Leo wasn't in the mood.

"I don't know what's come over you but since Silas Kelly returned to this town, you've changed and not for the better."

"And what does that mean?"

"It means you used to be sweet and now...you're...just, for lack of a better word, a ball-buster and I don't like it."

Frankly, Quinn took his observation as a compliment, even though he hadn't meant it that way.

"I told you, I have a job to do and I'm taking that job seriously. Silas is helping me as much as I help him. It's a mutually satisfying arrangement."

Her thighs still ached from being *satisfied*. Twice.

"I told Lester he ought to cut Silas loose and put his own detective on the case. This ought to be handled by a local anyway."

Outrage on Silas's behalf sharpened her voice, and she never spoke to her uncle like that but she was pissed that everyone seemed to think it was okay to tell her how to live her life. "Harrison Dex is an idiot. He couldn't find his ass with both hands. If Lester put Harrison on the case, the investigation would go nowhere and Rhia's killer would go free. Surely, you don't want that, right?"

"Of course not," he snapped. "But Port Orion doesn't need a Fed telling our deputies how to handle themselves in an investigation. It sends the message that we're somehow incompetent and that's a terrible thing to put on Lester when he's worked so hard to be a good sheriff all these years."

"Silas isn't doing that," Quinn retorted, baffled. "He's following his own leads and handling everything himself, freeing up the deputies to do their usual jobs of keeping the peace around here. Honestly, Uncle Leo, where is this coming from? You do realize I'm not a teenager anymore, right? And I'm sure as hell not a virgin, either, so if you're trying to protect my *purity*, that ship has long since sailed."

Uncle Leo's cheeks colored and he sputtered with embarrassment. "What's come over you, Quinnie?"

She softened when she realized she'd taken it too far. For God's sake, Uncle Leo couldn't even buy her pads and tampons when she'd started her period so he'd asked Lester's wife to do it for him.

"Uncle Leo, I love you but you have to stop trying to keep me a little girl. I grew up a long time ago. But if it makes you feel any better, I'm not looking to have a relationship with Silas."

"So you're not seeing him?"

"No, not at all," Quinn assured him. "We have an entirely platonic working relationship—" *that often ends with wild monkey sex* "—and that's all there is to it."

Leo lost some of his tension but he still looked like a nettled hen. "He's too old for you anyway. I guess I just jumped to the worst conclusion."

Quinn wanted to disagree that Silas was too old for her but that would only ignite her uncle's suspicion all over again. She liked that Silas was older. There was something to be said for maturity between the sheets.

Boys were all about getting off; Silas was all about getting her off.

Her breath hitched as her mind wandered. *Whoa...stay focused.*

"You worry too much," she said, patting her uncle on the cheek. "Nothing is happening between me and Silas."

It was a small lie but a necessary one. Her uncle Leo would have a heart attack if he found out that she was knocking boots with Silas.

She had no interest in hurting her uncle, but she also had no intention of stopping what she was doing.

And that included Silas—every chance she could get.

Brock Teichert came in with his parents in tow. They were understandably nervous and defensive.

"My son didn't hurt that girl," the woman said immediately as they were led into the interrogation room.

Brock, a big kid, roped with lean muscle, seemed equally jittery. He had guilty hands, Silas noted. Unable to stop fidgeting, Brock lowered his hands to his lap. "How long is this going to take? I have practice."

"I'm sure your coach will understand," Silas said. "Please, take a seat. Now, how did you know Rhia Daniels?"

"We went to school together."

"Was there anything more to your relationship aside from being schoolmates?" Silas asked, giving Brock the opportunity to come clean first.

"No. I barely knew her."

Nope, the kid wanted to play dumb—probably an act for his parents' benefit. Maybe the parents didn't care for Rhia and made it difficult for Brock to date her.

"Are you sure about that?"

"My son answered the question," the father said. "What's this about?"

Silas held Brock's stare until the boy's gaze darted away. "Brock, I don't think that's true," he said, casting a glance at the parents. "Now, let me tell you something… I'm really good at being able to spot a lie. It's what I do. And right now you're lying through your teeth. Just do yourself a favor and come clean. Whether you're guilty or innocent…either way it's going to come out in the wash so let's just cut to the chase."

"Leroy?" The wife looked to her husband, strain in her voice. "Should I call our lawyer?"

"Why would your son need a lawyer if he's done nothing wrong?" Silas countered congenially. "We're just talking right now, trying to get a few things straightened out."

"I don't like the way you're talking to my son," the wife said stiffly. "He's a good boy."

"I'm sure he is, which is why I want to get this part over with. It's really just to rule out that Brock didn't kill Rhia. One swipe of the cheek and you're free to go but, I would think that if you were innocent, you would be happy to help in any way you could...especially since Rhia was your girlfriend."

"She most certainly was not," the wife said indignantly. She nudged Brock. "Tell him that you and that girl were not dating."

"I've got a whole slew of witnesses that will say otherwise. Your son was seen with Rhia last weekend at a bonfire. Remember that, Brock?"

Leroy pulled a face, sensing that his son wasn't being honest with them. "Spit it out, son. What's he talking about?"

Brock looked to his dad, chewing his cheek. He went from defiant to resigned in a heartbeat. "Rhia and I had been dating for three months."

"Three months!" the mom gasped at the shock. "What are you talking about?"

"You were being such a bitch about it that I didn't figure you needed to know," Brock said mulishly.

"You watch your language," his mother said, wiping at angry tears. "I told you that girl was bad news. And now look at the trouble you're in."

"Stop, Mom. She's dead for God's sake," Brock said, embarrassed. "Give her a break."

"So why are we here?" Leroy asked, getting to the point. "Poor judgment in dating isn't a crime."

"No, you're right." Silas slid the court order across the desk. "This is a warrant for your son's DNA. We need a sample to determine paternity."

"P-paternity?" the woman gasped. "What?"

"Rhia was pregnant," Silas told her. "About six weeks."

Brock drew up with a start. "It wasn't mine," he protested. "We never even had sex!"

Silas expected the denials. He lifted the cheek swab. "Then this will show you are not the father. Open, please."

Brock allowed Silas to swab his cheek and then said, "Look, I don't know who she was shacking up with but it sure as hell wasn't me. That's what we were fighting about at the bonfire. She wouldn't give it up. Three months, man. For nothing. All I got was to second base."

The mom closed her eyes, looking green around the gills. Granted, it had to be uncomfortable to listen to your kid talk about his sex life—or lack thereof—but Silas didn't have the option of handling them with kid gloves, no matter how gentle Lester wanted him to be.

"Is that why you killed her?" Silas asked, deliberately provoking the kid. "She wouldn't have sex with you?"

"I didn't kill her!" Brock shouted, slamming his fists on the metal table, causing both parents to jump.

"Settle down!" Leroy barked then glowered at Silas. "Are you finished?"

"Seems you've got a temper," Silas said, capping the swab. "Did you ever hit Rhia?"

"Don't answer that," his father growled. "Unless you've got reason to hold my son, we're leaving."

Silas nodded. "Thank you for your cooperation. I'll be in touch."

Brock walked stiffly from the room with his parents

right behind him. Silas eyed the swab container, wondering if the DNA would come back that Brock was lying.

Or if Brock was telling the truth.

And if that was the case…who the hell had Rhia been sleeping with?

Chapter 17

Quinn chewed her nail, watching from behind the glass of the interrogation room.

Brock definitely seemed like a D-bag but was he a killer? Just going from first impressions, Quinn could put together a surface story.

Brock's parents didn't approve of Rhia and made it clear he wasn't to date her but kids being kids, Brock dated her without their knowledge.

But if what Brock said was true—that he'd never actually slept with Rhia—was it possible Rhia had been using Brock as a cover for whom she was really seeing?

Why would a teenager hide who she was dating?

Unless it was someone she shouldn't be seeing.

A teacher?

Rhia had been a pretty girl, popular. Easy enough to swivel a few heads.

But if it'd been a teacher, Britain would've known. That would've been something hard to hide from her best friend.

Quinn didn't think her illicit boyfriend was at the school.

Maybe someone she'd met on the internet? Tinder?

The door opened and she expected to see Silas but it was Harrison.

She hid her disappointment and smiled instead.

Harrison was a pain in her ass—always pestering her for a date—and he was becoming downright pushy about it lately.

"Working on a hot story?" he asked, lounging against the door frame.

Quinn smiled, quipping, "Always," and tried to maneuver around him but Harrison had more to say.

"I always knew you were thirsty but I never knew just how far you'd go to get what you wanted."

"What does that mean?"

He gestured to the interrogation room. "You're here with that Fed. Everyone's seen you around with him. Acting like you're some kind of team. Everyone knows reporters and Feds aren't pals so that tells me you're giving him something for his trouble. Hell, Red, if I'd known that's the way you wanted to play, I could've given you what you wanted. I've got all kinds of good stuff I can give you, starting with nine inches of solid steel."

Dream on. As if he was packing nine inches—five if he was lucky. Quinn met Harrison's stare. "You know this is called harassment, right? Keep it up and I'll have to report you."

He laughed, lifting his hands in mock surrender. "Down girl, just playing. Get a sense of humor, why don't you."

"I laugh when I hear something funny," Quinn retorted, trying to push past him, but Harrison wouldn't move. She glared up at him. "You're in the way."

Harrison bent down to whisper in her ear. "You know, someday you're going to need a cop to save your pretty little ass and I'm not sure anyone will be available. Sure would be a shame if anything happened to that sweet face, wouldn't it?"

Quinn fought the urge to step back and held her ground. "You're a dick."

"But I don't have to be. Just say the word and I'll be a gentleman. I'd be willing to do all sorts of things for you, sweetness."

Quinn wanted to tell Harrison that she had zero respect for him as a person but only marginally less as a cop. He abused his position regularly and if he wasn't related to a founding father of Port Orion, he would've been kicked out on his ass a long time ago.

But she couldn't say that.

Not yet anyway.

"Get out of my way before I start screaming my head off," Quinn said.

But quick as a snake, Harrison jerked her to him, pressing a hard kiss against her lips that made her want to vomit.

He released her and she nearly fell to her ass. She wiped her mouth, horrified. Before he removed himself, he said with a grin, "Someday you're going to learn that you're meant to be with me, Red. Someday."

And then he left her there, shaking and feeling violated.

It was just a kiss, she tried to tell herself. But she couldn't stop wiping at her lips because she could still feel the repulsive press of his mouth against hers.

The door reopened and this time it was Silas. "What's wrong?" he asked, immediately noticing her distress.

"Nothing. I'm fine," she lied, hating that her voice had a slight tremble to it. "Seriously, I'm fine. I just need some air."

She bolted past Silas and left the station as quickly as her legs would carry her. Air. She just needed air.

But even as she gulped big lungfuls, she still couldn't stop shaking.

She couldn't tell if she was shaking because she was angry as hell or scared.

Harrison had never been so aggressive—more of an annoyance—but this time was different.

She was much smaller than he was and he'd used that against her. She'd been powerless to stop him.

And it'd happened so quick that she hadn't had time to react.

Her hands were still shaking.

Just chill out. Focus. It was just a stupid kiss.

But tears were brimming to the surface.

And the minute Silas appeared, she wanted to run into his arms but she held back, needing to find solid ground before she involved Silas in something that wasn't his problem.

"Sorry... I just needed—"

"Some air, yeah, that's what you said. You're pale," he observed, regarding her intently. "How about telling me what's really wrong instead of lying to me?"

Quinn opened her mouth to offer another denial but the words wouldn't come. In fact, her mouth dried up and her throat tightened as more tears fell.

Silas guided her away from her car and straight to his. She didn't question, just climbed in and buckled up. She didn't care that people would whisper; all she wanted was to get away from Harrison.

Like, now.

Quinn had expected to return to Silas's hotel but when he took a detour, she didn't bother to question it.

After a short drive out of town, she realized they were heading down a private road. The forest flanked the road on both sides but soon she realized the road had curved back around, ending at a small cottage with private beach access.

Quinn looked to Silas. "Who owns this place?"

"Friends of the family. Marcia and Raymond Brown. It's their vacation house during the summer but it's all closed up for winter. I knew no one would be here and no one would be watching over our shoulders."

Quinn cast a grateful smile toward Silas for his thoughtfulness. "Thanks. I could use a minute to breathe."

"Me, too," he said, opening the door. "C'mon. Let's go inside."

Quinn followed Silas as he opened the small cottage. It smelled of dust and time, as if no one had been there in quite a while.

Silas made a fire in the stove while Quinn wandered the quaint house.

The worn hardwood creaked under her shoes, and the windows had that mottled glass look common to old-fashioned windows.

A small, hand-wound clock sat still, waiting for someone to wake it up with a gentle twist of the key.

Silas found a blanket and tucked it around Quinn then returned her to the sofa.

"What happened?" he asked, going straight to the point.

Quinn wanted to tell him even though she knew she shouldn't.

Instead, she said, "It's not your problem. I'll deal with it."

"You were shaking and pale as a ghost. You looked terrified. I haven't known you long but something tells me you don't scare easily. So, what the hell happened?"

Quinn swallowed, wishing she could just forget it happened. "I…it's stupid. I don't know why I'm so upset over it. Honestly, I just want to move on. It's not a big deal."

Silas's lips seamed together. He knew she was lying

through her teeth. But Quinn was embarrassed to have been so shook up by something so small.

Harrison had stolen a kiss. Big deal, right?

She forced a laugh. "Look at you, being my hero. That's so sweet. But I don't need a hero. I'm fine and I don't want to talk about it anymore, okay?"

Silas sighed and took a seat next to her on the sofa. The crackle of the fire was soothing but Quinn couldn't shake the queasy feeling in her gut.

"Let's talk about the case," she suggested. At least that would take her mind off Harrison's blatant assault.

But Silas wasn't so easily thrown off the scent. He reached over and caressed her cheek. She leaned into his touch, closing her eyes briefly. How easy would it be to open her mouth and just tell Silas what had happened?

Tears rushed to the surface and she knew if she didn't let it out, she would burst.

"Okay, fine. I'm only telling you so we can move on. It's no big deal but Harrison Dex kissed me in the surveillance room behind the glass. He's always had a thing for me and I guess he thought it was okay to just take what he wanted."

"Was this consensual?" Silas asked quietly.

"Hell, no, it wasn't consensual. He just grabbed me and smashed his mouth against mine. I thought I was going to throw up."

Silas swore under his breath. "I knew something was wrong. Why didn't you say something?"

"Because, I mean, it was just a kiss. Harrison is harmless, mostly. He's annoying but I can handle him."

Well, she could until today. That helpless feeling continued to linger and she hated it.

"It wasn't just a kiss—a man in a position of power assaulted you," Silas disagreed, his nostrils flaring ever so slightly. "Has he done this before?"

"No."

His strained silence weighed on her shoulders. She knew what he wanted to ask—*did you report Harrison?*—but he didn't and she was grateful.

"I'll handle Harrison when the time is right," Quinn said. "He's an annoyance. If he tries something like that again, I'll knee him in the balls."

"I'm sorry... I can't let this go."

"Why not?"

"Because the fact that he touched you without consent... it's sexual assault."

Quinn knew Silas was right. Harrison often abused his authority in small ways, nothing so dramatic as what he'd done to her, but little slips turned into big falls, which was what Silas was saying.

But Silas didn't have to live in this town in the aftermath.

"Trust that I'll take care of it," she assured him, though Quinn didn't actually have a plan; she just wanted Silas to stop. She reached for his hand and squeezed it. "Thanks for having my back, though. I could get used to this working-together-with-benefits gig."

He followed a faint scowl with, "You're making light of this to try and distract me but it's not going to work."

"Please, Silas. Let's just get back to the case."

Her plea seemed to reach him and he grudgingly backed down but she could still sense that red-hot ember, pulsing beneath the surface, just waiting for the right breeze to spark again.

"Not quite yet..." he said in a low tone, his gaze locking with tenderness on hers.

Silas pulled her to him, sealing his mouth to hers in a firm, cleansing kiss that wiped away the memory of Harrison and replaced it with one hundred percent Silas.

She melted against him, blissfully drowning in the sensation of being wholly safe and secure for the first time since that awful moment.

Silas slowly broke the kiss but held her gaze. He thumbed her bottom lip and said, "If he touches you again…"

"He won't."

"No. He won't," Silas promised with a dark edge that stole her breath. "Ever again."

Quinn shivered.

That worked for her.

Silas knew all the good reasons to distance himself from Quinn, especially in light of the startling information she'd shared about the detective.

The smart decision would be to take her assurances at face value and move on—he didn't have time to meddle in someone else's business—but the knowledge was like a burr under his skin.

"I just can't shake the feeling that there is something behind Sara Westfall's death that wasn't right," Quinn said, deep in thought, ready to move on. "Maybe I'm way too open to conspiracy theories but it feels too coincidental that Sara died after posting personal opinions on Spencer's death."

Quinn's musing pulled his focus. "The problem with looking for conspiracies is that you often find them—even if they aren't real. Be careful chasing after ghosts."

"I would've thought that you'd be on board with chasing down this particular lead," Quinn said.

"It just seems far-fetched," he admitted.

"So you don't think that whoever killed Spencer might've found a way to kill Sara as a way to shut her up? What if she accidentally stumbled on something and the killer got twitchy?"

"That's an awful lot of 'what-ifs.'"

"Stranger things have happened."

"Have they?" he teased.

"Yes," Quinn replied with a small sniff. "Truth is stranger than fiction."

He chuckled, his thoughts still preoccupied. Silas knew all the good reasons to drop the subject of the detective but he could still see Quinn's shaken expression and he knew she was making light of something terrible.

But before he could broach the subject again, Quinn asked, "Why did you bring me all the way here?"

The truth was he wanted to bring her someplace away from prying eyes. He was tired of the hotel, skulking around so as to avoid curious stares and the inevitable questions. But to admit that was to admit something was happening between them in spite of both insisting it wouldn't.

"A change of scenery," he finally answered. "And I thought you'd like the cabin."

"I do. Under different circumstances…this could be quite nice."

He agreed with a brief smile before sighing. "Yeah, it's been a while since I've been here. The offer is always there, but returning to Port Orion was never high on my list."

"I can only imagine." She inhaled a deep breath and let it out slowly as her fingers twined with his. "Maybe talking about the case isn't a good idea. Maybe we should just talk, get to know each other."

"You sure you want to do that?" he asked, enjoying the feel of her fingers entangled with his. "Things could start to get complicated."

"Only if we let them."

Easier said than done. Silas already felt knotted up over Quinn. "What do you want to know?" he asked.

"Ever married?"

"No. I guess this is where I say I'm married to the job

and the FBI is a demanding mistress, but if I say that then I might give you the impression that I'm giving something up by being a workaholic."

"Are you?"

"No. My job is fulfilling."

He sounded like a robot, parroting the right words, but there was something lacking in their delivery. What was he supposed to do? Admit that sometimes he wondered what his life might've been like if he'd pursued a less demanding career? Thankfully, the moments were few and far between but they were poignant when they came.

The fact was none of his brothers had married yet.

Maybe they all had the same hang-ups about loss.

"What about you?" he asked, turning the tables. "Why no boyfriend?"

"When you grow up in a fishbowl, you get tired of the same old goldfish swimming in circles around each other." Quinn pulled her hand free and adjusted her blanket before sharing, "You know, it just became clear to me that everyone was screwing everyone else. It was this big circle of who's sleeping with who, partners switching with each other like a damn square dance and I didn't want anything to do with it so I took myself out of the equation."

"You don't date?"

"Not locally."

Ah. "Well, there are advantages to that, I suppose," he said.

"Absolutely. I like that no one knows who I'm seeing and no one pokes their nose into my business. And aside from certain people, the guys have stopped pestering me. Funny thing, though, somehow a rumor started that I was a lesbian and suddenly, I was getting hit on by chicks at the bar. That was funny, but once I assured them that I enjoy a sausage and not a taco, they backed off."

Silas laughed. "Never tempted to play for the other team?"

"Oh, don't get me wrong. After a few drinks I may have thought about the possibility for a night, but in the end, I knew I was firmly dedicated to Team Sausage."

"That works for me," he said, leaning over to kiss her. There was something intriguing about Quinn that drew him deeper and deeper toward the very thing that he ought to be avoiding but he wasn't fighting it all that hard. "What other secrets do you have, Quinn Jackson?" he asked in a low, playful tone as he brushed another kiss across her lips.

"I'm lactose intolerant," she answered, smiling against his mouth. "So whatever you do...don't let me eat ice cream. Ever."

"What about cheese? I recall you ordering a cheese omelet that was more cheese than egg."

"Yeah, I paid for that later but there are some things you just can't give up."

"So what happens when you eat something with lactose?"

"Let's just say gastric distress on par with Armageddon. My uncle Leo says I should have to register with the government as a weapon of mass destruction."

At that Silas lost it, laughing so hard he nearly doubled over. "You're something else," he said, wiping at his eyes. "Fart humor. How'd you know that was my secret weakness?"

"Isn't it everyone's?" she countered, grinning. It was almost too easy between them, seductively dangerous. Quinn knew it, too. Their laughter subsided and Quinn ventured, "Silas...what happens if the killer isn't connected to Spencer's death?"

That question haunted him at night. He knew it was a possibility—hell, it was a probability—but the answer always remained the same. "I'll go home and resume my life," he said.

"It must be hard to live with the knowledge that you might never get answers," she said.

"It's more like a numbness in your brain. After a time, the pain fades to a dull ache, never quite gone, always pulsing in the background. But you learn to deal with it."

"What was Spencer like?"

Silas chuckled. "Like any other snot-nosed little brother who was always up your ass, wanting to do what you were doing."

"Were you close?"

"Yeah. All of us were. But I resented him a lot. Spencer was the baby. He always got away with shit that I didn't, and because he was closer in age to me, I always ended up his babysitter."

Silas fell silent for a moment. With the resentment came the guilt after Spencer was found dead. "If it weren't for me... Spencer would still be here."

"That's dangerous thinking."

He agreed but didn't change the facts. "I ditched him that day."

"You couldn't have known what was going to happen. Don't you tell parents not to think that way?"

Of course he did. But it was different when the mirror was facing you.

"I don't believe in fate. If I'd been there, none of this would've happened. That's the reality. I don't fight it anymore. I've accepted it. But it still sticks like a rock in my throat."

"Where is Spencer buried?"

"He isn't," Silas answered. "My parents had him cremated because they knew they weren't staying in Port Orion and hadn't wanted to leave him behind. To my knowledge, my brother's remains are in a vase in my mother's bedroom."

"Sometimes it's nice to have someplace to go, to feel close to the people we've lost. I always feel better when I visit my parents' graves."

Even if Spencer had been buried in Port Orion, it wouldn't have mattered. Silas would never have visited.

Quinn's soft smile mirrored her touch as she tapped his chest. "Your brother is here. Always. No matter where his remains are."

Silas fought the tears that burned behind his eyes. He caressed her cheek. "Who are you, Quinn Jackson?" he asked with subtle wonder. How had she dropped into his life without warning and yet…he couldn't seem to imagine his life before her. He brushed a tender kiss across her lips.

Silas didn't want to talk about Spencer any longer. He rose and helped Quinn to her feet. "Time for bed," he told her, leading Quinn to the bedroom.

The heat from the fireplace didn't quite warm the chill in the bedroom but a nice, thick quilt would keep them toasty.

That and their bodies pressed against one another.

Silas helped Quinn undress and they climbed into the soft bed, the old springs creaking slightly.

"I feel like I'm on *Little House On the Prairie*," she giggled from beneath the blanket.

Silas moved his hand across her smooth belly, loving the way she trembled at his touch as he traveled between her legs, cupping the moist heat.

"It's a good thing no one is around for miles…because we're about to shake the rust off this old bed."

Quinn giggled and wrapped her arms around him as he rolled on top.

Silas took his time, teasing her, showing her all the

ways he was beginning to care about her with the power of his tongue and hands.

Neither were ready to deal with the ramifications of the words.

Even if they were both feeling it.

Chapter 18

Silas dropped Quinn off at first light to pick up her car to avoid as many questions as possible, and Quinn was thankful no one saw her as she drove away.

Tiptoeing into the house, she yawned and headed for her bed, hoping to catch a few more winks before it was time for work but as luck would have it, Uncle Leo was already up.

And the thunderous expression on his scruffy face was pretty intimidating.

"Is this how things are going to be? No call? No check-in to let me know you're not dead on the side of the road somewhere?"

Quinn bit her lip, apologetic. "I lost track of time. I'm sorry, I stayed at Johnna's place last night and forgot my phone charger. Were you worried?"

"Hell yes, I was worried," he said, looking as if he'd aged ten years. "There's a killer on the loose and you're determined to put yourself in the thick of things. Why the hell wouldn't I be worried?"

"I'm so sorry for worrying you," Quinn said. "I'll call next time."

"Quinn…what is happening with you? It's like you're changing right before my eyes and I don't think I like what I see."

Quinn drew back, stung. "And just how exactly am I changing?"

"You're just so…reckless and inconsiderate. I don't even recognize you these days."

"I've always been reckless," she disagreed, but not because she wanted to own that argument but because she was hurt that her uncle was disappointed in her for whatever reasons he'd cooked up in his head as valid. "I will call next time."

"You look exhausted," Leo remarked with grudging concern as if he couldn't help himself. "Did you and Johnna stay up all night, gabbing?"

Yes, because I'm twelve, Uncle Leo. She held the quip back, knowing that to let that comment fly would only inspire more questions. Instead, she smiled and said, "Yeah, some habits die hard. I'm going to crash for a little bit."

"All right," Leo said, grabbing his coffee mug. "I have errands to run. Be home tonight, please. My heart can't take another long night of worrying."

She was truly sorry for worrying Leo. He was such a protective bear sometimes. Quinn never bugged him when he went on his Thailand photography excursions. Not that she could. He always seemed out of cell service when she tried.

Quinn always had to wait for him to call her, which he did, but sometimes days went by without a single call.

But Leo had always subscribed to the "Do as I say; not as I do" camp and that was nothing new.

She went to her bedroom and climbed into her bed, ready to fall instantly asleep but even though she was tired, sleep didn't seem in the cards.

Her mind was already buzzing.

Was it wrong that she wanted Rhia's murder to have some connection to Spencer's, if only to spend more time with Silas?

No, that wasn't the only reason, she told herself. Silas needed closure.

She couldn't imagine bearing the burden of all that guilt for so long.

Silas deserved a break.

He was such a good man.

And so different from anyone else.

Even the way he touched her was unlike any other man.

Quinn ought to focus on the case but her mind was stubbornly set on thoughts of Silas.

Strong, stoic, surprisingly funny—and sexy as hell.

Anyone would have to be blind not to see what Silas brought to the table.

She wondered how many broken hearts he'd left behind in his life.

Being married to the job…it was tough for any woman to compete.

What would people say if they found out that she was sleeping with Silas?

Oh, God. The tongues would fairly fall out of people's mouths.

In spite of the horrifying thought, Quinn grinned.

Let their tongues wag.

But most of all, she hoped that word somehow got back to Harrison. Maybe then he'd leave her alone.

What was she going to do about that situation?

Harrison had assaulted her.

Silas was right—there was no whitewashing what the detective had done.

But if she reported Harrison and the investigation went nowhere, she'd have to live with Harrison in the same town.

He could make her life a living hell.

So leave Port Orion, a voice said. *Leave all that bullshit behind.*

As much as she'd love to pack up and head for greener pastures, she wasn't ready to make the leap.

She didn't want to fail because she jumped too soon.

Failing and having to return with her tail between her legs would be worse than anything she could imagine.

Quinn shifted in bed, smiling faintly at the subtle ache between her thighs, reminding her of where Silas had been a few short hours ago, and she knew with resigned certainty that things had changed between her and Silas.

Changed in a way that would make it difficult to say goodbye when the time came.

They'd both been very clear that this was a no-strings-attached setup.

Watching Silas leave town, knowing she wasn't going to see him again, well, it set off a strange yearning that she wasn't ready to put a name to.

Maybe it was just the sex, she reasoned. The man could rock a bed.

True, great sex could bind two people temporarily but it would never last because you needed more than epic sex to make a relationship work.

Quinn groaned and kicked the bedsheets away. So much for sleep.

She grabbed her laptop and powered up. Searching for "Sara Westfall + Port Orion," she perused the links that popped up.

She sorted through pages of useless or irrelevant links

and then found a partially cached page of Sara's defunct blog, Port Orion Intrigue.

Everyone knows the corruption in Port Orion is legion but I'm not supposed to write about that. The secrets in this town could choke a horse. Do you know your neighbor? Do you know what he does at night when no one is watching? Sometimes to catch a monster you have to pretend to look the other way so you can gather the tools you need to win.

Quinn frowned with surprise. Sara had some strong opinions. She never named names, only used initials. Who was she talking about?

Did Little S find out something that X didn't want anyone to know?

Little S. That could stand for Spencer. Or it could mean someone else. There was no making sense of what Sara had written.

Frustration ate at Quinn. More ghost leads. What if Sara was a delusional alcoholic like Mick implied?

What if Sara had truly been trying to bring someone to justice?

Who the hell was X?

Quinn chewed her bottom lip. Corruption. Could it be... Sheriff Mankins? No. That wasn't possible. Lester was the sweetest man she'd ever known.

But whomever Sara was referencing was good at pretending.

What if the most dangerous person in Port Orion...was the one in charge of protecting it?

Silas stepped out of the shower to find Quinn at his hotel room door. Tucking the towel around his hips, he opened the door and she strode in, pausing only briefly to appreciate the view and then immediately started jabbering.

"I found a cached page of Sara's blog. The information was confusing at best but I wanted to tell you right away.

Something about it feels important. I know Mick implied that Sara was an alcoholic and maybe she was, but that doesn't mean she wasn't onto something."

"What did it say?"

"She only used initials 'X' and 'S' and it's easy to assume that 'S' means Spencer but I haven't a clue who 'X' could be. We need to talk to Sara's family and see if they had any idea what she was working on when she died. Also, I want to pull up the accident report and see if there's anything about her blood alcohol content. What if she wasn't drinking when she died, but someone made it look as if she were because they knew about her addiction? Seems an easy way to set someone up, don't you think?"

He loved how Quinn's mind worked even if she had a penchant for jumping to the most fantastic conclusion. "We'll follow up," he agreed. "Sounds worth a second look. But try not to get your hopes up prematurely. One thing I've learned in this job is that sometimes false leads seem more plausible the more you want a case solved."

"My gut says there's something there. Sara talked about 'corruption' a lot. Was she referencing politics? Law enforcement? Or was she just rambling after too many beers? I don't know but my Spidey-senses are tingling and I can barely see straight."

"Let me get dressed and we'll check it out."

Quinn nodded, distracted by her own thoughts. She tapped her finger lightly against her bottom lip, something he'd noticed she did when she was trying to piece through a puzzle in her mind.

"You know, at first I thought Sara was referencing Lester but honestly, that's just ridiculous. I've known Lester my whole life and he's the sweetest man on the planet."

"Let's see where the lead takes us," he suggested, mildly troubled by the thought, as well. Lester had saved him when no one else had been able to get through to him. In a way, he owed Lester everything. The remote possibility that Lester was involved…it turned his stomach but he'd follow any lead.

Dressed and ready, they made a game plan.

"I'll come with you to the station to pull the accident report," Silas said, but Quinn shut him down. Frowning, he asked, "Why not?"

"I don't need people talking about how we're buddies. Besides, it's a waste of your time to follow me around when you can chase other leads. We need to be efficient about this."

What she said was true but he didn't like her going to the station without him because of that grabby-hands detective. Of course, he knew if he said that, Quinn would pitch a fit so he kept that comment to himself.

Instead, he nodded and said, "Fine. I'll track down Sara's remaining family and see if I can secure a time to talk. In the meantime—" he pulled her to him, leaving her with one firm demand because it was nonnegotiable "—you will promise me that if that asshole tries anything while you are there, you will knee him in the balls and then report his ass, got it?"

Quinn bit her lip and nodded.

Satisfied, Silas brushed a kiss across her lips. "I mean it, Quinn," he murmured. "If he touches you again, I'll handle the situation for good."

She shivered a little in his arms but he knew it wasn't from fear. Her pupils dilated and her breath became short. His little hellcat liked a firm hand when it mattered. "You're so bossy," she said with a tiny smile that instantly sent a triple shot of lust straight to his groin. "But okay."

Silas smothered the urge to bend her over the bed for a quickie but it took an act of immense strength to release her from his arms.

Work now; play later.

Quinn grabbed her purse and left, giving Silas an excellent view of her perfect backside as she went.

He was fairly certain he could bounce a quarter off those pert cheeks.

His own breath felt trapped in his chest.

Get your mind off the girl, Silas.

Silas shook off the lingering hunger and pulled his focus where it belonged.

Time to use the FBI resources to track down Sara's family.

If anyone knew what the real Sara was like...hopefully, they were still around to share her story.

Leo stepped into his dark room and closed the door. Change was inevitable but Leo preferred the comfort of routine. He knew when he walked into his dark room exactly what was expected of him.

He'd always groused that there was no sense of artistry in digital manipulation, not like processing a photo with your bare hands, watching as it emerged like a newborn from the solution.

He was responsible for the outcome, the final product.

There was security in that knowledge because Leo knew photography.

Unlike other things in life that weren't so certain.

Port Orion was becoming a different place. People he didn't recognize passing by his storefront without looking twice, preferring the immediacy of digital over the artistry of film.

But Quinn was always accusing him of holding on to the past, teasing him about his archaic cell phone that neither texted nor did any of that fancy do-dah that he could do without.

There was value in disconnecting.

He closed his eyes and breathed deep the familiar scent of chemicals, letting the smell calm him.

This business with Rhia Daniels had upset the entire town.

This town didn't know Rhia.

Manipulative, cruel little bitch.

But he couldn't say that without putting a target on his back.

Rhia was a sweetheart, pretty as a picture and everyone's darling.

The corners of his lips turned down. Imagine the shock if he shared how Rhia had extorted him.

But that would open up too many questions.

Questions he wasn't ready to face.

A sharp pain pierced his chest. He rubbed at the spot on his sternum. Angina, his doc said, brought on by stress. Nothing to worry about. Just stress less.

Leo wiped at his forehead as he breathed through the pain, knowing it would pass. He and Lester were taking bets on who would croak first. Some days it felt as if he was winning that race.

As soon as this investigation was closed, everything would go back to normal.

At least that was the hope.

Chapter 19

Quinn walked into the station, signed in and strode forward as if her heart wasn't suddenly hammering against her breastbone.

She licked her dry lips and forced a cheerful wave at the officers she knew and ducked into Lester's office, breathing easy for the first time since entering the building.

Lester smiled when he saw her. Lester always had a smile for her. How could she entertain—even for a second—that Lester might be the evil Sara was writing about?

"What are you up to, troublemaker?" Lester asked.

"Just digging into leads," she answered, returning the smile before scooping up a handful of candies from the bowl on his desk. "You know, you shouldn't eat these."

"Oh, hush. Now, what do you need?"

"I need a copy of Sara Westfall's accident report."

Lester lost his smile to a frown. "Sara Westfall? Now, that's a name from the past. What do you need that report for?"

"Just something I'm looking into," Quinn said. "Do you think you can have someone pull it up for me?"

"Sure, I don't see why not. I just don't know why you'd want it. That happened ages ago."

"Did you know Sara?"

Lester coughed and shifted in his seat. "Not really."

"Seems no one did," Quinn said. "Did you know she had a blog where she talked about all the corruption in Port Orion?"

"Blogs," Lester said with derision. "What happened to people having better things to do than poking at other people? Now that you mention it, I do remember something about her stirring up mud with her silly internet stuff. I hope you're not thinking of following in her footsteps."

"Oh, no. I don't have time to blog. But I am curious as to what she thought she knew. Mick implied she was an alcoholic."

"I suppose he would know," Lester said. "He was her boss."

"True. But she was also three months in the hole to payroll. Why do you think Mick allowed her to take advances on her checks? Seems weird to me."

"That's between him and his employee."

"Do you think they were sleeping together?"

Lester offered a strained chuckle. "You are determined to shake the hen house, aren't you?"

"I guess so, if that means answers fall out."

"Now, what does Sara Westfall have to do with Rhia Daniels? Have you moved on from that case?"

"No, quite the opposite. I think they're all related."

Lester looked as if she'd lost her mind. "That's a reach."

"What if the person who killed Spencer Kelly was the same person who killed Sara Westfall and later Rhia Daniels?"

Lester frowned and wiped at his brow. "But why?"

"That's what I don't know yet," she admitted. "But I have a feeling that I'm getting close. When do you think I can get that file pulled?"

"Now, hold on, that was a long time ago, and I don't even know where it would be. All the archives are in a warehouse. You know I don't have the manpower to send someone on a search and rescue for an old accident report on a hunch. Come on, Quinn. You're killing me here."

"Lester, please. What if Sara was really onto something?"

"And what if she was just a crazy loon?"

Quinn drew back, surprised at Lester's cruel jab. "And what if she wasn't?" she returned quietly, trying not to be hurt by Lester's surly attitude. "Don't we owe it to the victims to follow all leads?"

"Darlin', you know I love you, but you're driving me batty with all these conspiracy theories. This is Port Orion you're talking about, not Las Vegas. We're a simple town with good, honest folk. Why are you trying to paint the place into something it's not?"

Good folk? Like Harrison Dex? Who got the job on the force because his great-grandfather was a founding father of the town? Whose own father was a shady, philandering realtor who couldn't keep his dick in his pants? Whose mother was suspected of embezzling funds from the Friends of the Port Orion Museum where she served as president? Were those the good folk Lester was referencing?

Quinn knew better than to say any of that. Lester preferred things quiet and smooth.

But she couldn't resist one final comment.

"If anyone is trying to paint a picture over the real one, it's you, Lester. Open your eyes. This isn't Mayberry and it never was. No matter how much you try to make it seem so."

"And you think dredging up an old case on the possibility—not solid proof—that foul play was involved is worth the pain and suffering it will cause?"

"Yes." She wasn't budging. "What about Sara's family? What about Spencer's family? Damn, Lester, what about Rhia's family? Aren't they owed whatever resource we can throw at them in the pursuit of justice?"

"We're doing everything we can," Lester snapped, slamming his hand down on the desk so hard she jumped. "You just need to be satisfied with what we can give."

Hot tears burned behind her lids. Lester had never yelled at her. In all the years she'd known him, never had he looked at her with such anger.

It hurt.

It was like having a beloved uncle suddenly turn on you.

Quinn rubbed at her nose to stop the tingling as tears threatened to fall.

"If you make me fill out a FOIA request for the report, I will," she said stiffly, rising. Swallowing the lump in her throat she added, "We're on the same side, Lester. Please don't make me the bad guy for demanding better for the victims."

As if finally hearing her, Lester exhaled a long breath as he shook his head. "I'm sorry for yelling at you, Quinnie. I'm not myself these days. I think the file is still in the building. For some reason, when we did an audit, a few files were inadvertently left out. That one just happened to be one of them," he admitted. "Harrison can grab it for you. Do you need anything else?"

The urge to tell Lester about his detective burned on her tongue. If she was going to say something, now would be a perfect opportunity.

But even as she wanted to tell Lester what a dangerous prick Harrison was…she didn't. Lester had enough on his plate. Instead, she smiled and said, "I'll wait in the conference room for the files."

And then she bounced.

If she knew Lester, she knew that he'd immediately discipline Harrison but he wouldn't fire him and that was what she was worried about.

That was like poking at a beehive.

Harrison would just wait out his punishment and then he'd be back—pissed off and looking for blood.

Lester wanted to spend the rest of his tenure as sheriff on easy mode. She didn't blame him—the man was past his prime and had earned some pasture time—but that didn't really help the citizens of Port Orion.

Harrison walked in and slid the file toward her. "All this fuss over a drunk. You're lucky. One more day and this would've been shipped to the warehouse," he said. She forced a small smile and reached for the file but he stopped her by covering her hand with his.

"You're so damn tiny," he said, dwarfing her hand with his big paw. "I could practically put you in my pocket."

"What are you doing?" she asked, pretending to sound bored when in fact, she was starting to sweat. "You're being ridiculous."

"What do you see in that guy?" he asked, lifting his hand only to grasp hers tightly. "You know he's not going to stick around. There's no future there. Now, me on the other hand…I got prospects. Lester is going to retire soon. Someone has to replace him."

"And you think that someone is you?" Quinn scoffed at the preposterous idea. "You're not remotely qualified."

Harrison squeezed her hand painfully before letting go. "I like that fire. You don't back down. Makes me wonder what you're like in the sack. I bet you're a wild thing. Do you leave scratches?"

Quinn narrowed her gaze. "You'll never know."

"We'll see about that."

What was he saying?

She swallowed the sticky lump caught in her throat but held her ground. Bullies were cowards. If she stood up to Harrison, he'd realize she wasn't easy prey. But the fact that he scared her after that last stunt was eating at her ability to remain strong.

"How do you sleep at night?" Quinn asked, dismissing him as she returned to the file.

But Harrison came around to stand behind her, leaning in to whisper in her ear, "I sleep just fine with dreams of what I'm going to do to you when you're finally mine."

Panic set her heart to fluttering. "If you don't get the hell away from me I'm going to start screaming my bloody head off," she warned.

Harrison chuckled and stepped away with his hands up in mock surrender. "Have fun with your little project," he said before leaving.

Quinn tried to calm her breathing but tears were threatening to fall. Damn him. She gathered the files and hurried from the station.

She couldn't stay there for another minute.

Silas called Quinn but when it went to voice mail, he left a quick message that he'd found Sara's sister and he was headed out to talk with her.

Why didn't she answer? His first thought went straight to that dickhead detective. It still burned that he was doing nothing to put that man straight but he was trying to respect Quinn's boundaries.

It bothered him that he felt so protective over Quinn. As much as he told himself to drop it and move on, his thoughts stubbornly returned along with a growl when he pictured Quinn's ashen expression.

He didn't like Quinn going back to the station without protection.

But seeing as she was determined to handle the situation on her own, there wasn't much he could do about it.

And that plain sucked.

Sara's sister, Emily, lived outside town on a small piece of property that overlooked the ocean. The view was tourist-friendly—meaning it was one of those places that begged for a selfie with the obnoxious hashtags, #bestviewever, #vacay, #watchthatfirststep, and Silas wondered why she chose to live so far away from town.

With a final scan around the property, he knocked on the front door.

A woman with frazzled gray hair and suspicious eyes answered, looking about as unwelcome as a hissing cat. "Who are you?" she asked, looking up at him with distrust. "What do you want?"

He produced his badge. "I'm Silas Kelly with the FBI. I was wondering if I could talk to you about your sister, Sara."

Emily blinked as if she hadn't been expecting his request but after another quick perusal of his credentials, she let Silas follow her into the house.

Cats darted from beneath sofas and chairs and the smell of ammonia pinched at his nose. He hated the smell of cats. A multitude of unkempt cats was the worst.

Emily sank into a worn chair and eyed Silas warily. "What do you want to know about Sara?"

Silas took a seat on the sofa, grimacing when he saw a crusted piece of cat crap on the sofa cover beside him. This place ought to be condemned. "Were you close?"

"I guess. She took care of me," Emily said. "Managed my trust for me."

A trust account. Silas realized Emily probably suffered

from some sort of mental challenge, which explained the multitude of cats and the dismal living conditions.

"I need to ask you some personal questions about your sister. Is that okay?"

Emily nodded as she picked up a cat and dragged it into her lap. The cat growled with displeasure but didn't try to flee. "She's been dead a long time now. Why the interest now? I tried to tell the cops that someone set her up but no one listened."

"Who do you think set up your sister?"

"Damned if I know. All I know is that she was onto something and whoever was guilty must've got twitchy because right before my sister was going to send all her information to you guys, she died."

"What do you mean?"

"Sara had a whole mess of papers, evidence she was going to send to the FBI because she knew no one in Port Orion was going to help her. But she died before she could."

"Sara had a contact with the Bureau?" he asked.

"No, not yet. She was waiting for the final piece of the puzzle. That's what she kept saying. And I think she got what she was looking for but then they killed her."

"Who?"

"Dunno." The angry pull of her mouth vied with the grief in her gaze, and Silas knew the frustration she must have felt, being so helpless. "All I know is that my sister was a good woman but no one wants to hear that. All they want to talk about is how she liked to drink. Yeah? So what. Drinking ain't a crime."

"Sara used to work for the newspaper but she also used to write her own blog about stuff going on in Port Orion. Do you remember that?"

"Yeah, she used to read it to me. It was good stuff. I liked Sara's stories."

"Do you know if they were real stories or made up?"

"Real," Emily answered with a definitive nod. The cat hissed and jumped from Emily's lap, scratching Emily in the process. She rubbed at the long scratch but otherwise didn't react. "Sara said there were lots of bad people in Port Orion and it was her job to tell the world but no one would take her serious so she started writing stuff on the computer."

"Do you know the names of the bad people?" he asked.

Emily snorted as if he was an idiot for asking. "Don't you think if I knew names I'd have told someone by now?"

He supposed that was true, though he suspected Emily had social anxiety, which probably kept her close to home.

"Has someone threatened to hurt you if you tell anyone what you know?"

"Sara spent all her time writing her computer stuff and she died for it. I don't need anyone coming around threatening me to know that it's better if I keep to myself."

"It's really important that you tell me what you know. If Sara was killed for writing something someone didn't want anyone to know, then she deserves justice and the only way to get justice is to put away the person or people who had her killed."

"Like it's that easy," Emily scoffed. "Don't you think that if Sara was able to, she would've?"

"Sara was alone. I'm not."

Emily sniffed, more grief creeping into her expression. "Sara was a good sister. She took real good care of me."

"It's been implied that Sara was an alcoholic."

Emily jerked an angry shrug. "What if she was? Does that mean what they did to her was right?"

"Of course not," he murmured but he needed to know more. "Did Sara have a drinking problem?"

"I wasn't an easy sister."

That was as much an admission as he would probably

get. Silas could only imagine the stress Sara endured as her sister's caregiver.

"Was she drinking the night she died?"

"No."

There was no pause in her recollection; Emily was solid in her memory of that night.

"Sara got a call and she left. She didn't tell me where she was going. And she never came back."

"Who administers your trust now that Sara is gone?"

"Sara set up an account for me. The money is put in my account each month. I never have to leave the house, except to check the mailbox at the end of the driveway."

Sara must've known she was playing with dangerous company and wanted to ensure her sister would be cared for if something happened to her.

"Sara mentioned someone with the initial of 'X.' Do you know who 'X' was?" he asked.

"Someone important. Someone who didn't like to be talked about."

"But did Sara ever mention a name?"

Emily fell silent. If Sara had shared details, Emily was determined to keep that information buried.

"Do you know who 'S' was?"

"That little boy."

Silas's chest tightened. "What little boy?"

"The one that died at Seminole Creek."

"Was his name Spencer?" Silas asked, his chest aching from the breath he was afraid to breathe.

"Yeah."

It was the first time Silas actually felt hope that he was finally on the right path. Even if the path was rocky as hell and likely to kill him.

"Sara felt real bad about the poor kid. She'd wanted to catch who'd done it to him."

"Do you think she knew who killed Spencer?"

"She didn't say but I think she was figuring things out. I think that's what the call was about. She seemed real excited when she left. That was the last time I saw her."

"Do you know why Sara was taking advances on her checks at the paper?"

Emily shook her head but she did share, "Sara was sleeping with her boss. Maybe he was helping her out."

Had Mick been paying for Sara's silence? Or was it completely unrelated?

"Do you have copies of Sara's blog backed up anywhere?" he asked, though he knew the chances were slim.

As expected, Emily shook her head. "I didn't have her password. Eventually, the account closed because I couldn't pay the bill."

"You never printed out a copy or anything like that?" he asked, grasping at straws.

"Maybe...but I don't know where it would be now."

Probably used to line the kitty litterbox by this point, he realized. As much as he wanted to shake the information out of Emily Westfall, he knew it wouldn't do much good. Emily had shared as much as she was able. "Thank you for your help," he said, rising.

Emily rose and shoved her hands in her pockets. "My sister was a good person. Better than me. She stuck around when I couldn't take care of myself no more. I hope you find who did this to her. She deserved better than she ever got."

Silas nodded and let himself out, breathing deep the fresh, salty air. Too many cats. One socially awkward woman hiding behind four walls, insulated from the world.

He didn't exactly get the answers he was hoping for but somehow the information he did get felt important.

Time to see if Quinn managed to get her hands on that accident report.

Chapter 20

Quinn grabbed Chinese food and met Silas back at the hotel. The food was more of a pretense so that she could occupy her hands because her stomach was pitching a fit.

She hadn't wanted to admit it but Silas was right; Harrison was a bigger problem than she realized.

But she wasn't in a position to do much about it. Not until this case closed.

Silas opened the door and smiled instantly. The warmth in his gaze made her wonder how she'd ever thought him cold. He practically burned with heat. When he looked at her with that combination of hunger and desire, it was a wonder Quinn could remain upright.

Yeah, weak in the knees—never saw that coming.

But it'd happened, so why fight it?

Silas pulled her straight to him for a searing kiss, barely pausing to register the box of food in her hand.

"Are you hungry?" she asked against his mouth, unaware of when the box left her fingers. Somehow Silas had relieved her of it and slid it onto the small table before walking her to the bed.

"Starved," he answered, pulling her shirt over her head. Her head fell back with delight as Silas's hot mouth blazed a trail down the column of her neck. "But not for Kung Pao chicken."

"Good, because I brought—" she gasped "—broccoli beef."

He growled and hoisted her into his arms to carry her the short distance to the bed. She shivered at the feel of all that muscle coiling beneath the skin, strong and virile.

Everything about Silas was masculine, from the way he held her gaze like a predator watches its prey to the way he managed to make her feel protected.

Silas helped her out of her jeans, pressing tiny kisses on each spot on her skin where a mark had been left behind, until he brushed a kiss across her covered mound, teasing her with his hot breath on her feminine folds.

She writhed, lifting her hips with short mewling pleas as he slowly sucked the thin fabric into his mouth, the combination of anticipation and pleasure mixing into a heady cocktail of need.

"Silas," she said, his name slipping from her lips like a desperate prayer, "I need you, *please.*"

"So sweet," he murmured as he gently pulled her panties free from her hips to toss to the floor. Silas gazed at her with total possession in his eyes. She shivered, secretly loving the unspoken exchange between them. Her eyelids fluttered shut on a groan as he buried his face between her folds.

"Oh!" Quinn moaned, losing herself to the exquisite mastery of Silas's touch. One finger—in and out—two fingers—in and out—now three all while driving her mad with his tongue.

Silas was merciless in his pursuit of her pleasure. Quinn

happily gave herself to him, sinking into that swirling abyss of abandon without reservation.

No one could touch her like Silas did.

Moisture leaked from the corners of her eyes as the extreme pleasure made her cry, her spread legs quaking without control.

"S-Silas!" She crashed into a wall, spinning out as wave after wave of sensation washed over her, every muscle clenching in a wondrous release.

"Oh God, I needed that," Quinn said, weak as a starved kitten. But Silas wasn't finished with her yet.

Silas thrust inside her, anchoring her hips as he drove into her tight sheath. As she knew it would, another orgasm began to build. Silas gave her no mercy and she wanted none.

Within moments Quinn lost herself to another wave, crying out as Silas found his release at the same time. Sweat dampened their bodies as they collapsed to the bed, breathing hard, hearts beating like frantic rabbits.

It was several moments before either could speak.

Silas quietly discarded the condom she hadn't even realized he'd put on—another reason she was addicted to him, he took control of every facet—and grabbed a bottled water from the mini fridge to hand to her.

She accepted it with murmured thanks and guzzled the water before falling back on the bed, content to lie naked as her body slowly stopped pulsing.

Silas finished his own water and tossed it into the trash before dropping into the chair at the small table.

"You know, this could become a habit."

Quinn smiled hazily and rolled to her side. "What makes you think it's not already?"

He chuckled but didn't dispute it. Silas peeked into the box and grabbed a spring roll.

"So *honey*, how was your day?" he asked half-seriously.

Quinn laughed but behind the laughter was the horrid memory of Harrison's threat. She swung her legs over the side to grab her discarded panties and shimmied them over her hips. "Fine. I got the report."

"Yeah? Let me see it."

Quinn gestured to the box as she slid her jeans on. "It's under the box."

Silas lifted the box the Chinese food was in and found the folder. He opened it up and started reading. The report was all of two pages with very little information that was helpful, which was what Quinn had already discovered.

"There's nothing here," Silas said with a frown.

"Yeah, I know."

"For a fatal accident, this report is pretty bare. Aside from an incredibly high BAC level, there's nothing else."

Quinn shrugged. "I guess they figured it was an open and shut case. I suppose this confirms that Sara was an alcoholic."

"She may well have been an alcoholic but according to her sister, Emily, Sara hadn't been drinking the night she died."

"What did she say?"

"Not much, just that Sara got a call and ran out of the house, excited. That was the last time Emily ever saw her sister."

"But that's not to say that she didn't stop at a bar first," Quinn reasoned. "I mean, it's hard to fake a BAC."

"Is it?"

His question stopped her short. "What do you mean?"

"It's just a typed report. Who's to say that anyone couldn't input that information and no one would be the wiser? Nor would anyone question it because Sara was known to drink."

Quinn gasped at the magnitude of what Silas was suggesting. "Do you really think someone would risk their career to falsify an official document?"

He chuckled at her shock. "Honey, I've seen people do a lot worse for less reason."

That left her reeling. This case was getting bigger and bigger. "How do we find out if the report was falsified?"

"Barring someone coming forward and admitting it? We can't. But Emily confirmed that 'S' was Spencer, which means someone didn't like what Sara was putting out there."

Confirmation of the identity of one of the initials left her giddy. "That's amazing. We're finally onto something," she said. "Now what?"

Silas's pensive expression worried her. "What's wrong?"

"We have a lot of tiny leads that ultimately run in circles. We're missing a key component and I'm running out of time to find something."

That caught her attention. "What do you mean?"

"My superior gave me the time to come here but if I don't come up with something solid, I'll have to leave and return to Chicago."

"You can't go," she protested. "We're finally getting somewhere."

"Maybe. Maybe not. Trust me, I want to believe with all my heart that we are onto something critical but I can't make a case out of bits and pieces of circumstantial evidence."

Frustration ate at her. He was right. They needed something big, a break of some sort to crack this case wide open.

"So you'll just walk away?" she asked.

"Maybe this case was never meant to be solved."

"You don't believe that."

"Hell, I don't know what I believe anymore."

Quinn heard the desperation in his tone, the frustration

that champed at his heels. This case was more than personal to him. It was everything.

To walk away with only the tease of closure...had to be excruciating.

Quinn rose and wrapped her arms around his neck as she settled onto his lap. "Then we will find something so big that you can't walk away," she told him, sealing her mouth to his.

Because of Silas, this case was more to her than just a ticket out of Port Orion.

She'd deal with the fallout later.

For now, she was playing for Team Kelly.

It was early morning. The dawn hadn't crested the horizon yet when his cell phone rang.

He was surprised to see it was his second older brother, Shaine.

"Did I wake you?" he asked.

"No."

"Damn. I'll call earlier next time," Shaine quipped with his signature smart-ass style but he sobered quickly. "Look, man, I heard that you're back in Port Orion. What are you doing? Chasing ghosts?"

"Maybe. Or maybe I'm onto something."

That piqued his interest. "Yeah? How so?"

Silas told Shaine all about Sara Westfall and how she died under suspicious circumstances, the blog and the current investigation into the recent murder of Rhia Daniels.

But Shaine stopped him with a sudden, "Wait a minute...you said this Sara chick wrote a blog?"

"Yeah, but it's long gone. We found a partially cached version but there wasn't much to go on."

"Yeah, I remember that blog," Shaine said, shocking Silas. "Well, I remember Dad following it pretty closely."

"Dad?"

"Yeah. In fact, it was one of the arguments he and Mom got into, because she hated that this reporter chick was using our tragedy to gain traffic on her website."

"Why was Dad interested?"

"Dad thought she might know something. He said Sara was smarter than she looked. Everything was cryptic but there was a message deep within the pages. He said she was probably afraid to come out and just say what she thought was happening, which considering how she died... maybe she was right to be afraid."

"I don't remember any of this," Silas said, baffled.

"Yeah, well, you were a kid and busy being an asshole most days."

No arguing that point. "Do you think Mom would remember any of what the blog said?"

"Don't know but it might be worth a phone call."

"I don't want to upset her unnecessarily," Silas hedged, hating the idea of giving his mother false hope if it turned out this lead went nowhere.

"Mom made her peace a long time ago. She's not as fragile as you think. Ask her. If she remembers anything, she'll tell you. If she doesn't, well, you're not out anything."

Valid.

"Is that why you called? To get me to call Mom?"

"No, but you really should call her now and then. She misses you."

"She's busy living it up as a widowed retiree in Florida," Silas disagreed, fighting against the crush of guilt.

"Call her, you big pussy," Shaine said. "Maybe it'll help."

"Thanks Captain Obvious," Silas said. "Enough about me, how's things with you and Poppy?"

"Can't complain." Silas could hear the grin in his brother's answer.

"Well hopefully she doesn't wise up and realize that she's getting the short end of the stick," he teased.

"There's nothing short about *anything* on me," Shaine returned with typical Shaine smugness. "Maybe that's an issue with you but I'm good over here."

"Dumbass. All right, so you're happy. Good. Glad to hear it."

They spent the next few minutes catching up, filling each other in on current events, but Silas left out the part where he was sleeping with the press. Shaine didn't need yet another way to bust his balls. Big brothers always had plenty of ammunition on their own.

Besides, he didn't know how to classify what was happening between him and Quinn without it sounding cheap and sordid.

He didn't want anyone to judge Quinn for what they were doing.

Not to mention, he wasn't entirely sure what was happening between him and that foxy redhead.

All he knew was that he couldn't stop thinking about her and when he thought of that asshole detective, he wanted to walk into the station and punch Harrison in the mouth.

Last night, Silas realized he and Quinn were worse than a habit; they were an addiction.

The idea of returning to Chicago without her...left him cold.

He also hated the idea of leaving her behind to fend off that lecherous dick all on her own.

Not that Quinn was some weak female who couldn't take care of herself, but sometimes Quinn underestimated the power of others.

That was a mistake that could cost her.

His thoughts returned to the case.

Who would have access to the accident report? The obvious answer was anyone in the station.

But also the coroner could've doctored the report.

The question is...why?

And who could he trust with what he'd learned so far?

As much as he hated to think about the possibility... what if Lester was behind everything?

The man had saved him.

Was he capable of the heinous crimes left in this killer's wake?

God, he hoped not.

But in the meantime, he would keep information close to the vest.

Chapter 21

Quinn was typing up her latest update when Mick walked into her office. Knowing what she did about Sara, she felt a little uneasy around Mick now.

"I think the Rhia Daniels case is cooling. The news vans are already starting to clear out. Maybe we should put our resources elsewhere until something pops up."

"The case is not cold," Quinn disagreed. "The case is hotter than ever. I'm just not in a position to reveal what I know yet."

"And what do you think you know?"

She wasn't deaf to the subtle sneer in his tone. Forcing a smile, she said, "Don't worry. When I'm ready to go public, you'll be the first to know."

"I'm your boss. Tell me now."

"Nope. Sorry."

"Excuse me?"

Mick wasn't accustomed to being defied. He ran the newsroom the way he saw fit and didn't take kindly to back talk. Too bad—Mick should've known that Quinn was nothing but back talk and sass on her best day.

"You're messing with your job, young lady."

She was walking on dangerous ground. But it was now or never. Stand up to Mick or else back down and never have the balls to chase her dream.

It was that simple.

The world was filled with men like Mick Creech and she wasn't about to run with her tail between her legs at the first sign of push-back.

Quinn rose and went toe-to-toe with Mick, which wasn't hard because he was rounder than he was tall.

"Why were you fronting Sara Westfall money from payroll? When she died she was three months in the hole," she tossed at him.

Mick's mouth dropped open a little but he recovered quickly. "Watch yourself," he warned. "You don't know what you're talking about."

"Actually, I do. It's all there in black-and-white. The numbers don't lie. It's just that no one thought to look, but that doesn't mean that the story isn't still there, just waiting to be written."

Mick blanched, his lip trembling a bit. "What story?"

"Maybe the biggest story of all…was Sara Westfall's death a crime of passion? Maybe she was going to tell your wife that you were sleeping together and you had to shut her up? I don't know, I guess I'll just have to go where the leads take me."

She was taking a huge chance. Her instincts told her that Mick wasn't a killer but he wasn't innocent, either.

"Don't go spreading gossip," he said, but his tone had lost its edge. He was scared. "That's not necessary."

"Of course not. I wouldn't dream of spreading rumors or gossip. But I wouldn't hesitate to write the truth…whatever that may be."

"I didn't kill Sara," he said, his gaze darting around the newsroom to see if anyone heard him. He continued in a low tone. "Yes, we were sleeping together and I felt bad for her because of her sister so I fronted her the money, which I paid back to payroll on my own, but I never killed her."

Stunned, Quinn tried to hide her shock at how quickly Mick caved. What a wet noodle. "Who was she writing about on her blog?"

"I don't know."

"You were sleeping together and you didn't know her secrets?" Quinn countered with disbelief. "Yeah, right."

"Look, we were just messing around. My wife...you don't understand...she's a cold, heartless woman. If she'd found out about me and Sara... I would've lost everything, but still, I didn't do anything to hurt Sara. I cared for her."

"So why are you so hell-bent on keeping anyone from digging into her accident?"

Shame crept into his expression. "I didn't want to chance anyone asking questions about our relationship. She was dead. Nothing was going to bring her back, so why dig up dirt? I just wanted it to go away."

"Someone killed her," Quinn said, disgusted at Mick's weakness. He was a coward. "Doesn't that bother you?"

"She was an alcoholic," he said almost desperately. "It was a tragic accident."

"Her sister said she wasn't drinking that night."

"Her sister is crazy," Mick shot back. "You can't believe a word she says."

"Why would she lie? She loved her sister."

"I...I don't know."

"Who doctored the coroner's report?" Quinn pressed in a hard tone.

"I don't know."

"You're lying." She narrowed her gaze. "Who are you protecting and why?"

A bead of sweat gathered on Mick's top lip. "Listen up, you'd better watch yourself. You don't know what you're getting into. Just... I don't want you to get hurt. You're a good kid—"

"I'm not a kid," she cut in coolly. "And I'm tired of this town trying to make me feel small and inconsequential. I'm ready to tear down the walls and expose whatever corruption is killing this town."

Quinn gathered her notes and stalked past Mick as he stuttered after her. Her heart was beating hard and she barely made it to her car before her knees gave out.

It'd been a hunch—a wild, desperate hunch—and it'd worked.

Mick was covering for someone.

Someone important.

Silas breathed deep and then dialed his mother's number. He didn't know why he was so reluctant to call his mom when it'd been his dad who'd been harsh after Spencer died.

But he supposed guilt was the culprit. Maybe he imagined it, but he always saw the echo of accusation in her eyes when she looked at him.

The fact that she lived in Florida now didn't change the residual issues that messed with his head.

She picked up on the second ring, a light laugh in her tone. "Honey? Is that you? Goodness gracious, I was so surprised when I saw your number flash."

"Hi, Mom," he said, rubbing at the sudden tightness in his chest. "How are you?"

"Pretty good. I just finished with my bridge circle and was going to enjoy a little pudding in the community hall. They have the best tapioca here, homemade even."

"That's great, Mom," he said with a small smile. He

enjoyed hearing how happy his mom was, but it made the purpose of his call that much more difficult.

"So what's this about? As much as I love hearing from my boy, I know you're very busy so you must have a reason for calling."

Guilt clawed at him. "Mom, I don't have to have a reason to call," he protested, though it was true. He hated that he was such a pathetic shit that he couldn't get over his issues and enjoy what time he had left with his remaining parent. "But since you asked... I do have a question for you and I hope it doesn't upset you."

"Oh, that sounds serious."

"I'm in Port Orion, investigating a case, and I discovered some leads that I need to check out. Shaine said you might be able to help."

"I'll help if I can, but it's been a long time since I lived in Port Orion. I doubt anything is the same anymore."

"More than you know," he said drily. "Do you remember a blog written by Sara Westfall?"

"The name is familiar."

"Shaine said that Dad followed her blog, thought that maybe she was onto something related to Spencer's death."

His mother drew a breath and said, "Silas...what are you getting yourself into?"

"Mom, a girl was killed in Port Orion about two weeks ago. She was killed in the same place and in the same way as Spencer. I think the two cases are related."

"Oh, honey," his mom sighed. "Let your brother rest in peace so you can finally let go."

"It's not about that, Mom," he said, quickly moderating his tone to mask his frustration. "It's about a killer who's getting away with murder because no one is looking for him." He drew a deep breath before continuing. "Do you remember the blog?"

After a long pause, his mother said, "Yes."

Relief almost made him weak. "What do you remember?"

"I remember that she was insinuating that Port Orion was engulfed in some kind of corruption ring but honestly, it was so wild and crazy I didn't have the stomach to keep reading. I told your father I thought it was unhealthy to read that garbage but he didn't listen."

"What if she was right?" Silas said.

His mother actually scoffed. "Honey, that's preposterous. A terrible thing happened to our family but that doesn't mean that the bogeyman is behind every door."

"Mom, I know you want to believe that everyone is essentially good, but I can tell you with great authority that the world is filled with terrible people. I believe Sara was killed because she accidentally stumbled on something that someone didn't want out and if that's the case...there very well might be a ring of corruption in Port Orion."

His mother sighed as if bothered by all this nasty business but admitted with great reluctance, "Your father printed out every page of that woman's blog. I stumbled across the papers when I was cleaning out the closet. Your father had already passed away and I thought about throwing them away but...I didn't. I can't even tell you why," she said. "Your father...he was a complicated man but I did love him."

Even though they'd divorced years before his father passed, Silas knew his parents had still loved each other at some level.

There'd just been too much pain between them for the union to survive.

"Anyway, the papers are in a box. I was going to toss them when I got around to it. I guess I just never did."

"Mom, I need you to email those papers. Do you know how to use your phone to scan documents?"

"I'm not a preschooler, Silas," his mother admonished. "I happen to be the secretary of the Bridge Birdies Club."

"My apologies," Silas quickly offered, but this was even better. "I'm going to text you my email address. I need you to scan those documents ASAP and send them to me right now."

"Silas, I can't just drop everything to run errands for you," she said, slightly perturbed. "I have an engagement in ten minutes that I can't be late for."

"Mom, I wouldn't ask if it wasn't important."

"Oh for goodness' sake, fine. I suppose I can be a few minutes late to dinner. I'll just have to ring Arthur and let him know."

"Arthur? Who is Arthur?"

"We don't like to put labels on things, but I guess the appropriate term would be boyfriend." She tittered and added in a giddy tone, "Just saying that out loud makes me feel like a kid again. Do you know, he actually gives me butterflies? I never thought I'd feel this way about some-one after your father."

Silas tried not to revert to a twelve-year-old. His mother had a boyfriend? Good grief, that couldn't be good for her bad hip. "Mom...aren't you a little...um, *mature* to be dating?"

"We'll see how you feel when you're my age," his mother said. "Now, I'll spare you the uncomfortable de-tails but at some point, you might want to come and visit. I think you would like Arthur quite a bit. He's a retired police officer from Naples, Florida. Isn't that something?"

He fought the urge to gag like an adolescent. "Sure, Mom," he acquiesced, if only to stop talking about it. He supposed he'd have to get used to the idea that his mother was still...*dateable*? "So you'll send those scans?"

"Yes, Silas," she answered, indulging him. "Say hello to your brothers for me."

"I will," he promised and clicked off, his hands clammy from gripping the phone too hard. His mother had the original blog pages. Of all the damn people who could be holding on to a vital clue...his own mother was the one.

He couldn't wait to tell Quinn.

This could be the break they were looking for.

Chapter 22

Quinn asked Silas to meet her at Gilbert Park. She was still so wired from her confrontation with Mick that she couldn't stop pacing.

Silas pulled up and she sprinted to his car. "You are not going to believe what happened at work today," she said before he'd even shut off the ignition.

"Why are we meeting here like two clandestine spies in a '90s movie?" he asked.

"Because I needed a change of scenery and couldn't fathom pacing that tiny hotel room of yours. Plus, I knew if we were somewhere private we'd end up having sex and I need to focus on what's going on right now."

"I've been thrown over for the case." He pretended to be hurt but he didn't blame her for needing to focus. Once he shared what he'd found, she would likely start jabbering like a woman possessed. "Get in. I have something to show you."

"I can't sit."

"Trust me, you're going to want to sit for what I have to tell you."

Quinn faltered, caught between her natural curiosity and her competitive spirit. She had pretty big news but Silas didn't cry wolf, which meant he must have something equally juicy.

"Fine," she capitulated with a groan and climbed into the passenger side. "What do you got?"

Silas produced five pages and handed them to her.

"What's this?" Quinn asked before reading. Then her eyes widened and she gasped. "Are you freaking kidding me? Are you a magician or something? How the hell did you get these?"

"You are never going to believe this but…from my mother of all people."

"Come again?"

He explained how he came to have the blog pages in his possession and all Quinn could do was wish she had that kind of luck on her side. "You were born under a lucky star," she said. "Have you read them?"

"I skimmed but I wanted to get them to you as soon as possible."

Quinn was torn between devouring the pages and sharing her own news. Silas sensed her indecision and helped her decide which to do first. "What were you going to tell me?"

Her hands lowered, papers momentarily forgotten, and said, "Mick was indeed having an affair with Sara but he swears he didn't kill her. He allowed her to take advances on her paycheck but he paid it back so no one would notice. However, I think he knows more than he's telling. He was freaked out, and not just because he was afraid of his wife finding out about his indiscretion all those years ago. He's protecting someone."

"He just came out and told you this?" Silas asked, dubious. "Why would he do that?"

"I may or may not have mildly threatened him," she admitted in a sheepish tone. "But I figured I had to do something wild to get him to admit to anything and he cracked like an egg. Much easier than I would've suspected."

"That was very dangerous," he said, surprising her with his disapproval. "I wish you would've talked with me before doing it."

Affronted, she said stiffly, "And why would I do that? I don't need your permission to chase down my own leads."

"You don't need my permission but you don't know enough not to get yourself killed by poking at the wrong people."

"Mick is harmless," Quinn disagreed, irritated that Silas was raining on her parade. "This was a big deal. Why are you brushing off my discovery?"

"It is big," he agreed in a patronizing tone that instantly set her nerves on fire. "But there are better, safer ways to get information rather than just rushing in, making a bunch of racket to see what crawls out from beneath the rock."

"I didn't do that," she said, stung. "I can't believe this. I thought you'd be happy that I cracked the case open a little wider."

"I am."

"You have a funny way of showing it."

"Look, if the corruption in this town is bigger than we realized, we could be dealing with more than one person, which makes this even more dangerous. I think you should let me take it from here."

"Screw you," Quinn said, seeing red. "No. Absolutely not. I can't believe you even suggested it."

"I don't want anything to happen to you," he said, trying to caress her cheek but she leaned away from him. He frowned. "C'mon, Quinn. Don't be a baby. I'm not playing around."

"What makes you think I am? You think I'm just doing this to pass the time? This case is my ticket and nothing is going to stop me from chasing after it. Not even you, Silas Kelly."

She spat his name and climbed from the car, still clutching the papers. Her previous euphoria was long gone. Now she felt ready to cry and she wanted to be far from Silas when that happened.

She'd thought Silas was different than everyone else, patronizing her big dreams and patting her on the head like she was a cute puppy.

Damn him.

Quinn managed to make it home before the tears really started falling.

She exited her car, papers still clutched to her chest, when she nearly dropped everything as she screamed.

Something bloody was lying on her doorstep.

Her scream brought Uncle Leo. He gasped. "What the hell is that?"

"I don't know," she said, swallowing as Leo bent down to take a closer look. "What is it?"

"Looks like it used to be a cat," he answered grimly. "Hold on, I'll get a bag and a shovel."

Quinn stepped closer, peering at the mangled mess. Someone had done this to scare her. Someone was sending her a message.

Uncle Leo went to scoop the carcass but the head rolled off its body to land in a juicy heap at her feet and she nearly threw up.

"Go in through the back door. I'll handle this," Leo said gruffly and Quinn didn't hesitate.

She ran around the back of the house and entered through the mudroom.

Good God, someone had tortured a poor cat to get to her.

What the hell was wrong with people?

Uncle Leo returned, shaking his head. "Who the hell would dump a dead cat on our doorstep?" he asked. "I better call Lester and let him know someone's playing games."

"No," she said quickly, not wanting Lester to know about this. "It's fine. Probably just a couple of kids with really questionable morals. I'm sure it's nothing."

But even as she tried to assure her uncle, her voice trembled and her entire body felt numb.

Never in her life had anyone threatened her.

She wanted to tell Silas but she couldn't.

Silas was an asshole.

"What's that in your hands?" Uncle Leo asked, drawing attention to the papers.

"Uh…research," she answered, clutching the pages more tightly. "Copies of an old blog that used to run in town."

"What blog?" Lester asked, his gaze narrowing with suspicion. "Not that fruit loop Sara Westfall's blog, right? There's no need to contaminate your brain with her nonsense. The woman was a menace. All she did was stir up fear and anger with her baseless accusations. Do yourself a favor and toss those in the trash."

She wanted to protest that it wasn't nonsense but her heart was still hammering and she just wanted to escape to her room to breathe.

"I need to shower," Quinn said, moving past Uncle Leo and ignoring his questioning glance. She didn't have the energy to fight with him when she was still in shock.

Once safe in her room, she smoothed out the papers, wiping her eyes as she tried to focus, but her brain wasn't cooperating. Her thoughts kept ping-ponging between Silas and the dead cat.

She'd mistakenly thought that Silas had believed in her.

But he still saw her as a kid, bungling around, more apt to hurt herself than do anything of value, and he'd proven it by reprimanding her for her actions with Mick.

Her vision blurred as more tears fell and she dropped back on her pillows, throwing her hand over her eyes as she sobbed.

Why was she so torn up?

So what? Silas didn't think she could handle the big league. Maybe she'd just been a diversion.

A fun bed partner while he searched out the leads, intending to leave her behind all along.

Ouch, that really hurt.

Quinn liked Silas—*really* liked him. But if he didn't have any faith in her…he was no different than anyone else in this town and she didn't need him.

And now someone was delivering dead cats to her door? What was next?

"Quinnie?" Uncle Leo's worried tone was muffled from the other side of the door. "Is everything okay? Want to talk about it?"

Talk about what? Her bad day or the dead cat? She didn't want to talk about either with Leo.

"I'm fine," she lied, sniffing back more tears. "I'll be okay in the morning."

"How about pancakes? Pancakes always seem to make everything better."

Screw the pancakes. I just saw a dead cat's head roll to my feet. Not exactly hungry.

But if she declined, her uncle would surely continue to pester her because Uncle Leo thought food solved everything, which was probably why Uncle Leo's doctor was constantly harping on him about his cholesterol.

"Sure," she relented, staring up at the ceiling. "Give me a few minutes, okay?"

"You got it."

And then Uncle Leo left her door, presumably to fix everything that was wrong with the power of flour, eggs, butter and syrup.

Would anyone ever take her seriously?

Or would she always be Cute Little Quinnie?

Quinn groaned into her pillow but she really wanted to scream.

Well, maybe she was looking at it all wrong…maybe someone didn't see her as Little Quinnie any longer because who delivered dead cats to people who weren't a threat?

If anything, the dead cat told her the opposite and in the state she was in, as disgusting as it was, she'd take that validation.

And that was the only way she'd manage to choke down pancakes tonight.

He blew it.

Man, he blew it hard.

He shouldn't have been so heavy-handed. Quinn didn't take very well to being given orders.

And he'd essentially crapped on her big news—and it was an interesting lead—but he was scared for her.

A growing knot in his gut told him things were about to get bad.

It was that sixth sense that Oppenshaw said he had that never steered the team wrong.

Of course, she was joking—the FBI didn't traffic with New Age bullshit—but he was rarely wrong when his gut started to twist.

And it was rocking and rolling right now.

If he was being brutally honest, he wanted to hog-tie Quinn, throw her into his hotel room and keep her there just so he knew she was safe.

Real caveman style.

Maybe he ought to be ashamed of how sexist he was being but the thought of Quinn getting caught in the cross-fire of a war she hadn't realized she was stepping into… it made his stomach ache.

So if Mick was sleeping with Sara and Sara wound up dead with a potentially doctored BAC on her accident report, that meant that someone in authority—or someone with ties to someone in authority—had managed to pull strings to keep things quiet.

But why?

And how did all that relate to Spencer?

Or Rhia, for that matter?

That was where things got muddy.

He wished he'd done more than skim those blog pages. Now he felt like an idiot for letting Quinn take them before he'd had a chance to really study them.

He realized, sheepishly, he'd imagined that they would read them together.

Yeah, that didn't happen.

He was letting his feelings for Quinn get in the way of the investigation—something he never imagined doing.

Quinn did something to him, turned him upside down and warped his thinking.

But there was no changing that fact now. As much as he wanted to deny it, he had feelings for Quinn that he couldn't ignore.

He wanted to protect her, wanted to keep her safe.

And her propensity for walking straight into the mouth of danger sent his anxiety skyrocketing.

If he didn't make amends, Quinn would just continue to ignore anything he said because she was pissed off and it might get her killed.

Sara might've been right—there had to be more than one person involved with Spencer's murder, if not the actual act but definitely the covering up of key details.

Who had the most to lose if they were caught?

He kept circling the obvious answer—Lester.

But it felt wrong.

Or maybe he just couldn't bring himself to admit that the man he admired wasn't a good guy at all.

Even the suggestion left a bad taste in his mouth.

So who else?

The deeper he got into Rhia's case, the more certain he was that Spencer must've stumbled onto something he shouldn't.

Spencer had always been a curious kid—precocious, even.

He'd had a smart mouth and a sharp wit, courtesy of three wise-ass older brothers.

Maybe he'd popped off to the wrong person? Maybe he'd seen something he shouldn't have.

He could've been in the wrong place at the wrong time.

And what about Rhia?

They'd already established that Rhia had secrets. She was sleeping with some mystery guy that not even her best friend knew of and she'd been stringing along her boyfriend as a front so no one asked questions.

Whoever Rhia was really sleeping with wanted to ensure that no one knew of their secret.

Was the need for secrecy enough to compel someone to kill?

Had they known about the baby?

What had Rhia planned to do about the pregnancy?

Keep it? Get an abortion?

Or had she just been a kid, in over her head, unsure of what she was going to do?

Chapter 23

X thinks he's safe but I'm just biding my time. I have to make sure all my ducks are in a row before I take down this monster. When I get scared I just try to remember how poor little S had felt—alone and afraid—and I soldier on.

Acid churned in Quinn's stomach as she read the blog pages, highlighting certain passages that seemed important. X could be a lot of people. *Please don't be Lester.*

It makes me sick to think that I live in a town that would protect X when he clearly has a perverse appetite. Did X do something to S before killing him? I shudder to think of what S must've gone through in his final moments.

I wish I could tell S's family that there's more than meets the eye going on in Port Orion but I can't...not yet.

I'm not very popular with too many people but screw them. They'll be singing a different tune when I expose the rotten underbelly of this godforsaken town.

Quinn tried to distract herself by studying the blog passages, which seemed more like diary entries than news stories. She didn't want to think about Silas and what he'd said.

But it was there, crowding her thoughts and pushing everything else aside.

Maybe she had been reckless with Mick. Silas's point was not lost on her but he could've handled it better.

Or maybe she would've reacted the same either way because she was embarrassed at seeming a rookie.

She wanted to be an investigative reporter—risks were part of the job.

So why did she feel like crap?

Probably all those pancakes; she rubbed at her belly with a wince. Her uncle Leo had tried to feed her problems away and she felt ready to burst.

Yes, she'd taken a chance that Mick could've called her bluff, and if by some chance Mick had been the dangerous one, she would've shown her hand but it hadn't worked out that way.

Sheer dumb luck, Silas would say.

The fact remained that Mick knew more than he was saying.

He was protecting someone—but who?

Mick knew someone had killed Sara and he'd helped cover it up by burying the story and perpetuating the idea that Sara was simply an alcoholic and her brain was likely soaked in gin.

That was despicable.

Terrible boyfriend.

Terrible husband, too.

Mick was pretty much terrible all the way around.

But was he a killer?

No, she couldn't see that. Mick was too soft and squishy around the edges to do something as brutal as take a life.

She returned to her notes, trying to see if anything else clicked.

Did she feel guilty for stomping off with the blog pages? Yeah, a bit. Silas had done a fantastic job of finding the pages and she'd taken off with them.

A sigh escaped as Quinn rekindled her focus, determined to find something of value in this gibberish.

What did she know at this point?

Sara had stumbled on something, putting her life in danger. Mick likely helped make the story go away when Sara was killed.

Rhia was sleeping with someone other than her boyfriend. Boyfriend was likely a front. Father of secret baby: unknown.

Rhia seemed a sweetheart but anyone who was willing to lie to that extreme was capable of more deception.

Quinn dropped the pages and let them scatter on her bed as she fell back onto her pillows. She was running in circles.

Nothing seemed any clearer—if anything she had more loose ends than ever before.

Sure, some of those ends were tantalizing but what did they all add up to?

She groaned and closed her eyes, fatigue beginning to pull at her. Nothing was jumping out at her except the driving need to apologize to Silas for overreacting.

And she was not doing that tonight.

Maybe tomorrow.

Maybe.

Seeing as Quinn had already stirred the hornet's nest, Silas figured it was time to visit Mick Creech with all the authority of the FBI behind him.

He walked into the newspaper front office as soon as it opened and flashed his credentials. "I'm here to speak to Mick Creech," he said, causing a flurry of baffled expressions by the office staff. He glanced at the attendant board and saw that Quinn wasn't in yet and he was glad. He didn't want her to think he was squashing her investigation again, but this had to be done.

A short, pudgy man with a balding pate appeared after he was given the message and after one look at Silas, he blanched but otherwise motioned for Silas to follow him to his office.

The man was already sweating as he dropped into his worn leather chair. "What can I do for you?"

"You can tell me what really happened to Sara Westfall and how her death pertains to the death of Spencer Kelly for starters," Silas answered, going straight for the jugular. "Or we could go to the station for a formal interview-slash-interrogation, which I'm guessing would make a fantastic headline."

Mick stuttered and tried to sputter a denial but Silas wasn't in the mood for this fool.

"At the station it is," he announced, rising, but Mick quickly motioned for Silas to stay.

"Sorry, sorry…this just comes as quite a shock. Give me a minute to breathe."

"I find that the truth is much less difficult to keep straight."

"Look, I don't know what you've heard but—"

"Cut the crap. I don't have the time or the patience to listen to you blather on with excuses. I want answers and I want them now."

"Answers to what? I can't give you what I don't have."

"Who are you protecting?"

"What are you talking about?"

"I'm not in a habit of repeating myself," Silas returned with a hard stare. "Who are you protecting?"

Mick shifted in his chair as if his ass was on fire. The panic rolling off the man was enough to fill the cramped room.

"Clock is ticking," Silas reminded him. "Who are you protecting?"

"Myself," he finally blurted desperately. He leaned forward and lowered his voice to an embarrassed hiss. "Look, I was having an affair with one of my reporters—a reporter who was unstable at best. It was a bad call on my part but I didn't have anything to do with her death. All I did was bury the story. I just wanted Sara to go away. I'm not going to lie and say that her death didn't solve a lot of problems for me, but I didn't kill her. You have to believe me."

"Why'd you front her money?"

"Because I thought she'd shut up and stop going on about that kid's death—"

"That kid was my brother," Silas cut in with a chilly look.

Mick quailed and jabbered an apology. "Of course, of course. No offense meant. It was a terrible thing what happened to your brother, but Sara was obsessed. She was going on and on about conspiracies and secret groups operating behind the curtain and it was just nuts. I mean, clearly, she was spiraling but I didn't know what else to do. If I didn't give her the money, she was going to start squawking about our relationship and it would've destroyed my marriage."

"You did all that to keep your wife from finding out that you were screwing around?"

He wiped at the sweat on his pate. "You can judge me all you want but you don't know what I stood to lose. Sara was a loose cannon and when she died…yeah, I was relieved, but that doesn't mean I had anything to do with her death."

As much as Silas wanted to pin Mick to the wall with something more concrete than being a crappy husband, his instincts told him he was being truthful.

More's the pity. He rather liked the idea of stomping on this little man.

Mick's lip trembled as he asked, "So…what are you going to do?"

"Cheating on your wife isn't a crime," Silas said dispassionately. "Neither is being a spineless dick."

Mick's lips pressed together as if he knew better than to argue.

"Why'd you tell Quinn that she was messing with people that were dangerous if you're not protecting anyone?"

"I was just trying to scare her off," he answered, swallowing visibly. "Quinn seems to be convinced Sara was right about the conspiracy theory and I thought that if I played into that delusion, it would work."

Seemed plausible. As Silas watched Mick sit in a puddle of his own sweat, he realized this man was no mastermind, nor was he an able accomplice. Anyone who would enlist Mick Creech as their accessory was adding a weak link to the chain.

This was a dead end. But he was going to make sure the man knew what would happen if he dared to mess with the redhead.

"Leave Quinn alone. If I find out you're pestering or harassing her in any way, I'll be back."

Mick licked his lips. "So, you're not going to arrest me?"

"For what? Like I said, you might be a weak asshole but that's not a crime. As far as your payroll indiscretions, that's between you and your employer. If they so choose, they can file a civil charge but seeing as so much time has gone by and you've already made restitution, it's not worth my time."

Mick sagged with visible relief. "Oh, thank God. Thank you."

Silas rose and left Mick, presumably to wipe up after himself, perhaps even to change his underpants.

While he was glad that Mick wasn't a direct threat to Quinn, it did raise the troubling question of whether Quinn was onto something...or if she was chasing wild theories like Sara had.

All he knew for certain was he needed to talk to Quinn, to sort out what'd happened last night.

He couldn't leave things as they were.

Even if a little distance between them was better in the long run.

Quinn managed to send a text to Silas to meet her at Reba's Diner as she left her house, purposefully avoiding the front door where the cat had been left.

She knew Uncle Leo had washed it down and removed the horrific sight but nothing would erase what remained in her memory and she really didn't want to keep reliving it.

The dead cat had shaken her up, more so than she wanted to admit. For one, she felt sorry for the cat but two, she shuddered to think what kind of psycho would do that to send a message.

She slid into the booth farthest from the door and closest to the kitchen so the noise would drown out their voices.

Maybe she was being paranoid but she figured, at this point, she had good cause.

Silas appeared, looking sharp as ever and for a brief moment she lost the anxiety that'd been with her all night and just enjoyed the view.

But as soon as Silas slid opposite her, sudden tears filled her eyes.

Alarmed, Silas reached for her hand, which she allowed him to grasp, in spite of being in public. She needed the comfort of his touch, if only to ground her.

"Someone left a mutilated cat on my doorstep last night," she said, throwing it out there because there was no way to pretty it up and she just wanted to get it over with. "It was pretty disgusting."

"When?" Silas asked, his grip tightening with concern. "Did you see anyone?"

She shook her head. "No, it was late, after I left you at the park. I was pissed off and not paying attention. I almost stepped on the damn thing. I screamed when I realized what it was and my uncle took it away."

"Did he throw it in the trash or keep it?"

"Ew? Why would he keep it?"

"Forensic evidence."

Quinn grimaced. "No, he tossed it. I couldn't believe someone would do that."

"Has this ever happened before?"

She cut him a sardonic look. "No, generally people don't leave nasty, rotting dead things at my door. This was the first time."

"Then it's related to the investigation," he concluded, which was the same assumption she'd come to. "Either we're getting close or someone is panicking. They're trying to scare you."

"Well, I hate to say it but it worked. I was freaked out. The cat's head rolled off and nearly landed on my toes."

"Classic psychologic warfare. They're saying this could be you."

"Which has to mean we are on the right track."

"Perhaps. People tend to react foolishly when they are scared."

"I can understand that. I wanted to run straight to your hotel. For the first time in my life, my house didn't feel safe."

A beat of silence passed between them and Silas reluctantly let go of her hand. They both started to talk at once but Silas let Quinn take the lead.

"I'm sorry I overreacted about what you said. I guess

it was reckless and it could've blown up in my face. I'm tired of taking the safe route. I want to shake things up. I figured if I couldn't handle someone like Creech, how was I ever going to handle bigger fish?"

"Little fish have teeth, too," he reminded her.

"True. Do you think it was Creech who left the cat?"

"No. That man has no spine."

"How do you know?"

"I paid him a visit this morning. He's got no connection to anyone important. He was trying to save his own ass by trying to scare you into dropping your investigation."

"That little prick," she muttered, shaking her head. "What a weasel."

"Yeah, but he doesn't have the stones to actually gut an animal. He's all talk, no conviction."

Quinn tried not to read too much into Silas going to her editor. He was following a lead, nothing more. But the warmth spreading in her belly made it hard to stop smiling.

Silas caught her gaze and a wordless exchange flowed between them.

"I'm sorry for the way I handled myself yesterday," he said. "I was worried and I overreacted."

"It's okay. I mean, no, it's not okay but I get it. I shouldn't have gotten so butt-hurt about it. You had valid concerns."

"Quinn, I'll be honest, I don't know what I feel when it comes to you. I find myself doing and saying things I would never do any other time when it concerns you or your well-being. I know it's not my place to worry about you or question your methods. But when I think of you in danger…it does something to me and I lose my objectivity."

"Careful, I'm terribly charming," she warned playfully,

if only to keep from fluttering like a girl with a crush. "I've been known to break hearts."

"I believe it," he said with a hint of a smile that she found irresistible.

"We should get something to eat and then head out," Quinn said, forcing herself to break eye contact. Another second and she might fall completely in love with the man who was leaving soon.

Sensing her withdrawal, Silas followed her lead. "If the cat killer brings another present, call me. I don't care what time it is. Whatever you do, don't touch anything. I want to see if anything can be found forensically."

"Okay," Quinn promised but she really hoped she never saw something like that again. "So where are you going today?"

"I have to check in with my boss, make sure I'm still good on leave time and then I'm going to pop over to the coroner's office, see if the paper trail on Sara's accident report got waylaid anywhere along the chain. And you?"

"To the office. I have to actually get some writing done. But now that you've gotten Mick off my back, it shouldn't be too bad. I just have some odds and ends to take care of. Boring crap that's still part of my job."

"Such as?"

"Such as typing the senior lunch menu," she admitted with a blush. "Yeah, real scintillating stuff. Making a difference out there in the world."

"Well, for the senior citizens who plan their daily activities around the lunch menu, I'm sure it's very important what you do," he teased.

"Ha ha," she returned. "I'll meet you back at the hotel afterward."

He smiled, liking that plan.

Her blush returned, only this time she met his smile with one of her own.

What would she do when Silas left town?

Quinn had a terrible feeling it was going to hurt more than she realized.

Silas was…quickly becoming her favorite part of the day.

And night.

Chapter 24

Quinn thought perhaps Mick might come to her office but when he was noticeably absent from the building, she wondered if that was a good thing or bad.

If only she'd been witness to the show. That would've been worth the cost of admission.

She sighed with a small smile and turned to gather her paperwork to start her work when an unexpected visitor appeared in her doorway.

Pastor Simms knocked lightly, his kindly face a welcome change from the usual people who ended up at the office, usually to complain about something.

"Pastor Simms, what are you doing in my neck of the woods?" she asked, smiling as she gestured for him to come in. "Is it time for that story on the new sound system for the church already? I thought we had more time."

"No, no, you're good. The sound system isn't being delivered until next month. No, I came down here to see if I could talk to you on a more personal level."

"Oh? That's intriguing. On or off the record?" she teased.

But Pastor Simms was quite serious when he answered, "Definitely off the record," as he gently closed her door for privacy.

Now things were getting serious. "What's going on?" she asked, concerned.

"You've always been a bright girl with a hunger to go places. I knew the moment I saw you, you were going to make a name for yourself and with your talent... I have no doubts you'll get to wherever you hope to go."

"Thank you?" Quinn said, a little baffled by the direction of the conversation but her gut was tingling in warning. "I appreciate the compliment."

Pastor Simms nodded as if he was glad he prefaced what he was about to say. "The thing is, as talented as you are... I wonder if you've taken the time to consider the cost to the people around you for your ambition."

Oh, this argument? Coming from Pastor Simms? Crimine, was there a Facebook group out there coordinating attacks on her integrity? She wanted to quip something harsh such as "You have to break a few eggs to make an omelet," but she held it back, if only out of respect.

"And where is this coming from?" she asked.

"Rhia was a good girl. Sweet, kind, generous...and her family is grieving. We need to let her parents have closure."

"I agree. That's why I'm determined to find who *killed* her. I feel that's the best kind of closure."

Pastor Simms cast an aggrieved look her way and said, "Yes, of course. But what good does it do to broadcast that the poor girl had made a mistake and gotten pregnant? Hasn't the family suffered enough?"

"Someone killed Rhia and her unborn baby," Quinn said. "They need to be brought to justice."

"But what if that justice is never served, in spite of all

the dredging that happens in chasing this story? Some people are never brought to answer for their crimes and we have to trust that God will do that for us."

"I'm more of an *in-this-lifetime* supporter of justice. No offense."

"In a perfect world, Rhia's killer would be apprehended quickly and quietly with as little pain to her loved ones as possible. But we don't live in a perfect world so we have to be aware of how our actions affect others. I was a classmate of Spencer Kelly's. I remember how his death affected this town. None of us were ever the same."

"Least of all the Kelly family," she reminded him. "But I can guarantee you that closure is the best gift the grieving family could hope for. The questions can finally stop."

"Yes, yes, but is it really necessary to drag Rhia's name and reputation through the mud to get to where you want to be?"

"I'm not dragging anyone through the mud," Quinn retorted, freshly offended. "Forgive me, Pastor Simms, but I don't understand why you're coming to me with this. It's none of your concern how this investigation is handled."

"Oliver and Violet Daniels are members of my congregation. It's my duty to speak on their behalf."

"Do you always go out of your way to speak for your church members?"

"No, of course not. Only the ones who I feel need my intervention."

"And why would they need your help?"

"Rhia was a very special girl. The Danielses are a wonderful family. Their pain is my pain."

"That's admirable of you," Quinn murmured but something didn't feel right. Pastor Simms mistook her reflective silence as one of acquiescence and pressed his point further.

"Rhia was a very private individual, much like her parents. She wouldn't appreciate her business splashed all over the local news. I'm not asking you not to do your job," he clarified. "Just to exercise empathy as you do what you feel is necessary. You are affecting people with the pain your articles cause. Please think of that."

But Quinn wasn't going to back down, not even for Pastor Simms. "If we don't print the truth, the killer wins. Justice isn't served by remaining in the shadows. It's my job to throw light on the dark corners where the bad guys hide and I aim to continue doing that. I'm sorry for any pain it may cause the Daniels family."

"Are you?"

Quinn held his stare. "Yes."

Pastor Simms nodded as if disappointed in her decision. "Well, that's all I can do, I suppose. I appreciate your time."

He started to leave but Quinn stopped him with another question. "You seemed to know Rhia pretty well. She was really involved with the church from what I hear."

"She was an angel. She was very special. God broke the mold when he made Rhia."

Quinn smiled as if she agreed and Pastor Simms let himself out.

As soon as he was gone, Quinn dropped the fake smile and leaned back in her chair, her gut churning.

Something about that didn't feel right at all.

Something about the way Pastor Simms had said *angel*.

It hadn't felt *fatherly*.

It'd felt like something…a lover would say.

Good God.

Was it possible that Rhia's secret lover was Pastor Simms?

Pastor Simms was young, and the age difference between him and Rhia was the same as that between Quinn and Silas.

And he was attractive in a soft, gentle sort of way.

Rhia had spent a lot of time around the man—with her parents' blessing.

What if the entire time the Danielses believed Rhia was helping Pastor Simms with God's work, she was really just working Pastor Simms behind the pulpit?

It was a good thing Quinn wasn't very religious because she was fairly certain she might go to Hell for even thinking something so dirty.

But it clicked.

It made all sorts of terrible sense. Pastors weren't infallible. Rhia had been beautiful. Sins of the flesh and all that nonsense.

Holy crap. They needed a DNA sample from Pastor Simms.

She had to tell Silas.

Grabbing her jacket, she bolted from her office like the devil was on her heels.

Silas was about to leave his hotel room for the coroner's office when an urgent knock as his door had him reaching for his sidearm.

When he saw it was Quinn, he immediately let her in. "You're early, I was just heading to the coroner's."

"That can wait. We have to get a DNA sample from Pastor Simms," she said in a rush, her eyes sparkling with excitement. "Like, now. Immediately. Can you make that happen?"

"If I have probable cause," he answered slowly, knowing it was going to be a bitch getting the judge to sign off on another DNA sample for this case on flimsy evidence but he'd pull strings if the reason was compelling enough.

"Hold on to your shorts but I think Pastor Simms is the father of Rhia's baby."

He narrowed his gaze. "What makes you think that?"

"He came to my office to basically tell me that I should

think of the family when I'm writing about Rhia's murder and that it wasn't necessary to print that she was pregnant. In a sense he accused me of pandering to the salacious nature of the story instead of trying to break the case respectfully."

"It's not your job to be respectful," he growled.

"I know. If he wasn't such a nice guy I would've tossed him out and told him to kiss my ass but Pastor Simms really is sweet."

"If he's so sweet what makes you think he was sleeping with an underage girl?"

"Good question. Call it a hunch? It was the way he talked about her. I got this icky vibe like he was talking about a lover, not a member of his church. And it makes sense. If he's the father, of course he's not going to want me poking into that angle of the story. He could lose everything. Don't you think a secret baby is cause enough to murder?"

"I do." Silas agreed, thinking fast. "Maybe he's banking on God's forgiveness."

"Trust me, I hate thinking that Pastor Simms could be capable but everything feels right. How soon could you get a warrant for his DNA?"

He exhaled, thinking fast. "I could have it by this afternoon but my request is going to go over like a lead balloon with Lester."

"Well, too bad. This case is too important to this town to dance around politics."

"True enough, but that still won't soften the potential backlash. I take it Simms is a popular pastor around here?"

"Yeah, I guess so. I mean, I'm not exactly a church-goer but the townsfolk seem to like him."

"What if your vibe is wrong and we embarrass the town pastor for nothing?"

Quinn cast him a quizzical look. "Are you going soft on

me? If he's innocent, he should be willing to do whatever it takes to clear his name and find Rhia's killer. Innocent people have nothing to worry about, right?"

"Yeah, that's the general idea."

"Then, everything should be fine."

But Silas knew if it turned out that Simms was innocent, there would be plenty of people with things to say. Public opinion shouldn't have a place in an investigation but he'd been doing this long enough to know that enough false leads could kill an otherwise solid case.

However, he was beginning to see that Quinn had a nose for details so he was going to trust her instincts and hope they weren't misplaced.

"I'll place some calls," he told her.

"Good. In the meantime, I'm going to hang around the church and see if anyone else caught Pastor Simms and Rhia acting a little too chummy."

"Be careful."

"Of course."

She started to leave but he grabbed her hand and pulled her to him. "Wait."

Her gaze widened and her breath shortened but she held his stare. "Yeah?"

"I mean it. Be careful out there," he said without making a big production about it. "I don't want anything to happen to you."

"I'll be fine," she assured him. "Get that warrant."

He brushed a firm kiss across her lips, resisting the urge to linger. "I will. What exactly are you going to do at the church?"

"I'm going to poke around and see what happens. There had to be someone there who saw something that wasn't quite right. Maybe I can persuade them to tell me what they know."

He knew better than to caution her; he just had to have faith, ironically.

Quinn left as quickly as she came and he was left to shake off the immediate heat that permeated his bones whenever Quinn was in his arms.

The woman was an enigma—one who was fast becoming his favorite mystery.

What was he going to do when this case was over?

Don't build bridges you don't have to cross just yet, he told himself. *Particularly when you already know the answer.*

Besides, this case had just taken a giant leap and he wasn't going to be left behind.

Chapter 25

Quinn walked into the church and saw it was empty but when she heard faint giggling from multiple sources, she followed the sound to the back offices where a day care operated.

Gladys, the older woman who served as the church secretary and Pastor Simms's right-hand lady, smiled at Quinn's entry.

"Quinn Jackson? What are you doing here today?" she asked.

Quinn drew a deep breath and forced a smile. Either she was going to be thrown out or Gladys would prove to be the catalyst they were hoping for.

"Can I talk to you about something serious?" she said, gentling her voice. "It's…sensitive."

"Oh, dear," Gladys said with a deep frown. "Hold on just a minute." She turned to the children and clapped her hands. "Movie time," she announced, gathering the kids into a circle with pillows and blankets before turning on an animated movie. She motioned for Quinn to take a seat with her away from the children. "What can I do for you?"

"I...I don't know how to say this without being offensive but I have to ask something that might make you uncomfortable."

Gladys waited with apprehension, her softly wrinkled face reminding Quinn of a stereotypical granny in a fairy tale.

Or one of those dried apple dolls wearing gingham.

"It's about Rhia."

"Oh, goodness, bless that poor child," Gladys said immediately. "Such a tragedy."

"Yes, definitely. But I'm sure you've heard the latest news..."

"Oh, yes," Gladys breathed, shaking her head at the scandal. "Pregnant. She was so tiny, it would've been hard to tell."

"She was only six weeks along," Quinn reminded Gladys. "Likely, she wouldn't have started showing for a while."

"Yes, that's true."

"I've heard that Rhia and Pastor Simms had a special relationship. May I ask...did you ever see anything inappropriate happen between Rhia and the pastor?"

Gladys's appalled expression answered that question. Now all that remained was to be thrown out for suggesting something so perverse of their Godly leader.

But Gladys swallowed and looked conflicted, struggling with something. "Why would you ask?"

"Because...Pastor Simms came to see me today and he seemed less like a pastor and more like a...lover when he talked about Rhia. It set my alarm bells off."

"Oh, dear," she murmured, fluttering her hands as she twisted them. "I don't want to talk out of turn. Sometimes things seem what they really aren't and reputations can be ruined."

"That's also true, but when our intuition tells us that something is wrong…it's usually right. What did you see?"

Gladys looked as if she was going to be physically ill. "I don't know," she admitted. "It was late on a Friday. I came back to the church because I forgot my sheet music for the Sunday service and I wanted to practice the following day. I heard something in the pastor's office and thought perhaps a cat had gotten into the church again. But I stopped when I realized it wasn't a cat making those noises."

"Were they having sex?" Quinn asked.

Gladys blushed and stammered, "I-I don't know. It was very late and afterward I wasn't even sure I'd heard what I did. It was all very embarrassing. I shouldn't have come back so late. It was my fault for forgetting the sheet music in the first place."

"Was Rhia with Pastor Simms?"

Gladys's agonized expression said what her mouth wouldn't.

"Did you ever talk to Pastor Simms about what you heard?"

"Goodness, no. I wasn't even sure of what I'd heard. A few days later I was positive I'd let my brain play tricks on me. I wasn't about to ruin a good man over something I wasn't even sure I'd heard."

"Why are you willing to tell me now?"

"It's been a terrible burden. I prayed for days about it. Then I made a promise to God that if he wanted me to say something, he would make it happen. If no one came asking questions, then I would forget it ever happened because that was God's will. You being here…tells me that God wants me to share what I know."

Quinn tried not to scoff at the woman's logic, but it infuriated her that Pastor Simms could've gotten off scot-free if Quinn hadn't asked the right questions at the right time.

"Do you think he killed Rhia to keep their secret? Sooner or later the truth would've come out."

To that Gladys was adamant. "No. Pastor Simms may have succumbed to the temptation of flesh but he is not a killer. He is a Godly man who cares about his flock— perhaps too much—but he is not capable of murdering someone."

"Are you sure? People do things they might not otherwise when they are desperate."

"He did not kill Rhia. I know that in my bones."

"Would you ever have imagined that Pastor Simms was capable of sleeping with an underage girl in his congregation?"

"No."

"And he did that. So maybe…is it possible you don't know what Pastor Simms is capable of at all? It could be that he's been fooling everyone into thinking he's a good man when in fact…he's a predator."

"No. I can't believe that. I won't believe it. Now, I've said everything I can. I've done as I promised God. I won't say anything more to further blacken that man's good name."

And just like that, Gladys shut down, shuffling off to provide snacks for the children as they watched their movie as if she could distance herself from the stain that Quinn threatened to paint on the church.

Well, she was about to unleash a shit-storm with this latest development.

If Pastor Simms was guilty of fooling around with a kid, yet not guilty of killing her…someone out there was likely to get real nervous.

They were getting closer to the truth.

Quinn could feel it in her bones.

Nothing could stop her now.

* * *

The warrant was easy enough to obtain but Lester wasn't too happy about it.

However, he didn't stand in the way, either, so that was a good sign. Probably because both Brock and Oliver's DNA results had returned negative for paternity.

This case had aged Lester in ways that shocked Silas. He could only hope it wasn't guilt that was putting the extra lines in Lester's face.

Silas walked into the interrogation room and found Pastor Simms looking edgy. "Can I ask what this is about?"

"We need your DNA," he answered, going straight to the point. "It'll be quick."

But Pastor Simms leaned away as Silas approached him with the swab. "What for?"

"To rule you out as a suspect," Silas answered.

"A suspect? In what?"

"Rhia's murder."

The pastor whitened and his eyes widened. "I didn't kill Rhia," he protested, horrified. "How could you think that I'm capable of something so heinous?"

Silas settled on the edge of the metal table. "Desperation will cause people to do things they might never consider otherwise."

"And why would I be desperate?" he asked but a bead of sweat had collected on his upper lip. "I have nothing to hide."

"Good. Then you won't mind giving us your DNA."

"I don't feel it's necessary," the pastor said, eyeing that swab as if it were a cobra about to strike. "I've already told you—"

"What exactly did you tell me, Pastor? The entire truth?" He wagged the swab. "I think not." His voice hardened. "Now open up."

"And if I refuse?"

"Then this little paper gives me permission to hold you down and jam this swab in your mouth forcefully," Silas answered simply. "Your choice."

Defeated, the pastor opened his mouth and allowed Silas to swab his cheek. Silas capped the sample and handed it off to an awaiting deputy.

"See? That wasn't so hard."

"This is mortifying."

"Since you're here, let's chat."

Pastor Simms cast Silas a dark look. "About?"

"About you and Rhia Daniels."

"I've already told you my relationship with Rhia was platonic."

"Yeah, and I'm pretty sure that little swab is going to say otherwise."

Pastor Simms's gaze darted. "And what is that going to prove?"

"That you were the father of her baby."

Pastor Simms shuddered, his shoulders sagging. Silas allowed the silence to press on the man, letting him sink further into his own muck.

Face it, preacher man, you've been caught.

"Why'd you sleep with a sixteen-year-old girl?"

Pastor Simms looked as if he was going to lose his lunch.

"You were in a position of authority and you took advantage of her."

More silence.

Silas sighed and bluffed to get his attention. "Okay, I can arrest you right now for sex with a minor at the very least. Do yourself a favor and tell me what happened and why you killed her. Was it a crime of passion? Desperation?"

The trick worked.

"I didn't kill Rhia," Pastor Simms blurted out as if the suggestion was anathema to him. "I loved her."

"People kill ones they love all the time," Silas said, unmoved. "Tell me what happened between you. If you didn't kill her…who did?"

"I don't know. I didn't even know she was pregnant. I would never hurt her. We were going to wait until she turned eighteen and then I was going to ask her parents for her hand. I wanted to marry her."

Bingo. Confession.

"But you didn't wait until she was eighteen, did you? Couldn't keep your pervy hands off that young body. Pastor Simms, that makes you a pedophile."

He shook his head as if he couldn't accept that judgment. "I loved her," he maintained stubbornly. "And she loved me. We wanted to build a life together."

"She was a child."

"Rhia was more mature than most girls her age," Pastor Simms protested. "She seduced me! Not the other way around."

"Do you know how many times sick men like you have tried to convince me that their victims were some kind of highly sophisticated seductor? Too many to count. Let's try that again. What happened between you and Rhia?"

"Are you going to arrest me?"

"Yes. But if you cooperate, maybe you can get a lighter sentence. That's about all I can offer but sometimes shaving off a few years is worth it. Do yourself a favor and do the right thing."

Simms fell silent, his lip trembling.

Silas twisted the screws a little more. "If you really loved Rhia, you'd want to do the right thing."

Simms jerked a nod. "Okay. I'll tell you what I can but I swear to you I didn't kill her."

"Let's just start at the beginning," Silas encouraged, needing to get him talking.

"She needed volunteer hours for a school project and she came to me looking to see if I needed any help around the office, like an intern. I've known the Danielses for years and I was happy to help."

"Sounds aboveboard. When did that turn into doing the dirty in your office?"

Pastor Simms choked back a cry. "Must you use such vulgarity? What we did was—"

"Sex. Plain and simple. Don't waste time trying to put a prettier label on it."

"I didn't intend for anything to happen," he said, distressed. "Believe me, I felt sick about it afterward."

"But you didn't stop," Silas supplied.

"I tried," the pastor insisted. "I did. I told her it wasn't right, that we shouldn't, but…she just kept coming after me. I am an imperfect being and I succumbed when I shouldn't have but believe me when I say, I truly loved that girl, even as illicit as our relationship was. I would never hurt her."

Silas jerked his thumb toward the door. "Is that swab going to match?"

The pastor looked defeated. "Yes."

"You were the only one she was sleeping with?"

"She was a virgin when she came to me."

"How do you know that?"

Simms blushed. "Because I could tell. There was… blood our first time."

Not entirely open and shut on that score but if Simms thought his DNA would match, there was no need to dig any further into Rhia's sex life until proven otherwise.

He knocked on the window and deputies walked in. "Forrest Simms, you are under arrest for unlawful sex with a minor. Anything you say can and will be used against you in a court of law. If you cannot afford an attorney, one will be provided for you. Do you understand these rights as I've explained them to you?"

Simms bobbed a miserable nod.

"Take him away, boys," Silas said to the deputies, who then put Simms in handcuffs and led him away.

Same story, different pervert trying to justify actions that had no defense. God, he hated pedophiles.

He joined Quinn in the surveillance room.

"Somehow that didn't feel as satisfying as I thought it would," Quinn admitted, chewing her bottom lip. "Do you believe him? That he didn't kill Rhia?"

"I don't know. He lied about his relationship with the girl to protect his own self-interests. Who's to say that he wouldn't lie about killing her, too?"

Quinn nodded but seemed troubled. "Yeah, I guess you're right. Why don't I feel better about this?"

"Sometimes the truth sucks," he answered.

"What do *you* think? Do you think he killed Rhia?" she asked.

"I think we should just follow the evidence and see where it leads us. Speculating is what gets people all twisted up."

Detective Douche-bag walked by and cast a flip smile Quinn's way and she turned away pointedly. Just knowing what that guy did made Silas's blood boil.

She sensed his rage and cooled him with a look. "He's small and petty. We have more interesting things to chase after. Can you check and see if any additional DNA evidence has come through on Rhia's case? I need to run by my uncle's shop and talk to him. I know he's going to be really bummed to learn about Pastor Simms."

He nodded and watched her go. Silas met the detective's gaze with a hard one of his own. A wordless exchange passed between the two men like two dogs circling each other before a fight.

Who would back down first?

As expected, Harrison did.

So maybe he's not as dumb as he looks. Damn, he was hoping Harrison would bow up on him. Silas could use a punching bag.

Another time.

Silas walked into Lester's office but was shocked when Lester looked angry enough to eat nails.

"Shut the door."

Silas followed the sheriff's gruff instruction. "Something wrong?"

"Something wrong? Everything is wrong, you little shit," Lester grumped, his scowl deep enough to drown kittens. "What the hell is going on around here? Since you've come around, all hell has broken loose and now you've got the pastor arrested for fooling around with that girl?"

"I asked for a DNA sample. He confessed to sleeping with her."

"You badgered him into a confession," Lester persisted. "Forrest Simms is a man of God!"

"No, he's a man," Silas corrected the sheriff. "Plain and simple. Subject to the same temptations as the rest of us. He messed around with a kid. Somehow I doubt *God* would be okay with that."

Lester's fight seeped out of him as he stared down Silas. "What's happening to my little town?"

Silas didn't have the heart to tell Lester that Port Orion had never been immune to evil.

And Lester should've already known that.

"Look, Mick Creech buried the story about Sara Westfall's accident. There's a possibility that someone tampered with the accident report."

"What makes you say that?" he asked, wiping at his brow.

"Because Emily Westfall said the night her sister died, she hadn't been drinking. She'd gotten a call and blazed out of there, seemingly to meet whoever had called but she ended up dying instead."

Lester shook his head. "Son, surely I don't have to tell you that Emily Westfall isn't right in the head? She's not a credible witness."

"That's why I wouldn't put her on the stand but her testimony is enough for a second look at the report."

"For crying out loud, would you like to tear down all our old cases?" Lester said, scowling. "I'm starting to wish I hadn't given you carte blanche on this case."

Silas didn't want to be disrespectful to the man but Lester was digging his heels in for the wrong reasons. He didn't want to turn over stones, nor did he want to reopen old cases and Silas needed to do exactly that.

"Were you patronizing me when you said I could look into Spencer's case?"

"Hell, of course I was. I know you need closure. I thought this would do that for you. I had no idea you were going to turn my town upside down and backward in an attempt to find what was likely a goddamn transient who's long gone by now."

Lester's face turned florid, his eyes hot.

Silas's temper reacted in kind. He leaned forward to meet Lester's gaze. "Someone is out there, someone in Port Orion, who is doing all sorts of bad things right under the radar. Someone killed Sara Westfall to keep what she knew from coming out. Someone might've killed Rhia Daniels for the same reason."

"And Spencer?" Lester returned caustically. "Was a little boy snooping around, getting caught doing something he shouldn't have? Do you hear yourself? You're trying to make connections where there aren't any!"

"And you're too damn old to see that there is something wrong going on in this town!"

"So far all I've seen you do is rile up good people, spread fear and discontent and disrupt a good way of life. You might've hated this place but the people who still live here are pretty happy with it."

"This isn't a vendetta against Port Orion," Silas said. "If anything, I'm trying to protect this place from a killer who is hiding in plain sight."

"You haven't come to me with a shred of evidence that would convince me that anything other than your one-sided need for vengeance is at work."

"Do you attend Pastor Simms's church?"

"Every Sunday," Lester answered with a stubborn tilt of his chin.

"Then you're in no way positioned to remain objective," Silas pointed out. "I get it, you're attached, but you have to stop being emotional about this and start looking at the facts. Something doesn't pass the smell test and you know it. Stop sticking your head in the sand and be the damn sheriff. The people need you to stand up for them."

"I have always stood up for my community," Lester said.

"Well, show me. All I see right now is a man who's too tired to care about solving crimes and just wants to wave and smile in parades."

Silas knew the minute the words left his mouth, he'd pushed too far.

Lester shot from his chair, his eyes blazing. "Get out! Get out of my office right now! I'm not going to listen to another minute of your bullshit. I defended you, stood by you and made sure you didn't turn into a worthless pile of crap after your brother died and this is the thanks I get? *Out!*"

Silas had lost any ground he'd gained. The best course

of action was to go but not before he left Lester with one final piece of leather to chew. "I'll go. But before you start blustering that I'm out of line for suggesting that you're turning a blind eye to what's going on right beneath your nose, you ought to look into your lead detective's behavior. He attacked Quinn right here in your station and he's going to do it again because he knows there ain't *nobody* who's going to stop him, least of all, you."

Silas left Lester in blustering silence.

He may have just screwed everything up but if he was going to be forced out of this town, he was going to make sure that Quinn was safe before he left.

Even if she's going to be pissed as hell when she finds out.

Chapter 26

Quinn left the station to talk to Uncle Leo. She wanted to be the one to break the news about Pastor Simms.

She walked into the shop, smiling faintly at the familiar smell of lingering chemical solutions and stopped a minute to appreciate her uncle's talent.

Leo loved his Thailand photographs. The lush green canopies and the local wild fauna as well as the people, were his passion. He said that his time in Thailand always reinvigorated him and he certainly always seemed happier when he returned, almost dreamy at times.

Uncle Leo had an entire series on orphans that'd won him some awards. Not surprising, their little eyes had looked so haunting. Even now, each time Quinn looked at his wall, those eyes told a sad story.

That was the mark of a true professional.

Quinn always thought her uncle had the chops to work for *National Geographic* but he preferred to stay local.

Such a good man, sacrificing his opportunity for the love of his small town and of her, of course.

Leo appeared from the dark room, wiping his hands. "This is a surprise," he said, smiling. "Are you here on an official capacity?"

"Actually, sort of," she answered, biting her lip as she tried to find the gentlest way to break the news. "I have something to tell you and I didn't want you to hear through the grapevine."

"I don't like the sound of that," he said, worried. "Is everything okay?"

"An arrest was made today in Rhia Daniels's case," she said, placing a hand on his arm.

Uncle Leo's gaze widened. "Who?"

"Pastor Simms."

"No." Leo sucked a sharp breath. "Not possible. Pastor Simms is a good man."

"Well, that remains to be seen. He was arrested for unlawful sex with a minor. Silas believes the pastor was also Rhia's baby-daddy."

Leo made a look of distaste. "Honey, please. Let's be a little more respectful. But to your original statement, I can't believe it."

"I know, that's why I wanted to tell you myself. I knew it would be a shock."

"Shock isn't the word. Why do they think he would kill her?"

"Maybe he was terrified that their secret would ruin him?" she suggested. "Either way, unless the pastor has a really good alibi for the night Rhia was killed…it doesn't look good for the man."

"That's a damn shame." Leo shook his head sadly. "The sins of the flesh catch us all."

"That was very Old Testament."

"I suppose Silas wasn't too happy to find out that Rhia's death was probably not related to his brother's murder."

"Oh, I wouldn't say that," Quinn disagreed. "Granted, our evidence is more circumstantial than concrete but we've uncovered some incriminating bits of information, suggesting that Sara Westfall was murdered by the same person who killed Spencer Kelly."

"Oh? Such as?"

"Sorry, can't tell just yet." She smiled, patting his cheek with love. "But you'll be the first to know when I can spill the beans."

She turned to leave but Uncle Leo caught her hand. Quinn turned with a smile. "Are you okay?"

Uncle Leo's grip tightened and her smile faltered as something she didn't quite recognize flared in his eyes but it was gone in a blink. A heartbeat later he was back to the man she knew and loved, causing her to question if she'd seen anything at all.

"Yes, yes," he said, dropping her hand. "I'm just being a sentimental old man. Go on. I'll see you at home."

"Okay," she said as she left but Quinn couldn't shake the odd feeling that her uncle had wanted to tell her something.

She called Silas, planning to suggest lunch but he told her to meet him at the hotel instead.

Thirsty little devil, she thought with a smile, guessing that a little nooky was on the agenda for lunch but when she arrived, he looked neither cuddly nor approachable.

Unless a grouchy bear was considered cuddly.

"What's going on?"

"Lester threw me out of the station."

Her mouth gaped. "He did what?"

"He kicked me out."

"Why the hell did he do that?" she asked, confused.

"I pushed him too hard. But something had to be said."

"I don't understand. What did you say?"

"It was about the pastor. I think he really would've been content to look the other way and when I got the search warrant for the DNA, he knew there was no way he could and it pissed him off."

"But Lester has always been a straight shooter," she protested, uncomprehending the version of events as Silas was telling them. "Why wouldn't he want the pastor brought in?"

"Because it rocks the boat of his quiet community. He doesn't want to do the hard work anymore and, hell, I'm not blaming him for wanting to cycle out to his retirement on a slow ride to shore but I can't ignore evidence that's staring me in the face."

Quinn's heart ached for Lester but she was conflicted, too. "What if…" God, she could barely manage the words; they felt like sacrilege leaving her lips. "What if the reason Lester doesn't want anyone poking around is because… he's the one who's guilty?"

The grim set of Silas's lips told her he worried about that possibility, as well but Silas admitted, "I've got nothing tying Lester to the murders, though, and I sure as hell can't drag the sheriff in for questioning. I might as well fashion the rope to hang myself with if I try a stunt like that."

A thought occurred to Quinn. "My uncle and Lester are very close. Best friends for as long as I can remember. When I went to talk to my uncle about the pastor, he seemed… I don't know, odd."

"Odd how?"

"I can't explain it and I feel terrible for even mentioning it. I feel all I've done is dangle half-chewed leads in front of this investigation without anything substantial to go to press or court with."

"Don't ignore your gut," Silas told her. "If your uncle knows something, we need to find out."

"I'm just saying, if Lester was up to something bad,

my uncle is such a good man he'd try to protect his best friend. Even if he shouldn't."

Quinn wanted to wash her mouth out for saying something so evil but that look her uncle had given her...it'd sent a warning tingle down her back, something she'd never experienced with Leo.

"Maybe it's time I talk to your uncle."

"No," Quinn said quickly. "I'll do it. I don't want him to think he's being interrogated. He's a good man, Silas. I don't want to upset him."

"Fine. You try and see if your uncle will talk but if he doesn't, you have to let me try."

Quinn nodded though she hated the idea of Silas going after Leo. Silas could be very abrasive and she didn't want her uncle to bear the brunt of all that Kelly intensity.

Silas's scowl grew deeper as he said, "There's something else I need to tell you."

"What is it?"

"I told Lester about Harrison."

"You did what?"

"If Lester throws me off this case and withdraws his invitation to help, I'm not leaving you with that asshole without some kind of protection."

"Why did you do that?" she said, her ears growing hot. "I told you I'd handle it."

"Yeah, well, I handled it. If Lester was serious about doing his job, as he was when he took offense with what I had to say, he'll can Harrison or at the very least, scare the crap out of him so he doesn't go near you again."

"Silas, I can't believe you. I told you I didn't need you to be my hero," she said, trying to hold her temper in check but she was mortified that Silas had told Lester her business. "I am fully capable of handling Harrison. When are you going to learn that I'm not some weak female who needs a man to protect her?"

"Look, I did what I did and I don't regret it. You can be mad all you want. I'd do it again."

Quinn wanted to slap his face. "That wasn't your place."

"Probably not. I did it anyway."

She could tell by his set jaw he wasn't going to budge. He believed he did the right thing and he wouldn't back down, no matter her feelings on the subject.

Quinn grabbed her purse and left the hotel before she did something stupid.

If Silas was kicked off this investigation, that would mean finding the true killer would be up to her.

She wasn't going to waste precious time fighting with Silas.

Not even when she wanted to show him just how much he'd stepped over the line.

Rain check, Kelly. Rain check.

Silas watched Quinn go and didn't try to stop her. She was pissed, just as he knew she would be but he didn't care.

He wasn't about to leave Quinn to Harrison's continued harassment.

Men like Harrison didn't stop until someone made them. He knew Lester wouldn't, not in his current frame of mind, and Silas wasn't willing to take the chance that Harrison might get his hands on Quinn again.

So, yeah, Quinn could be pissed as a wet cat and she would just have to deal with it because he didn't regret his decision to spill the beans.

He ought to check in on the coroner but he was too agitated. After about an hour of trying to focus on his notes, he gave up and decided to get some air.

Grabbing his coat, he stalked out, needing something to take the edge off.

Silas found himself at The Pier, and as he sat at the bar,

nursing a beer, he tried to let his mind quiet, if only for a blessed minute.

He should've handled Lester with more finesse. Poking at anyone's ego was a fast track to disaster but he'd been so angry that Lester was ignoring key evidence that his mouth had popped off.

That wasn't his MO. Usually, he was known for keeping it together, even under extreme stress, but there was something about this town that collapsed his ability to compartmentalize.

His gut said they were close to something big. But the clues were ephemeral, dancing in and out of the light without substance.

Sure, catching Pastor Simms with his pants down was a win but as much as he'd like to pin Rhia's death on the man, he had a feeling Pastor Simms did not, in fact, kill the girl.

Maybe Simms really did feel as if he loved her—not that it justified his actions—but if that was true, what would his motive be for killing her?

What if Simms really did love Rhia Daniels and the paternity came back as a match, that would mean Simms had lost the woman he loved and his child.

None of those variables added up to murder.

And there was absolutely no correlation between Simms and Spencer or Sara Westfall.

Silas swore under his breath and downed his beer, signaling for another when an older woman with dyed platinum hair in a high ponytail sat gingerly on the stool beside him.

"You're that FBI agent, right?" she said, her gaze darting.

"Yeah," he answered, withholding a sigh. He didn't want to talk to locals. He just wanted to enjoy his beer, get a nice buzz and go sleep it off. "And you are?"

"Can I talk with you?"

"About?"

"Not here," she said, pursing her lips slightly. "Your hotel room."

Silas smothered a groan. He didn't have time to deal with this. "Look, I don't want to hurt your feelings but—"

"I'm not interested in screwing you," she cut in, lowering her voice. "I have information that you might want."

That changed things a bit. "Such as?"

"I'll be at your hotel in ten minutes." And then she left.

Cryptic and annoying, he thought regretfully as he stared down at the remainder of the beer that he wouldn't get to finish. Tossing cash onto the bar, he decided to see where this would take him.

True to her word, the woman was there, in the shadows, waiting for him. The fact that she knew where he was staying was a little creepy but he let that slide.

He opened the door and she slunk past him, motioning for him to shut the door quickly.

"Okay, you got me here. Now, what are you so afraid of telling me?" he asked, curious. "First, who are you?"

"My name is Jessa Almasey. My daughter was Rhia's best friend."

"Why are you here, Jessa?"

"It's about Rhia. I didn't want to say anything because I didn't want Britain to get mixed up in all this, but I can't keep quiet any longer. Before I say anything I want you to know that I loved that kid like my own. She could talk to me in a way that she couldn't with her own mother and I would never dream of breaking her trust, but I feel I have to tell you what I know."

"Please do," he said, listening with laser focus. "I'm all ears."

"I'm not sure where to start…"

"How about I help you out?" Silas didn't have time to

mess around. "Did you know Rhia was sleeping with the pastor?"

Jessa looked miserable. "I knew she had a terrible crush on him but I wasn't aware they were sleeping together, though it doesn't surprise me. Rhia had a way of getting what she wanted from people."

"What do you mean?"

"She was…persuasive. Maybe a little too spoiled for her own good. I tried my best to guide her but she was a wild child. I worried about her. She thought it was fun to poke at certain people."

"What do you mean?"

"Rhia…she…well, at first I thought it was just silly high school stuff but then I realized she was playing mean games with people in town."

Impatience sharpened his tone as he said, "What kind of games? With who?"

"Last year Rhia won an amateur photography contest. It was all over the newspapers and even a few regional ones and everyone was so proud of our little Rhia. But one night I overheard Rhia talking to Britain, telling her that the photos hadn't been hers. She'd taken the credit for someone else's work."

"Why?"

"I don't know. But she wasn't the least bit sorry about it. In fact, she said whoever she had over a barrel would do just about anything to keep his secret. She thought it was funny."

"Did you talk to Britain about it?"

"I tried but Britain just waved away my concerns, saying that Rhia had been kidding and that I shouldn't eavesdrop."

"Did you tell her parents?"

Jessa shook her head. "No, I didn't want to ruin our relationship. You have to understand, I'm a single mom, trying to do the best that I can, and my daughter is my life. I wasn't going to do anything to come between her and her best friend."

"Why didn't you go to the sheriff when Rhia died?"

"It seemed wrong to smear the poor girl's memory. It was bad enough that she died. I was prepared to just let her rest in peace."

"So what changed your mind?"

Jessa licked her lips. "I'm afraid for Britain. What if whoever hurt Rhia comes after Britain because they were friends? Everyone already believes they were joined at the hip. It's a natural assumption that Britain might know Rhia's secrets. The more I thought about it, the more scared I became."

"Why all the secrecy?" he asked.

"Because this is a small town," Jessa answered. "People talk. I didn't know who I could trust. Everyone knows everyone else. I just want this to be over. I'm thinking of taking Britain and moving to Seattle. My parents live there. Maybe a fresh start is what we both need."

"Do you know whose photography she stole?" he asked, watching her keenly. The woman was practically vibrating with anxiety.

She nodded.

"Who?"

"Leo Jackson, the owner of Looking Glass."

Silas narrowed his gaze as the import of what Jessa had just shared sank in.

Quinn's uncle.

Ah, hell.

Could "X" stand for Leo?

Chapter 27

Quinn returned home, still angry, but her temper was slowly cooling. She knew Silas had acted out of concern and he wasn't the kind of person to stand by and do nothing when he knew someone was in danger.

She liked that quality about him.

But what really tipped the scale against him was that he'd done so without taking her feelings into consideration. She'd expressly asked him to let her take care of Harrison but he'd ignored her request, doing what he felt was right in spite of her wishes.

Was that a major character flaw? Was Silas a misogynist who secretly thought women were weak and frail creatures?

Silas would learn that she may be small but she was a firecracker.

Quinn walked to the kitchen and grabbed a beer from the fridge. She wasn't a big drinker but she needed something to take the edge off.

For every step they took in the right direction, something shoved them two steps back.

The frustration was enough to choke a horse.

Uncle Leo wasn't back from the shop yet so she had time to formulate her questions. It was bad enough that she had had to break the news to Uncle Leo about Pastor Simms; she had no idea how he would react to her questioning about Lester, his best friend.

A strange sound came from Uncle Leo's office and she realized the fax machine was jammed again. She'd tried to convince Uncle Leo to buy a new machine but he liked to hold on to things and resisted change.

She flipped the light and went to the old machine, opening the top and pulling the paper free that was stuck in the rollers. Quinn threaded the paper back through the rollers and went to the computer to restart the feed.

Uncle Leo had his email linked to the fax machine because he hated reading on the small screen, saying he preferred to read his emails on paper.

She went to log on but found the computer already on. Quinn smiled, knowing her uncle must've left it on before leaving for the shop.

"So absentminded," she murmured with a chuckle as she opened his email program to reset the fax. Finished, she went to log off but her eye caught a different folder on the desktop. Uncle Leo wasn't very organized but he was fastidious about his computer desktop.

It was simply labeled "Them," which was an odd choice for a folder.

Curious, she double-clicked to see what was in the folder.

Quinn blinked as she realized it was filled with photos. Not odd for a photographer, but what she saw caused her belly to cramp as her breath caught.

Pictures of boys.

Young boys.

Naked.

She covered her mouth to keep from throwing up.

A familiar photo jumped out at her.

One of the Thailand orphans with the sad eyes.

Only this time the boy was posed provocatively, wearing a fake smile but his eyes remained the same—reflecting a broken soul.

"No," she breathed, unable to believe what she was seeing.

She quickly clicked through more.

What remained of her last meal was threatening to bubble up in her throat.

What was she looking at?

She couldn't reconcile what she was seeing with what she knew of her uncle.

The man who had loved her, taken her in when her parents died, the man who was a kindly bear of a man who never had a cross word or a bad thing to say about anyone...

A horrified sob erupted as she continued to click through the photos. Why didn't she stop? She couldn't. Her finger kept dragging her through each file until she thought she might faint from the breath she was holding.

But one set of photos was different.

A smiling boy, a gap-toothed grin, wearing a Port Orion Bluejay baseball jersey against a backdrop she recognized as Seminole Creek.

"Oh, God..."

Spencer had been wearing that same shirt when he'd been found. Quinn remembered the detail from the crime scene photos.

Why did Leo have pictures of Spencer Kelly?

And then she nearly vomited.

Spencer, eyes closed, his mouth slack as a tiny stream

of blood seeped from the corner, deep red hand prints circling his windpipe.

"No. No. Nooooo..."

She rose on shaky legs to use the restroom. This couldn't be happening. This had to be a nightmare.

Quinn fell to her knees and retched, her stomach heaving as she puked her guts out.

She fell to her behind, her head resting on the cool surface of the bowl as she fumbled to flush the toilet.

What the hell was happening?

Uncle Leo wasn't capable of the filth she saw in that file.

But why else would he have it in a secret file titled, "Them"? She'd been on his desktop a million times before. Why was it there now?

The odd expression on Leo's face the other night came back to her. He'd wanted to tell her something.

Was this it?

Had he been ready to confess?

If he had, he must've chickened out and tried to collect evidence to get rid of it.

Leo must've been moving files and forgotten it was on the desktop. Lately, he'd become more absentminded, preoccupied.

Now his behavior seemed suspect.

Everything seemed suspect.

And what was she supposed to do with this information? If she told Silas, he would arrest Leo.

The details of the arrest would spread like wildfire.

The headlines would read, "Local Photographer Caught With Child Porn" and it would kill her.

But wasn't it her duty to report him?

Did Lester know about her uncle's perverse appetites?

And the biggest question...did this discovery mean that Leo had killed Spencer, Sara and Rhia?

Please, God, no.

* * *

The following morning Silas awoke to a quiet knock on his hotel room door. He rose to find Quinn, her eyes swollen, her nose red, and he thought the worst.

"Did Harrison hurt you?" he asked, ready to shoot the man in the balls.

But Quinn shook her head and reached into her purse to hand him a flash drive.

"What's this?"

Her voice was strangled as she said, "The break in the case we've been hoping for."

Silas accepted the drive and motioned for her to come in. Expressionless, she walked over to sit on the bed. Quinn had lost all of her fire, which scared him.

"What's on this drive?"

But she couldn't form the words.

"Quinn...what is this?"

The tears started fresh. She dropped her head into her hands and started sobbing. "All night, I played those images in my head and I didn't know what to do. I love him. He raised me but I-I don't know why he has these pictures. I don't kn-know what to do. This will ruin him."

Silas plugged the drive into his laptop and clicked the folder.

His spirits sank as he realized what he was looking at.

The shock was written all over Quinn's face—she'd had no idea. But people with secrets were adept at hiding what they didn't want people to know.

"There are pictures of S-Spencer on there," she whispered.

His heart stopped and he had to force himself to click through the photos until he found the ones of his little brother.

Smiling, wearing his Bluejays shirt, unaware that his life would end that day.

Tears blinded him as rage whipped through him. He tried to tamp it down so he could think straight. He needed a warrant. He needed to call his brothers. He needed…his gaze went straight to Quinn and realized what he needed to do the most was be there for the woman who'd just lost everything in her world.

Ignoring his need to arrest Leo right then and there, he went to Quinn and gathered her into his arms to hold her tight. She clung to him, still sobbing.

"How could I not have known?" she cried.

Silas smoothed the wild red of her hair. "Because he didn't want you to know."

"But I should've sensed something, should've realized something was wrong. All those pictures of kids…that's why he goes to Thailand? He told me he was volunteering at an orphanage! I want to throw up. I *did* throw up! And I want to throw up some more. I want to scream. I want to demand answers but I'm afraid of knowing the truth. What if he killed all those people, Silas? What if my uncle is someone I never knew at all?"

"Let's take this one step at a time," he said softly. "Your uncle needs help."

"He's n-never touched me that way. Never done anything inappropriate with me. I-I don't understand."

The files were all of boys. Quinn had to know what that meant.

"I'm going to have to go to Lester and tell him. After the fit he threw over the pastor, I doubt this information is going to go over any better."

"What's going to happen to my uncle?"

"He's going to be arrested," he answered as gently as he could. "A search warrant will be issued for his home."

"My home, too," she reminded him in a stark whisper. "People will be going through our things, like we're criminals."

He knew there was no way to soften the blow. Quinn was shell-shocked as it was; what was coming would put her over the edge.

Silas wanted to be there for her but he also needed to get the ball rolling. "Did your uncle know you'd seen this file?" he asked.

She shook her head. "I put everything back the way it was and went to my room. By the time he came home, my door was closed and he assumed I was asleep. But I couldn't sleep. How could I? I'm lost right now, Silas. What am I going to do?"

"Stay here. I don't want you to watch your uncle get arrested," he told her. "The things that are about to go down... I don't want you to get hurt any more than you already have."

"I can't avoid what's coming," she said, wiping at her eyes. "I work for the newspaper. This is fresh blood in the water. The headlines..."

"Stop thinking that way. Take it one step at a time. But in the meantime, I want you to stay here, okay?"

She nodded but he wasn't sure she was listening. Her stare had glazed and her reactions dulled. With any luck, she'd crash for a few hours, at least. Rest would help clear the thought process.

And she'd need her wits about her.

Things were about to get ugly.

Chapter 28

Silas walked into Lester's office with a somber expression that immediately set his whiskers on edge.

"Did you come to apologize?" he asked gruffly.

"No, sir."

"Then what do you want?"

"I came to let you know I am arresting Leonard Jackson for the murder of my brother, Spencer Alexander Kelly."

The breath left his chest. "What?"

"We've found evidence connecting your friend to Spencer's death as well as evidence that he may have been involved with Rhia's murder, as well. As a courtesy, and out of respect for you, I came to tell you first."

"Leo Jackson? Are you sure about this?"

"Positive."

Silas placed a flash drive on the desk and gestured. "Plug it in and see for yourself. I should warn you...the photos are disturbing."

Lester snatched up the drive, not willing to accept his

best friend was a killer of any sort. "This is bullshit," he muttered, mostly to himself but a thread of fear had begun to squeeze his heart, causing his angina to flare up.

He rubbed at his chest but stilled the moment the flash drive opened and a treasure trove of horrors unfolded before his eyes.

"Where did you get this?"

"Leo Jackson's home computer. Quinn stumbled on it and brought it to me."

"Where is Quinn?" he asked.

"Safe. I have her resting. She's understandably distraught."

The pain in his chest intensified, causing him to fall forward. "Goddamn it," he muttered, squeezing his eyelids shut as he waited out the pain.

"Lester...what's wrong? Are you okay?"

"J-just give me a minute," he gasped through the clenching agony. "It's just a-angina."

"I'm calling the ambulance," Silas said, ignoring his protests. Within minutes, paramedics came pouring into the office in a flurry of motion.

This was all his fault. He should've known. He should've seen it coming.

Dimly, he heard the paramedics barking orders and he was hoisted onto a gurney.

An oxygen mask was fixed to his face as he was loaded into the ambulance. "You're suffering a heart attack, Sheriff," a young paramedic told him. "Stay calm and we'll have you at the hospital in minutes."

Leo Jackson killed Spencer Kelly.

After all this time, the truth came out.

He closed his eyes and saw Leo, twenty years earlier, right before the Kelly boy was murdered. Jumpy, easily agitated, looking as if he was going to be caught at any second doing something he shouldn't.

Lester had joked Leo needed to get himself a girlfriend, to relieve some of that stress.

He'd had no idea he'd been fighting his perverse nature.

But if Leo had blood on his hands...so did Lester.

It had seemed a small thing.

Sara Westfall was stirring the muck of the town, making insane accusations that made everyone edgy.

In the wake of Spencer's death, it seemed a mercy for the townsfolk.

It'd taken all of three seconds to adjust three little letters followed by a colon.

From BAC: .02

To BAC: .20

In a few clicks, Sara had gone from sober to raging drunk and no one asked questions.

Everyone knew Sara had been an alcoholic. Death by DUI had seemed an inevitability.

Leo had urged him to make the change. "You gotta think of the town and everything they've been through. Sara is a cancer. We need to nip it."

He should've known then that something was up but Leo had made a good point, had seemed so earnest in his concern, that Lester had made the decision to change the report.

Such a small thing...

Better for the greater good.

But as it turned out the true cancer had been whispering in his ear under the guise of friendship.

He groaned as his old heart simply broke.

His last thought before blacking out... *I should've retired when I had the chance.*

Silas brought three deputies with him to arrest Leo Jackson. He wasn't taking any chances with the big man in case he started throwing punches.

He thought of Quinn and how her world had just crumbled to dust and he wanted to shout at the man responsible for ruining what she knew as her life.

But he couldn't do that.

He needed to stay on course, implacable.

Silas knocked on the front door but after several knocks, he realized no one was home.

"He's probably at the shop," Silas told the deputies with a frown. He'd hoped to do this away from curious onlookers, for Quinn's sake.

Silas made a quick call to Quinn. "Your uncle wasn't home. I want you to stay at the hotel. Don't come to the shop. You don't need to watch us arrest him."

She sniffled and agreed, hanging up quickly.

Silas grimaced at the pain she was in.

Time to get this over with.

They arrived at the shop and found it open but seemingly empty.

The deputy told him, "There's a dark room in the back."

Silas nodded for the intel. "Leo Jackson?" he called out. "Come out with your hands up. We don't want to make a scene. Come quietly for the sake of your niece."

Leo emerged, haggard but wearing a resigned smile as he dropped a gas can from his fingers.

Silas swore under his breath. "Don't shoot, he's doused in gasoline."

To Leo he said, "It doesn't have to be like this. Don't let Quinn's last memory of you be like this."

"You think she's going to remember me as anything but a deviant?" Leo said, his mouth quivering as he wiped the gasoline from his eyes. "This is all that's left."

"Let's talk," Silas said, trying to get the man to calm down before he set the entire building on fire. "You love this town. You don't want to do this."

"No, I don't want to do this," he agreed. "But I have to."

"You need help."

"Nothing can help me."

The desperation in Leo's eyes was dangerous. The man had nothing to lose.

"Why'd you kill my brother?" he asked, knowing if he didn't ask, the question would haunt him. "What did he do to you?"

"Nothing."

"Then why'd you kill him?"

"Things went too far," Leo answered as if that made total sense. "It was before I realized I could control it if I had an outlet. I was able to maintain. But when he…he started screaming. He didn't like my games anymore. I had to shut him up. I was just trying to scare him. But I went too far."

"That's why you go to Thailand, isn't it?" Silas said. Thailand had a reputation for child sex trafficking. American tourists bought children without an ounce of guilt or threat of prosecution because the government looked the other way, happy to have American money in the economy.

"They love me there," Leo said. "Always happy to see me. Always ready to be my friend for the cost of a lollipop."

Silas tried not to grimace with disgust. He'd heard the stories from agents on specialized task forces. It was a detail he couldn't stomach.

"And Sara?"

"Sara was spreading terrible lies."

"Were they lies?"

"As far as anyone was concerned," Leo said, a faroff look in his eyes. "And she was a drunk. Drunks kill themselves in accidents all the time. Brake lines fail at inopportune times."

Silas swallowed. "And Rhia? What was her crime?"

Rhia's name roused him as he spat, "That little bitch.

She went snooping through my private things, pretended to be interested in photography so I would let down my guard. She discovered my secret files then forced me to say my photos were hers so she could win that contest but that wasn't good enough. She wanted more. She wanted money or else she was going to expose my activities. I couldn't have that. I had to protect Quinn."

"She was extorting money from you to keep your secret," Silas said. "It must've been hard to play the concerned citizen."

"You have no idea, but I would do anything for my Quinnie."

"Even come in quietly, to spare her the pain of this standoff?"

"You and I both know I won't last in prison. I'll die there. Violently. I know men like me are the bottom of the social pyramid. I'd rather choose my death than wait in fear for it every night."

Selfish bastard. He was going to do it.

But before he could say anything else, Quinn's voice at his back had him swearing internally. She was supposed to stay at the hotel!

"Uncle Leo, what are you doing?" she said in an anguished whisper. "Don't. Please."

"Quinnie…go home. Don't watch." His voice shook. "I love you, Quinnie. I really, really do. I tried to manage it. Lord, I tried. Somehow things just spiraled out of control. I never meant to hurt you. Not ever." He drew a halting breath. "I love you. You're a good girl. I wish I could've done better. Take the world by storm. There ain't no one in this world who can do it as good as you."

And then in slow motion, Silas saw the lighter flick and a flame erupted as Quinn screamed. Silas managed to catch her before she ran straight into the flaming ball of fire that'd become Leo Jackson.

Silas dragged Quinn to safety as the building quickly became engulfed. Fire trucks came rushing in as deputies secured the streets.

All Silas could do was hold Quinn as she collapsed against him, sobbing as if her heart had shattered.

Chapter 29

Several days had passed in a blur as Quinn had hid in her house, refusing to leave her bedroom.

Johnna had stopped by but when Quinn had been unresponsive, she left with a promise to return later.

She never did.

But Quinn wasn't hurt by Johnna's defection.

No one wanted anything to do with Quinn after the revelation that Leo Jackson had been a perverted monster, living right among the good folk of Port Orion, completely sheltered by their ignorance.

Gigi had written the news story, not her.

It was a conflict of interest, but she had no heart to do so anyway so it hadn't mattered.

Silas was the only one who refused to leave her side.

He cooked for her.

Made her shower.

Held her at night.

But she felt nothing.

"You don't have to stay," she finally said one night as he settled a bowl of hot soup in front of her. "There's nothing keeping you here now. All the murders have been solved. Yay for closure."

She didn't even have the strength for the level of sarcasm she was going for and gave up.

"Sometimes we think the truth is going to set us free when it really just drags us down," he said quietly.

Quinn swung her gaze to Silas. "What do you mean?"

"All this time I thought knowing the truth would help me sleep at night but the nightmares are worse. Now I know what happened and I can't forgive myself."

"It's not your fault Spencer ran into a predator," she returned dully. That predator being…her uncle. She still couldn't say it out loud.

"No. But I should've never sent him away. If he'd been with me…he would still be alive."

She couldn't argue that nor did she try. "I guess that's the cost you were talking about. The cost of knowledge. Sometimes ignorance really is bliss."

Silas changed the subject. "Lester is out of the hospital with new hardware in his heart. Doctor said he's going to recover fully as long as he changes his diet, limits his stress and starts exercising."

"Good luck with that," Quinn said, wiping at the sudden tears that tended to show up at the most inopportune moments. "Damn it."

"It's okay to cry."

"No, it's not. Who am I crying for? The monster or myself? If I cry for my uncle, I'm the monster. If I cry for myself, I'm a selfish bitch. How can I love a man who was so bad? I can't grieve for him. I'm not allowed."

"He wasn't a bad man to you," Silas explained, understanding her struggle. "To you, he was loving and kind. And that's all you need to remember."

"But everyone knows."

"Yes. But that doesn't change who he was to you."

She laughed almost hysterically. "It changes everything." Quinn pushed away the soup and rose. "I need some space. Can you go, please? It's been days. I need you to go."

"No."

"Get out."

"No."

Quinn balled up her fists and screamed. "Get *out* of my house!"

"I'm not leaving you like this."

"I'm not a child. I don't need you to babysit me."

He didn't answer, just regarded her with an expression that raked nails across her heart.

"Don't," she warned. "Just don't. I don't want this. I don't want you. I don't want anyone. I just want to be left alone!"

And still he stood, weathering her rage, accepting her abuse.

"Are you deaf?" All the pent-up rage and grief exploded and she ran at Silas, fists swinging. "I said get out, get out, get out!"

He caught her easily even as she tried to destroy him, lashing out with pure agony at everything she'd lost. She screamed until she was hoarse and still he held her tightly.

"I'm not leaving," he said, squeezing her in his arms, holding her so she couldn't hurt herself or him.

Quinn gasped as the fire burnt out of her soul, leaving ash. She lost the strength in her legs and he hoisted her up. "Why did he do those terrible things?" she whimpered, crying against Silas's chest. "Why, Silas? Why?"

"I don't know," Silas answered, choking up with raw emotion. "I don't know."

"Why don't you leave me?" she groaned. "I'm toxic. You deserve to get your life back."

"Shhhh," he said against her crown, rocking her like a baby. She cuddled up to him, her hand tucked beneath her chin, so tiny.

His whispered answer, "I won't leave...because I love you," was the last thing she heard before falling into a fitful sleep.

Everything had changed.

Nothing would ever be the same.

This was what she'd wanted but she'd had no idea the cost.

Sawyer, Shaine and Shaine's fiancée, Poppy, arrived in Port Orion three days later, each cashing in immediate sick leave or vacation time, whatever they had on the books to get there.

Their mom had opted to stay in Florida, saying she'd said her goodbyes to Spencer long ago and seeing Port Orion again would only open old wounds.

Silas understood and didn't try to convince her otherwise.

Quinn had offered her place for them to stay so they didn't have to get a hotel room.

It'd been a while since he'd seen his brothers, even though they kept in touch on the phone.

The minute his older brothers walked into the house, Silas felt the tears coming.

They embraced, a knot of Kelly boys, bound by shared grief.

Sawyer, the oldest brother, broke the embrace first, wiping at his eyes, as well.

"You did it, little brother," he said with love and respect. "You managed to do the impossible."

Silas accepted his brother's praise but out of consideration to Quinn, didn't go into detail.

He introduced Quinn to Shaine, Sawyer and Poppy. She shyly welcomed them and they went to the living room to talk.

Shaine jumped in first, as was his style. "Quinn, I just want to say how sorry I am that you've had to go through this ordeal. I can't imagine how you must be feeling."

She shared a look with Silas then returned to Shaine with a small smile. "I'll be okay. Eventually. Silas has been my rock."

Shaine smiled. "At least he's good for something. As a kid, we all had our doubts."

Poppy sent Shaine an incredulous look, "Cut the guy some slack," she said then apologized to Quinn. "Sorry, I'd like to say Shaine's not usually like this but that would be a lie. But from what I hear, this is totally normal between these knuckleheads."

Quinn actually laughed and Silas's heart tripled in beat. Hearing her laughter was worth enduring the insult from his brother. Hell, he'd let Shaine roast him alive if it made Quinn smile.

"I'm going to get some coffee," she announced and Poppy offered to join her, both leaving the room. Silas knew they were allowing for some privacy so he could talk with his brothers.

Silas gestured after Poppy, saying to Shaine, "She's a keeper."

"As is yours," Shaine agreed then teased, "I never knew you had a thing for red hair."

"Neither did I."

They chuckled softly, each processing the newfound facts in their own way. It was easier to talk about superficial stuff than to delve straight into the pit they were all circling but it had to be done.

Sawyer shook his head. "When you called…I couldn't

believe it. After all this time…it was Leo Jackson. He took my senior photos."

Shaine jumped in, "And he set himself on fire? Man, that's wild. That takes some cojones."

"Hey, watch yourself. Quinn loved her uncle very much. This has been a terrible transition."

Shaine immediately apologized. "You're right, man. I'm sorry. I just can't wrap my brain around everything. It's a lot, you know?"

"This case had more twists and turns than a country road. If it hadn't been for Quinn, I would've derailed several times. She's an incredible investigator. She's got great instincts."

"So what happens now?"

"I want her to come to Chicago with me," he said, braving his brother's disapproval.

But he received none.

"I think that's a good idea," Sawyer said and Shaine agreed.

"Where's the lecture that she's too young for me or I shouldn't get involved with people from a case…?"

"Yeah, if I thought any of that would work, I might try to offer it as advice but I can see right now none of it would matter. You love her. It's written all over your face. The way you look at her, the way you track her every move, the way you worry. You practically have hearts and butterflies floating around your head."

"It's that obvious?"

Both brothers nodded.

Honestly, he was relieved. "Good. I wanted you to meet her first."

"Before you ask her to move to Chicago with you?"

Silas laughed nervously. "No, before I ask her to marry me."

"Are you serious?" Shaine asked.

"As a heart attack," Silas answered. "I know it's sudden. But this is real. She's the only one I want."

"And how does she feel about it?"

Quinn's soft voice trembled with tears as she answered from behind them.

"She feels lucky."

Silas met her gaze, his heart beating so hard he thought he might pass out.

"So it's settled?" Silas asked, his own voice breaking. He was in great danger of bawling like a baby. "You will be my wife?"

"Before I answer, I have one question."

"Ask."

"Will you stand in my way of whatever career choice I choose even if you hate it or think it's dangerous?"

He ground his teeth but shook his head, making a promise. "I will support whatever decision you make. I will always have your back."

Quinn wiped at her eyes and smiled. "Good. Then let's do this and get the hell out of this town. I'm ready."

Sawyer kicked at Silas's shin. "This is where you go kiss your woman and seal the deal, you jackass."

Silas didn't have to be told twice.

He kissed her long and hard, loving her from the tips of her red hair to the points of her painted toes.

Port Orion had taken something precious from him but it'd given him something to treasure in return.

Silas could finally put Spencer to rest.

And just like Quinn…he was ready for whatever was to come.

Epilogue

Quinn rubbed at her arms, listening to the rain and wind lashing at the windows in their apartment.

"Man, they weren't kidding when they called it the Windy City. Are the storms always this bad?"

Silas smiled. "Yeah. You get used to it. Wait until it starts to snow. Makes driving to work real fun."

Since moving to Chicago, Quinn had settled in with Silas but she hadn't decided what she was going to do with her life, and Silas had given her the space to figure it out on her own time schedule.

Each time she'd started to send out résumés to the newspapers and news stations, she'd held back.

She loved writing but after Port Orion, she'd lost her taste for chasing leads.

Still, the need to write continued to nag at her so she'd started journaling. At first, it'd been a way to vent the pain that'd lingered but soon it became a cathartic way to deal with her feelings.

And to find forgiveness.

The wound remained tender and probably would remain so her entire life but she was able to talk about it without breaking down.

Not that she opted to do that very often but when she did, she held it together.

Mostly because she knew Silas had her back.

The ensuing investigation into Rhia, Sara and Spencer's deaths had erupted into a firestorm of big stories with reporters coming at her from every angle.

In light of everything, Lester had finally retired but not before firing Harrison Rex for conduct unbecoming an officer after he'd confessed to his actions against Quinn, as well as the intimidation tactics he'd used with the dead cat. Quinn wished she'd had ringside seats for that show. She would've brought popcorn.

Thanks to a convincing letter Quinn had written to the Board of Supervisors, Port Orion had decided to open up the search for a new sheriff outside town and had found a suitable candidate from Seattle.

But as more reporters hounded her for an interview, to tell her side of the story, the more Quinn distanced herself from journalism as a career choice.

Being the pursued was a completely different perspective and she surely hadn't enjoyed it.

She understood why Silas had been biased against her at the beginning.

But Quinn knew only she could tell the story as it was meant to be told, how it *had* to be told.

So, that's what she did.

At first, written long-hand then transcribed onto the computer and before she knew it, Quinn had written the narrative. She basically opened a vein and let it pour out, messy and heartbreaking in the hopes that she could be reborn from her own ashes.

It'd been the most difficult and the most rewarding journey in her life.

And now, producers were coming to her with offers to turn her story into a movie.

She still hadn't decided if she wanted to go that far.

The book was finished; she felt complete.

That chapter of her life was finished.

Closure, as Silas had said, was a beautiful gift if you were willing to work for it.

And she'd worked her ass off.

Nothing was going to stop her.

Most certainly not the past.

A slow smile found her lips as Silas walked into the room.

She had too much to look forward to in the future.

* * * * *

*If you loved this novel, don't miss other
suspenseful titles by Kimberly Van Meter:*

*TO CATCH A KILLER
GUARDING THE SOCIALITE
SWORN TO PROTECT
COLD CASE REUNION
A DAUGHTER'S PERFECT SECRET
THE SNIPER
MOVING TARGET
THE AGENT'S SURRENDER
DEEP COVER*

*Available now from
Harlequin Romantic Suspense!*

#1935 COLTON'S SECRET SON
The Coltons of Shadow Creek • by Carla Cassidy

After his notorious mother escapes from prison, Knox Colton is temporarily placed on leave from his job as a Texas Ranger. With nowhere else to go, he returns to his hometown of Shadow Creek, Texas, and there discovers he's the father of a nine-year-old boy with the woman he's never been able to forget.

#1936 NANNY BODYGUARD
Bachelor Bodyguards • by Lisa Childs

Lars Ecklund is on a mission to safeguard his nephew and rescue his missing sister. He finds help in the tiny but tough Nikki Payne, a fellow bodyguard at Payne Protection Agency, who is as wary with her heart as she is good with a gun. But when faced with a sleazy adoption lawyer, assassins and a baby, they must also contend with their feelings for each other or risk losing their hearts—and lives!

#1937 OPERATION ALPHA
Cutter's Code • by Justine Davis

When teacher Ria Connelly comes to Foxworth about a troubled student, operative Liam Burnett doesn't know what he's in for. But Ria refuses to back down and leave him to his lonely exsistence, even when the secrets they uncover threaten them both.

#1938 LAST CHANCE HERO
by Melinda Di Lorenzo

Ten years ago, Donovan Grady died in a car accident. Or so Jordynn Flannigan believed. Now he's back from the dead, and his only goal is to keep her alive and safe from the people who forced him to fake his own death all those years before...

Allison raised her head with every intention of stepping
away from him. But his arms pulled her closer to him and
his lips crashed down on hers.

The kiss erased all rational thought from her mind.
Instead, all her senses came gloriously alive as Knox's
mouth made love to hers. His tongue swirled with hers as
his scent suffused her, and the heat of his hands on her back
invited her to melt against his broad chest. Their bodies fit
together perfectly, as if they had been made for each other.

He finally left her lips to slide his mouth down the column
of her throat. As her knees weakened with desire, rational
thought slammed back into her. She jerked back from him,
appalled by how quickly, how completely, he could break
down all her defenses.

His eyes radiated a raw hunger as he held her gaze
intently. "Despite everything that has happened between

us, I still want you. There's always been something strong between us, Allison, and you can't deny that it's still there."

No, she couldn't deny it, but she also wouldn't admit it to him. "It doesn't matter." She took two steps back from him, needing not only to emotionally distance herself but to physically distance herself, as well.

"That kiss was a mistake. I don't feel that way about you anymore." Okay, maybe she could deny it, but she could tell by the look in his eyes that he didn't believe her.

"In any case, anything like that between us would be foolish and it would only complicate things. We aren't going there again, Knox, and now I think it's time we say goodnight."

She breathed a sigh of relief when he nodded and turned to walk to the front door. Her legs were still shaky as she accompanied him.

"I'm sorry about my little breakdown," she said.

He turned to face her and before she could read his intentions he grabbed her and once again planted a kiss on her lips.

It was short and searing and when he released her his eyes sparkled with a knowing glint. "The next time you try to tell me you don't feel that way about me anymore, say it like you really mean it," he said, and then he was gone into the night.

Don't miss
COLTON'S SECRET SON by Carla Cassidy,
available March 2017 wherever
Harlequin® Romantic Suspense books
and ebooks are sold.

www.Harlequin.com

HRSEXP0217R